Praise for Eric Garcia's mysteries featuring dinosaur private eye Vincent Rubio

CASUAL REX

"A funny book. I can't remember an author pulling off a more difficult premise, unless it's T. Jefferson Parker."　　　　—*Los Angeles Times*

"[Eric Garcia's] X-Files take on the classic detective tale will appeal to both mystery and SF readers. Here's a series with dino-sized legs."
　　　　—*Publishers Weekly*

"Garcia, whose rollicking debut, *Anonymous Rex*, jazzed up the detective genre, returns to the land the dinosaurs share with contemporary bipeds. . . . Seamless, wonderfully clever world-building, a little dino-depravity, and an abundance of tongue-in-cheek humor to keep things rolling along."
　　　　—*Booklist*

"Great fun."　　　　—*Library Journal*

"It's so hard to resist stomping around in dinosaur metaphors in reviewing *Casual Rex*. But the book . . . is too good, too funny and too inventive to get bogged down in Jurassic jargon . . . dripping with tongue-in-jaw wit, snappy action, funny lines and plot twists. A genre-bending, species-bending, gender-bending romp of a mystery . . . What's really intriguing is Garcia's commentary about society and historical events as seen through dinosaur eyes. . . . It's obvious Garcia had fun with *Casual Rex*. Readers will too."　　　　—*The Columbus Dispatch*

"A prequel that's as daringly, darkly loopy as *Anonymous Rex*."
　　　　—*Kirkus Reviews*

"Garcia's manic energy and chutzpah are infectious, and it's good to see Vincent Rubio back on a case."　　　　—*The Miami Herald*

continued on next page . . .

Anonymous Rex

A People *Beach Book of the Week*

"First-time novelist Eric Garcia pulls it off, keeping the laughs frequent and the plot intriguing. After a few chapters, it seems downright logical to believe we're surrounded by a cast out of *Jurassic Park*. Apart from showing off a splendidly warped imagination, Garcia provides a solid mystery."

—*People*

"Awesomely funny. Witty, fast-paced detective work makes for a good mystery, but the story's sly, seamlessly conceived dinosaur underworld contains all the elements of a cult classic. A."
—*Entertainment Weekly*

"Debut novelist Eric Garcia pulls off this parallel dino world to a T (Rex). [His] descriptions are delicious . . . inventive and imaginative. He cleverly avoids what could have been a one-joke book with charm, sly humor and a terrific narrative pace."
—*USA Today*

"What would the world be like if the dinosaurs hadn't gone extinct? As this very funny book shows, for one thing, L.A. would be even weirder than it is now."
—Dave Barry

"Garcia has come up with an imaginative twist to the detective fiction genre."
—*Daily Variety*

"If a novel, by definition, is new, rare, and strange, then Eric Garcia's *Anonymous Rex* is the most novel novel I've ever read. By turns hilarious and chilling, this is a terrific joyful read."
—T. C. Boyle

"Audacious and imaginative. You might not believe any of this thirty seconds after you close the covers, but while it's going on you're going to be dazzled by Garcia's energy and chutzpah."
—*Publishers Weekly*

"Garcia plays it almost completely straight, respecting all noir traditions, and comes up with lovely touches."
—*Chicago Tribune*

"A 'noir-asaurus' of a novel, bellowing for attention, the first and only of its breed in the dinosaur detective genre. Garcia has written something so strange, so bizarre, that he's to be admired just for the attempt. And he not only pulls it off, he also actually makes you wonder why someone hasn't thought of it before. Garcia's tough guy deadpan is perfect for navigating his outrageous lost world, and the easy, familiar tone is probably what makes the premise so simple to swallow. Garcia talks the talk, and more importantly, he smirks in all the right places."
—*The Miami Herald*

CASUAL REX

A NOVEL

ERIC GARCIA

BERKLEY BOOKS, NEW YORK

A Berkley Book
Published by The Berkley Publishing Group
A division of Penguin Putnam Inc.
375 Hudson Street
New York, New York 10014

Copyright © 2001 by Eric Garcia
Book design by Caroline Cunningham
Cover design by Daniel Rembert
Cover photograph by Marc Tauss

Published by arrangement with Villard Books,
a division of Random House, Inc.

Published simultaneously in Canada.

PRINTING HISTORY
Villard Books hardcover edition / March 2001
Berkley trade paperback edition / March 2002

Visit our website at
www.penguinputnam.com

Library of Congress Cataloging-in-Publication Data

Garcia, Eric.
    Casual Rex / Eric Garcia.
        p. cm.
    ISBN 0-425-18339-4
        1. Private investigators—Fiction. 2. Dinosaurs—Fiction. I. Title.

    PS3557.A665 C37 2002
    813'.54—dc21

                                                              2001043205

PRINTED IN THE UNITED STATES OF AMERICA

10 9 8 7 6 5 4 3 2 1

For my beautiful daughter, Bailey Jordan,

who snuggles up close to me

and whispers all the really good lines

"Two leaves of basil. Folded, not torn."

—RUBIO, VINCENT RUBIO

CASUAL REX

1

mprovision is the modus operandi when you work with Ernie Watson.

"You doin' okay, kid?" he asks me, and all I can do is mumble back a reply—shag piling pressing up and into my mouth, my nostrils—as I'm momentarily assaulted by the stench of six thousand pairs of shoes and one incontinent household pet. "Stay down—I almost got the damn thing."

As an insistent burglar alarm whines away in the background, Ernie fumbles with the system's plastic keypad, doing his best to shut the contraption up, or at least send it to a better place. Ten seconds have passed, and in twenty more we're as good as bait for the neighborhood security patrol. Fortunately, they don't carry weapons. At least I think they don't carry weapons.

"The code," I say. "Put it in already."

"I did—"

"You didn't. It's still beeping."

"I did. And it's wrong. The code's wrong."

A leap to my feet—Bruno Maglis today, clearly the inappropriate attire when one is breaking and entering, but at eight A.M. this morning I expected a non-felonious workday—and I'm beside my partner in a beat, punching in the code over his protestations. Ernie's a crack PI, but it doesn't change the fact that his eyesight's slowly dropping off the low end of the scale—last time, he insisted to the ophthalmologist that the reading chart was mocking him, by God—and most likely he's simply hitting the wrong numbers.

There: 6-2-7-1-4-9-2. Just like it said in the Rolodex on the new hubby's desk. We found the code scrawled down as a phone number listed for a Mr. Alvin Alarming, and you can bet the farm it took the stellar mind of a T-Rex to come up with that brain-twister. I take my time and carefully depress the numbers on the keypad in their proper sequence.

The beeping continues. Twenty seconds down. This ain't good.

"Hey," I say, "the code's wrong."

Ernie fixes me with a cold, familiar stare. I grin. "Damn," Ernie mutters, "he musta changed it."

"Maybe *she* changed it—"

"No." Simple, monosyllabic. I don't argue.

Fifteen seconds. My gaze slides toward the doorway we came through, then out to the driveway and the suburban streets beyond. No security patrol so far, but that doesn't preclude an imminent arrival. The time has come to beat a hasty retreat, exit stage left, mission aborted. I was getting hungry, anyhow.

But before I can grab Ernie by the lapel of his blue bowling shirt and haul him out of the building and down to Pink's for a chili dog with extra onions, he's somehow managed to tear off the face of the keypad, exposing the simplistic guts of this seemingly complex security system. Wires spill out like loose spaghetti, electricity snapping through the open gaps, and Ernie shoots a queasy glance in my direction. "Get down, kid," he says. "And stay there."

No argument here. Over a decade of snoop work with the guy,

I've learned that when Ernie gets that pained, cramped look—
that *I've-just-licked-a-human* grimace—it's time to listen up and
listen hard. I drop to the floor.

An array of stunted claws flash out from Ernie's suddenly
exposed paw, latex human fingers flapping loosely off the wrist. A
flick of the forearm, a sweep through the air, and those four
sharp razors slice their way up and through the assortment of
high-tech wizardry bolted to the wall. Sparks fly, showering Ernie
in a wash of miniature fireworks, but he stands his ground and
holds tough despite the burn marks spreading across the surface
of his polysuit.

The alarm, if anything, grows louder.

Moving with some real urgency now, Ernie grasps a severed
wire in each hand and twists the two exposed ends around each
other into a single sparkling braid.

Light. Hissing. A small explosion, perhaps.

And silence. The distinct smell of sulfur hangs in the air.
Wires and buttons and lights and computer chips lie in a small
mountain of rubble on the foyer carpeting, and I have to stamp
out the smoldering mess with the bottoms of my designer shoes
in order to prevent a small fire. The things I do for this job . . .

But Ernie is triumphant, arms aloft, the latex fingers on his
left hand clutching the exposed claws of his right, jumping up
and down like the winning pugilist after an early-round knockout. There's glee in that little dance, in that smile spreading
across his face. I know that smile. There's no getting past that
smile. That's pure Ernie.

"Nice job," I say. "You gonna fix that before we go?"

Ernie shrugs. "Don't know how."

"So there goes the covert entry."

"Yep. There it goes."

"You got a kick outta that, didn't you?" I ask.

A short laugh, almost a choke, as Ernie turns his head, avoids
making eye contact. "I sure as hell ain't sad, kid."

We move farther into the house.

Tight hallways and small, sectioned rooms are the norm in this wood-paneled home, a restored throwback to the cobblestone-wall and modular-furniture days of the late seventies. The rooms practically pulse with disco backbeat. A vaulted ceiling rises above the main living area, in which a Steinway grand piano lies dormant, a thin layer of dust having settled across the keys.

"She still play?" I ask.

"How the hell should I know?"

"I thought maybe you—"

"No."

Rows of framed photographs hang side by side in the main hallway, some of them old, most of them recent, all of them dinos in disguise. In the back of one group shot—a family reunion, I gather, from the striking clan resemblance—I believe I can make out a familiar guised face, a familiar squat body. No time to check, as Ernie's already through the hall and into a bedroom.

"What are we looking for?" I ask. Ernie's on his knees by the side of a California King Craftmatic adjustable bed, hurriedly rummaging through a battered oak nightstand. Books and old receipts fly onto the floor as my partner digs through the drawer with an intensity bordering on frenzy. This is not a careful archaeological expedition, to say the least.

No answer. I tap Ernie on the shoulder, and he barely flinches. "What are we—"

"I'll know it when I see it," he says.

I sit on the edge of the bed, and it nearly sinks to the floor under my meager weight. I don't even hear the creak of springs, as they must have given up the long, hard battle some time ago. This must be the side that the new husband sleeps on; T-Rexes, frame notwithstanding, are not known to be light snoozers.

Ernie has successfully transferred the entire contents of the nightstand's upper drawer to the floor, and as he starts in on the lower one with the same troubled deliberation, I realize I'm going to be in for a long evening. Once my partner gets his mind set on something, there's little short of a cannonball or a side of mutton that can stop him.

"I'll go stand guard," I offer.

"For what?"

"In case they come back."

"They're at the opera."

"Maybe they'll leave after the third quarter," I say, and Ernie waves a hand in my general direction. I take this as my cue to leave, destination already in mind. A squadron of little demons resting inside my belly are clamoring for their evening feast, scratching at the lining of my stomach with their pitchforks, and I can't deny the monsters for much longer. The kitchen, therefore, is the first stop.

Clean. Sparkling. And well appointed. I am a particular fan of the Sub-Zero fridge: easy to open, and, thanks to its excellent layout, easy to raid. Being careful not to disturb the other contents, I pluck a leftover leg of lamb from the bottom shelf, snag a bottle of hot mustard, and make my way to the kitchen table. The demons intensify their poking and prodding, and my stomach growls in protest.

A munch, maybe two, and then it's no more time for food as a pair of lights swing across the peach curtains that line the front windows of the house. Headlights, I'm sure of it, accompanied by the unmistakable purr of an import automobile.

"Ernie!" I call out, achieving new dino land speeds as I race down the hall. "We've got a problem—"

But he's engrossed in the same project as before, this time rummaging through an old bureau set against the far wall. In the few minutes since I'd left him, a miniature tornado must have localized itself in this bedroom: the floor is covered with knick-knacks and loose sheets of paper, strewn about in every direction. "I think I'm onto it," Ernie says, oblivious of the F5-size mess he has created.

"Not anymore, you're not onto it," I tell him. "They're here."

"I know," he says wistfully. "I smelled her two minutes ago."

Even though the inhabitants of that car must have been ten blocks away two minutes ago, I have no cause to doubt Ernie's schnoz in cases such as this. Still, we have to vamoose. I grab Ernie by the shoulder, but he shrugs my hand away and continues digging.

I can hear two pairs of feet clomping up the front walkway, and now I, too, can smell them—one scent strong, musky, thick, and cloying, a bargain-basement cologne; the other is full of lilac and warm oatmeal.

And now the key is turning, opening the lock in the front door, and it won't be long before the rightful owners of this house walk into their foyer and step directly into a homeowner's nightmare represented by a pile of charred plastic and silicon that used to be their primary means of defense against intruders great and small.

"Ernie, we can't wait around—"

Front door creaking, opening, a matter of milliseconds—

"—for you to sniff this thing out, whatever it is—"

"Found it," says Ernie, his voice even, almost melancholy. I try to take a gander at the small, yellowed piece of paper in his hands, but he's already out the sliding glass door, leaving me to wade through the bedroom wreckage. I'm barely onto the patio when I hear the chorus of gasps and angry voices emanating from the foyer, but by then I'm at full tilt and rising fast. Past the pool, into the yard, over the fence in a single jump (with a little more effort than it used to take, I must admit), and hauling my carcass through the neighbor's backyard, Ernie a good ten yards ahead.

We're in my beloved Lincoln two minutes later, panting hard and catching our breath as we keep an eye out for anyone who may have seen or followed us. But the only movements in the shadows are your basic suburban staples—basketball nets swaying in the breeze, lawn flamingos falling off their rusted metallic legs, neighborhood cats prowling their turf, cruising for a good time—so it seems that for the moment, at least, we have escaped unnoticed.

The stomach succubi are displeased with my recent unexpected exercise, and are threatening to return the little lamb I was able to shove into my mouth to the land from whence it came. I swallow hard, trying to maintain some degree of professionalism. The last thing I need is to spend the rest of the evening cleaning up the Lincoln's front seat.

Ernie's engrossed in reading the sheet of paper he pilfered from the house, and after a time I ask him, "You wanna show me what you got?"

He folds the paper once, twice, then stuffs it into his front shirt pocket. "Let's get outta here."

"Best plan I heard all day." I turn the key and the good old American engine rumbles to life, breaking the stillness of the night. As I flick on the lights, Ernie reaches over and flicks them off again.

"I kinda need those."

"Go down her street," Ernie tells me.

I shake my head. "That ain't smart, Ern." I pointedly turn the lights back on again. "We got lucky once. We'd be asking for trouble—"

"Keep the lights off, no danger. C'mon, kid. For me."

I'd argue—really, I'd be more than happy to—but I can predict my own defeat ahead of time. So in order to save myself a few hours, I wall off the argumentative part of my brain behind some strong mental brickwork, flick off the lights, and drive down the street.

The front door is open, every light in the house in full-on blaze position. The exterior halogens have popped to life as well, and the home glows with nuclear intensity. I take my time coasting through the shadows, barely touching the accelerator.

Snippets of sound from inside—"the jewelry . . . did they get the . . . where are your rings . . . check the safe . . ."—accompanied by a side order of rancorous scents. The block is slowly filling with the smell of chestnuts roasting on an open fire, but for dinos that aroma means fear and anger as opposed to Jack Frost nipping at your nose.

The lady of the house, perhaps sensing our presence, perhaps simply in need of a break from the difficulty of accepting a home invasion, steps out of her doorway and onto the front porch, staring off into the night. Does she see us? Possibly. Does she recognize us? Unlikely.

It's been some time since she's had her guise professionally aged—I can tell even from this distance that the wrinkle set usually required for the early fifties hasn't yet been sewn into her face—and as a whole, she looks similar to the last time I saw her, more than three years ago. Short blond hair puffed into a tight little ball against her head, a collection of mid-range jewelry adorning her small, thin wrists. Eyes covered in blue shadow, lips more pink than red, and the traces of good nature turning up the corners of her mouth even amid all this danger and disappointment.

"She's still got that smell about her, don't she?" Ernie says, and his wistful tone pulls me into a similar reverie. A soft pat on my partner's back, and this time he doesn't move my hand away. We issue a collective sigh.

"A real sweetheart," I say.

"You don't gotta rub it in."

"Rub what in?" I ask. "You said she had a great smell, I said she was a sweetheart. Am I wrong?"

Ernie scratches his chin, massaging the stubble he so carefully applies once a week. He'd thought about getting that facial hair kit from Nanjutsu, the one in which the hairs actually grow *through* the skin at a predetermined rate, but decided that the beard replacement packs (at least one every two weeks) weren't worth the cost. "No, you ain't wrong, kid," he says. "She's a sweetheart all right."

In a single move, Ernie reaches into his pocket, extracts the slip of paper he took from the house, and tosses it into my lap. I open it slowly, the old, worn pages crackling beneath my fingers, and hold it beneath the small light from the LED clock display.

A marriage license. Louise and Ernie's marriage license, to be specific, and I fold it up as reverently as possible and hand it back to my partner, who is still unable to take his eyes off his ex-wife standing in the doorway of what used to be their house.

There's a moment when I think she's looking right at us, a moment when I think her eyes and Ernie's eyes make some connection, when I think I can hear her saying *It's okay, I understand,* but then she turns, walks back inside, and closes the door. The front lights are extinguished moments later.

"Drive on home, kid," Ernie says to me. "Don't stop for gas."

· · ·

When Ernie says "home," he means our office, the corner suite on the third floor of a building in Westwood that has neither adequate water pressure nor a proper mail-delivery system. Half of the time I find myself plucking envelopes out of the mud beneath our outdoor mailbox, and when I return to the office I'm barely able to wash the grime off my hands thanks to a six-drop-per-minute water flow.

The sign out front reads WATSON AND RUBIO, INVESTIGATIONS, and although I've never put up a fight about the order of the names—never cared one way or the other about it, in fact—Ernie nevertheless offers to flip-flop status with me at the end of every year.

"This is your big chance, kid," he always jokes with me. "Rubio and Watson's got a helluva nice ring to it."

Not interested.

On this night, the mailbox has been properly filled, and though there are at least ten envelopes and a package lying in the dirt below, I can't find any down there addressed to us. Mr. Toggle in 215 is going to have quite the fit, on the other hand, and though he's a human, that man can roar like a Stegosaur with a hangnail.

Elevator's broken again, so it's the stairs for us. Two flights, both short, but Ernie's starting to pant. Pack a day of the long ones will do that, and I can't understand why he doesn't quit; it sure as hell ain't the nicotine keeping him there.

The door to our office is ajar, a thin band of light streaming into the darkened hallway. Thin, tinny music escapes from within, some big band bopping away on our subpar, tweeter-impaired stereo. Ernie and I approach cautiously, sticking to the shadows, backs pressed against the rough exposed concrete walls.

"Thought I told you to close the door," Ernie whispers.

"And I told you to turn off the lights," I whisper back. If I had a gun, I'd be reaching for it. As it is, the fingers of my left hand are fumbling with the glove on my right, ready to whip out the claws should push come to slice.

Edging closer to the door, Ernie motions for me to flank him on the other side. I hold up three fingers, then two, then one. Time to grind the teeth.

A well-placed kick sends the door flying back on its hinges, and like two hyperactive feds busting in on a raid, we leap into the open doorway, claws at the rough and ready.

"Hiya, fellas. What took you?"

There's a pudgy-faced midget sitting on my desk, dangling his squat legs in the air, kicking his feet to the beat of the music, leafing through the papers scattered across my desktop, and running a stubby index finger below the words as he reads. He's got manicured nails and a tailored suit and decidedly black hair. Greasy black hair. Dripping, greasy, black hair. As the door bangs loudly against the side wall, the little guy shoots us a grin that is supposed to look ashamed, but doesn't quite make the grade.

I slam the door closed behind me and storm my way up to the minuscule marauder. "You can't do this, Minsky—"

"What?" he asks. "What'd I do? What's the problem?"

Ernie flashes out with his claws, waving them past Minsky's angelic expression. "You were about five seconds from meeting your ancestors, that's the problem."

"What, you were gonna kill me?"

"The moment ain't passed yet."

"Hey—hey—wait—I didn't break in," says Minsky. "How can I break in when I own the building?"

I have no urge to get into a discussion over landlord-tenant rights at this point in the evening, so I cock an eyebrow at Ernie—one of our little "back off" signals when interrogating witnesses—and he slowly steps away, retracting his claws. Minsky smiles.

"How's it going?" he asks. "Business good?"

"Whaddaya want?" I say. Formalities and chatter with this fellow have been known to eclipse entire weekends, and I have sleep to catch up on.

"Can't a landlord check in on his favorite tenants?"

"No." A firm grasp beneath each armpit and I lift the undersized Hadrosaur up and off my desk, depositing him on the ground. Now his head reaches no higher than my waist, which makes me a little more comfortable with his presence. It's odd to see such stunted growth in a dinosaur nowadays, but forty-five years ago, back when Minsky was growing up, a lot of us neglected the dino side of nutrition. Fast-food burgers and tacos may nourish a human child, but it takes a little more than that to raise a healthy Hadrosaur.

"You guys have the rent?" he asks.

"Rent ain't due for another two weeks," Ernie says. "I got it all in my calendar." He puts a firm hand behind Minsky's back and begins ushering our landlord toward the door. "You be sure to come back and see us then. Better yet, I'll drop the payment in your box, and you don't have to come near the joint at all, okay?" I open the door as Ernie grasps Minsky by the seat of his pants and prepares to toss him into the hallway.

"Wait, wait," he squeals. "I've got a question—I've got a case—"

"Sorry," Ernie says, "business hours are over."

But Minsky's squirming in Ernie's grasp, flopping like a fish on the hook, trying futilely to push his way back into the room—picture a Peewee League linebacker trying to get by the Miami Dolphins entire offensive line—and I can see that Ernie's doing his best not to break up laughing.

"What the hell," I say. "Let him in."

Ernie reverses the direction of his throw, and Minsky stumbles back into our office. With precise, deliberate motions, he straightens out the paisley tie that doesn't quite match his otherwise well-tailored suit, reassembles his dignity, and struts confidently back toward the desk. At this moment, the thought hits me that Minsky's guises, custom-made as they must be for his extraordinarily small frame, must cost a fortune. Are we overpaying in rent? Is the dental business that profitable?

"I've got this mistress," Minsky begins, and Ernie and I sigh as one. I push back from the desk and stand up.

"Goodnight, Minsky," I say, fully preparing to take up where Ernie left off, flexing those muscles that might be best for midget-tossing.

"It's different this time," he says.

"It's always different. Hell, it's never different," I say, my volume climbing, rising along with my ire. "You get yourself in some hot seat with a floozy and want us to bail you out with the missus."

"No, please, you don't understand. . . . Her name's Star, and she's an Allosaur. I found her up on Sunset. She's fantastic."

"Teenage runaway?" I ask.

"Not exactly. Well . . . she's nineteen. So, technically, yes, she's a teenager, but she's not a runaway per se. She's more like an entrepreneur."

Ernie's picking his fingernails with a letter opener, but he looks up at this. "A hooker."

Pain slides across Minsky's face as if Ernie had slapped him a good one. "Never! What—why would you say that?"

"You said you found her up on Sunset Boulevard, she's not

'exactly' a runaway, and she's an entrepreneur. Do the math, Minsky."

"I'll have you know that Star is not a prostitute, thank you. She sells maps."

"Maps?" I ask.

"To the stars' homes."

It takes some time before Ernie and I are able to stop laughing.

"I'm glad you find her profession amusing," Minsky says once our hysterics have dwindled to the occasional chuckle. "But she makes a good living, and she's smart, and she's kind, and she's the sweetest girl I know."

"Fine," I say, cutting short the love sonnet. "So if she's so sweet and you're so damned happy, why come to us?"

Minsky lowers his head, his voice somehow dropping past the midget register, lowering a full tone. "I think she's stealing nitrous from me."

"Sweet girl."

"And ether."

"Real sweet girl."

"And maybe some prescription pads, I'm not sure."

Minsky may be one of the premier dino dentists in Los Angeles, and he may have the corner on the filed-down-tooth and human-molar market, but he's got a lot to learn when it comes to women. This is the fourth mistress we've heard about in the last two years, and I am quite sure that there were many more who floated by without getting a mention. Then again, maybe I'm the one who's got a lot to learn; Minsky's certainly fulfilling his reproductive duty a heck of a lot more often than I am.

Still, they always seem to screw him over.

"Whaddaya want us to do?" I ask.

"Find her."

"You don't know where she is?"

"Not . . . not exactly."

"Maybe this *is* the ideal relationship," I chuckle.

"And I want you to find out if she's stealing from me."

"And if she is?"

"Confront her. Or stop her. Get the stuff back."

"Why don't you just ask her?" says Ernie. "Ain't that what rela-tionships are based on? Trust and honesty and all that crap?"

Minsky shrugs, a toss of his teensy shoulders. Is he shorter than he was a minute ago? "I'm afraid if I ask her, if I tell her to stop . . . she'll leave me. Or . . ."

"Or she'll tell Charlene about you two." Charlene is the wife. The jealous wife. The jealous wife six times his size.

Minsky nods. "Yes." He's growing smaller by the second. Any moment now, I expect him to shrivel into a pea and wink out of existence.

Ernie and I glance at each other, allowing our eyes to lock for no more than half a second. It's all we need nowadays, a momen-tary chance to read the other's thoughts on the matter, and then the issue is settled before the client even realizes that the ques-tion has been asked.

"We'll do it." I sigh, and Minsky looks up, beaming with gratitude.

"Really?"

"Give us a week or so," Ernie says.

"How much?" asks Minsky, reaching back for his billfold.

Another glance between me and Ernie, and I say, "Three months' rent."

"Done," says Minsky.

"And two free visits," Ernie adds. "I gotta get a new M-series set of caps for my lower left. Maybe a new bridge, too."

Suddenly, Minsky's hopping off the couch, waddling up to my desk. Without a hitch, he leaps on top, kicks a few papers out of his way, and stands over Ernie, who obediently opens his mouth for the doctor's small, skilled hands. Minsky purrs over the worn set of false teeth he finds within.

"I can fix you up with the new Impresario brand," he says. "Real sweet set of choppers, George Hamilton model. No prob-lem." Suddenly, Minsky turns his attention toward me and shuffles across my desk, kicking up even more paper as he moves in for the kill.

I back off. "Thanks, but . . . thanks, no, I'm fine."

"Come, Vincent—oral cleanliness is next to godliness," he says, stubby arms reaching out for my clenched jaw.

"And I'm a dental atheist. Back off, little man."

Minsky shrugs and hops down off the desk. "I appreciate this, fellas."

"We're gonna need info," says Ernie.

I scribble down some necessities on the back of an envelope and hand them to Minsky. "Full name, date of birth, where she's from, maybe some pictures."

"X-rated?" he asks.

"G is fine."

And with that, Minsky is gone. I set to cleaning up my desk, picking up the papers that have dropped to the floor, and Ernie takes off his coat and hangs it on a brass hook set into the back of the door.

"You believe that guy?" Ernie asks me.

"Poor son of a bitch."

"Every six months he's in here with another sob story about one of his dames."

"Some guys . . ." I begin. "Some guys . . . they don't know how to handle themselves. They don't know where the line starts and where it ends."

"I'll tell you what it is," Ernie says. "He thinks his answer is in women. Minsky thinks that Minsky isn't Minsky unless he's with a woman."

"Can't live that way."

"A guy can stand alone," insists my partner. "A guy *should* stand alone."

"You're right, Ern. You're right."

We clean up the rest of the office in silence, and say our goodnights. I freshen up in the small bathroom down the hall, and when I return—my face still wet, water dripping down the false bridge of my latex nose, small puddles forming on the floor—I find Ernie curled up on the couch, shoes off, a rough wool blanket pulled tightly beneath his chin, a small throw pillow clenched between his arms, and a light snore buzzing out from behind his thick lips.

I drive home alone.

'm in the office late the next morning, thanks to a Hemp for Humanity rally in front of the monolithic Federal Building, which towers over Wilshire Boulevard down near UCLA. Traffic was backed up for a mile in all directions, which isn't so odd for Los Angeles, but because the air conditioning in my car isn't up to snuff, I had to keep the windows rolled down for fresh air, and the incessant folk music and strong scent of extralegal substances blasting out from the rally quickly threw me into a particularly foul mood.

Ernie's not in; the blanket has been folded up and put away, I see, and the couch has been fluffed and primped back to proper buoyancy. It's been at least six months that Ernie's been sleeping in the office, and I don't bother him about it anymore. If the crumpled ambiance of his new bachelor pad in Hollywood doesn't allow him to get in a good night's sleep, who am I to tell the guy any different?

A note on my desk, large but neat letters drawn across an

entire sheet of yellow legal paper. DENTIST APPOINTMENT reads the letter, and I don't think he went to Minsky's for that checkup they discussed. More likely, he's checking out our client's office, maybe his home, maybe the love nest where Minsky and his teenaged Allosaur shacked up. Take him at least an hour, maybe more. This should give me time to straighten out the burgeoning pile of paperwork that's threatening to throw off a seismic tremor and completely bury my desk beneath an avalanche of demand letters and eyewitness accounts.

A knock at the partially open door, and I turn to see a familiar face—recently familiar, in fact—peeking in from the hallway. "Is . . . is Ernie here?"

Warm oatmeal and lilac flood the room, and instinct takes over as my mind stages a temporary strike. I find myself shaking my head, sitting my rump down on the edge of the desk. My arms fold across my chest of their own accord. "He's out."

"Oh. It's good to see you, Vincent." She steps inside, knockoff Chanel handbag slung across one shoulder. Wrinkles still missing where wrinkles should be.

"It's good to see you, too, Louise." We trade strained grins. "How's the new husband? Terrence, right?"

"Terrell."

"Sorry. Terrell. He's well?"

"Under the circumstances, yes. He's got some respiratory problems."

"T-Rexes often do."

"Yes," she says. "We do."

Silence for a moment, as I try to figure out if we're breaking any specific code of conduct, veering off on any moral tangent, simply by being in the same room together without Ernie present.

Louise speaks first. "We're not—I mean, you're not . . ."

"Mad at you?"

"Mad at me. Yes. You're not—"

"No. No, of course not." I grin, in order to prove my sincerity. At least, I hope it comes across as sincerity.

"Thank you. I'd understand if you wanted to . . ."

"I don't. It's between you and . . . I mean, you divorced Ernie, not me. I'm not involved."

Louise seems to accept this, and takes my lack of ire as a cue to step farther into the office. I extend a hand toward the couch and she takes a seat. A moment later, she wiggles her bottom, reaching under her rump as if to scratch in a decidedly unfeminine fashion. Her hand comes up with a dark night mask.

"This looks like Ernie's," she says.

"Looks like it."

"Does he—is this where he's sleeping?"

"Once or twice a month," I lie. "On late nights."

This could go on forever. Louise could sit on that couch and I could perch on the edge of my desk and we could talk about Ernie—rather, we could *not* talk about Ernie—for days, exercising whatever part of our brains that specialize in strained cocktail-party chatter, but I have a quick breakfast and the aforementioned paperwork to get to, so I come out with the standard question that always gets the clients moving in or out of the door in a real hurry:

"What can I do for you, Louise?"

A steady stream of tears rolls out of the corner of her left eye, welling in the joint formed between natural scaled skin and latex polysuit. If I didn't know Louise as well as I do—eight, nine years now—I'd think that she was crying, upset perhaps at her reason for coming to see me, perhaps at the situation between her and Ernie. But Louise is just one of those unfortunate dinosaurs for whom the lachrymal glands are still overproductive, even after millions of years of evolution worked this kink out of the rest of our systems. This is nothing more than the near-literal representation of crocodile tears, and I've handed the woman enough handkerchiefs over the years to know that this isn't sadness; it's just salt water.

"Excuse me," she says, dabbing at the corner of her eye with a tissue. "I leak sometimes."

"I know. Do you want to wait for Ernie to come back? He should be here—"

"No," she says abruptly. "I'd prefer if we spoke, just you and me. At first. Then maybe you could pass it on to Ernie, okay?"

I nod and take a seat behind my desk, attempting to straighten the papers back into some semblance of a pile. "Start from the beginning, Louise. That's my best advice."

A deep breath, shoulders rising quickly, then gently falling back into place, and she's ready to lay it out. "Last night, someone broke into our house."

And don't I know it. It takes a special effort, drill-sergeant tactics, to convince my facial muscles to retain their neutral placement.

"I'm so sorry," I say, tone remaining perfectly even. "Did they steal anything?"

Louise shakes her head. "Not that I know of. They destroyed our alarm system, ransacked the bedroom, made a terrible mess of the kitchen." Actually, I thought I'd left the kitchen rather tidy, despite the leg of lamb abandoned on the breakfast table, but I've always had a slightly more lax standard of neatness than my peers.

"So you weren't home."

"Thank God, no. I can't imagine what those monsters would have done."

"The world is full of them," I say, nodding with what I hope comes across as mellow resignation. "Did you call the police?"

"Of course," she says, and my heart takes a small jump backward. "But they couldn't find anything of use. They were dinos, we think, and apparently guises don't leave good prints."

"I see. So how can we be of help? You want us to take a look, try to grab some smells, see if we can find out who did it?"

"Oh, I think we know who did it," she says, and suddenly I'm thinking it wouldn't be the worst idea to keep a defibrillator here in the office. Was this the whole purpose of her visit—to face me one-on-one and confront me with my misdeeds? I usually have no qualms about breaking or entering or "borrowing" or any number of assorted illegal activities Ernie puts me up to, but it's the betrayal of whatever friendship Louise and I have going that puts me on edge.

"How do you know?" I ask, involuntarily pushing my chair back from the desk. "If the police found nothing . . ."

Louise is somber, locking her gaze with mine. "I know because . . . I know."

I hold that look, refusing to flinch away. Play this out till the end. "Then why don't you tell me?" I suggest, hoping she'll do exactly the opposite, that she'll get up and walk out of the office. "Tell me who broke into your house."

"The Progressives," says Louise, and my circulatory system pulls out of the pit stop and races back into action.

"The Progressives?"

"They're a . . . a religion. A cult, I guess."

"I don't follow you. What kind of cult?"

"I don't know. They're all dinosaurs, I know that. A dino cult."

"And why would they break into your house?"

"To get money, maybe?"

"But they didn't take any money."

"Because I don't keep any in the house. That's probably why they wrecked it."

"Why would they break into *your* house, Louise? Why not my house, or Ernie's house?"

"Because I know them. Rather, they know me. Rupert is one of them. He's a Progressive."

"Your brother?"

Louise nods. "For about two years now. I didn't tell anyone when he was getting into it, partially because it scared me, but . . . Honestly, I was hoping that it was a passing thing."

"A phase."

"A phase, yes. He's had enough of them. Remember the hang gliding?"

I can't help but chuckle, and I'm glad to see that Louise joins in. "Of course I remember it," I say. "And the bungee jumping and the trips to India and the Peace Corps and the spelunking. Rupert's a good soul, but a little lost."

"And then a couple of years ago he started selling whatever he had left—his bike, his share of Mom's house. He'd ask me for money, and wouldn't tell me how he was spending it. And now he thinks he's found himself," Louise says. "He says he's found Progress."

"What's that mean?"

"I have no idea. I wish I did." Louise delves into that magical purse of hers—how anything other than a single tube of lipstick could fit in that small compartment I'll never know—and comes up with a folded sheet of paper. "I got this letter two weeks ago, and I've been beside myself since." She hands it over, and I unfold it and take a gander.

In a strong, heavy-handed script, the letter reads:

Dear Sister,

When, in the course of our shared events, it becomes necessary for one portion of the family of Raal to assume among the creatures of the earth a position different from that which they have recently occupied, but one to which the laws of the ancestors and of the ancestors' ancestors entitle them, a decent respect for the opinions of dinokind requires that they should declare the causes that impel them to such a course.

I hold these truths to be self-evident: that I am like no other creature on this planet; that I have a natural beauty inherent within all the family of Raal; that I have a moral and genetic obligation to the ancestors; that I have the capacity to understand myself as myself.

The time will come, in a few short weeks, to retrieve our heritage from the fossil pits of time. I have found Progress, and Progress has found me. My blood is becoming pure as I accept the wisdom and ways of Raal

and our forefathers. Until you too accept yourself as a product of the product of the ancestors, I will not see you again. I love you.

Your brother, Granaagh

"Granaagh?" I ask.

"I don't understand it either. The ancestors, that part about the genetic obligation, this Raal character, retrieving their heritage—it's all beyond me. When I got the letter, I was so worried. It had been months since I'd heard from him, but this . . ." She's starting to cry again, but this time it's actual tears streaming out of those big brown eyes. I'm torn between staying at my desk and joining her on the couch. I remain in place.

"The last two weeks, all I've been doing is looking for him. I've been everywhere. Phone calls, letters, faxes . . . No one knows where he is, even his old friends down at the mission where he used to volunteer. They got letters like mine."

"And the cops?"

"I told the police," she says, "but they say they can't do anything. Religion is . . . religion. They can't touch these places unless they break the law, and Rupert's in his twenties, old enough to make his own decisions."

"I'm very sorry about your brother," I say. "He's a good kid. Mixed up, but a good kid. Anything I can do to help . . ." It's a cursory offer, nothing more, but my mouth has this annoying tendency to speak before it's conferred with the brain.

"I want you to find him," says Louise. "I want you to find him and get him to come home."

"Whoa, whoa, wait up," I say.

"You said you'd help—"

"Sure, but . . . Slow this down a second. Let's even say I can find him, right? That letter doesn't sound like he's the most rational guy in the world right now. Who's to say he'll go with me?"

There's a telltale pause—long enough to make it seem like

she's thinking the question over, short enough so that I know she's already thought it through way before she stepped into my office, that this was the real reason she came to see me today.

"Then I want you to kidnap him."

In the two seconds it takes for me to formulate a proper, polite way to say that there is no way on earth I'm going to commit what amounts to a major felony in order to remove a full-fledged adult from a situation he has presumably chosen for himself, that there is no possibility of Ernie and me taking on a case that, if the right charges were pressed by the wrong people, could land us jail time and a hefty fine, that I can't even begin to think about the circumstances under which a kidnaping, even in a situation as odd as this, could possibly be justified, Ernie opens up the door to our office and charges inside.

"She cleaned Minsky out real good," he announces as he lumbers toward his desk, not bothering to glance over at the couch. He drops a file folder on the seat of his chair and proceeds to rifle through it.

I clear my throat. "Ernie—"

"She got the ether, all right, and some nitrous, and some prescription pads, but I searched the doc's office, and I checked with his secretaries for a listing of what's usually in the storage cabinets—"

"Ernie—" I try to interrupt. Futile. I look at Louise—she looks back—we both look to my partner, who's still got his back turned.

"—and they gave me a whole list of things. And guess what? The crazy bitch took a whole bunch of dental drills and scrapers, too. That's freaking insane, right? I mean, what's she gonna do with fifteen metal scrapers?"

"Hey, Ernie—"

"Wait a sec, Vincent, you gotta see this list. You won't believe—"

"Hello, Ernie." Louise this time. Soft, kind, deliberate.

Ernie clams up and slowly turns on his heel. I can almost make out the knot forming in his throat; wrinkles appear in the manila folder as his hand clenches, knuckles widening.

"Louise."

"You smell well," she says, and I'm worried that I'm going to have to sit around for a replay of our earlier conversation.

Ernie nods at Louise's compliment, doesn't return it. "How's Terrence?" he asks.

"Terrell," Louise and I say as one, and I'm blasted by a vicious look from Ernie. I back off and let them take the conversation down whatever path it needs to go.

"He still doing construction work?"

"He's a contractor," Louise says defensively.

Ernie looks to me. "You two have a lunch date?"

I knew it would come down to accusations eventually; the earlier feelings of guilt well up. "No, Ern—she came by to ask—"

"I need something investigated," says Louise, rescuing me. Now Ernie can hear his ex-wife out, listen to each word carefully and patiently, then toss the idea on the skids, and we can get back to looking into the Minsky affair.

Ernie moves out from behind his desk, each step slow, conscious. "Whatever we can do to help." From here, I can see his nostrils flaring—he's trying to get a whiff of her, catch the aroma that he loves so dearly.

"Rupert's joined a cult," she says plainly. "I want you to find him, and, if he won't come home with you, I want you to kidnap him."

No hesitation from Ernie. "Certainly."

Certainly? *Certainly?* I must be throwing off pheromones at an unnatural level now—some dinos can smell themselves, but I've never been able to—because Ernie holds up a hand in my direction, a clear signal that I should clam up and calm down.

"Louise, Ernie and I really need to talk this over," I say. "But if you come back tomorrow—"

"No need," Ernie interrupts, moving closer to his ex-wife. They're only a few feet apart now, and each is clearly into smelling the other. "We can take the case."

"Thank you," says Louise. "I gave Vincent all the details."

"Good. We'll see what we can do—"

I hop forward and wedge myself between these two conspirators. "Now wait just a second," I say, but Ernie sidesteps me and opens the office door.

"—and give you a call once we have something concrete."

More tears coming out of Louise's right eye again, and this time I can't be sure if they're chemically or emotionally produced. "I can't thank you enough," she says. "Whatever it costs—"

"No charge," says Ernie, and now it takes all the strength I can muster to keep my eyes from blasting out of my head like a cartoon character who's accidentally ingested half a ton of chili powder. I grab a hold of the side of the door, if only to keep myself from shooting into the stratosphere.

Louise issues Ernie a peck on the cheek, a polite "Bye, Vincent" to me, and then she's out the door and down the hall, and Ernie's back behind his desk. When the red haze of rancor has faded from before my eyes and my blood pressure has returned to triple digits, I find Ernie sitting calmly at his desk, highlighting the dental inventory sheet he brought back from Minsky's.

"This is a *partnership*," I begin, keeping myself at a moderate pace so that I might choose each and every word with caution and clarity. "If you do not understand the concept of *partnership*, perhaps I could explain it to you. Shall we get a dictionary?"

Ernie looks up from his work. The whites of his eyes—the only dino part I can see of him right now, as the brown contacts he's wearing cover up the natural blazing green of his Carnotaur irises—are choked with red veins wiggling and squiggling in every direction like a first-grader's art project. Even through the thickness of his latex mask, his cheeks look sunken and hollow, and his entire body refuses to remain in a perfectly upright position; his shoulders slump, pointing down to the floor.

"For Louise" is all he says, and it's enough to stop the final dribbles of steam from pouring out of my ears. "For Louise." *For Louise* should be Ernie's motto, etched into his forehead like a pair of monogrammed Mickey Mouse ears, and though I cannot fully empathize with my partner, I can understand the power of those words, if only because I've never had a Louise to do anything for.

"We're talking felony here," I point out. "Kidnaping's a step beyond anything you've tried before."

"We might not even find him, Vincent."

"And if we do, then what?"

Ernie shrugs. "Then we tell him that his sister loves him and misses him and we want to help. Rupert might come along willingly."

"And the odds on that?"

"There's lots of definitions of 'willingly,'" Ernie says, some sparkle returning to that defeated body. "And there's lots of ways to make fellows think they're willing. Look, I don't want to break the law any more than you—"

"Hah!"

"—so first we try to talk sense into him. If that doesn't work, you and I drop back and discuss what's next." Ernie's eyes are wide open now, part of his tried-and-true trust-me-I'm-honest face.

"So, we discuss, a serious discussion—like, a *discussion* discussion—you and me, before we get into the heavy stuff? Promise?"

Ernie nods. "Promise."

I hold out my hand, and we shake on it. A mere formality, but my partner and I don't have to make deals like this very often, so it seems right to mark it with such a canonical gesture.

I walk back to my desk, feeling victorious that I was able to pressure Ernie for once, that I was able to force him into a binding agreement. Then I replay the scene in my mind, piece by piece, and quickly come to realize exactly which way the ball bounced. "I just got talked into this, didn't I?"

"Like a tourist in a trinket shop," says Ernie, and returns to his highlighting.

There are any number of ways to approach Hollywood Boulevard, but for pure shock value, the key is to strike at the heart of the beast, right where the cheese factor is highest: the intersection of Hollywood and Highland Avenue. That's Limburger Central, baby, with a side of extra stink. You cruise on up the street, passing Santa Monica and Sunset, all-for-a-dollar stores slowly replacing the discount movie-prop and video-editing services, and by the time you hit the Boulevard, you're a primetime player in a full-fledged Warhol/Escher urban nightmare. There are the usual tourist hot spots, of course, but it's the locals who make the original sin city worth the pricey parking lot fees.

Things have changed, I'll let that much slide—it's not the eighties anymore, when Mohawks were to Hollywood Boulevard what crew cuts are to the Marines, but the hairstyles are still plentiful, large, and kaleidoscopic. Many of the denizens of the area have found new, impressive ways to express their self-loathing, primarily by locating body parts to pierce that were previously unknown to medical science. The hate-the-world sneer, so popular only five short years ago, has recently been replaced by the I've-seen-it-all smirk, which is less visually disconcerting, but still troubling nonetheless. And the clothing is still a hoot; though ripped jeans have been usurped by ripped leather, the end result is the same: ragged clothing, soiled flesh, and a brown-tinged aura that acts as a bumper sticker—DON'T BOTHER ME, I'M DANGEROUS. Heck of a town.

Dinos, as a rule, do not frequent this part of the city; we find it difficult enough to live our double lives without having to dis-enfranchise ourselves from the rest of the world by choice. Still, there are exceptions, and I've smelled a few of our kind among the runaways and hustlers lining the gold-sprinkled streets. This, by the way, is not a colorful description—a number of years ago, the Hollywood Chamber of Commerce actually voted to embed flecks of gold plating into the asphalt of the Boulevard itself, so that the city streets could truly be said to be paved with gold. Delusional, to be certain, but that's why I love coming up here.

"I hate coming up here," Ernie says to me in the car. It's round about three in the afternoon, and we've just finished up doing some preliminary investigation on Star, aka Christine Josephson, Minsky's little fruit tart. She's sweet, all right—the kind of sweet that'll rot you from the inside out. Three lockups in juvie, two arrests as an adult, no small cookies when you're only nineteen.

"We're in, and then we're out," I say. "All I wanna do is talk to Jules, and we're done. If anyone has a handle on this Progressives thing, she will."

"She creeps me out."

"She creeps everyone out. Bite your tongue and try not to kiss her."

Dingy golden stars pass by underfoot, each engraved with the name of a so-called celebrity. Some are famous, some slightly less so, some have been plucked from the *Encyclopedia Obscuria*, but they've all paid to get there. The sordid secret about the Walk of Fame is that there's no particular distinction in having one of these hunks of bronze, apart from the honor of knowing that your studio paid ten grand to the city of Hollywood. That's all it takes—a picture of Salmon P. Chase on a little green bill and you, too, can be pissed on by some of the most erudite bums in the universe.

We pass by Danny Kaye (Ornithomimus) and Bob Hope (Compy—actually, the only one I've ever laughed *with* rather than *at*), and a host of other dino-cum-celebrities, and eventually arrive at the famous Hollywood Wax Museum, where twenty-four hours a day you can witness the spectacle of wax slowly melting under ultraviolet light. It's not as exciting as it sounds.

I pay the husky female attendant my eight dollars—"Highway robbery," mumbles Ernie—and as the woman turns around to give us our tickets, I take a deep whiff near the back of her neck. I'm rewarded with the musky odor of fermented yeast and peanut shells. This chick's a walking baseball game, but at least now I know she's a dino.

"Is Jules in today?" I ask, spinning around to make my scent glands readily available to her.

"I don't wanna smell ya," she barks. "I gotta smell the crap walking down this street all day long, I don't need any more."

"Just tell us if Jules is here," says Ernie.

"Yeah, it's here today." A push of a small button beneath her console and the front door to the museum buzzes open. "It's in the back."

"I know where to go," I say and lead Ernie into the darkness.

We pass through the chamber of terror—this is where it all gets a little spooky, mind you—and once we're over the shock of how similar the Michael Jackson sculpture has become to LaToya's over the years, we enter the actual Hall of Horrors, replete with larger-than-life figures of Frankenstein, the Wolf-man, and more than a few real-life serial killers.

We make our way to the back of the museum, passing a few tourists along the way—mammals, all of them—until we reach the pièce de résistance, a diorama with attendant wax sculptures depicting the fighting medical men of the 4077th, the lovable team from M*A*S*H. Not content with having extended the Korean War three times longer than necessary, Hawkeye, Radar, and the rest of that wacky crew now invade reality every day via six thousand pounds of wax and a couple of shaky-looking plastic army tents.

"Last I saw her, she'd moved the workstation back here," I say, leading Ernie past a partially melted B. J. Hunnicut and toward one of the small tent facades. A quick series of knocks on the "false" door on the front of the tent, and after a few moments, a muted scuffling emanates from the other side.

"Turn around," comes a raspy voice, shot through with sultry overtones.

"It's me, Jules. It's Vincent."

"Then you know the rules, lover. Turn around."

A small compartment slides open near the door's peephole, and I willingly place the back of my neck against the wire mesh, presenting my scent glands for inspection. A strong inhale from behind the screen, a moment's whiff of delight, and a second later the lock turns.

As the door opens, I notice that some form of unnatural human perfume is at work in this place, nearly overpowering Jules's natural lemon chiffon aroma. She must be slathering on the Obsession again, a filthy mammalian habit she can't seem to break. We walk through the door to find Jules strutting back toward her workshop, wiggling that tight guised-up rear as she goes. She's sporting a pair of form-fitting black jeans this afternoon, along with a sleeveless blouse that's got all but two buttons undone. Long, curly black hair hangs down to that small waist of hers, and the legs stretch in all the right directions. For a human female, Jules is a knockout.

Too bad she's a Velociraptor, and bad over again that she's male.

"Close the door, fellas," purrs my favorite dino drag queen. "So sweet to see you."

"I'm gonna be sick," Ernie mumbles to me, and I fix him with a hard glare. It's not rare for dinosaurs to be homosexual, but the spectacle of a male dino wearing the guise of a human female is just too much double deception for most of our kind to take. There's persecution and there's persecution, but ostracism knows no bounds for a dino who's crossed genders. As a result, Jules spends most of her time in this cramped, musty back room, practicing her special brand of guise reconstruction away from the public eye.

Moving quickly after our host, we head down a short corridor and soon enter the workshop. Great multicolored balls of wax line the wooden floor of this simple, spartan studio; the concrete walls are bare of decoration, and an intricate shelving system hangs down from above, bolted into the ceiling via strong iron clasps. Within these drawers and cabinets and compartments are the tools of Jules's trade—scalpels, syringes, putty knives, and mallets—along with a few samples of her work so that she might give customers a chance to see in advance what they'll look like once their requested procedure is complete. Photographs line the walls, intricate close-up work detailing the before-and-after nature of her profession.

"You come for your lips, Vincent doll?" Jules asks me as she takes her place behind that wide oak table. "Mmm, we could fatten those up a bit, make 'em smooth and kissable."

I smile and say, "Not why we're here, Jules."

"Of course it's not why you're here, but a little help every now and again doesn't hurt a man, does it? Us ladies aren't the only ones who need the nipping and the tucking. Ten-minute procedure, tops." She beckons me closer, and, always amused at her little antics, I obediently step toward her open hands. A slight tug at the top lip of my mask as she brings up a long, red fingernail, tracing it along the fleshy underside. "One cut down the main line, then I implant, say, twenty cc's of wax, re-sew, even it out, and suddenly you're a dreamboat."

"Forget the lip job. We need some information," Ernie blurts out.

Jules falls back behind the desk, landing hard on her simple wooden stool. Her eyes meet mine—dazed, a little hurt.

"It's not that we don't think you're a great plastic surgeon," I explain. "We think you're the best. But we've got an appointment. Soon. We just don't have the time."

"I *am* good," she pouts.

"I know you are."

She turns to Ernie, eyelids blinking, flashing at strobe-light speeds, bottom lip puffing out, turning it all on. "And you, big boy?"

Ernie looks to me, and I pointedly look away. No help here; Ernie's never been the most tolerant of fellows, and though he's certainly an old dog, there's a few new tricks he's gotta learn.

"Fine." He sighs. "You're good. You're the best. Can we get on with this?"

All smiles now, Jules reaches out and pinches Ernie's cheek. "We sure can, lover."

"Have you ever heard of the Progressives?" I ask.

A wad of phlegm slaps onto the concrete floor, and it's a stunned moment before I realize that Jules is the culprit. "Why would you want to know?" she mutters.

"Guess you've heard of 'em," Ernie says. "What can you tell us?"

"Only secondhand information, darling. I hear what I hear from my friends on the street, but my friends on the street aren't always the most reliable queens in the world."

"What could make them reliable?" I ask.

"A little bit of basil, a little sniff of snapdragon," singsongs Jules, smiling all the way. "Unfortunately, the drag business isn't what it was five years ago. Did you know they're shutting down the Shangri-La next Saturday? It's becoming a coffee shop, of all the horrible things. Times are tight for my little friends, the poor dears."

"They're good, they'll find work."

"They're the best, but the best doesn't work for free, darling."

She's avoiding the issue; this is what Jules does when she's uncomfortable with the conversation at hand. But two twenty-dollar bills are soon making their way from Ernie's wallet to the oak table, and when I give him a little nudge, he adds one more to the pile. Jules scoops up the money, folds the bills in half, and tucks them inside her shirt, presumably into some bra we are unable to see.

"You don't want to deal with them," she begins. "They've screwed up a lot of good dinos."

"That's why we're looking. Go on."

She sighs, but the lady knows she's got to talk once the money's been put away. "Started up about thirty years ago by some nutcase vacuum salesman," she begins, formalities having been dispensed with. "Built it up out of the back room of his little store up in Pasadena, but over the years they got more and more converts. Business folk. Finance folk. Entertainment folk. Anyone with money, or access to money, anyone looking for a way outta their regular life. From what I hear, they've got their tendrils all through the city by now."

"What's this guy's name?"

"Don't remember. Doesn't make a difference anyway, honey, 'cause he's dead. Caught some bug and bit the big one 'bout ten years back."

"Bummer. Coulda been a good start."

"You wanna start somewhere, sugar, go sign up. The Progressives have a storefront down by Hollywood and Vine," she says. "My friends tell me they've got quite the operation going out of there."

I shake my head. "Can't be. Been by that corner a dozen times and I've never seen it."

"And if you tell people that this isn't a wax museum," says Jules, "if you tell 'em that it's just a front for black-market guise surgery, how fast do you think they'll call the loony bin on your sweet behind?"

"Go on."

"It's a tourist crap shop on the outside. Three T-shirts for ten dollars, plastic Hollywood signs, fake California license plates with your name on it. They're all over the Boulevard, but this one's got a little something extra where something shouldn't be."

Ernie can't hold back. "Bet you know that real well."

Jules doesn't mind the crack. She blows him a wet kiss, tongue waggling through the air like a panting dog. "Your friend is catty today, Vincent," she says to me. "I like that in a man."

I let it go—no need to wring the tension rod even tighter—and say, "Let's pretend we're interested in talking to one of these Progressives. Say we're interested in finding out more about the group. We walk into the tourist shop and . . . what? Is there a code word?"

"You've been in this business too long, Vincent. No code word. In fact, you don't even have to walk inside. Those cats are always on the prowl, waiting outside the shop, smelling the air for dinos walking by. They catch a whiff of one, they invite you inside the store, and that's when the fun begins."

"Fun, eh?"

"It helps if you look lost."

"Maybe we should buy a map."

"*Spiritually* lost. Emotionally lost. Pretend you've just lost your job and your house kind of lost. Pretend your dog ran away kind of lost. Pretend your wife's left you kind of lost."

At this, Ernie spins and stomps back toward the door. "Come on, Vincent. We've got what we came for—"

"Ernie, wait—she—she didn't—"

"Forget it," he growls. "I'm done with this shit. Let's go."

"I'll meet you outside," I call after him. I hope he's heard me, as he's already through the door, into the museum, and winding his way past Hot Lips and Frank on his way toward the exit.

"Did I say something wrong?" asks Jules.

"Not so you'd know it. His wife . . . He's grumpy right now. Don't mind him."

"I won't. So . . . how's it going, sweetie? Got any hot punches on your dance ticket?"

I shake my head. "No one like you, Jules. Listen, I spoke with your father, like you asked me to."

"Oh." Her hands begin to fiddle with the instruments by her side. She absentmindedly rolls a ball of wax around the table, gaze averted from mine, as if by not looking she can shield herself from the truth. "And?"

"And . . . it's the same as it was."

"He won't see me," she says, trying to keep the warble out of her voice.

"No. He won't."

Jules issues a game little shrug, tossing her hair back across one shoulder. "Well, it's his loss, right?"

"Exactly. His loss." I'm not good at this comfort thing. I should probably put out my hand for her to take. I should probably put an arm around her shoulder. I should at least convey my apologies for not being able to convince her severely opinionated father that his only son is not a freak of nature, that he's just doing what he feels is right in a world where not only do the sexes masquerade as one another, but the species can't even keep their tails on straight. But as it is, I just stand there mutely, waiting for Jules to let me out of the awkward situation.

"Go on, Vincent," she says quietly. "Go join your cult."

Our destination is about six blocks down from the wax museum, and in a driving town, that's practically a marathon. Only time you'll find most Angelenos walking that far is when their car runs out of fuel six blocks from a gas station. And even then, the resourceful ones find a way to have a few gallons delivered to the side of the road.

Schwab's Drugstore is gone. Brown Derby? Vanished. Diners and celebrity hot spots and places to see and be seen? Vamoosed. Not quite the entertainment crossroads it once was, the corner of Hollywood and Vine now boasts four fine establishments: a liquor store, an empty lot, a gas station, and High on Hollywood, the tourist trap Jules told us about.

"You didn't have to be so mean to the gal," I complain as we make our way past yet another SPACE FOR LEASE sign.

"Yeah, and she—he—whatever—didn't have to bring up Louise leaving me."

"She didn't even know about Louise. She was just giving an example."

"Oh." He clams up.

"See, not so high and mighty now, are you?"

"Don't push me, kid."

"Excuse me, brothers—" This, coming from behind us, accompanied by the distinct scent of pine. "Brothers, would you like to have a word about our shared interests?"

Ernie and I hit the brakes on our little argument and turn as one, coming face to face with tidy incarnate. This is, without a doubt, the most clean-cut individual I've ever seen east of La Cienega Boulevard. Short, cropped hair, blue worker's shirt, tan khakis, and a sparkle in the eye that tells me we've got nothing short of a full-blown live-wire nut-job standing in our midst.

"Our shared interests?" I say, playing it cool. Ernie and I decided on the hike down here to give ourselves into their little game, but only after a hard sell.

"We're the same, the three of us," says the dino, and though I know it's not possible, it's as if he sends me a little pheromonal wink, an extra burst of that pine and baby-oil scent.

Ernie huffs, "There's lots of us around, pal. We're not tourists, we don't want to buy your toys."

"It's a free service, brother," he says. "No charge whatsoever, and I promise you'll learn more about yourself in thirty minutes than you ever thought possible. There is more to this than trinkets and T-shirts, I assure you, brother. Come inside, we can speak."

"About?"

"About each other. About our common ancestry."

Now we're talking. Rupert's letter to Louise was littered with references to ancestral mumbo-jumbo. "Ernie, you interested?" I ask. We've made a conscious decision to use our real names— our first names at least—because the last time we tried out undercover names we kept slipping left and right. Ernie was supposed to be Patch and I was supposed to be Jimmy and the number of times we referred to each other incorrectly ran into the dozens. Fortunately, it was just a routine roust on a two-bit counterfeit toenail operation, so despite our slips, the bad guys were too small-time to notice.

"What the hell," Ernie replies. "We got time to kill."

The clean-cut dino grins—the lip stretch not too wide, not too thin, and somehow very sane—and says, "Follow me." We do so.

Jules was right—the tourist shop is both incredibly tacky and not much more than a front. The storage room leads to a back office that leads down a flight of stairs and to a rusty metal door set into the wall below.

"Where the hell are we going?" asks Ernie.

"The subway," says the dino, and the door swings open without a creak.

I'm proud of my hometown, if only for its excesses. The Los Angeles subway system is widely recognized as one of the most fraudulent, wasteful, and potentially dangerous uses of public tax money since the good old bacchanalian orgies of the Roman Empire. At least in Nero's time you could get yourself drunk, laid, or both; in the LA subway you can mostly count on getting yourself dead. The genius engineers who came up with this radical mass-transit plan neglected to take into account the fact that the ground out here has a tendency to move without the courtesy of giving two weeks' notice, and that subway tunnels don't take well to being rerouted by shifting tectonic plates. As a result, nearly everyone in the city derides the notion of riding the subway, leaving a select few individuals to adopt it for their own use. It should come as little surprise, then, that the Los Angeles subway system has become a haven for the city's burgeoning dinosaur population. New York has alligators swimming the sewers beneath its streets; we have Stegosaurs.

"I caught *your* name, Ernie," says our guide as he leads us out onto a platform adjacent to the subway tunnel, "but I didn't catch your friend's."

"That's Vincent. And you?"

"You can call me Bob," says the dino. "For now."

I can't let that pass. "Is there something else we should call you?"

"No," he says. "Bob is fine."

We hop down into the subway tunnel—looking left, left, and left again—and climb up onto a walkway that runs parallel to the tracks. Dim overhead lighting illuminates the path for a good twenty feet before it drops off into murky darkness.

"Is this safe?" I ask, peering down at the tracks below.

"We're fine up here," says Bob. "Don't worry about the third rail."

"The rail, hell. What about the trains?"

"There are no trains in Hollywood yet. They're still working on getting the downtown system running straight." Which means we're in the clear for at least the next few decades.

Out of the shadows in the distance a silhouette detaches itself from the wall and angles toward our party. Instinctively, my muscles clench up, as I sense the real possibility of an ambush. No one knows we're down here, and there aren't many who would care to go hunting for us if we didn't show up in the real world for the next few years. Next to me, I feel Ernie tense as well.

"Good afternoon, Sreeaal," says Bob, waving a hand in the shadowy figure's direction. The last word is more of a shriek, a strangled roar, than an actual string of letters, and I take it to be the other gentleman's name.

"Good afternoon, brothers." It's another blue-shirted, tan-Dockered Progressive, I can see now, and he's got that same wholesome aura floating about his perfectly groomed body. There's an urge rising in me to rub my hands through the subway muck coating the walls and transfer some good, honest filth over to these two dinos, but I imagine it would bring a rapid end to the proceedings. "Are your friends interested in their ancestry?"

"I'm interested in getting outta the subway," says Ernie, and the two Progressives laugh as one unit, too loud, too long.

"You have a strong spirit, brother," the newcomer says to Ernie, to which my partner emits an audible grunt. Then, to Bob: "Be well, Baynal," this last name yet again nothing more than a throaty growl. Before our guide has a chance to return the salutation, the dino is past us and lost in the shadows once again.

"He didn't call you Bob."

"No. He didn't."

"You wanna explain that?"

"My true name is Baynal. Bob is my slave name."

"Your slave name." Is my sarcasm poking through?

"The name that I have taken on in my mammal form. We're all just slaves to our guises. Progress shows us that."

"I'm sure it does," I say.

"Don't you ever feel it?" he asks. "That you're a second-class citizen? That you have to hide your natural beauty every day, that by imitating the mammals, we're slowly becoming them? That through their very nature, they're controlling us—how we act, how we dress, how we think?"

"Never gave it the once-over," says Ernie.

"So it's . . . Baynal," I clarify, trying to fit my voice into that terrible shriek of a name.

"Correct. But call me Bob if it makes you feel more comfortable."

"I'll do that."

I decide this might be a good point to go fishing. "I like your outfit," I tell Bob. "I knew someone who dressed just like that. . . . What was his name, Ern?"

"You mean Rupert?"

"That's right," I say. "Rupert Simmons. Swell fella, wore those same clothes as you and your friend."

If there's a reaction from Bob, I can't discern it in the darkness of the tunnel.

We eventually leave the subterranean world through another unmarked metal door, climb a flight of stairs, and arrive in a large, well-lit room separated by row after row of solid gray partitions.

It's like any other modern office space, and I fully expect to see Garfield cartoons and family snapshots tacked up on the barren walls. But there's nothing in these cubicles but a contingent of guised-up dinosaurs, each speaking on their own separate phone, jabbering away at a low, easygoing pace. Dino smells flow down the makeshift corridors, mixing and merging with one another into a soupy pine melange.

"Big place," I say. "Who runs the joint?"

"Just some friends." We enter a small, glass-walled room. "Please, take a seat. You'll find some pastries on the table behind you."

Sure enough, there's all manner of tasty dessert treats lining the shaky card table set up in the corner, and I've almost downed a scrumptious-looking fruit tart and a cup full of punch before I remember that even though I'm playing an innocent rube, I can't fall too deeply into character. I know nothing about this place or these people, including whether or not they have a tendency to drug their new recruits. "You know, I had a big lunch," I say. "I'm not very hungry." Ernie echoes my sentiments.

"Fine, then," says Bob, his expression not changing in the least, "let's get started. I'm sure you'll be amazed—I know I was."

Ernie and I sink into cushioned leather seats around a solid wooden desk, pointedly making ourselves as comfortable as possible. As Bob opens up a large wooden cabinet on the far wall with a shiny brass key, Ernie leans over and whispers, "You get a load of this place? There's money here."

"Question is, where'd they get it?" I mumble back. "Not selling snow globes on Hollywood Boulevard, I'll tell you that much."

With a grunt and a heave, Bob lifts a lead box no more than two feet square out of the cabinet and hauls it over to the top of the table. It lands with an audible thunk. "It's small," he says, "but quite heavy." A moment later, the cabinet is locked up tight once again, and Bob seats himself across from us.

"Who's first?" he asks.

Ernie scoots his chair forward. "Whadda we gotta do?"

"I'll need you to remove your gloves, first of all. The tests must be administered to natural dinosaur flesh. Latex is a poor conductor, to say the least."

"I'll do it," I volunteer. My underclaw's been itching to come out for some time now; it's been at least three days since I disrobed completely, and if I don't wash under this guise sometime soon, I'm going to have my own little fungus circus to take care of. Can't have that—I look terrible with a rash.

Feeling for the buttons hidden beneath my fake mammalian flesh, I work the silicon knobs around and out of their holes until the gloves loosen of their own accord. Then it's just a matter of a light pull with the other hand and I've got the freedom to release my claws into the air. My underclaw is sticking slightly, chattering along its tracks like a stuttering, sputtering go-cart, and I should probably have that looked at by a dino doc at some time in the near future.

"You have a beautiful natural skin," says Bob. "It's a shame you have to cover it up all day."

"Not much of a choice there," I say. "Council doesn't look kindly on a Raptor strolling down Wilshire, huh? My tail might knock out some window displays."

"And if you could go without a guise?" asks Bob. "What then?"

"Pointless question," I respond.

"Hypothetically, then. If you could just rip it off and go natural . . . ?"

"What, all day? If I could . . ." It's an intriguing proposition, I must confess—the freedom to open up and expose my skin to the air, to banish all worries about these girdles and straps and buckles that constrict my flesh and impede my natural movement, to use my tail and my legs and my body the way it feels it *should* be used. "If I could, I would," I admit. "But I can't. So I don't."

Bob's grin is infectious; I find myself smirking along. "Good," he says. "Let's begin."

With a flourish, Bob whips off the cover to the metallic box, exposing a ridiculous gadget time-warped out of the space movies of the 1950s. It's the decapitated head of Robby the Robot, only with an array of lights and buttons and switches and knobs and meters set into the side, each currently dormant save for a single pulsating button.

"This is an Ancestrograph," says Bob, extending his arm, palm upright. He turns to me. "Please, give me your hand."

My initial reaction is to refuse, but I've already come through the subway and down into an undisclosed location with the guy; if he wanted to put me out of my misery, I imagine he would have done so by now. I place my hand in his—the grip firm, insistent, but not painful in any way—and he leads my index finger, claw extended, toward a small, dark opening at the top of the box.

"Retract your claw, if you could." I do so. "Good. It's not usually a problem, but claws have been known to jam the machine. Better safe than sorry." More than happy to comply. It would most likely hurt my singles-bar pickup techniques if I had to walk around with an Ancestrograph permanently attached to my hand.

As my finger disappears into the hole, the device emits a perceptible hum; accordingly, a series of green lights flick on and the needles of the meters start to twitch. Meanwhile, the metal surrounding my finger begins a palpable drop in temperature, and within thirty seconds my once-warm digit is well on its way to becoming a fish stick. I look up at Ernie and issue a game little grin. "Piece of cake," I say. Ernie looks dubious.

"This is the first phase," says Bob. "It's testing your pheromones."

"It's smelling me?"

"Not exactly. That slight cooling sensation you feel is starting a process of condensation. Whatever hormones are seeping out of the pores in your finger are being turned into liquid form by the low temperature, which the machine can then test."

"Test for what?" I ask.

"Purity," is the only reply. I do not ask for an elaboration.

A minute of this, and now my finger is starting to turn numb. Is this their little scheme—frostbite me to death, piece by piece?

If he asks me to put any other body part inside that hole I'm going to whack him to next Tuesday.

But just as I'm about to complain, a moment before I yank my digit from the hole and go back to good old-fashioned interrogative techniques involving browbeating and bloodshed, I feel a sharp prick at the tip of my finger.

"Hey!" I shout, my arm flexing backward involuntarily. Pain, small and sharp, accompanied by fluid. Bringing my hand up for inspection—sure enough, there's a small stream of blood trickling down toward my palm. "What the hell was that for?"

But Bob just grins that maddening grin and says, "Taking a blood sample, Vincent. We can't do an Ancestrograph without a blood sample."

"Obviously," drawls Ernie, holding back a chuckle.

"You could have told me."

"And then you wouldn't have done it. As it is, I'm going to have a harder time getting your friend here to go along now."

"Damn straight," says Ernie.

But it doesn't take much in the way of persuasion to convince Ernie to do what all the other cool kids are doing. Bob removes my samples from within the guts of the box—I try to peer inside, but can't make out anything other than a few wires and some diodes—and recalibrates the machine. Ernie unwraps his hand and repeats the procedure, but his anticipation of the pinprick allows him to stay stone-faced when the pain comes. Makes my earlier protestations look foolish, but I bet if situations were reversed, he'd have cried like a Compy.

"We done yet?" Ernie asks.

"Nearly." Bob unveils a new machine attached to the wall— a Pheromonitor, I am told, which looks like a cross between a condom dispenser and a blood-pressure gauge—and places the small vial holding my bodily fluid samples into a receptacle in the bottom. "Let's see what we've got here," says Bob, flipping a switch on the side.

Lights flicker, engines whir, and the vial is snatched up in a furious rush of air. I watch the murky liquid inside being sucked up to the tune of a bubbling vacuum, and the needles on the machine's meters begin to convulse.

Bob clicks his tongue and says, "Oh, this is very . . . interesting. . . ."

I find myself actually leaning forward, trying to decipher the seemingly random blips and beeps of the machine, tracking the needle jumps, attempting to interpret this strange mechanical language. "What's it saying about me?"

"It's determining your ancestral purity," explains Bob. "Over time, each of us has gotten further and further away from the pure dinosaur lineage. We've become mongrels."

"I don't see how," I say. "My parents were Raptors. Their parents were Raptors. None of us can produce kids unless it's with another of the same breed, so I'm as pure as they come."

"I don't mean breed purity, Vincent. I mean dinosaur purity. Every day we put on these costumes is another day we lose part of ourselves. Here, see for yourself."

A long sheet of white accountant's paper has scrolled out of the bottom of the machine, black numbers set in bold, even type filling the page. It's all data and figures and mathematical hoo-ha, but at the very bottom of the page there is what amounts to a declaration of my inadequacies as a member of the greatest species on earth: 32% DINOSAUR NATURAL.

"Thirty-two percent 'dinosaur natural'? What the hell's that supposed to mean?"

Bob says, "Many of us are very upset to learn how far we've fallen—"

"Damn right, I'm upset. Stupid machine—"

"But for every problem, there's a solution. I'll let you in on a little secret—when I had my first Ancestrograph, I was only twenty-nine percent natural."

"You don't say." Doesn't make me feel that much better, to be honest. I'd hope I'm at least a good twenty percent higher than Bob here on any standardized test.

"But now, with a little Progress, my last test read at sixty-seven percent." Bob beams with pride.

And I can't help but find myself a little intrigued by the notion of raising what seem to be arbitrary numbers produced by an obviously rigged machine. "How'd you do it?" I ask.

"Oh, it's not an easy journey," Bob assures me. "But it is a possible one, and the most rewarding experience there is. Here, let's see how your friend measures up, and then we can talk some more."

"I'm on the edge of my seat," Ernie deadpans.

Ernie's fluids take a path similar to mine, and when all the sound and the fury is over and done with, he's listed as 27 percent natural. No two ways about it—I gotta gloat a little. "Beating you by five points, buddy."

"So what's all this mean?" I ask, giving Bob the opening to make the sale.

"It means we can help you," he says. "It means that although your impurities are strong, there's still hope."

I make a show of nodding, thinking it over. "You say 'we.' Is this a business?"

"No, no," says Bob, who has begun to put the machines back into their proper places. "Think of it as a club."

"A club."

"A social club. With benefits." Bob opens another drawer and pulls out two leaflets printed on muted green paper. "Here, each of you take one." The top reads *You're Invited to a Special Event* in a strong, flashy font. "It's short notice, I know—tomorrow night—but I think you'll get a lot out of it."

"What kinda event?" asks Ernie.

"We meet every once in a while to discuss dino-related issues, that sort of thing. It's like a cocktail party. Free food, free drink, music, good friends. A lot of fun, really. And tomorrow night, we'll have a special lecture from Circe."

"Circe?" I know that name from the few weeks I spent studying mythology for the botched Therakropolis case—don't ask, don't ask—but the exact nature of the creature involved eludes me.

"Circe is ninety-six percent pure," says Bob.

"You don't say."

"She's become something like a president to the club. A fascinating lady. Perhaps I can arrange an introduction."

"That'd be super."

Bob gives our hands a hearty shake and says, "As you can see from the invitation, the party is up in the Hollywood Hills. There's driving instructions on the bottom."

I peruse the invite. All's in order. "Sounds like a swell shindig."

"So . . ." says Bob, "can I count you two in?"

No need for signals between us this time; Ernie and I know we're at least halfway into where we want to be, and much faster than we had ever imagined. Finding Rupert and the end of this case is but a mere step or two down a well-paved path.

"We'd love to come to your party," Ernie says, and the deal is done.

. . .

Later, after Bob's taken us back up to the street via a separate exit and subway tunnel, Ernie and I hop into the car and make our way down Highland. There's dirty work to be done before the party, and though I hate to deceive my partner, sometimes it's necessary. He doesn't always know what's best for him, the old biddy, and I'm often the one who has to drag him into this decade kicking and screaming.

So I wait until we pass Santa Monica Boulevard, then veer the car sharply into the right lane. That's when it hits my partner—rather sooner than I anticipated, actually, and I hope he doesn't try to leap out of the automobile and make a break for it. Ernie knows full well where I'm taking him, and he fixes me with his best why-hast-thou-forsaken-me stare.

"C'mon, kid, you can't do this to me."

"If we're going to a party in the Hills tomorrow night—"

"It's not a party," says Ernie, his voice rising with something approaching panic. "It's a cult meeting. I got lots of stuff to wear, Vincent."

"I can't let you go to a party—I can't even let you go to a cult meeting—looking like something outta the Sears catalog from 1978. Not if you're gonna be standing by me."

We pull onto Melrose.

5

The place: The Hills of Hollywood, one vertical mile north of the Boulevard. The time: Round about seven in the P.M. The mood: Tense. The clothing: As stylish as it is uncomfortable. I'm driving, Ernie's complaining, and all is right with the undercover world.

"We get in, we listen to their shpiel, we find Rupert, we get out."

"Works for me, Ern."

"And then I get outta these goddamned silk pants."

I shake my head. "It's not silk—it's linen. It's very in."

Ernie doesn't care; he pulls petulantly at his Calvin Klein shirt and Armani slacks like a five-year-old dressed up for Sunday church. I drive on.

In the twenty-four hours between our marathon session down the corridors of Melrose Avenue—during which time Ernie was introduced to the wonders of all sorts of clothing whose designers do not advertise for Kmart, and whose fabrics do not trace their origins to the Poly or Ester families—and our "club meeting" with the Progressives in the Hollywood Hills, we did some more grunt work trying to track down Minsky's babe of the week. It's not rare that we work multiple cases at the same time. A PI's plate is never, ever full; if it's piled too high, we just get another set of dishes.

First step was trying to find a home address, and though this was easy enough with the help of Dan Patterson, a Bronto friend of mine on the LAPD, the rat hole that Star Josephson used to live in has been red-tagged and condemned by the Board of Health. I guess we could have gone in, tried to case the place, but great cracks had made their way down the exterior walls and across the roof of the building, like crevasses in a glacier, and the whole structure looked ready to collapse under its own weight. Unfortunately for us, even the more daredevil mammals and dinos had abandoned the joint, and roaches don't give out forwarding addresses, so we were on our own.

We had a few pictures—Polaroids, mostly, snapped by Minsky in a fit of hormone-fueled lust—and we showed 'em around with all the vigor we could muster, eliciting gasps from old ladies and knowing leers from young gents.

"I know the tramp," one particularly foul-smelling Compy told us. His name was Sweetums, and he was a pimp working the dino hooker trade up on Sunset. I've used Sweetums before, mostly to find missing girls, as he's the kind of pimp who makes them go missing in the first place. Not your midafternoon tea kind of fellow, but he knows what he knows, and he always needs cash. Poor sap's got a furious saffron habit, and that delicious toxin doesn't come cheap. "I seen her cooling her heels out on the Boulevard."

"And you tried to take her in," I said.

"Take her in, break her in, it's all in the game," cooed Sweetums.

"You're a saint. Just tell me where to find her." I emphasized my last point with two folded twenties, and Sweetums snatched them between his teeth, shaking the bills around like a dog with a chew toy.

The pimp licked his lips and pocketed the money. "Last visit I paid her was at the St. Regis Hotel. Sweet piece of tail . . ."

"St. Regis?"

"Up on Franklin," said Sweetums. "Rents by the minute."

The St. Regis manager wasn't too keen to give out info on the hotel's guests, but it only took a sawbuck to affect hotel policy. Yes, she'd been staying in the hotel, and yes, she had a room on the third floor, but no, he hadn't seen her in over a week. But there were no foul smells emanating from under the door, so he didn't feel a need to contact the police, especially since she paid for an entire month up front.

By the time Ernie and I decided to sneak around the back of the St. Regis and break into the tart's hotel room, it was nearing five o'clock and we had to get back to the office and change for the Progressive party.

"Star can wait," Ernie pointed out. "Dames like that, they might move around, but they don't *go* anywhere."

Now, two hours later, Ernie's probably wishing we were still tracking down the mistress, if only because he could do so in a workshirt and chinos. But not here—not now—not faced with the kind of extravagant opulence that would send a Saudi sheik running for his interior decorator.

This is not a house in front of us. I'd even hesitate to call it a mansion. It's a gargantuan affair, white marble on top of white marble, pillars and columns and a whole sampler of Greek architecture thrown together into a single, monstrous parody of the Acropolis.

"You seeing this?" I ask Ernie, but all he can do is stare, slack-jawed, at a home that, even by LA standards, is fantastically ostentatious.

We drive up to a large wrought-iron gate set off to one side of the house, and a uniformed guard emerges from a large white door. The setting sun bounces off the marble, reflecting a steady stream of light into my eyes, throwing the guard into sharp relief.

"Can I see your invitation, please?" he asks, and though I'm dazzled by the sunlight, I'm aware enough to catch the scents of popcorn and model airplane glue coming from his direction.

Ernie produces the flyers and hands them to the guard, who inspects them casually and reaches behind him for a button. "You're cleared. Just go right on into the main house."

The main house. "You mean—this isn't—this thing here—"

"This is the guardhouse," he says. "And sometimes a ball-room. But mostly the guardhouse."

Suffice it to say that the main house is to the guardhouse what the planet Jupiter is to my ass. Contemplating its size is like attempting to get your brain around the concept of infinity—not much point, and it's only going to wind up in a migraine. It's nice to see that they've kept the architectural parody going, and that this Goliath of a domicile would be right at home in ancient Athens, provided, of course, that they hadn't spent all their money fighting off the Spartans.

Ernie and I park the car amid a cornucopia of makes and models—there's two hundred cars here if there's a dozen, and still the lot is barely half full—and trudge our way up a set of stairs set into the side of a hill.

"I wanna know where they get this money," says Ernie, panting a bit from the climb.

"Where'd *they* get it?" I say. "Hell, I wanna know where *I* can get a piece."

Even before we reach the front door—twenty feet high, shining alabaster, brass doorknobs the size of my head—and even before it opens for us of its own accord—swinging wide, no creaks, no rustles, just a smooth, simple glide—and even before we step into a hallway filled with archaeological treasures and works of art I am sure no human has ever seen before—original portraits by Modigliani, Rubens, Pollock, all dino masters—

Ernie and I pick up on the array of scents twisting and braiding around one another into an olfactory licorice whip, streaming out of the house, bursting from beneath the doors, the windows, squiggling out from behind the insulation. The smells come at us with force, as if exploding from within, shoved along their way.

"Welcome, brothers," comes a soft voice as Ernie and I step into the hallway, our shoes clacking on the marble floor below. "May I take your belongings?"

A thin female Ornithomimus holds out her hand, beckoning us closer. "We came empty-handed," I apologize. "Shoulda brought a gift, right? I'm lousy at party etiquette."

The Ornitho laughs, her cheeks bouncing fetchingly. "By belongings, I mean your guises. May I take them?" She points to a sign above her head: PLEASE CHECK YOUR COSTUME AT THE DOOR.

I issue a game little laugh, but my partner is not amused.

"Can't believe you made me buy this crap," Ernie grumbles as we undress in a shuttered room next to the guise check. "You set me up with all this silk and leather and fancy shoes, and we ain't even supposed to wear our guises here, let alone this shit. Almost a grand for one outfit, and it's wasted."

"You'll have it for the next time."

"Ain't gonna be a next time, I promise you that. After tonight, I bonfire this garbage."

We disrobe, then begin the real task of removing our costumes. Ernie and I help each other with the G-series, and quickly remove the rest of the trusses and buckles ourselves. My mask is sticking a little, the epoxy I applied yesterday morning a bit too strong for the job, and it takes a thin layer of my own hide with it as I rip the fake face away.

Ernie might be getting up there—though he's never admitted his age to me, he's at least fifteen years my senior, I'd bet—but back in his natural form, you wouldn't sense anything over-the-hill about the guy. His Carnotaur muscles are quite evident beneath his dark brown hide, and I know he's not squeamish about using them when the droppings hit the fan.

We hand our guises over to the Ornithomimus, and she carefully places them on a row of hangers, one for each series in the costume, tagging them all with the same number so as to keep the set together. I'm number 313, and Ernie's number 314.

Carefully, she places the hangers holding our costumes onto what looks like a dry-cleaning rack behind her and presses a blue button set into the wall. Two tall, thin doors swing wide and the rack begins to move, the hangers going with it, disappearing into a room beyond. For a second, I can make out row after row of human skins hanging in orderly fashion like a ghastly war experiment, limbs drooping limply to the ground. Then the doors close, the Ornithomimus sits back down, and we're directed down the hallway and to our right.

It's a ballroom like any other, no big deal, nothing impressive, except this one is inside a house and larger than all the apartments I've ever lived in put together. About three hundred dinosaurs mill about unguised, a veritable slime-fest of pheromones choking the air, staining the walls, the ceiling. Gonna be hell for whatever team of housekeepers has to clean this place out Monday morning.

I see Raptors and Stegosaurs and Brontos and Ankies and Hadrosaurs and pretty much every one of the sixteen species that survived the Great Showers sixty-five million years ago, and though I can't find a Compy in here at the moment, I'm sure I'll come across one when I least expect—or want—to do so.

And standing among it all, fifty feet tall if it's an inch, a centerpiece to make all other centerpieces hide their heads in shame: the perfectly preserved, expertly assembled, fossilized body of an ancient ancestor. It's a T-Rex—an original—a party-goer who showed up at the door sixty million years too early and couldn't subsist on cocktail-hour nibbles for that long. The modern dinos in the room mill around the dead giant as if it's not even there, barely giving the skeleton any notice. Odd—I thought these freaks worshiped the ancestors. Shouldn't they be bowing? Chanting? Offering up a virgin or two?

Making my way through the stifling crowd, I notice something missing, though it takes me a second to put my finger on it: no plates. There's always appetizers at these functions, and more often than not I find myself trying to balance delicate cocktail conversation with a goblet of water (or wine, at human events) and a plate full of toast and spread. Here, the dinos have the drinks, but they don't have the food. Across the room, near the dance floor, I see a Hadrosaur carrying a covered silver tray. I approach.

"Care for an appetizer, sir?" he asks, and I nod hungrily.

I expect the waiter to whip off the cover with a flourish, but all he does is open a small slot at the top of the tray and look at me expectantly.

"Perhaps I didn't make myself clear," I say. "I'd like something to eat."

"Yes, sir," he drawls, "and that's why I've opened the slot."

"Isn't it easier to just take off the cover?"

Surprise and confusion on his face, one of those looks I get from witnesses sometimes when they think I've had a few too many blows to the head. "Goodness, no, sir. They would escape."

Escape? I've never seen a cocktail wiener with feet before. Enough with this. I reach out and shove my hand down that hole—

And into a writhing pile of spaghetti.

I yank my hand back with enough force to send the tray smashing to the ground, the cover popping off with a furious clatter. A mess of small black snakes, each no more than a half-dollar around, varying in length from six to twelve inches, slither out of their confines and quickly spread throughout the ballroom in all the cardinal directions, eliciting a cavalcade of carnal shrieks and screams. The waiter fixes me with a hard stare.

"Why did you have to go and do that, sir? Now we'll have a feeding frenzy on our hands."

And indeed we do. While a few of the other dinosaurs in the room are acting much as I did—jumping backward, avoiding the beasts at any cost—the majority of them are snatching up the critters with their bare hands and shoving them into their mouths, past their jaws, swallowing them whole if need be. Laughter and roars of culinary ecstasy fill the air, and I find myself ashamed for having been rattled by what isn't even a rattler. They're garden snakes, nothing more, and despite our tenuous genetic link, none of my brethren have any qualms about digesting the buggers wholesale.

Ernie comes up behind me, mumbling through his lips. "Good party," he says.

I turn to find a small, green tail—still wiggling, mind you—poking out from between my partner's lips. I hold back my strong desire to cringe.

"That a snake?" I ask.

"Newt," he mumbles, and finishes it off with a hearty swallow. "Been a while since I had fresh meat."

As the last remaining appetizers are rounded up and summarily digested, Ernie and I take a spin around the room, scoping out the crowd, sniffing for familiar scents.

"He's not here," Ernie tells me.

"You remember what he smells like?" I'm surprised. As far as I know, the last time Ernie and Rupert saw each other was well over five years ago.

"Coffee, maybe . . . dessert tray . . . Can't say as I definitely remember," says Ernie, "but I know I'd recognize the boy if I smelled him. Hell, he spent half a year living at our place after he got back from that god-awful India trip. Smelled like curry for a few months—I remember that for sure, so I should be able to pick it up."

A trio of dinos scurry out of a pair of swinging double doors and begin setting up audio equipment at the back end of the dance floor. A microphone, some speakers, and a host of electrical cables snake out from beneath eighteen-inch risers, which are quickly bolted together to form a makeshift stage. It's all very Woodstock, and I feel the strong urge to flick a lighter and scream out a song request. Minutes pass, and Ernie wanders off for more food. Meanwhile, I'm watching these Raptor roadies go to town when I feel a tap on the rough hide of my shoulder.

"This turf's covered, Rubio. You're steppin' over the line."

The voice isn't familiar, but the tone certainly is. Ooze on top of grease with a generous helping of smarm. I turn, trying to fix some type of grin to my face. It's the kind of thing he'll expect, and though I don't care whether or not I alienate the guy, I've got too much business to attend to without catering to his whining.

"Sutherland," I say, catching a strong whiff of that burnt-milk-and-spoiled-egg scent with which this rival PI is unfortunately saddled. "What the hell are you doing here?"

"I got cases, see," he says, drawing out his lines in a horrific Cagney impression. "I got a job to do, and to do it right."

"Can the nightclub act," I suggest, "and stick to the day job."

He drops the accent and asks, "Your partner here?"

I nod over toward Ernie, who gives Sutherland a perfunctory nod and raises another newt—this one struggling, kicking, not ready to meet his reptilian maker—in salutation.

"So," I ask, "what's the story? You're on a job . . . ?"

"Undercover work," he whispers. "Real hush-hush. I get a lot of the big jobs now, you know."

Now that he's hot-to-trot with the boss man's sister, sure he gets the big cases, despite the fact that Sutherland is probably one of the least-qualified private investigators I've ever come across. This guy couldn't find Go on a Monopoly board.

"So Mr. Teitelbaum thinks I'm a great detective . . ." he rambles on, ". . . and wants to start talking—get this—*partner.*" He emphasizes this last part with a tight forehead scrunch, a difficult move when the area above your eyes isn't much other than a few bony plates fused into a marginally flexible mass. Ankylosaurs have difficulty expressing emotion visually. Think Al Gore. "So long as I finish off this case right."

"So that's why you're here. For this big case."

"Right. But it's real secret, so keep it under wraps, willya?"

"What am I gonna say?" I ask. "You didn't tell me about it."

"Exactly." He looks relieved.

"I mean, it's not like some kid got mixed up in this Progress thing, went all nutso and broke off ties with the outside world, and the family came to the office and wants someone to break 'em out. . . ."

Suddenly crestfallen, cheeks blanching of color, shoulders drooping into sharp slopes of defeat, Sutherland slams a fist into his open palm. "Goddamnit! God—damn—it! I knew Teitelbaum would send another team in, I goddamned knew it!"

"No, no, he didn't—"

"Now we gotta split the fees, right? You're taking half—your partner gets the other half—damn it all . . ."

"Hey, hey—"

I'm sorry, but Mr. Sutherland can't be reached right now. He's lost in the depths of self-pity. Please leave a message. "Look— you take it, Rubio. I don't need to be here. I'm no good at this—"

"Lower your voice and quit whining."

"I should have been a doctor. That's what my mother wanted me to be."

"Sutherland—Sutherland! Shut up and listen to me." Amazingly, he does so. I've noticed that we're drawing a crowd, so I pull the hack off to one side and lower my voice to a loud whisper. "We're not here for Teitelbaum."

The beginnings of relief. "You're not?"

"No. And we're not on your case. We've got a private matter, probably similar to yours, but not the same thing. You can keep your stupid fees."

"I have a mortgage to pay," he says, a semblance of color— appropriate shades of brown and green—returning to his face.

"I know you do."

"I have kids."

"I know." They are ugly made flesh. "They're adorable."

"Oh. Oh. Oh, good. Thank you."

"No need to thank me. Go get a glass of water and have a

seat. Put your head between your legs, take deep breaths." I pat the PI on the back and urge him toward a nearby waiter. "Grab a newt, I hear they're delish." Sutherland trots off, and I can't help but chuckle a bit.

Ernie walks over and I clue him in; he shakes his head in resignation. "See, kid, we ain't so special. I betcha half the dinos in here are dicks on the job. Wherever you got confused kids, you got parents willing to shell out dough to look for 'em."

The roadies in the corner have just about finished setting up and plugging in all the audio equipment they've lugged out onto the dance floor, and it's not long before a tall, muscular Iguanodon strolls onto the stage, long neck spikes glistening in the spotlight, the wooden risers creaking beneath his considerable weight. His hide is a deep emerald green with not a miscolored fleck on it, and though I don't usually feel complexion envy, I can't help but stare in awe at the sheer natural beauty of those scales.

A tap on the microphone, the requisite squeal, and in a resoundingly deep voice, the Iguanodon says, "Welcome, brothers and sisters."

"Welcome!" comes the overwhelming reply, the shouts buffeting me in all directions. I notice that a good quarter of us remain silent, bouncing back and forth on our feet, unsure of what to do. Recent converts and potential inductees, I would imagine.

"If everyone would take a seat . . ." And with this, the majority of dinosaurs in the room plop onto the floor without ceremony, and I'm shocked to find that the marble doesn't crack and buckle beneath the sudden assault.

"Please," says the Iguanodon, speaking directly to those of us who remain on our feet. "Anywhere is fine, no chairs are needed here."

Shrugging, Ernie and I take our positions on the floor. It's relatively cold, but nothing new to me—my desk chair is broken at one armrest, and dumps me onto the office hardwood once every few days. Most of the time I'm too lazy to drag myself back into the seat, so I do the rest of the day's work from that position instead.

"Before we begin," continues the Iguanodon, "I'd like to welcome and congratulate all of you who were at our convocation last week and decided to return and learn more about yourselves and your ancestry. I'd also like to welcome those of you who are joining us for the first time. It's a long journey from where you are now to where you could be, but it's the most rewarding, fulfilling journey you can take." Seems I've heard that somewhere before.

"My name is"— and here he gives one of those elongated, strained growls that has no mammalian equivalent whatsoever— "but until you get the hang of it, feel free to call me Samuel.

"We'll have punch and more to eat after the talk today, so be sure to stick around and get to know your fellow dinos. We're nothing as one million, but everything as one." I consider asking for a clarification on that point, but Ernie bats my hand down even as it rises of its own accord.

And now, as the Iguanodon steps down off the riser, a spotlight illuminates a Velociraptor musical trio set up on the opposite side of the dance floor. They're wielding instruments the likes of which I've never seen before, and, as they begin to play, I realize that I've never heard the likes of it, either. There's a long, stringed instrument that could pass for a bass, but its composite elements are nothing more than a stick and what looks like an elongated tendon or ligament. Some sort of conch shell, easily ten times larger than average, serves as a blaring horn, and a set of flat rocks, expertly banged upon by the largest of the dinosaurs, serves to create a rhythm. They all croon together, a series of growls and whoops coming across as lyrics, and though it's easily the most horrific cacophony I've ever heard, though the crowd is barely even swaying back and forth, I can feel an electric hum of intensity growing within them. They love this stuff. This younger generation has no taste; someone should introduce them to the blues.

Another spot, this one green, swings up the wall and holds on a set of double doors high above the stage. There's no balcony there, just a closed portal set into the wall. I'm surprised I hadn't noticed these before, but my attention had mostly been diverted toward the floor since the snake incident, on the off chance that one of the appetizers had escaped and would be looking to make a home somewhere on me. The band's number picks up in tempo and volume—rocks banging louder, horn honking harsher—and the tense passion in this crowd rises.

A whisper from my left. "She's coming . . ."

And the doors fly open, slamming into the wall behind with tremendous force. The dark corridor beyond is suddenly filled with the green spotlight, and then, a second later, a ravishing female Raptor leaps to the edge of the doorway, balancing precariously thirty feet above the ballroom floor. From here, I can make out the long, delicate lines curving through that supple body, the graceful swan curve of the neck, the tremendous definition in the underclaws, the meaty slab of a tail, and that shining, almost iridescent hide soaking up the rays from the spotlight and blasting it back out at the crowd, blinding us with its brilliance.

Before I have a chance to mumble my amazement, the Raptor raises her snout to the sky and lets loose with a bone-chilling wail, the corners of her mouth turning up, up, and out, teeth snapping at the ceiling, tongue waggling through the air. The crowd, as one, leaps to their feet and begins a furious round of applause as the Raptor flexes those powerful yet delicate leg muscles and leaps away from the wall, falling toward the dance floor below. I can't bear to watch.

But it's a perfect landing as she uses her tail to take the brunt of the force, and a moment later she's standing at the microphone, soaking in the crowd's adulation.

"Welcome," she says, her voice feminine yet oddly deep, a tightly spun web of varying tones. "Welcome, brothers and sisters."

"Good entrance," Ernie mumbles to me.

"For those of you who don't know me," says the Raptor once the crowd has quieted down and returned to their seated positions, "my name is Circe, and I've been on the road to Progress for many years now. It's been a hard path, but a fulfilling one, and I believe I am closer to the ancestors now than I have ever been before. I believe that we can *all* be closer to the ancestors now, if we can only believe in ourselves and in our shared history. We can all learn to Progress from where we are now."

Circe motions toward Samuel, the Iguanodon whom we'd seen earlier, and he wheels over a large television set attached to a familiar-looking machine.

"Ancestrograph," I mutter to Ernie, and he nods.

The crowd had begun to murmur, with either approval or disdain, I can't tell which, as Circe retracts her claw and places the first delicate finger of her right hand into that dark little hole. The Iguanodon presses the appropriate buttons, and the contraption spins to life, working whatever voodoo and hoodoo it needs to do to come up with that nonsensical number. Soon, Circe's fluids are transferred to the vacuum tube, and the lights, meters, and needles start their crazy little dance.

Hush from the crowd. They're holding their breath. If they pass out, maybe I can raid the kitchen and find some real food.

After a burst of static, the thirty-six-inch television screen lights up with the pronouncement on Circe's purity: **96.8%** DINOSAUR NATURAL.

A new thunderous round of roars and howls echoes throughout the ballroom, and I can only hope that either the walls are soundproofed or whatever neighbors live within a few miles of this home are under the impression that MGM is filming an *Out of Africa* sequel nearby.

"Please, please," says Circe, clearly basking in the glow of admiration while still maintaining a distinct air of humility, "take your seats, take your seats. I have a story to impart to you. I want to tell you all how we came to be where we are today."

"This oughta be a doozy," says Ernie, and we settle in for a good listen.

I t is a story from not so long ago," Circe begins, "though to some of you whose purity has become muddied over the years with human effluvia, it may seem like ancient history. But remember—ancient history to the mammals is nothing more than yesterday to us.

"I first heard this story from our great founder Raal"—this name my best approximation of the grunt she emitted—"and he heard it from his parents, who heard it from their parents, and so on. It has lived through the ages, and now I pass it on to you."

"This Raal must be the vacuum salesman," Ernie mumbles to me, and I'm impressed at how well he pronounces the difficult dino name. "The one who started up the cult and then died off."

"Less than one million years ago," continues Circe, "our ancestors were faced with a problem. A certain branch of the hominid family, a species which they had been watching carefully for some time, had begun to evolve along a different path than that of their close relatives, the great apes. The change had become more significant, more pronounced over the last few hundred thousand years, and the great Councils were concerned that the evolution was somehow speeding up, that these hominids whose braincase was quickly enlarging might soon learn a form of communication, and with it, create a society. This was something never before seen in the course of our shared history: a potential rival.

"But the Council members urged caution. Surely these . . . monkeys could pose no threat to our well-being. They were gangly, they were dumb, they were loners, for the most part. And they were small, much smaller than we were. Even though we were no longer the size of the Great Ancestors, our forefathers of a million years ago still stood taller and broader than the dinosaur of today—ten, twelve feet at the minimum."

"How's she supposed to know this?" Ernie grumbles to me.

"It's a story. You heard of stories, right?"

Circe goes on. "But it soon came to light that one band of humans had indeed organized itself and begun to live in a loosely based nomad society around the area that has now become Ghana. There was concern that the other hominids would do likewise within the next ten or twenty thousand years, and that something ought to be done about it.

"The most vocal of those urging action were three brothers, whose names and races are unfortunately lost to us. But these brothers were widely known to be the strongest, bravest of their kind, to have battled other natural predators with great skill and valor, and so it was decided that they should attempt to make contact with that first group of hominids.

"The first brother was a genial fellow—kind, giving, and always had a knack for putting others at ease. The second was uncommonly large and powerful, and some say he stood higher than the trees in the forest. And the third was particularly cunning, able to wrap his mind around the sharpest of problems. They were a perfect choice.

"The brothers wanted to go together—that had always been

their way, and that indeed was how their own forefathers had defeated an attempted coup by a dinosaur faction earlier that eon. But the Council had mandated that each of the brothers would go singly to the valley of the hominids, and, as we know, when it comes to the Council, rules are rules. We may have evolved some in the last million years, but the Councils have not." Laughter here from the audience, and I find myself chuckling along, caught up in the story's flow.

"The first brother set out for the valley and, after a long and arduous journey, found his way to the outskirts of the hominid camp. These prehumans were living out in the open back then, not even bright enough to cover themselves with a simple lean-to or hut. The first brother hid in the forest and watched them for days, trying to figure out how best to communicate with these new creatures. After some time, he decided that the best course of action would be a direct and simple approach, perhaps with some pantomime thrown in for good measure.

"At dawn one morning, he strolled into the valley, head held high, trying to win them over with his best smile. He wanted to welcome them to the race of sentient beings, to glean their intentions toward the valley and toward the dinosaurs, and to see if they would be interested in forging a friendship.

"He was massacred on sight."

An electric shock passes through the crowd, rocking us all backward as one. Circe's voice hit a hard note with that last part, a flick of vitriol hitting hard on the word *massacred*, and it did the job right.

"When a few days had passed, and they had yet to hear from the first brother, the second was sent out to see what had become of him. He reached the valley quickly and proceeded to do the same as his sibling before him—hide in the forest nearby and observe the creatures before making his move. But that night, as he watched from a distance, he saw the whole tribe of hominids feasting on his brother's carcass, shoving gnawed bones and bloody entrails into their disgusting, greedy little mouths.

"Without thought, without any preparation, the enraged dinosaur rushed into the clearing, teeth bared, claws slashing out, and fell upon the unsuspecting hominids, bloodlust erasing all thoughts of danger or consequence.

"He killed twelve of them before he, too, was slaughtered.

"Now quite some time had passed, and neither of the brothers had returned. The Council had no choice but to send out the final one of the trio, and he set out willingly, eager to learn what had become of his siblings. But the third brother was the cunning one, the cautious one, and he took his time coming to the valley. He examined every trail, every path, attempting to get a true feel for how the hominids acted and hunted and ate and lived.

"So by the time he arrived at the valley and, like the others before him, hid in the woods to watch the hominids from afar, his brothers had already been consumed and their bones picked clean. All that remained of them were a pair of partially intact skeletons scattered across the valley floor.

"Perhaps because the remains of his brothers were unrecognizable to him, or perhaps because it was simply his nature, the third brother did not become enraged. He did not set out immediately to destroy the creatures, nor did he step down into the valley in the hope of forging a peace treaty between the species.

"What he did was come up with a plan.

"He tucked his tail between his legs and secured it there with a soft, flexible sapling, tying the edges around his waist. He covered his body in mud, slathering it across his scales, so that his natural hide looked like nothing more than that of any other creature who hadn't bathed in some time. He retracted his claws. He broke off the two teeth that showed even when his mouth was closed, snapping them at the base. He pulled back his ears and touched up his eyes and covered his snout in a homemade mask of twigs and branches. He slathered himself in feces, so as to obscure his natural smell.

"The next morning, costumed up in the first guise ever, he walked out of the forest and into the heart of that hominid camp, sat down in the middle, and grunted along with the best of them. His costume was shabby, of course, and nowadays would seem downright ludicrous, but the humans were slightly dumber then than they are now, and they accepted the dinosaur as one of their own. That night, he even went so far as to partake in the marrow of one of his own brothers' bones, so as not to raise suspicion. He looked like a hominid, he acted like a hominid, and he smelled like a hominid.

"And that night, when all of those upright mammals had gone to sleep, the third brother crept up to each and every one of the creatures, and cleanly, quietly, and efficiently slashed them all to death."

A great cheer goes up from the audience, as if we're personally welcoming the great and conquering dinosaur back from the battle. Circe raises her arms for silence.

"Now—can anyone tell me if this dinosaur, who tricked the humans by guising himself up as one of their ilk, was a hero?"

A few hands pop up instantly—brownnosers, no doubt, who've heard this story before and know the appropriate response. I chuckle at their eagerness to impress the teacher, but my laughter soon dribbles to a stop when I see that long, green finger being pointed in my direction.

"You," says Circe, and there's no doubt that she's turned her attention to the one Raptor PI in the room who isn't interested in playing twenty questions. "Tell me, was he a hero?"

Gotta stammer, a little hemming and hawing. "I don't—I, ah—"

"Gut instinct. Hero or not?"

"Hero," I say. "He killed those who had killed his brothers. Revenge factor right there." I assume this is the correct answer, considering that the whole story seemed to be primarily up-with-dinos intensive.

"True," says Circe, and the class goody-goodies fix me with envious glares. "But in doing so, did he not compromise his identity? Did he not force himself into an unnatural position?"

"Yeah, sure," I say, "but it's nothing different from what we're doing now."

An ooooh from the crowd—including Ernie, the bastard—and I realize quickly that I've just made Circe's point for her. But that smile she shoots my way smoothes over all possible feelings of ill will, and I find myself gravitating toward those beautiful pointy teeth and that shimmering green hide.

"What that one dinosaur started one million years ago as a means to avenge his family's death has become our way of life. Some may say he was a hero, but we believe he was nothing more than the catalyst to our eventual downfall."

Murmurs of agreement as those head-of-the-class shoe polishers turn their noses up in my direction and go back to their business of being superior.

"I don't tell you all of this to make you angry," Circe says to the audience. "In fact, I don't tell you all of this to make you feel *anything*. That's not my job, to tell you how to feel, to give you . . . propaganda . . . . despite what others might say. But it is important for each and every one of you to know who we are and where we came from, and why the dinosaurs of today are so much different from our true ancestors."

Sure, I got it, but she didn't have to make me feel like a problem student.

"Pooched that one pretty good, kid," jokes Ernie. I don't respond.

"This is where the issue of purity comes in," Circe continues. "How natural are we as dinosaurs? How far have we strayed from our lineage? Stories tell of the days when our pheromones would carry for miles, when we could sense large packs of one another across entire seas. Now we're lucky if we can sniff each other out across the dinner table."

Around here is when she launches full force into a lecture

about purity and naturalism and the torture we dinos put ourselves through every day, both physical and emotional, in order to blend in with the so-called ruling majority. I learn, over approximately one hour's time, how the costumes we put on actually absorb certain chemicals, sapping us of our natural pheromones; how studies have shown that over prolonged exposure in a guise, a dino's brain waves will actually become more similar to that of a mammal's; how our Jekyll-and-Hyde, persona-by-necessity lifestyle has splintered us into thinking of ourselves as sixteen separate races of dinosaur, as opposed to one single species. It all makes a heck of a lot of sense, especially when it's coming from the beautiful, sensuous snout of Circe.

Ernie is not quite as taken by this creature as I am; he uses the claws from one hand to pick at the other, occasionally looking up and nodding in mock enlightenment.

It's another half-hour, perhaps, before the speech is all good and done, and another ten minutes after that before our applause settles down. As the band begins to play again—this time, the music jibing a bit more with my jangled ears—Circe takes leave of the stage, disappearing among a crowd of well-wishers.

"That was a big freaking waste," Ernie says. "I didn't smell him the whole time."

"Smell who?"

"Rupert."

"Rupert who?" I ask, and Ernie slaps me in the back of the head. Now it all comes rushing back—the ex-wife, the brother, the fact that I'm standing in the central room of some sort of cult. Whatever brain-fog I fell into during Circe's speech dissipates, and I shake my head a few times to clear the last cobwebs.

Ernie puts a hand on my shoulder, catches my eyes with his. "You all right?"

"Never better. Let's scram."

But it's not quite that easy. A receiving line has been set up by the door, Circe greeting her visitors and bidding farewell to the departing guests. Three beefy dinos, Samuel the Iguanodon one of them, stand by her side, watching the crowd with what is certainly dubious intent, insisting that anyone who wishes to leave first pay their respects to our esteemed hostess. There's something just short of paranoia in those eyes, and Ernie and I realize that it's best to go with the flow. We take our place in the back of the line and slowly make our way forward.

"You catch that?" Ernie asks me after a few minutes spent shuffling forward six inches at a go.

"Catch what?"

"That scent—the cappuccino-flavored one."

I flare my nostrils as wide as they will go and take in a deep breath of the surrounding air. A rush of pheromones invade the olfactory nerves, and I have to close my eyes, my ears, shut down my other senses, in order to concentrate on separating the wildly varying scents. Yes . . . Somewhere in there, intertwined with the pine nuts and the oranges and the ocean breeze, is a distinct smell of after-dinner coffee drink, flavored lightly with cream, maybe a hint of chocolate.

"That's him?" I ask. "He's a mocha?"

"Can't be certain, but I think so."

We take a quick scan of the room, trying to direct our snouts toward the different dinos standing about us so as to isolate their individual scents. This is not simple—the practice of direct-line smelling is more art than science, and some would claim more hocus than pocus. The line continues to move forward, and we continue to come closer to our brief audience with Circe.

"Quick run past the dame, we shake hands, say our thanks, and then we get ready to track him. Clear your nose, for what it's worth."

It's another twenty minutes before we reach the front of the line, Ernie ahead of me. I'm anxious to get this part over with so that we can find Rupert, take him home, and close the case so that I can get in a good workout tomorrow morning. It's been three weeks since I've played my *Richard Simmons Sweatin' with the Stegosaur* tape, and my hind thighs are feeling a mite paunchy.

I stand back as Ernie approaches Circe and issues what I imagine to be polite thanks and some insincere toadying. I fully expect to repeat the performance.

But when I'm actually standing in front of her, when I'm fully face-to-face with that voluptuous Raptor body and those full Raptor lips, it's hard for me to even stammer out "Thank you."

"I hope I didn't embarrass you," she says. "With my question."

"No, it's—I learned a lot." And then, like the babbling moron I have instantly become, I repeat, "Learned a lot."

There's an intoxicating aroma streaming out of Circe's pores, and it's more than just the strong whiff of a Raptor female that's got me going. At this close distance, my head is spinning from whatever magical smells are dripping out of her body; Circe's essence smells of the natural intoxicants—basil, oregano, cilantro. Never before have I encountered a dino with such pheromones, and I doubt I will again. The room tilts to the left, and I try to adjust my head in order to counterbalance. It doesn't work.

"What's your name?" she asks me.

"Vincent," I say. "My name's Vincent." Then, because I haven't made quite enough a fool of myself this evening, I give it one more go-round. "That's me. Vincent."

I'm being drawn in, somehow. Circe is three feet away, then two, then one. Those eyes, that snout are encompassing the whole of my vision, and the scent grows stronger. Even beyond basil and its brothers now, moving into thyme and rosemary and fennel—all of the most powerful herbs I've ever known—the scents are invading my head via these two wide nostrils, taking long, powerful strokes up my sinuses, spawning upstream toward my brain, and every care and worry in my head liquefies at once, pouring out through my ears . . .

"Vincent, it's wonderful to meet you," she says, and I can feel my lips curling into a goofy smile. Part of me is quite aware of this transformation from a detached private investigator to a drooling, dribbling schoolboy, but the other part is happy to lower the safety bar and hang on for the ride.

A hand on the back of my head—and Circe draws me closer, tighter. Is she going to kiss me? I pucker, waiting for the sweet feeling of flesh on flesh, but my head is pulled past those lips, past that perfect left cheek, and around to the back of the neck. I get it. I get it. I prepare to hold my breath. Can't do this.

No time. Before I even have a chance to ready myself for that delicious smell-taste of Circe's pheromones, I am hit full-on by a tidal wave of condiments cascading over my body, drenching my senses in a herbological assault.

And then I'm no longer in a house in the Hollywood Hills; I'm no longer standing in a receiving line, bent awkwardly and possibly obscenely over our host, my nose pressed to the back of her neck. In fact, I'm no longer in the City of Angels or its environs, and I'm no longer in this millennium.

Instead, I'm running through an endless forest, the trees overhead scraping the sky, leaves the size of Chryslers, my legs blurring as they churn faster and faster across the muddy ground, a warm wind whipping past my hide. A sweet wail fills the night and I find myself calling out in my own Raptor-tones, answering in some language that, although I have never heard it before, trips naturally off my tongue.

Circe is beside me, running strong.

A cliff approaches in the distance, and we increase our speed, some primal need accelerating our run into madness. There's no slowing down now, no stopping as the cliff looms larger, the overhang and infinite drop below coming sharply into view. A turn of my head, a look toward my companion, and she grabs my claw in hers and smiles as we leap high into the air and off the cliff, rising higher and higher before gravity takes its toll and we begin the inevitable plummet . . .

We make love on the way down.

7

"incent! Vincent!" A voice coming from somewhere in the forest. My eyes are closed. I am peaceful. The birds are singing, the lizards are licking, and all is well and good.

"Don't make me knock your block off, kid. Snap to, we got work to do."

It's Ernie. Why is Ernie in the forest? Where did Circe go? Reluctantly, I open my eyes, squinting at the bright light that invades my vision. Has the sun come up already?

Hallway chandelier, glowing bright. Works of art, framed with skill and class. The ballroom is behind me, and Circe continues to receive her guests.

"I smelled him back this way," Ernie says. "We gotta get tracking."

"Ernie," I say, my mouth thick, still stuffed with the meaty air of that prehistoric world, "was I . . . ? I mean . . . did you . . . When you said goodbye to Circe . . ."

"Nice enough gal," he says. "For a cult leader."

"No—I mean, did you smell her?"

"Sure, I smelled her. Kinda herby, right?"

I know it's not possible for a dinosaur to regulate her smells—our gland production is simply a product of our metabolism, chugging away at a steady pace. It can't be flexed like a muscle; at least, that's what I've always been told. But that last burst of Circe's scent, the one that threw me over the edge and out of this space-time continuum—that wasn't normal pheromone production, by any standard. And even if it were, Ernie would have experienced the same thing that I did; and judging by his nonchalant reaction, nothing went on for him in that receiving line except a polite handshake and see-ya-later. But she definitely did something there, something strange and different and unnatural and yet decidedly *right*.

I decide not to bring it up right now. Ernie's correct—we have to get tracking.

We're just about to leave the mansion when a familiar voice calls us back into the hall. "Gentlemen, your guises?"

Of course. We trot back to the Ornithomimus, Ernie mumbling to me, "Let's hurry up. I think I smell him, but the scent's fading."

We toss our tickets at the guise-check girl and wait impatiently as the multitude of costumes slowly rotates around toward the delivery slot. I tap my claws against the marble counter, the clack-clack-clack mimicking that of the dry-cleaning rack. No time, no time.

"Three-thirteen and three-fourteen," she says, and we snatch the costumes without a second thought, throw them on, and hightail it out of the mansion. As soon as we hit the open night, I'm dismayed to find that the LA air is as dry as usual, making pheromone detection difficult. The thicker the air, the more water there is clogging up the surrounding atmosphere, the longer any given smell remains available for tracking. This is why no one ever goes missing on Miami Beach.

Still, there's something of that Starbucks scent wafting

toward us from behind the mansion, so we follow the odor as best we can. A beautifully landscaped path leads us around one of the many corners of the house and onto a sloped walkway paved with giant stepping-stones. Small sprigs of grass pop up between the grouting, interspersed with the occasional weed. Probably tasty, but no time to sample.

As we follow the smell of congregated dinos, the path grows more convoluted, twisting about in a knot of missteps and jumbled directions. The woods have sprung up around us as we've walked, and the weeds are thicker here, the ground poorly maintained. Soon the stepping-stones give way to cracked slabs of asphalt, which give way to broken rocks, which give way to nothing but dirt. The smell of pine, though—and inside it, a thimbleful of cappuccino—has intensified.

A hundred yards or so into the forest, I can make out a set of monkey bars, rusted over but still usable, and ten old tires placed in football-training fashion along the ground. There's a rope swing and a twenty-foot hurdling fence, and the ground is covered in natural dino tracks, both three- and four-toe alike.

"Playground?" asks Ernie.

I shrug. "Everyone needs a little release, right?"

"You think they're keeping kids here?"

"Could be. Some of these cults you hear about, it's whole families."

Ernie shakes his head, top lip turning up in a sneer of disgust. "Can't keep kids in a place like this," he mutters.

"What, at a mansion in the Hollywood Hills? You're right, such squalor."

But there it is again, the coffee and the pine, and it's not another hundred feet of walking before Ernie and I catch sight of three large bungalows set between the trees. Like the brothers in Circe's story, we hide behind the oaks and watch the natives go about their routines for a few minutes. Dinosaurs wander about in their natural states, protected by the leafy canopy overhead, and much as it was in the ballroom, all of the species are represented. I even see a few Compies this time, scurrying back and forth across the compound like rats searching after a bite of cheese.

"You see him?" I ask.

Ernie shakes his head. "Don't remember what he looks like unguised. We've gotta go in for a closer smell."

"And they'll pick us out right away."

"Not necessarily," says Ernie. "They've got new converts coming in every day, right? Who's to say we haven't just joined up?"

Can't argue with that. We hop out from behind the tree and strut into the camp, every step announcing that we belong, we belong, we belong.

"Evening, brothers," says a Coelophysis who's busy stripping bark off a nearby tree.

"Evening, brother," I return, and we pass by with a merry wave.

"See," says Ernie. "Easy."

A quick tour around the camp with our nostrils flared wide and it soon becomes evident that the conglomeration of smells, while closer to us now, makes individual detection difficult, if not impossible. At least we've got the species narrowed down, but there are easily ten T-Rexes in sight, and any of these dinosaurs could be Rupert. Unfortunately, they seem to band close together, and it would take close quarters before we could make a positive identification on any one of them.

"We could just walk up and ask for him," suggests Ernie.

"And then he'd see us—see you, at least—and he'd spook. Cut and run is my guess."

We wave to a passing "brother," and Ernie takes another glance at the group of T-Rexes sitting by the third bungalow. "I'm sure it's one of them," he says. "There's gotta be a way."

A moment later, a small Compy whizzes by, humming under her breath. I reach out a claw and snatch her by the shoulder. "Excuse me, sister," I say. "I was wondering if you could do me a favor. Please."

"In a hurry, brother," she replies, and tries to zoom past. But I exert a little more pressure, and the Compy stays put.

"Please," I reiterate. "It would mean so much for your Progress."

That gets her. Although I'm sure I made absolutely no sense, especially in what is bound to be a hyped-up lexicon of jargon and catch phrases, I've caught her attention nevertheless.

"Good," I say. "Could you find . . ." I'm searching for the name, sending my memory back to that meeting with Louise, reading that heartbreaking letter that her kid brother sent her way, skipping past the mumbo and the jumbo and eventually finding the signature. *Your Brother, Granaagh.*

"Could you find Granaagh?" I say, scratching my throat in what I hope is the proper Progressive pronunciation.

"He's right over there," says the Compy, pointing to the crowd of T-Rexes in the distance. "See—"

"Yes, but we're in a hurry. Please, tell him that Circe wants to see him by the monkey bars."

"The monkey bars?"

"The—ah—the play set . . . near the swings—"

"Oh," says the Compy, "the mammal bars." Then, with whatever suspicion that little brain can muster: "You say Circe wants to see him?"

"That's what she told my friend here."

The Compy thinks it over, the minuscule cogs and wheels in that brain turning at 10,000 rpm, threatening to overheat, the tiny face scrunching up even tighter, and she finally says, "Okay. I'll tell him."

"He's gonna recognize us the second he gets here," I say once we reach the playground.

" 'Course he will. Then we reason with him."

"Is reason a quality you'd ascribe to most of these Progressives, Ern?"

My partner shakes his head at me, clucking his tongue loudly.

"I never shoulda let you get that Word-a-Day calendar. 'Ascribe.' What kinda word is 'ascribe'?"

Before I have a chance to defend my vocabulary, there's a scuffling from the trees. The leaves part, and a smallish T-Rex—six-two, six-three, still much larger than myself, mind you, but on the puny side for the so-called King of Reptiles—makes his way into the clearing. He squints through the darkness, cupping a hand over each eye. "Miss Circe?" he asks.

Miss Circe. Ain't that cute? "Evening, baby brother," says Ernie, stepping out of the shadows and into the meager rays of moonlight that fight their way through the LA haze.

Rupert doesn't run. He doesn't scream. He doesn't even change his expression much—maybe a little sag at the eyes, perhaps a slump to the stance, but that's about it. "Good evening, brother Ernie," he says. "I suspect my sister sent you." A small smile lights up his face, and there's the Rupert I remember from days of old. The kind of kid who could somehow be good-natured, but serious about it.

"Hey, Rupe. Sorry about the deception."

"No apology needed. I trust you enjoyed the lecture."

"You knew we were there?" I ask.

Rupert nods solemnly, and there's that infectious grin again. "I've known Ernie's scent since the day he first started to court my sister. Yours, too, Vincent, from all the times you came to the house to mooch food at dinner."

"Louise—she's real worried about you." Ernie takes a few steps toward his ex-brother-in-law and the T-Rex stands his ground. "She's crying herself to sleep every night since that letter, doesn't know where the heck you are."

"Then you may tell her I'm in good hands. Tell her I'm being cared for and that I'm learning the truth about myself. If she cares about me, that should stop her crying."

In all honesty, Rupert looks to be in much better shape than I ever remember seeing him before. Once upon a time, he was a gaunt, pale specimen of a dino; but now, despite his lack of height, he's managed to fill out that gangly body into what looks like a strong, muscular frame. His hide, like all of the Progressives, is clear and shiny, his tail long and firm, and his sharp claws glint in the moonlight. He's the picture of T-Rex health.

"It ain't that easy—tell him, Vinnie."

"He's right," I say, also making my approach, keeping a watchful eye on those claws of Rupert's. "I spoke with her for quite some time, and though we understand that you're comfortable here, and though we understand how the Progressives have helped you—really, we do—that doesn't mean that you can't further your learning at home. She's got space for you there, a nice bed, lots of love—"

"I get all the love I need here," says Rupert. "I have a place to sleep. I have space. It's not a question of location, it's a question of my Progress. Here is where I need to be."

Rupert's head cocks to one side, then the other, tick-tocking back and forth, as if he's hearing something in the woods and can't quite make it out. "I have to get back to the camp," he says. "It's been nice to see you two. I hope you'll stay and learn more about your ancestry."

He begins to clomp back through the bushes, and I turn to Ernie. "Great. Like I said, he ain't interested. Now what?"

"No idea."

"We can't leave now. We gotta do something."

Ernie looks to Rupert, who's nearing the edge of the clearing, and calls out, "Wait a second! Please, brother!"

It's the "brother" that does it again—a magic word if ever I've seen one, abracadabra be damned. Rupert stops, turns on his heels, and slowly walks back to us. His tone is even, but masking a growing impatience.

"Yes, *brother*?" Tinged with a hint of sarcasm this time.

"I want to show you something," says Ernie, and I'll be damned if I know what he's up to.

Rupert starts, "I'm not going back with you—"

"No, no—" interrupts Ernie. "You can see it from here. Look."

Ernie points into the distance, just beyond the mammal bars and the tire course, into a small copse of oak trees. Rupert dutifully turns around and squints his eyes, peering into the blackness of the night.

"I don't see anyth—"

The next thing I know, Rupert's on the ground, unconscious, Ernie's standing above him holding a large branch, and I'm just about as lost as a platypus in a beauty contest.

"Grab his legs," Ernie tells me. "I'll get the arms."

A chorus of words form in my throat but refuse to breach the barrier of my lips. As a result, I choke for a while, making small gasping sounds while staring at Rupert, who has yet to regain consciousness.

"Quit panting, kid," says Ernie. "Don't need *you* passed out, too. Rupert's gonna wake up soon enough, and we gotta get him to the car."

"You didn't—you can't—" I begin, and finally opt for, "We didn't discuss this!"

"We did discuss this," Ernie says calmly. I believe at this point that he would make an excellent sociopath. "We discussed this very scenario."

"We said there was a chance that he wouldn't go along with us—"

"And he didn't," says Ernie.

"Right, he didn't. And then we said we'd discuss what to do."

"And we did. You said 'Now what?' and I said 'No idea' and you said 'We gotta do something'—that's verbatim, kid—so that was the discussion, and then I came up with my plan."

"And your plan," I say, "was to knock Rupert unconscious with a big tree branch and kidnap him."

"Yes. Well, the tree branch was improvised, but . . . more or less, yes."

The kid's beginning to come around, I see—the eyelids are fluttering, the hands beginning to clench, small mewling sounds emerging from his throat like a lost litter of baby kittens crying out for mama—and I have to make a decision, quick.

Clearly, there will be another time for anger, a choice moment for me to lash out at my partner for violating what I thought was a sacred trust, but one way or another, I'm going to make a concerted effort to remain pissed off at Ernie this go-around. In the past, he's skipped away on an apology and a smile, but this time Ernie ain't getting off the Vincent Rubio blacklist any time soon, no sir.

"*You* take his legs," I say, hoisting Rupert's arms into the air. "You're the one who got us into this, so you're the one who gets to smell his feet on the way down."

The small studio apartment located just above our office in Westwood is not, by any means, soundproofed, a fact that has recently come to our attention by way of some very personal experience. For the past two days of Rupert's incarceration up there, we've heard all manner of banging, shouting, and a fair number of expletives, most of which have yet to make much sense. At least I've got some good words to mutter under my breath next time I'm audited by the IRS.

Tell the truth, I can't understand what all the fuss is about. Sure we've got him locked up against his will, sure he was knocked on his head and dragged through a dirty, muddy forest, sure he was put in the trunk of a Lincoln Mark VIII and driven over potholed alleyways, but the guy's got water, a place to sleep, and all the take-out food he could ask for. We even ordered in from Twin Dragon one night, and MSG does not come cheap.

"You gotta eat," Ernie told him.

"You gotta drink," was my refrain.

"Thank you, no," was his only response. He'd shut us out entirely for that first day, begging off all manner of nourishment with a polite refusal and a tight little grimace. The plan was to get him to a state of acceptance, lull him into an easygoing frame of mind, then drill it into his head full-bore that he wasn't a Progressive—he was just a kid who needed help, with a sister who loved him—but all this *no thank you* crap was throwing a monkey wrench in the works.

"Maybe we need professional help on this," I suggested to Ernie that first morning.

"What's a shrink gonna do that we can't?"

"Get him to eat, maybe."

"I can do whatever one of them fellas can, kid. Watch and see."

But such macho answers didn't help Rupert, and Ernie's protestations and hour-long lectures bounced off deaf ears. It was a Tony Robbins moment (an Ankylosaur to be sure, like John Tesh or Rosey Grier—no natural human could possibly be that massive) gone horribly, horribly wrong. Rupert simply sat there and stared at us staring at him.

"This gonna help your Progress?" Ernie asked him. "Eating nothing and drinking nothing and saying nothing's gonna wind you up dead, and you think being dead's gonna help?"

No answer. Sarcasm and rhetoric were either beyond the boy or beneath him, and Rupert simply sat cross-legged on the floor or the fold-out sofa bed, prepared, if need be, to wither away just to spite us.

We didn't tell Louise. She didn't need to see him like this.

By afternoon of the second day, the basic pangs of hunger must have overridden whatever meager philosophical constraints had bound Rupert to his prior convictions, and he was more than willing to eat the copious leftovers from the previous day's meals. He wolfed down two orders of pad thai and a generous helping of spicy fried chicken from KFC before excusing himself to the bathroom, where I believe his stomach revolted at the unnatural combination.

"Will you talk to us now?" Ernie pleaded, but he was asking too much.

"At least we got him eating, Ern," I pointed out. "Talking can come later."

Later on, we attempted another amateur deprogramming session, consisting mainly of us knocking on the door, telling Rupert he was crazy, and being told to go away.

Still, we felt it better not to tell Louise. Yet.

We both slept over that night, worried that Rupert would attempt to break out of the apartment, even though we'd done our best to make sure such a thing was impossible. Boards on the windows, locks on the doors, phone cord taken out of the wall, and any means of communication with the outside world pretty much sealed off from his use. I felt like a criminal, locking him up in that manner—and, sure, technically, we were—but enough of it rang true as something good and right that I forgot about the felony and carried on with the plan.

So Ernie and I were both there the other morning when Rupert decided to abandon the peaceful part of his resistance and get down to the nitty-gritty of making himself a real nuisance. He started banging on the floor, the walls, the doors, shouting our names at the top of his stuffed-up lungs (he's got a cold now, of all things), threatening us with civil action and bodily harm. Clearly, this couldn't last for long, as the other denizens of the office building would be arriving for work shortly, and it would be unseemly to have a T-Rex shouting for all the world to hear that the two dinos on the third floor had kidnaped a twenty-two-year-old and are currently in the process of holding him against his will. That's the kind of thing that attracts attention, even in LA.

This time we called Louise.

She came over twenty minutes later, cheeks flushed from either anticipation or the sudden exertion of guising herself up and rushing down to Westwood.

"He's a little argumentative right now," I warned her. "You may not get anywhere."

But Louise said she had to try, and we respected her decision. So, for the last three hours, she's been up there with Rupert, presumably talking him down, and hopefully talking him out. Ernie and I have been twiddling our claws down here on the third floor, unable to help and unable to research the other cases that badly need our attention.

"Hey," I suggest, "I could run down and check out that lead on Minsky's babe. Won't take a half-hour."

"I need you here," Ernie says to me. "In case he tries to bolt."

So I sit. And I wait. I clean my claws. I read the paper. I clean my claws again. I go downstairs and run them through a patch of mud, just so I have something to do. I clean my claws for a third time.

Eventually, there's a knock at the door, and Louise steps inside. The human makeup she's so expertly applied to the mask of her guise has run in great streaks down her cheeks, staining the latex a deep purple. We both rush to her aid, but I back off and let Ernie bear the brunt of the consolation.

Between weeps, Louise explains that Rupert didn't say a syllable to her, that she didn't even know if he had heard a word she said, and that he'd barely even registered her presence the whole time she was up there. "It's not him," she says to us. "I don't recognize my own brother."

I look to Ernie, and he shrugs. I've yet to chew him out good and proper for starting these shenanigans in the first place, so the lug knows he owes me one. It's time to get this thing settled, once and for all.

"Louise," I say, "how would you feel about bringing in a professional?"

· · ·

"I've heard about those guys," Sergeant Dan Patterson is saying to me over the phone less than ten minutes later. Dan's my contact at the LAPD, a one-time private detective who took the jump to law enforcement once he tired of the freelance life, and probably the best Brontosaur I know. We take the occasional fishing trip together when both of our schedules mesh and we get some spare moments—that's once in the last two years, mind you—and aside from his prowess as an officer of the law, he's an incredible fisherman to boot. A hundred-and-fifty-pound bass would be nothing more than a laugh and a throwback for Dan Patterson, but he's kind enough not to begrudge me my catches of minnows and guppies. "These Progressives got a place up in Hollywood, right?"

"Right. But what I need from you now," I say, "is a name. You must have worked with cults before, maybe heard about someone who can deprogram a member."

"Risky business."

"You know someone or not?"

Dan says, "Not offhand, but I can ask around. Actually going through with it, though . . . that's a different story. Usually you gotta kidnap the guy first, and that ain't always what you'd call legal."

Silence from my end. I fear it's telltale.

"Vincent, you still there?"

"Hm? Yeah, yeah, kidnaping's illegal, I know. Can we forget about that part right now?"

"Do I wanna forget about it?"

"You do," I say, and to my great relief, my good friend on the LAPD is quick on the uptake. He's got a see-no-evil, hear-no-evil policy when it comes to his friends, an attitude that has saved my green butt from the county poke countless times.

"Done and done. You give me a little bit of time, maybe I can round up someone for you. Any preferences—male, female, that sorta thing?"

"Someone fast," I say, worried for the future of the furnishings in the upstairs apartment. If anything's dented beyond repair, Minsky's gonna take it out of our ever-dwindling security deposit. As it is, he has only the most glancing knowledge of what's going on up there; we told him the weeklong free rental of the empty studio was in lieu of further "research fees" for his case, and he reluctantly agreed to back off.

I hang up with Dan and give Ernie and Louise the good news. "He's going to find us somebody," I tell them. "Just a matter of time."

From upstairs, I hear a sharp crack and believe it might be the legs of the sleeper sofa being snapped in two. "Just a matter of time," I repeat optimistically and sit down to order up some lunch.

Six hours later, the phone wakes me from a light snooze and a dream about licorice whips and bottomless elevators. The infernal device has already rung three times within the last few hours, but each time it's been for a purpose unrelated to the case at hand. Two were wrong numbers, and the third was another lead on the Minsky affair, from Sweetums, the dino pimp. He'd claimed to have seen Star hiking her way back up to the St. Regis, but as I was confined to quarters for the evening, I was unable to follow up on the tip. He whined and pleaded with me to messenger him a bit of informant cash in advance, but the rules are the rules: I don't wire money and I don't write checks. Western Union is dead to me—don't ask, don't ask—so he'll have to wait for the moola.

I answer the phone, still a little groggy from the catnap. "Rubio."

"Y'all lookin' for a little help down there, I hear." The individual words are not quite that clear—running together like a stream of thick molasses, drawn out into a long drawl, as if the speaker has slowed his 45 rpm voice box down to $33\frac{1}{3}$—but after some thought I'm able to piece together enough of the syllables to make out an actual sentence.

"This is Vincent Rubio," I repeat. "Can I help you, sir?"

"I said that word is out that y'all are in need of a professional service. I might be able to provide such a service."

The meaning behind the words cuts through my stupor, and I blurt out, "You're the cult guy?"

"If that's what y'all choose to call me, then yes, I'm the cult guy."

I backpedal now, not wanting to foster any ill will. "No, I didn't mean—we can call you whatever you want—"

"Cult Guy is a fine name, son. I've been called much worse, believe you me. But if you'd like to refer to me by my Christian name, it's Dr. Beaumont Beauregard."

I almost prefer Cult Guy better; at the very least, it doesn't make me want to fall headlong into a laughing fit. I steady my lips and repeat the name out loud, trying to stifle the giveaway trill of my voice. "Dr. Beaumont Beauregard, thank you for calling. I'm Vincent Rubio."

"I gathered. And, son—I know my name's amusing to folks, so it's okay to laugh. You don't go through grade school with a name like Beaumont Beauregard without finding out it's funny somewhere along the way. Makes it any easier, you can just call me Bo."

I nod, then realize he can't see me over the phone. "I'll do that, Bo." I feel an instant camaraderie with this deprogrammer, and he hasn't even set foot in my door. "How do you know Dan?" I ask.

" 'Scuse me?"

"Sergeant Patterson," I amend. A lot of people refer to the cops by their rank and last name only; it's a sign of respect, and I make a mental note to do similarly in the future. "He gave you my number, right?"

"Sure did," says Bo. "I'll tell ya—when you've been doing this as long as I have, there's not an official in the country you *don't* know. It's a messy job I do, but ain't nothing more rewarding than returning happy kids to their families. Tell me, what's that situation out there lookin' like?"

When I'm all done running down the basics, Bo asks what group Rupert got himself mixed up in. "Progressives," I say. "They're Hollywood-based, and—"

"Hollywood-based, hell," he says. "Them folks is all over the world."

"You've heard of them, then."

"Son, I am practically an expert."

"I don't know if we're talking about the same Progressives," I say. "I doubt they're national. I mean, I'd never heard of them before—"

"They practice ancestor worship, am I right?"

"Yes . . ." Then again, so do most of the so-called true dino religions. Truth be told, the standard human Bible—Exodus, Numbers, and the rest of 'em—isn't exactly revered in our society as the holiest of books. We've got churchgoing dinos, sure, and a number of them really get into the holy rolling, but it's more of a cultural and ethical consideration than anything else. Our species has been around long enough to know that if Adam and Eve existed, they did so quite some time after my forefathers were long fossilized, so, at the very least, the Bible's missing about six thousand chapters before Genesis even gets going.

"And these Progressives you're talking 'bout," continues Dr. Beauregard, "they've got themselves enough money to choke one of them Arab princes, am I right in that as well?"

I concede that he is.

"Then you and I are talking 'bout the same group, son."

He's sold me. The only remaining questions I have are how much Dr. Beaumont Beauregard charges—a prince's ransom, and up front, but Louise has the bucks to cover it—and how soon he can be in Los Angeles. Quicker the better, because the sounds of splintering wood from upstairs have intensified over the last few hours.

"Next flight outta Memphis is first thing tomorrow morning," he tells me.

"Memphis, huh? You treat Elvis?" I joke.

"Don't poke fun at the King, son. Man with a heart that big, did such good for people . . . Ain't his fault if he needs a little help getting outta where he shouldn't be."

Bo's got me surprised once again. "Elvis is one of your patients?" I ask him.

Dr. Beauregard snorts into the phone, and I can almost feel the wet spittle dripping out of my receiver. "Don't be daft, boy," he says to me. "Elvis is dead."

Somehow I know that two thousand miles away, Dr. B. is shooting me a sly wink.

. . .

I'm back up on Franklin Avenue in Hollywood a short while later, ready to make a full frontal assault on the St. Regis Hotel. Ernie's agreed to baby-sit our special package for the evening, freeing me up to do some investigative work on the Minsky case without having to worry whether or not our bird's gonna stick to his cage while I'm gone. Seemed like a generous gesture from my partner at the time, but now that I think about it, I realize that he just wanted a few extra hours with Louise. They've gotten chummy again, and I've got to keep an eye on those two.

Three flights up, I'm winded. Four and I'm panting. Five, and I'm wondering if I should have had an EKG the last time I was at Doc Zalaznick's. Since when did flophouse floors get so tall?

By the time I make it to the sixth-floor landing, I've got to take a second for a breather—and I thought *Ernie* was outta shape. Dragging myself down the hallway, I take a quick listen at the door of room 619. Creaking, mumbled grunts. The music of intercourse. This should be fun.

A well-placed kick at the intersection of doorjamb and knob, and the flimsy wooden door flies inward, slamming into the wall behind. The man on the bed—a mammal, a filthy little human—withdraws from the guised-up hooker beneath him, clutching a mass of the stained, filthy sheets in his trembling grip.

"What the—who—"

I don't bother responding—at least, not with my voice. A quick bounce forward and I'm in the room, knocking whatever I can off the nightstand and dressing table, hoping for a loud, disorienting crash. The sight of this pig violating one of our kind—

even as low-down, disgusting, and cheap as this streetwalker might be—is enough to send me into overdrive.

"Five seconds," I say, trying to keep my voice to a dull roar. My teeth are itching to break free, my claws flickering in and out behind their gloves.

The human is confused. His penis has quickly gone limp, dangling between those pasty white legs like a useless little worm. Viagra is no match for a pissed-off Velociraptor. "Wh—what?"

"Okay, *no* seconds." I take a step forward and remove a large gold ring that adorns the third finger on my gloved right hand. This is to indicate that I will be using my fists at some point in the near future.

This john's seen enough mob flicks to get the signal—tell the truth, that's where I picked it up—and he doesn't even bother dressing before grabbing his clothes under one arm, scurrying out of the room, and down the stairway, flabby butt cheeks flopping with each step.

I turn my attention to Star, who has yet to move from the bed. Her naked human costume glistens with whatever she's passing off for sweat nowadays—I tend to use genuine Nakitara Perspiration Bulbs, but I've heard of poorer slobs resorting to water from the Pacific, or, in a pinch, their own urine. Disgusting, what some dinos put themselves through in order to save a few bucks.

"He was a good customer," she drawls. A line of drool stretches from her mouth down to her chest, and it takes all my concentration to focus back on that too-pale, drugged-out face. "He'll be back." Her bubblegum and fresh-sod scent drops in and out, spiking and falling, spiking and falling.

"What is it?" I ask, coming closer, slapping her cheeks to try to convince a bit of color to return. "You on the basil?"

She laughs—it's a typical streetwalker cackle—and pushes me away. "Basil is so over, asshole. Cayenne's where it's at this year. Cay-yaaaaan . . ."

Another slap, this one more for the pleasure than the efficacy. "Where'd you put Minsky's stuff? You fence it?"

No answer. Instead, she leans over the side of the bed, flicks out her uncapped tongue—didn't the human john notice it was a bit too long, a bit too dexterous?—and takes a sloppy wet lick off the top of the nightstand. A rust-colored line of cayenne has been sprinkled there, but it disappears into those taste buds two seconds later.

I open the nightstand drawer and find a pharmacy of plastic baggies filled with cayenne pepper and some other noxious herb I don't immediately recognize. Rosemary, maybe? I open the window—struggle with it, in fact, the damned thing probably having been stuck shut since the Paleolithic—and a warm breeze flows through the room, circulating the stench into new and interesting places. I open the plastic bags and pour the rest of the tramp's drugs into the alleyway below, an herbal cascade drenching the trash and cracked asphalt.

She starts whining again and tries to lift herself off the bed. "That's my stash, you bastard."

"Correction. That *was* your stash." I push her back with a flick—her skin nothing more than brittle tissue, muscles weak and useless—and she falls down hard. "I wanna know what you did with Minsky's stuff."

"Who?"

"You know who I'm talking about. Minsky, the guy you've been seeing."

"I see a lotta guys," she says, and tries to pull me toward the bed. "I could see you, too. We could do it right." She pulls back a corner of her guise at the neck, exposing a hide whose natural color has been obscured by a sickly pallor.

I hold down my gorge, pull away easily, and take a seat in a rickety chair. "Minsky. His ether. The instruments. Talk."

"Oh, the midget!"

"Now we're on the same page."

She gives me a sly once-over. "Lemme get this straight. You think . . . you think he *cares* about all that crap?"

"Lady, thinking ain't part of my job. Just tell me what you did with it and we don't need to get into any unpleasantness." I make a show of unsnapping my gloves, preparing my claws, taking my sweet time in order to make my intentions obvious.

But Star isn't going for my tough-guy act. "The midget don't care about his drugs," she says, hopping off the bed—human breasts drooping lasciviously off that pale chest—"believe me. You wait a second, you can ask him."

The hell is she talking about? "The hell are you talking about?"

With exquisite timing, there's a knock on the partially opened flophouse door, and a familiar stunted arm pops through the doorway, grasping a bouquet of roses. "Sweetie," calls the heliuminflected voice, "did I come too soon?"

I rush the door, grab that arm as tight as I can, and yank hard, dragging Minsky off his feet and into my face. "Give me one reason why I shouldn't give you a rose-bouquet suppository," I growl.

That little body sets to trembling, but I refuse to back off. Minsky, dressed in a fine wool suit and ridiculous tiger-stripe tie, glances back and forth between me and his mistress, as if one or the other of us will somehow disappear and leave him in a good, happy place.

"I—I—she didn't—"

"What the fuck are you doing here?"

"She—I didn't mean to—"

"You sent me to find her and get your stuff back," I say.

"Please," Minsky pleads softly. "Not in front of Star—"

"You know she was making it with a human when I got here?"

Not even a cringe from the dentist. He's probably known about her interspecies dalliances for some time; maybe he even gets off on it. The realm of dino depravity knows no bounds. "Please," he says again. "You don't understand."

"Then explain."

Minsky looks to Star again; I can tell he'd be more forthcoming if she weren't in the room. "Scram," I tell her, tossing a dollar bill at her feet. "Go get yourself a soda."

The tart picks my dollar up off the floor, crumples it into a ball, and tosses it back in my face. I try not to flinch as the rough paper scratches my cheek. Then, still costumed but otherwise buck naked, she strolls out the door—running her hand across Minsky's chest as she goes—and into the hallway, disappearing from sight.

I throw Minsky onto the bed and he goes down hard, the rusty springs creaking beneath the force. "You been wasting my time," I bark. "Ernie's time, too. You think this is the only case we got? You think we do this 'cause we're nice?"

"I didn't—I told you guys the truth—she stole those things from me—"

"And?"

"And . . . and nothing. She stole them, I was mad, I wanted you to get them back."

"So it's okay now. The stealing, the lying."

"No, it's—yes . . ."

"Because you're still fucking her."

Minsky looks away. I grab his fleshy cheeks with one hand and turn him back around. Our eyes meet for a second—embarrassment, pain, desire—but he quickly averts his gaze once more. "I can't help myself," he admits. "I just can't stay away."

With but a flick of my wrist, Minsky goes flying backward again, bouncing off the bed and landing hard on the floor. I've spent enough time on this dog of a case already without throwing more good time after bad. "Tell you what you *can* stay away from," I say. "My office."

I slam the door and don't look back. Two flights down, I pass an open doorway, a familiar cavalcade of shrieks and moans emanating from the room within. It's Star again—I know it without looking in—and in some petty way it makes me a little happy that

Minsky has to wait upstairs twiddling his underclaws while his love of the month is three flights down, shtupping a stranger for fifty bucks.

Strike that. It makes me *very* happy.

. . .

It's one week later, and, for the most part, things have quieted down around the offices of Watson and Rubio. Louise has ceased her vigil in our offices and returned to her home; we've promised to call her the moment anything breaks. Ernie misses her presence, I can tell, and he finds at least two pretenses every day to dial her number and fill her in on some insignificant detail of the case. I wonder if Louise's new husband knows Ernie's been calling. If so, I wonder if he cares.

The last twenty-four hours have been blissfully silent, but the days before were filled with an unwelcome cacophony of screams, roars, and blasts of anger from the studio apartment above. Rupert Simmons was not taking well to deprogramming.

Dr. Beaumont Beauregard—Bo, as I call him now after a week of fetching fast food and diet peach iced teas for the guy—showed up on our stoop the morning after I got back from the St. Regis Hotel. He's a big 'un, the doctor is, a good ol' boy in the finest plantation-owning tradition, with a shock of white hair and a similarly colored mustache and goatee—Nakitara brand, Colonel Sanders #3. Smelled mainly like a foil-covered chocolate bar, but I thought I may have detected some wheatgrass in there as well.

"You Rubio?" he asked me when I approached and offered a hand with his luggage.

"Dr. Beauregard?"

He grinned and grabbed his own bags, easily hoisting the heavy suckers without so much as a grunt. "No need to waste your time with these, son. Ain't nothing but books, anyway. All my clothes I got on my back."

I got my first smell of the doctor right then, and commented on what I thought to be a pleasant aroma.

"Don't know what you're talking about, son."

"Your smell," I said. "Your scent. I'd guess you were an Ankie, but I'm not too good at this."

Again, no recognition. Had I made a fatal error and somehow contacted a non-dino deprogrammer? Would Dan have been dense enough to give me the name of a mammal?

I tried again. "It's okay. We're all . . . we're all of a kind here. No one eavesdropping. All I'm saying is I like your scent."

Bo threw me an exasperated glare, then softened it to one of mild annoyance. Lowering his voice, though there was no one else within a hundred yards, he whispered, "Listen—if I'm gonna have to convince a patient to come back to the real world, if I'm gonna be telling him that he ain't one of the ancestors, I can't be walking around talking dinosaur the whole day. Long as I am in this guise, I am as human as the next fella. You got that?"

Ernie, Louise, and I camped out in the office below while Bo and Rupert went at it upstairs in what sounded like the world's greatest pro wrestling grudge match. If I thought I knew banging and screaming before . . . Let's just say that it was chamber music compared to the struggle—both physical and emotional—that has been taking place upstairs for the last few days.

Every day at one and at six, Bo would emerge from the apartment, sweaty and slick beneath his guise—though of course we weren't allowed to mention the costume in any way—and put in his fast-food order for the day. Hamburgers, hot dogs, the odd taco or two. Rupert's meals, on the other hand, were carefully prepared banquets concocted by his sister, slaved over for hours in the small kitchenette attached to our office, and more often than not returned untouched come nightfall.

Louise was losing weight. She was losing sleep. And she was losing her sanity. We were relieved when she finally bailed out two nights ago.

So it's just Ernie and me who are around to look up in shock when Rupert appears at the door to our office—well-dressed, a little thin, but seemingly sane—and says, "I feel better now."

Bo, standing just behind him, glows with pride. "It wasn't easy," he says. "No, sir. But we're over the hard part now. It's all level ground from here on in."

"Are you sure?" I ask. "I mean . . . everything's . . . better?"

"I understand what happened to me," says Rupert. "I understand what the Progressives were trying to do to me, and I'm glad that you got me out of it. And that's a step."

"And the other thing?" prompts Bo.

"Right," says Rupert. He approaches Ernie and me, and, in an effort that must stretch his arms to their maximum limit, envelops us in a group hug. My face squishes up against his shoulder, and since it would be bad manners to back off, I deal with the pain. "Thank you for rescuing me."

"Anytime, kid," says Ernie, and I second the emotion while pulling away. Enough with the huggy-huggy.

"Could you maybe call my sister?" asks Rupert. "I don't want her to worry."

"Course we can," I say, but Ernie's already on the phone telling Louise to hurry her little self on over to the office.

That night, we all head out for a celebratory dinner at Trader Vic's, the Polynesian joint near our office, and the tiki torches and huge fruit drinks with uncommonly large parasols serve as a perfect reflection of our elevated mood. Dr. Bo proves to be a fascinating conversationalist, and we learn about his exploits curing cult members all over the world. A few sprigs of basil are passed around the table as a further means of enhancing our good feelings, but Bo forbids Rupert to take any of the weed. Probably a wise choice.

Still, I feel that I can't let the night end without a proper toast. Plucking a sprig of basil from the side of my pu-pu platter, I thrust it into the air and say, "To Rupert, for coming back to us."

"To Rupert," is the chorus that echoes me, my dining companions holding aloft their own herbal buddies.

"And to Bo," I continue, "for leading the way."

"To Bo." We munch up. We feel good. It's a happy day.

And so it is that on March 19th at eight forty-five in the evening, Rupert Simmons was successfully deprogrammed from the dinosaur cult known as the Progressives and returned to his friends and family, a happy, healthy, and well-adjusted Tyrannosaurus Rex.

. . .

And so it is that three days later, Rupert Simmons is dead.

The funeral is a lovely affair, done up with all the taste and black velvet the Simmons family could rustle up on such short notice. There's an open coffin—mahogany, with gold inlay— Rupert inside, looking to all the world like he's just getting in a good forty winks. There's a preacher, droning on about the youth of society, about how they take so much for granted, yet are so reluctant to ask for help. There's Louise and her elderly father, a smattering of aunts and uncles, all looking pale and weak and shattered and, more than anything else, confused.

Louise found him. At least, that's what Ernie told me, and I have no reason to doubt either one of them. As it is, Louise has been somewhat incommunicado for the last few days, dealing with the petty tasks that the death of a loved one brings on: phone calls to the mortuary, to the clergy, to caterers. Duties that are best left to someone else—anyone else—are unfortunately the domain of the bereaved, and as a result, I've gotten in barely a word of condolence to my partner's ex-wife.

And then there's the whole issue of guilt. If not a sea of it, a river, perhaps.

Rupert's note read BECAUSE I HAVE NO MEANING, and that was the end of that. Five words, each one a little BB pellet into my heart. The self-blame game goes like this: had he not been deprogrammed, had he not been locked up, had he not been taken from the Progressive compound and thrown into my trunk in the first place, Rupert Simmons would be alive and well today. Worshiping his ancestors and prattling on about the truth behind Progress, sure, but at least he'd have vital signs and a healthy, active scent. As it is, his smell has disappeared from the corpse in the box before me, and I can barely bring myself to stop sniffing for that cappuccino and cream.

"And so we see," the preacher is saying, "that life is not a gift. It is a privilege granted to us. . . ."

Seconal. One of the few mammal-oriented drugs that has similar effects on our kind, and that's what they found, a big bottle of it clutched in Rupert Simmons's right hand. He hadn't even undressed before downing somewhere around 2,000 milligrams, roughly twenty times the recommended dosage for these sleep inducers, which means he entered the world of the dead still tied up beneath the buckles and the girdles and the zippers and the latex. Maybe it was a message to all of us: *See what you did? See how you made life so unbearable for me?* Maybe it wasn't. No way to know, since a note reading BECAUSE I HAVE NO MEANING leaves a lot open to interpretation. I think I like it better that way.

An elderly gentleman to my left smelling of stale graham crackers and codfish covertly hands me a small stash of basil, like a fan passing a joint at a rock concert. I take a nibble, instantly feeling the slow mellow rush spreading through my veins, warming me up from the inside out, and pass it on to Ernie, who samples and continues the chain. This is how we deal with death: an herb, a gnaw, and let's move on with the whole ugly shebang. The preacher, though—a human, I gather, from the way he won't quit babbling—isn't hip to the scene.

". . . and so it is with young Rupert, who in death cannot tell us why he felt he had no meaning in life. . . ."

It had been going well, or so we thought. Rupert was back in his old apartment, meeting up with his previously estranged group of friends, and had been talking about finding a job with a nonprofit organization. "One of the environmentals," he told us over the phone two days after that dinner at Trader Vic's. "Saving the rain forests." And as I've still got a few relatives back in South America eking out a living beneath the jungle canopy, I thought it a fabulous idea. Bo told us that a job search was one of the first stages of reintroduction to everyday life, that it indicated that the patient—that Rupert—was interested in rejoining society. He'd even expressed interest in volunteering for a cult-awareness group for young at-risk dinos, another idea we all greeted with enthusiasm.

Plus, he was talking to his old high school girlfriend for the first time in a few years, and they'd already made plans to go out on a pre-pre-date at a local Spanish tapas restaurant. Again, Bo was optimistic: "A little nookie don't hurt anyone." What's more, Louise said he'd begun playing the guitar and cooking dinners again, and already a blush of normalcy had returned to his eerily youthful hide. Thumbs-up status on all accounts.

Doesn't sound to me like he had no meaning. Then again, some folks have a talent for putting up a good facade even when their infrastructure is shot through with rotting beams and crumbling struts. Rupert must have been one of them.

On the night of March 21st, Rupert had invited his sister and her husband to come over the next morning for one of his special brunches, a meal the young T-Rex was known by his friends and family to have perfected during his world travels. All manner of ethnic foodstuffs went into these elaborate presentations— quail's eggs, green pancakes, sushi, tandoori shrimp—and he somehow managed to combine the disparate flavors into a meal that would make Wolfgang Puck's naturally brown hide tarnish green with envy.

Terrell—big as a house, dumb as the stucco—wasn't able to make it to brunch that morning, so it was just Louise, alone and unprepared, who found herself confused when the doorbell didn't bring her brother. And it was Louise who found herself pounding on the door after a few minutes had passed with no answer from within. And it was Louise who eventually got the landlord to unlock the door, and it was Louise who found her brother, dead, slumped across an unmade bed with a bottle in his hand and a five-word suicide note by his head.

While Louise wept and held her brother in her arms, the landlord—an Ornithomimus who was drunk off his ass on cilantro but functional enough to use modern appliances—dialed the dino division of the cops and the morgue, and soon enough the place was swarming with badges. They scoped the scene, took samples, and, once a rapid inquest had been processed at Dan Patterson's request—a result, of course, of my own request—declared the death to be what we all knew it was: a suicide.

Dr. Beauregard was beside himself with guilt, calling nearly every day from Memphis to proclaim his sorrow at Rupert's passing.

"I can't believe this happened," he kept saying. "The boy seemed so . . . His behavior pattern never indicated . . . This just ain't right. . . ."

We didn't blame him. At least Ernie and I didn't blame him, and Louise certainly professed to bear no ill will toward the doctor. Still, he sent flower arrangement after flower arrangement, even spicing up a few with the odd medicinal herb here and there, anything to assuage Louise's sorrow and his own feelings of failure.

He even sent back the check for services rendered. Now *that's* a doctor for you.

"Please follow me outside for the interment," the preacher is saying, finishing up his epic tribute to a dino he barely even knew, "where we will return young Rupert to the ground from whence he came." I've never understood this—are we supposed to be made of dirt? I consider raising my hand, but the preacher has already moved past me, down the aisle and into the bright light of day.

"Vincent!" Ernie hisses. I look over—he's cocking his head toward the back of the small funeral crowd. Behind the array of foreign and domestic automobiles is a long stretch limo, five-window style, green as the hide on a Hadrosaur's behind.

"That just pull up?" I whisper back, and Ernie nods.

A chauffeur, duded up to the nines in an emerald tuxedo, hops out of the driver's seat and runs around to the passenger door. It's quite the jog. With a flourish, he pulls open the door, and I only wish I were more surprised at what gets out.

It's Circe, and she's dressed to mourn. Long black overcoat, green velvet dress down to the perfectly sculpted latex ankles, sensible pumps padding through the damp dirt below.

"What the hell's she doing here?" Ernie asks, a bit too loudly. A number of the bereaved turn to shush us, but Ernie does a stupendous job of ignoring them.

"She must have thought of herself as a friend," I say, finding myself defending the leader of the Progressives. "Friends come to these things."

"Friends don't brainwash each other."

"Nothing you can do about it. I'm sure she wants to pay her respects, that's all."

Ernie starts to rise from his seat—"I'll show her respect"—but I'm able to grab his forearm and force him back down before he starts anything unseemly. The progress he's made with Louise over the past few weeks has put him in a much better mood; causing a scene at her brother's funeral might land him back in the mammal house for good.

"Let it go," I counsel. "Let her watch, and let her leave."

And that's all she seems to do. Circe takes her place at the back of the gathering, and as the preacher continues his endless sermon, I can almost feel her stare boring through the back of my head, as if she were trying to crawl into my brain and gaze out through *my* eyes, to place herself in my position. But every time I turn around she's looking somewhere else, seemingly focused entirely on the clergyman and his dubious words of wisdom.

"Ashes to ashes," the preacher is chanting as the gears turn and Rupert's coffin is lowered into the ground, "dust to dust . . ." It's a human ritual but serves us well nevertheless. The days of burning our corpses or letting them sink to a watery grave are all in the past. We're just like the mammals, nothing more than pack rats when it comes to our dead nowadays, secreting them in boxes underground as if we might want to dig them up again should they come in handy at some point in the future.

As the funeral comes to a close and the group disbands, Rupert's friends and family empathizing with one another in a huge cat's cradle of consolation, I feel a familiar presence rise up behind me. It's the smell that gives it away, more than anything else, that wild concoction of herbs accompanied by an intense burst of pine boiling out of her pores—a common dinosaur scent somehow elevated to another level.

"I didn't expect to see you here," I say even before I've finished turning around.

"Nor I you," replies Circe. She's at least three inches taller than me—new ground for a dame—and I find myself unable to look away from that gaze. "Do you have a cold?" she asks.

She's referring to the fact that I'm pinching my nostrils closed with two fingers from my right hand, doing my best to shut out that intoxicating scent. The last thing I need right now is another trip back to the Jurassic. Then again, maybe it's the first thing I need. As it is, the evolutionary process hasn't completely local-ized all of my scent-sniffing glands in my nose; scents are still partially the domain of my taste buds, and I can smell every inch of this Progressive leader each time my tongue comes in contact with the pheromone-laced air.

"Yes," I reply. "My sinuses are all a mess. Forgive me."

"Did you know him well?"

"On and off," I explain. "Friend of a friend. Last time I saw him was the night that the . . . *club* . . . met up at your place."

Her laugh is high, airy, and if it weren't for the circumstances, she would most likely let it transform into a full-fledged giggle. "Oh, it's not my place," she says. "It belongs to all of us. Tell me, did you enjoy yourself the other evening?"

"It was . . . educational," I say.

"That is what we strive for," replies Circe. "Then again, all work and no play . . ." And for a second, I'm pretty sure I can feel her pinching my rump. But her hands aren't anywhere near my derriere, and a quick 360 spin shows me that I must be hallucinating. I clamp my nostrils tighter, shutting out the last remaining olfactory vestiges of those evil weeds. "Perhaps you might like to come to another session."

I'm about to reply in the negative—the strong negative, the desperation negative—when my fingers fail me. Muscles loosening up, blatantly disregarding my orders to clench, engaging in full-scale mutiny even as my brain screams at them to fall in line. But soon my nostrils are wide open and flaring of their own accord—I'll have to add them to my blacklist of misbehaving body parts—and sucking in Circe's sweet scent.

"I'd love to come back," I find myself saying. Somewhere, Ernie's calling for me to come to the car, to say goodbye and to hurry up, and somewhere else I'm telling him to hold on one second. But right here and right now it's just me, a verdant goddess named Circe, and the tallest, thickest, most fragrant jungle anyone's seen this side of the Triassic. Trees burst from the ground, soaring into the sky; vines surround us, reaching out with their leafy fingers, caressing our bodies as they entangle me and this perfect female Velociraptor in a vortex of lush foliage. We're not running this time, but even standing still I feel that sense of urgency, that raw natural power welling up within, bursting with pure energy. Holding my face—holding hers—tongues whipping out, lashing at one another, teeth clashing in the furious rush for pleasure, growls and roars forming deep within our throats, call-ing out in a language I don't even know—

And suddenly I'm back in my Lincoln, driving out of the main gates of the funeral home.

". . . which is why I have to suspect her motives," Ernie is say-ing. "I'm not telling you she's wrong or she's evil or anything, but I want you to watch out."

"Right . . ." I respond, trying to get a bearing on the conversa-tion. Where was I just now? *Who* was I just now? "What was that part about watching out, again?" I ask.

Ernie slaps the dashboard. "Damn it, I knew you weren't lis-tening to me."

"I *was*—I *was*—it . . . You wanted me to watch out . . ."

"For Circe," he supplies.

"Why?"

Ernie doesn't even try to suppress a sigh. It bursts out of his lips, a long, drawn-out wheeze of frustration. " 'Cause every time you talk to her you get all googly-eyed."

We do not discuss it further. The rest of the ride home is uneventful, but when we arrive back at the office and step out of the car, a funny thing happens: I find myself unable to control my lips. This is not your basic Vincent Rubio careless talk—this is a fully undeveloped thought coming to the forefront, blindsiding me even before I have a chance to choke off my throat and cut off the air to my own vocal cords.

"You wanna check out another Progressive meeting?" I hear myself saying.

Ernie takes a step back, ducking as if I've swung a bat at his head. "I don't think you said what I think you said."

"It might be fun. See what they're really all about."

"Kid, you feeling okay?"

And that's all the time it takes to regain control over my rogue brain. I throw the offending part in the stockade and shake my head, attempting to banish all remaining inklings to a nonintru-sive nook in my noggin. "Just thinking we could do some more snoop work, see if any other kids are messed up in this," I lie. I wish I could tell Ernie the truth, that I don't know where either the thought or the words came from, but I fear that'd freak him out more than the fib. Certainly gives *me* the willies.

"Forget about it," says Ernie. "And forget about all the Progress crap. It's over. Progress is behind us."

"Progress is behind us," I repeat. I think I will make that my mantra for the week, once an hour, twice before bedtime. And if, after all that time and all those repetitions, I can still smell that powerful, pleasurable, pungent scent—as I can now, on my clothes, in my hair, on my skin, behind every bush and every tree and every passerby—then I will make it my mantra for the next month. And the year. And the decade, if need be. Yes, it's settled.

. . .

It's been a quiet few weeks in the office. Minsky hasn't bothered us in quite some time, instead leaving short messages of apology on our machine, which we listen to, laugh at, and erase. Louise, meanwhile, is managing to work through her grief with a little help from Ernie, who sees her and the new husband a few times a week for dinner. It's a little weird if you ask me, the ex hanging out with the new couple all the time, but if Terrell doesn't complain, I certainly won't. I get the feeling that the guy isn't home a lot, and maybe Ernie is providing some comfort for his ex-wife at a time when she desperately needs it. Maybe he just wants to screw her. Don't ask me; I'm no shrink.

Teitelbaum, the T-Rex who owns and runs TruTel Enterprises, a massive PI firm here in the basin, was kind enough—hah, he doesn't even know how to *spell* the word *kind*—to throw a few cases our way. I'd like to say that we reciprocate, that Ernie and I occasionally find ourselves so swamped with work that we have to pass on clients to others, but it's simply not the case. We do okay for ourselves—I've got a home, nice clothes, a car that's nearly paid for, and I get in the occasional special stash from time to time—but it's not like we can afford to be trading cases back and forth with the big boys. As it happens, Teitelbaum doesn't expect us to hand over our clients. He just wants our souls.

"Two thousand in fees, flat deal," he announced, flipping a case file onto the desk in front of me. I'd come down at six in the morning at Teitelbaum's request, and I wasn't in the mood to be lowballed by Jabba the Hutt.

"Missing-persons case, right? That could take months."

"Yeah, and . . . ?"

"And two thousand won't begin to cover it."

"Do what you want," he told me, knowing exactly which body part—well, parts—he had me by. "I can give it to Sutherland."

"He's a hack."

"He's a *cheap* hack. And he doesn't bitch like you do. You want it or not, Rubio?"

I agreed to the fee. Ernie would kill me for doing it, but I had no choice. We're hard up for cash.

So we're running down some missing persons, we're trailing a few deadbeat dads, we're spying on a few salacious spouses. Still, it's a job, and it pays the bills. Even with Teitelbaum skinning us alive.

If the jerk's going to take half of our fees, though, I'm going to make sure to use his facilities as often as possible. As a result, I find myself spending a perfectly lovely Los Angeles spring afternoon—temperature in the low seventies, not a cloud in the sky, smog in remission for the week—holed up inside a darkroom, squinting at blurry negatives and nearly passing out from the overpowering smell of photographic chemicals.

The guy we're trailing is a Raptor, a two-bit con artist who makes a play out of taking old ladies for a run and then splitting town with their cars and their cash. Unfortunately for him, he scammed the grandmother of Tommy Troubadour, a local lounge lizard with reputed ties to the mob—the dino one, I mean—and I can only hope he'll enjoy eating his meals through a straw for the rest of his life.

Here's a nice photo of the slimy Raptor now, coming out of an '89 Oldsmobile with a member of the Social Security set on his arm. His greasy black hair contrasts horribly with her blue coif, and even through the black-and-white of the photo it's a painful sight. The contrast isn't quite right, though, so I dunk the print again, waiting for the images to sharpen. I should be timing the developing process with a stopwatch, but sometimes I like to feel my way around the procedure instead. Photo-developing for snoop work always takes me somewhere between the spiritual intuition of the artistic process and the workaday photoboard cut-and-paste of a third-grade science fair project, and I like to take my time and find a decent midpoint.

I'm almost to where I want to be—there's the image now, coming in nice and clear, the son of a bitch's face center-frame and ready to be identified—when the darkroom curtain pulls open, a blast of fluorescent light nearly blowing me off my feet.

"What the hell—" I shout, trying to protect a string of negatives that have yet to be developed. "Shut the outer door first, you moron."

"Ooh, man, Vincent, I am so sorry." I can't see who it is behind the glare, but it only takes a second to place the voice. Sutherland. "I am so, so sorry."

"I got it, you're sorry. Now shut the fucking door!" I hate to resort to vulgarity, but the cretin isn't reacting to direct commands.

"Right," he says. "Right, right." And finally, the light from outside is extinguished, leaving us in red-tinted darkness. He grins sheepishly, points to the print in my hands. "Photo looks okay."

" 'Course it looks okay, it's developed already. I got three rolls back there strung up you might have just burned out."

"I am so sorry—"

"Enough. Do you need something, Sutherland?"

He doesn't even have the self-respect to look away or seem ashamed when he responds. "Please. I'm not too good at this."

I grab a cartridge of exposed film from Sutherland's hand and help the guy begin the developing process—hell, I'd do it for him if it would get him out of here any quicker.

"So," he says as I pull his film from the canister, "how's tricks?"

"Tricks are fine. If you're gonna stand around, you might as well watch what I'm doing. Maybe you'll learn something."

"Certainly, absolutely." Sutherland makes a play out of taking great note of my movements, humming and yes-ing under his breath, but I know the guy's just putting on a show. None of this is going to stick with him; his brain is Teflon-coated. But meanwhile, he's standing behind me all the while, rancid breath combining with that rotten-egg scent to create a horrorshow of unequaled proportions for my sensitive snout.

"Listen," I blurt out after an unbearable five minutes have passed, "why don't I just do this for you, huh? I'll leave the photos here, you come back and pick 'em up later."

"Would you?" he asks innocently, and I know that I'm being played for a chump. But it's a small price to pay in order to secure the return of my privacy and a relatively odor-free environment. "That's . . . that's great of you, Rubio. Tell ya what. I'll take you to that herb joint up on Franklin later tonight, my treat."

"Not necessary," I say. "Not my kinda place." I know the establishment of which he speaks; it's a small run-down dive of a basil bar where the waitresses are hooked on the very stuff they're doling out. Vacant eyes and lazy tails are the name of the game at the Pesto Palace, and it just serves to depress me every time I step inside. The Hollywood bars have that effect on me, for some reason, and I make it a point to avoid them as much as possible.

"Hey," he says, "how'd y'all do at that wacked-out Progressive thing?"

I shrug and say, "We made out. Did what we came there to do. You?"

"A whole mess," he says. "Don't get me wrong—I got my info

all right, and Mr. Teitelbaum was real happy with me. Real happy." He reaches into his pocket and withdraws a wallet stuffed to bursting with receipts and coupons. From within the depths, he extracts a business card and hands it to me. HORACE "HAPPY" SUTHERLAND, it reads—and I've never known the guy's first name or this moronic nickname until just now—EXECUTIVE SECOND VICE PRESIDENT OF INVESTIGATIONS. "That's almost like partner," he confides.

"How pleasing."

"But a lotta weird shit went down after I got back, I'll tell ya." Sutherland shoves that wallet back into his pants pocket and makes to leave. But something in that last sentence has grabbed me. Maybe it was his tone, his quick delivery, or maybe it's just a buried suspicion of my own snagging a reason to show its ugly face, but I reach out and grab Sutherland by the shoulder.

"What do you mean, 'weird shit'?"

"What do you mean by what do I mean?" He pulls away, eyeing me carefully.

"Don't start with—look, you said weird shit went down, I'm just asking what it was. Idle chitchat."

Sutherland sighs, tries to turn away again and meets up with my body wedged between him and the blackout curtain. "It was a mess," he says. "You don't want to know. Just wasting your time."

"Humor me." With every moment of stalling, I've become more interested.

The Triceratops shrugs and takes a seat on the developing table—his butt spilling over the sides, pants nearly dipping into the pool of chemicals—and opens up. "We had this case come in, some woman whose daughter had disappeared. Only this note left behind said she'd found Progress and all that jazz."

I've heard of such things. "Go on."

"When you saw me at the party, I was there looking for the girl. Picked up on her scent, followed her when she went to the powder room, and had a little confrontation. First she claimed to be someone else, said I was crazy, but I'd smelled her old sheets from her bedroom at home, and this here is one dino who doesn't forget a scent. It was her all right, and so I pressed her and I pressed her and I pressed her and finally she admitted it, but wouldn't come back with me. My orders were not to get physical, so I let her go. Disappeared into the crowd and I couldn't find her the rest of the night. Good appetizers, though.

"So I returned to the office, relayed my information, and they sent in a team to extract her—that was their term, *extract her*—from the compound. A few days later, I hear they've got her at home and she's all better, Mr. Teitelbaum gives me a promotion and a raise, and everything's hunky dory."

"Seems fine to me," I say. "Nothing messy there."

"That's what I thought. Then I get called into the big man's office a few days ago, and he tells me that the girl is dead, and I have to submit all my documents from the trip. I mean, all my notes and everything. Like I keep these things—pain in the ass, right? So I have to go digging through my files—"

"Wait a second," I interrupt, my mouth having taken a few seconds to catch up with my suddenly racing thoughts, "did you say she was dead?"

"Hm? Yeah, ain't that a shame? We get her outta that cult, turn the girl's life around, and then poof, she's gone."

"How'd she die?" I'm up off the stool now, volume raising, voice echoing in the small chamber.

"You're very excitable today, you know that?"

"Sutherland . . ." I snarl.

"Car accident, it was a car accident."

"Oh." I don't know what I expected, but a car accident wasn't on the list.

Sutherland notices my disappointment, and elaborates further. "She hit a pole."

Now we're talking. Next to the overdone overdose, the single-car accident is the bread and butter of the suicidal set. "Was she by herself?"

"Solo accident, that's what they said, out on some deserted road up near Angeles Crest." He's talking the mountains, the Angeles Crest National Forest, a favorite spot of serial killers thanks to the excellent canopy coverage it provides a rotting corpse. Suicides like it up there, too—something about getting away from the smog and the noise and the heat and the traffic and just hanging out with a blue jay and the wind for your last minutes on earth, I suppose.

"I'll see you later," I hear myself saying, even as my legs are moving me past Sutherland, past the safelight and the developing table and the trays of chemicals, and through the inner blackout curtain.

"Wait!" Sutherland cries out. "What about my pictures?"

"Take 'em to the Fotomat," I reply. The outer door opens— bright light poking sharp needles into my eyes, but I pay it no mind—and then closes behind me, and I don't even know if the hack PI can hear me anymore. Tell the truth, I don't really care. I've got something else developing.

Ernie said it was all just a coincidence. I said it might be. Ernie said I was wasting my time. I said I might be. Ernie said that the two dead dinosaurs were only that, two dead dinosaurs, and not connected in any way. I said they might be.

But it hasn't stopped me from going to the coroner's.

"All I need is a list of suicides and accidents over the last few years," I'm saying, trying to get past Dr. Kalichman's initial reluctance to let me into her files. "Just the dino ones, won't take long at all."

"No can do."

"You wrote the reports, you can give me the information."

"Of course I *can*," she tells me. "But I'm not supposed to."

I whip out two twenty-dollar bills and throw them onto the autopsy table between us. They flutter down onto the chest of a well-preserved human corpse, where they sit untouched. Dr. Kalichman raises a single eyebrow in my direction.

"I'm not looking to be bribed, Mr. Rubio."

"Sorry," I respond, plucking the bills off the body and shoving them back in my pocket. "Force of habit. And please, call me Vincent."

"Fine. Vincent, I can't give you the report."

"Look," I say, "we've known each other for how long? Years, right? We're colleagues, in a way. Colleagues do *favors* for each other." I emphasize this last part, particularly to remind Dr. Kalichman that I did some complimentary detective work for her a few years back when she thought her husband was fooling around on her. He'd been working too late down at the Natural History Museum, cataloging fake fossils, a job that had never previously necessitated anything more than a standard forty-hour work week. Their joint bank account had been gradually depleted of funds, marked by withdrawals of sizable chunks of cash. And he'd recently been reluctant to engage in marital relations, all of which led Dr. K. to her assumption of infidelity. Didn't take more than a few nights of surveillance to find out that he wasn't sneaking out at all hours of the night to meet his mistress but was instead heading down to the track every afternoon and gambling away their mortgage money, then hopping down to Tijuana at nights in order to recoup his losses by riding a mechanical bull for spare dollars thrown at him by the other tourists. At the very least, he was too damned tired to screw his own wife. I think they're in counseling now.

"I know what you're getting at," the coroner replies, a flush coming to her cheeks, "and I thank you for your help in that matter. I do. But it would be breaking some serious rules to give you—"

"Then don't give it to me," I suggest. "Don't give it to me at all."

". . . Okay . . ." She's confused now, and I'm comfortable with that.

"Isn't it about lunchtime?" I suggest. "Don't you have that lunch meeting with the rest of the morgue set? That meeting a few miles away? Take about two hours or so?"

Dr. Kalichman sighs, but it's a sure sign of acceptance, and I know I'm in. "Be careful with the files," she says, "and put everything back the way you found it."

"No problem. And the next time you need snoop work, it's on me."

A few minutes later, she's gone, the door is locked, and I'm digging through the files, flipping past endless names of the deceased, checking a third of the way down the first page for the small green dot in the margin that indicates a corpse of reptilian heritage. After that, I let my eyes drop to the bottom, where Dr. Kalichman or one of her assistants has marked the assumed cause of death. I then cross-reference all the suicides, accidents, and unresolved cases with the date of demise written up at the top and toss out anything more than two years old. I'm sure there's a smorgasbord of interesting information I'll be losing out on by using this method, but I'm not getting paid for my time, and I've got to draw the line somewhere. Even hunches have their limits.

An hour later, I've got twenty-three names in twenty-three folders whose information matches my criteria, all stacked in a teetering pile at my feet. I guess I could use this as my base set, take down the names and numbers and make my phone calls, but I get the feeling that there's something else I'm missing, some way in which I can cull out the slag.

Gender? Nah, the Progressives are quite fair when it comes to their unisex recruiting policies. Just the two cases I know about—Rupert and the girl that Sutherland was after—prove the point right there. Income? It seems to me that a cult would be interested primarily in those members who could drain their families of whatever reserves they had—much in the way that Rupert had consistently funneled cash from Louise into the Progressives' coffers—and there's no doubt in my mind that they didn't come to that fancy mansion and the workstation in the subway by selling miniature "Best Grandfather" Oscar statuettes on the Boulevard, but these autopsy reports don't have a window into the victim's financial status.

What's left? Hair color? Sexual preference? Age?

Well there's a key, right there. Seems to me that most of the Progressives I saw at the meeting were in their younger years, only a very few even approaching middle age. The oldest one I saw, in fact, was Samuel, the Iguanodon who introduced Circe, but I'd consider him one of the cult's organizers; certainly, he was no ordinary member. Youth is my cross-referencing tool, without a doubt—there might be the odd case of the octogenarian seeking spiritual fulfillment, but by that point in life, most of us have had our heads screwed on tight and rusted over for a good many years.

I run a quick hippie check on the list, culling out anyone over thirty, which brings the pile down to a manageable twelve unlucky souls. I hurriedly scribble down the names and phone numbers of the closest relatives, and doing so further cuts the list to nine, as three of the victims left behind no known survivors. I carefully replace the files in their proper order—filing never having been one of my strong suits, I must admit, so I can only hope that whatever mistakes I made in alphabetizing don't gum up the works too badly—take my leave of the coroner's office, and close the door tightly behind me. Wouldn't want folks snooping around where they shouldn't be.

.   .   .

After a bit of arguing and more than a bit of guilt, Ernie's agreed to check out four of the names; I take the remaining five. My first two phone calls are not answered, and I'm reluctant to leave messages for what are most likely still-grieving parents regarding children who are years in the grave. No need to pick at old wounds for no good reason. The third one, however, goes through three rings—I'm getting ready to hang up again—and then abruptly—

" 'Lo?"

"Mr. Levitt?"

"What are you selling?"

"I'm not selling anything," I respond.

"Oh," he says, a bit surprised. "Good. I don't wanna buy anything. I got that waffle maker already, and I don't like it."

"I'm not selling anything, Mr. Levitt. My name is Vincent Rubio, and I'm a private detective."

A grunt. "Don't need detective work. Don't wanna buy it." A pause. "But if you want, you can tell me about it."

"No, no," I explain, "you don't understand. I'm not selling you anything."

"That's what they all say."

"Who?"

"The salesmen. They say they ain't selling, and then they start selling. I'm on the phone six hours a day. Am I happy with my appliances? Do I want a six-pack of abs? What kinda equity do I have in my home? Everybody's selling. You're gonna start selling soon."

"I promise you, I won't." And if he's so sure I am, why is the guy still on the phone with me? "I just want to ask you a few questions."

"What about?"

"About Jay."

A hiccough on the other end. Silence, but in the background, I can hear a television, blaring out some sort of infomercial. Someone is very excited about a cutlery set.

"Mr. Levitt?"

"I hear ya," he says after a few seconds. "You wanna sell me somethin' for my son, I bet. He don't want nothing, either."

Exasperated, I stammer, "I—how do I explain this—I don't want to sell you anything. I am not—I repeat, *not,* a salesman. I just want to know about your son. Before . . . before he died."

More silence, and this time I think he might have hung up on me. I repeat his name a few more times, and now I can't even hear the television anymore. I'm about to chalk it up to a no-go and replace the receiver—

"You wanna come down to the house?" asks Mr. Levitt. "I can make us waffles."

. . .

Mr. Levitt's home in the suburban city of Thousand Oaks, a quiet residential town about forty-five minutes outside of Los Angeles with rolling green hills, friendly neighbors, and a surprising lack of smog, is at the same time cluttered and immaculate. Littered with the conquests of a thousand telemarketers, the house is stuffed to the gills with doily-cutters and ribbon-curlers and wall-painters and burger-flippers and chicken-roasters and twist-tie-twisters and a host of inventions over which the fellas down at the Patent Office probably had a good chuckle for a year or two. But every single inch of these semi-useless appliances—and the house in general—shines like the chrome on a schoolboy's new ten-speed.

"You have a lovely home," I say as I enter the door and nearly trip over a defunct appetizer-serving robot.

Mr. Levitt eases himself into an old BarcaLounger in the front living room, and I take a seat on a sofa draped in a blue slip-cover, itself coated with a slick substance that makes it quite difficult to remain seated in one place.

"That's Protect-o-Gel," says my host. "Fella came 'round the house last month sold it to me. Keeps the slipcovers from getting stained. Makes 'em waterproof."

"I see. Fascinating." And disgusting. It's like sitting on Vaseline. Most likely, it *is* Vaseline.

Mr. Levitt sets a cup of tea in front of me, served in a gyroscoping mug that I've seen advertised on television. It's supposed to make it easier to drink coffee and drive at the same time, wholly useless in a stationary environment, but as my butt won't stay still on this sofa, it might actually come in handy. "I've got the waffles cooking back in the kitchen. And I'm dehydrating some fruit if you'd like to stick around."

"Thank you, no," I say, and then, seeing the crestfallen look come across his face, amend it to, "We'll see."

Mr. Levitt is a small dino—a Coelophysis or Compy if I had to guess—whose recent lot in life has only served to shrink him even more. The human guise he's wearing over what seems to be a meager infrastructure only accentuates this sense of loss, the face etched with wrinkles deeper than I'm used to seeing on guises of dinosaurs twenty years older. Perhaps he ordered them from Nakitara to suit his grief. I knew a widow once who was so distraught over her husband's untimely demise in a tragic reaping accident that she purchased sixteen sets of Bette Davis Eyebags from the Erickson guise company in Sweden and shoved them all beneath her ocular cavities so that her outer appearance might properly reflect her inner misery.

"I wanted to ask you about your son," I begin.

"About Jay."

"Yes, about Jay. He took his own life, I understand?"

"He was a good boy," says Mr. Levitt, nodding his head as if to agree with his own statement. "Never caused me any grief. Some kids, they're skipping school, doing the basil, speaking back to their elders. Not my Jay."

"Of course not." Mr. Levitt seems to be stuck in nostalgia mode, and I don't want to do anything to shake him out of it, but I don't have unlimited time out here in the 'burbs. I need to return to the Westside at some point and resume making phone calls. "I'm sure he was a great boy."

A sharp *ping!* from the kitchen, and Mr. Levitt pops up from the easy chair. "Waffles are done," he says.

"That's okay, I don't need—" But he's out of the room already.

Now, I'm not here to feel sorry for anyone—at least that wasn't my original intent—but I can't help but commiserate with one of the most definitive descriptions of loneliness I've seen in quite some time. My eyes wander around the room, taking in the multitude of gadgets and devices that have taken the place of Mr. Levitt's only son.

No less than six cuckoo clocks line the walls, four of them different in size, shape, and color, but two exactly the same—he must have accidentally purchased this model a second time without realizing it. Each of the clocks is set to a different time, I notice, and since I left my own watch at home this morning, I'm thoroughly confused as to how long I've been sitting here, trying not to fall off the sofa.

"Those are my favorites," Mr. Levitt says of the clocks as he enters with a plate full of pancakes. "They keep me company. Like a bunch of old friends."

Yep, there's the pity train, arriving at the station right on time.

He places the pancakes down on a small coffee table that doubles as an aquarium—no fish inside, just water, some plastic plants, and a multicolored ceramic castle—and invites me to take one.

"I thought you said you were making waffles."

"I am. The pancakes were done first." He grabs one off the plate and begins to take small nibbles. Never one to be rude, I do likewise. They're rubbery.

"Like I said," Mr. Levitt continues, "Jay was a good boy. Ran with a nice crowd."

"Mm-hm," I mumble through the pancake.

"Very clean-cut, I always felt. Especially today, what with the punk look most of these kids are into."

I don't want to throw the guy more out of time-alignment than he already is, so I decline to tell him that the punk look has been dead for decades. "Did he ever mention a religion?" I ask. "Maybe he was getting into spirituality?"

"No, no, nothing like that. We've always been something of lapsed atheists around this house."

"These friends . . . did they seem odd at all?"

"Odd? No, sir. Very nice boys. Very clean-cut." There's that word again. I center on it.

"Clean-cut, huh? In manner, in style . . . ?"

"Sure. Dressed real nice, too. Guises always looking tip-top, hair not too long. Very respectful of the elders. Always made sure they were respecting the elders."

Now we're getting somewhere. "Is that what they said—respecting their elders? Did they maybe say 'respecting their *ancestors*'?"

A little light blinks on behind Mr. Levitt's eyes. Someone's home after all. "Yes . . . yes, that sounds familiar. In fact, I believe that's exactly what they said, now that you mention it."

On the right path, no doubt about it. "Do you mind if we talk about Jay in detail, Mr. Levitt? About his death?"

"Those waffles will be ready soon," he mumbles.

I want to let myself be distracted, I really do—it's no fun getting information out of someone I have no reason to hurt—but I'm too close to back off. "Was he acting strangely in the days before his death? Had he left home, maybe been taking some of your money?"

"He was a good boy," Mr. Levitt repeats, volume rising, agitation creeping into the tone. "He never stole a thing."

"I understand that. I do, really. But what I'm saying . . ." A breath, collecting my thoughts. "Had he ever talked about Progress? About Progressing?"

Possible recognition from my host, but there's no time to tell. A second *ping!* from the kitchen, this one louder, tinnier, and Mr. Levitt is up again and out of the living room. I sit back on the sofa, trying desperately to maintain some purchase on the slick surface, and close my eyes. This conversation has been a little more strenuous than I expected, and I hope Ernie's having more luck talking with a family he contacted in Newport Beach whose child met with a similar fate. At the very least, he's probably not being fed as well. I take another bite out of my pancake.

Mr. Levitt returns from the kitchen, a heaping plate of waffles stacked like an Aztec pyramid held out before him. Wordlessly, he places the waffles next to the pancakes, then straightens back up and walks out of the room again. Have I pushed him too far? Have I offended the poor guy? This wasn't in the plan at all.

A few minutes later, after the sounds of ruffling and rumbling from a back room, Mr. Levitt returns holding a crumpled sheet of white looseleaf paper. He shuffles across the room in a zombie shuffle, feet dragging through the blindingly clean shag carpet, and wordlessly holds the paper out for me. I take it by one corner, guessing already what this might be, and give it a read.

In a sure, even script made with a crisp felt pen, the note reads simply: THERE IS NO POINT IN GOING ON WITHOUT PROGRESS.

"We were supposed to go bird-watching," Mr. Levitt says as I return the note to his shaking hands. "I'd woken up early, got the cameras and the binoculars all packed and ready to go, and then went to wake the boy. He'd been all excited those last few days, talking about how his life was looking up, how he was feeling better about himself, and so I figured he'd do good with a nice photo safari. Everyone does good with a nice photo safari. . . ."

"And then?" I prompt.

"He—he never woke up," Mr. Levitt chokes out. "I kept trying to wake him, real quiet like, but he didn't move. In his hand . . . in his hand were some of my sleeping pills, I guess—"

The note—the mention of Progress—Jay's "clean-cut" friends—his reverence of the ancestors—all of this tells me exactly what I came here to find out. The rest of it is just a sob story, no doubt quite tragic, but not important enough to the case at hand to keep me here any longer.

"Thank you for your time, Mr. Levitt," I say, trying to rise from the sofa without giving myself a hernia in the process. My guise is tight today—must have been packing down those french fries during Rupert's incarceration in the upstairs studio—and it's difficult enough to move around without having to lift myself off a vat of Jell-O.

But Mr. Levitt is persistent, if nothing else, trotting after me as I walk to the door. He's suddenly become animated, more alive in this last minute than he has been for the whole half-hour I've been at the house. "Please, stay," he implores. "I've got some cookies in the Quick-Bake, won't take more than two and a half minutes at full setting."

"I wish I could," I explain, "but I've got to get going. I'm very sorry to have disturbed you."

"I understand," he says in a low, uninflected monotone. "Everybody leaves." Without another word, he turns away and sulks back into the living room, sits on the slipcovered couch, and slides off onto the floor, where he lies, motionless, in a fetal position.

Ah, Christ. I'm not a statue.

We play Parcheesi for a few hours. I win every game despite a thorough misunderstanding of the rules, but Mr. Levitt beams from ear to ear the entire time. I'm not in this business to make people feel good, and in fact I'm causing distress more often than not, but in those instances when I can work in a good deed—what my Jewish Allosaur friend calls a *mitzvah*—I'm more than happy to add it on, free of charge.

The waffles are terrible.

. . .

"Overdose of sleeping pills, probably Seconal," I tell Ernie once I've returned to the office later that evening. "And a suicide note that indicates he'd left the Progressives."

"Do you one better," replies my partner.

"How?"

Ernie whips out a photograph of a young, well-dressed woman, no more than twenty if she's a day, standing in the middle of a speedboat on some unidentifiable lake. There's a small birthmark right near her navel—a trademark of the Nakisoba Corporation, an offshoot of the larger Nakitara guise manufacturer. They're also into high-tech electronics, computers, publishing, the film industry, and personal sexual protection, but that's neither here nor there. The girl in the photo seems happy enough, smiling and waving at the camera, one hand poised on a raised hip.

"And she would be . . . ?"

"Crystal Reeds," says Ernie. "Diplodocus, and heir to the Reeds pencil fortune."

"There's a pencil fortune?"

"Well, not so much anymore," Ernie admits. "Been going downhill since computers hit big, but they still do a nice business with schools. Point is, the family has money."

I say, "And lemme guess—they were losing a big chunk of it to the Progressives."

"Even better. They lost their house, too. They'd put it in Crystal's name for some obscure tax purposes, and in a fit of religious ecstasy, she signed it over to the group. Six months and about two hundred thousand in legal fees later they got it back, but it was the end of the end for her parents.

"They sent in these two dinos up from Nevada who claimed to be specialists in extraction, and sure enough, they got her out and into a safe house for deprogramming."

"They were shrinks?"

"No, they were just the extraction team. The family hired some therapist from back in New York to shake the Progress out of her. Stier, they said his name was. Dr. Frank Stier."

"Wonder if Dr. Beauregard knows him," I say.

"Point is, they had this girl in a safe house because the parents were all worried about rival pencil-makers trying to take advantage of their situation—I didn't mention that they might like to get themselves checked out for paranoid delusions. And then, a few days after she's supposedly cured, she winds up dead."

"Suicide?"

"Nope," says Ernie. "Botched robbery attempt."

"That's a good one."

"Wait, you gotta hear it. They'd put the girl into one of the pencil operation's warehouses down in Long Beach, set her up in the furnished office on the second level overlooking the warehouse floor. That night, cops say, some burglars broke in, she tried to put a stop to it, and they offed her. Shot her up so bad they could barely identify the body."

I grab a pencil off my desk and take a look at it. NUMBER 2, it says. And sure enough, at the bottom, right near the eraser, small green type reads: REEDS PENCIL CO. Ten similar pencils lie scattered in the plastic tray of my organizer. Maybe there is a fortune there, after all. "Nothing so odd about that," I say. "Long Beach has burglaries every day."

"Sure it does," replies Ernie. "And that's the point—the criminals down there aren't greenhorns. They know what they're doing. They know what goods go to what floor, and the pencil warehouse—not exactly a cash cow—was surrounded by sixty others just like it, except they were stocking furniture, consumer electronics, jewelry . . ."

I toss the pencil back onto my desk and stand up. It's late, I need sleep, but there's enough pressing on my mind to force me back into some semblance of action. I lay it out for Ernie. "We've got three deaths—two by overdose, one in a car—that occurred in otherwise healthy, young individuals just a few days after their departure from the Progressives. We've got witnesses who say that the victims were feeling well just before they met the Reaper, that they didn't seem depressed in any way—"

"And, at least in Rupert's case," Ernie chimes in, "one suicide victim who didn't even have a prescription for the drug that supposedly killed him."

"This is new."

"I just found out today," Ernie says. "Did a search at damn near every pharmacy in town. No prescription on record, and the vial they found in his hand was both empty and unmarked."

"Is this enough for you?" I ask my partner. "Are you ready to give up on coincidence and join me in conspiracy?"

"Do I have to dress up again?"

"You can wear whatever the hell you want," I tell him. "Go naked for all I care."

"Shut up and get in the car, kid."

By the time we've made our way out to Hollywood and begun the climb up through Laurel Canyon, I've worked up a pretty good head of steam. I'm incensed enough that there might be a cover-up going on here, but even angrier that I may have been taken for a fool. Rupert was under my care when he died—okay, technically he'd been declared officially sane by Dr. B., but that doesn't preclude the fact that it was me who got him into the mess in the first place—and I don't take well to playing the chump.

"I want you to stay away from that . . . that woman," Ernie tells me. "Let me do the talking."

"No problem," I say, though I know that the problem is actually very real and very large. Ignoring Circe when I'm in her presence is like ignoring a polka-dotted elephant doing a samba through the Russian Tea Room. She's been on my mind more and more often since the last burst of pheromones at Rupert's funeral, and I've got to admit that more than a few dreams have been haunted by that ethereal presence and those savory seasonings.

We arrive at the outer gate to find it, predictably, shut, and the guard, predictably, stubborn. It's the same fellow from the last time, but he doesn't recognize us.

"We were here a few weeks ago," I say. "For the meeting. The *meeting.*"

His hand doesn't move toward the gate button. "Don't care if you were here for the Pope's birthday party"—and I wouldn't be surprised if this had been the venue for such a shindig—"you still can't come in without a pass."

"Can you make a phone call? This is all I'm asking."

"If you don't have a pass—"

"One lousy phone call!" I yell, then drop my voice back to a lower register. "Tell Circe it's her friend from the funeral, that's all. She'll—"

"Please turn your car around. This is private property, sir, and I don't make the rules."

"I appreciate that—"

"I don't think you do," interrupts the guard. Now he's moving toward us, and instead of the typical dino gesture of threat— baring of the teeth, unsnapping of the gloves—he actually pulls his jacket aside and flashes a gun. A gun, of all things!

"That's disgusting," says Ernie, unable to help himself. I can see distaste well up past his throat, making for his tongue, his lips. There's a great aversion to unnatural weapons, especially among the older generation of dinos, and Ernie's no exception.

But the guard doesn't move an inch, doesn't even try to cover the weapon up. He feels no shame. "You fellas wanna move along now?" The gun glints in the remaining sunlight, the barrel shiny and new. Probably never been fired, but I can't take the chance that his lack of practice guarantees bad aim.

Ernie leans across me and out of the car window. "Now you listen to me, you chickenshit piece of a Compy—you pick up your little phone there and tell the boss that two gentlemen from the other night are asking to see her—"

"No can do," says the guard. "Turn the car around. I'm not going to ask you again." His hand moves slowly toward the weapon on his hip, coming to rest lightly on the butt. With a grunt, I push Ernie off my lap and back into his seat. I get into enough daily trouble thanks to my partner, I don't need to be shot for trespassing by a rent-a-cop who thinks he's the dino answer to Charles Bronson. "Maybe we can go back to Hollywood Boulevard," I suggest to Ernie. "Get our friend Bob to wrangle us another invite."

Too late. Unsnapping his seat belt in a smooth, single movement, Ernie pops the locks on my Lincoln and leaps out of the passenger seat, volume at eleven and rising. "Bullshit! Get on your phone, apefucker, and call up to the house—"

I'm up and out of the car, but not before Ernie and the guard have met face-to-face in front of the hood, human-guised noses no more than a centimeter apart. If they were to take off their masks and facial straps right now, their snouts would certainly bump into each other, causing two ugly nosebleeds.

"Hold up," I say, trotting around to get between these two hotheads. "Hold up."

But simultaneously each puts out an arm to block my way, and the combined force sends me sprawling back across the hood of my car—scraping my leg on the ornament—and onto the asphalt on the other side.

I look up just in time to see Ernie spitting out his bridge—the worn, human dentures clattering to the ground like a prizefighter's mouthpiece, kicking up dirt where they land, the bright, sharp teeth snapping hard against one another—as the guard reaches for his gun, fingers grasping the butt tightly, pulling it up and out of the holster, taking dead aim on my partner and best friend's unprotected chest—

I should probably scream here. *No*, or *Stop*, or something of that sort, which can be so moving when played back in slow motion.

The phone rings.

Ernie's midair bite comes to a halt, leaving his mouth in a confused, half-open grimace. The guard relaxes his grip. The phone rings again. Backing up slowly, keeping a quarter of an eye on me but the rest on Ernie and his rows of sharpened teeth, the guard reaches into his booth and lifts the handset. "Yes? Yes, ma'am. Yes, they . . . No, he was going to . . . Yes. Yes, ma'am. I understand. Thank you."

We get a pass. We get an apology. We get super-detailed instructions on how to drive up to the main house and where to park. We make the guard repeat them three times even though we already know full well how to get there. We spin the wheels and kick dust in his face as we drive off.

The little smattering of daylight that remains before the sun drops over the hills reflects off the marble columns of the main house, throwing the whole thing even further back to its ancient architectural roots. Ernie and I trudge through the parking lot—surprisingly, there are quite a number of autos parked here—up the hillside stairs, and into the main corridor, fully prepared to check our costumes. But the Ornithomimus from the other night's meeting is not at her assigned spot, and the guise-check room is locked up tighter than the waterproof sealant on a Naki-tara Gold series Latex Bonding Package #9.

"We're not always so informal," comes a voice from down at the other end of the corridor. "We like to be natural, sure, but it's a hassle if you're running errands in the outside world all day." An Iguanodon—unguised—is walking toward us, familiar in some way. It's the deep voice that gets me, the one two shades lower than that of James Earl Jones—who is, by the way, one of the dinosaur community's most prized actors. I saw him do *Othello* once in an all-dino cast, and to see such a masterpiece performed the way Shakespeare intended it—with an Allosaur in the title role—was nothing short of breathtaking.

Got it now—he's the one who introduced Circe at the party the other night. The memory returns just in time, for as the Iguanodon approaches, I'm able to stick out my hand and say, "Samuel, right?"

"Yes. Circe sent me to come get you. Please, follow."

We trail after Samuel, his tail swishing mesmerizingly back and forth along the ground. Even though I've been told it's not necessary, I feel an urge to rip off my guise and go naked and free, but we don't stop in any one place long enough for me to unfasten any of the buckles. Ernie notices what I'm trying to do and slaps my hand away. "Leave your damn clothes on," he mutters. So old-fashioned.

The house becomes mustier as we make our way through, and whether it's from dust bunnies or something blooming nearby, my sinuses are starting to act up. A few sneezes later, I take a handkerchief from my pocket and wipe down my nose, dismayed to find that nothing's coming out; I must have misaligned the nostril holes again, which means by the end of the day, I'll end up with a lovely trail of mucus gumming up the works beneath my mask. It's times like this—the misalignments, the pinched buckles, the poorly tightened straps—that make me want to throw myself headlong into the Progressive lifestyle, to rip it all away and go running wild, much as the ancestors must have done in the carefree days when the mammals were more interested in swinging from trees and having sex with anything that moved than they were in eradicating other sentient species from the planet.

We wend our way through another series of corridors, passing through countless doors and passageways, everything set off by more of that dino artwork. Many of them are unfamiliar, as I've always been something of a Philistine when it comes to the visual arts, but some of the pieces are nevertheless familiar to me, due to whatever cultural concepts have filtered into my brain by chance over years of osmosis. I know that for every mammalian piece that Modigliani put out, for example, he produced at least one in a more naturalistic state. *Woman with Child* was meant for humans to marvel at; *Bronto Lies Down* was painted strictly for our persuasion. And, lo and behold, there it is on the wall, resplendent in its verdant hues. And it is, no doubt, the original.

I try not to sneeze on it.

A series of winding staircases are next, a double helix of steps curving round and about one another, and after what feels like a climb through the Andes, we arrive at the top floor and a tight, narrow corridor leading to a single door at the end of the hall.

"Vincent," cooes Circe as we enter a room filled with cushioned chairs and throw pillows scattered on the plush carpeting below. It's the 1970s version of a harem, only green instead of pink, and a shade too bright to be accidentally tacky. "It's so good to see you again. Better times, yes?" A flowing green gown covers her otherwise naked, natural Raptor hide, a slit in the back cut out for that sensually curved tail. "And Mr. Watson, a pleasure."

We're each given a hand to shake and a peck on the cheek, and I must admit that my body instinctively dives in for a whiff of that maddening scent. Strangely enough, it's barely present. I expect to be transported to a world of Pterodactyls and Diplodoci, but I find only a hint of cilantro and marjoram, hardly enough to send me back in time even five short minutes. I'll get more accomplished this way, sure, but I can't say I'm not disappointed.

"Lovely room you have here," I tell her. "Very . . . comfy."

A little lip-curl, a bat of the lashes. "It's my lounge. I come here before large events, to . . . prepare, if you will."

"Large events?" I ask.

"Yes. I'm sad to say, but we've had some misfortune of our own," purrs Circe. "A dear friend has passed on—"

"I'm sorry—"

"She was very old, her time had come. She was at peace with the ancestors. But the funeral is downstairs in a few minutes— we do seem to meet at these occasions, don't we?"

"We could come back," Ernie suggests, some vestige of social graces clinging to his investigator's tone.

"Please, stay. I have a few moments. Now, what can I do for you boys?" asks Circe, curling her tail up and around her body. She's got incredible control over that thing—it glides through the air with ease, flicking out at my knee, almost teasing it while she speaks.

"My . . . friend and I have been talking," I begin, "ever since that first night. About Progress, about what you believe in, what you stand for."

"Good, good. We encourage discourse," she says.

"And then the funeral, when we saw you . . ."

Circe nods empathetically. "Yes, quite a shame." That tail of hers still on the move, still making for me. I try to evade, but that thin slab of flesh manages to work its way down to my feet and up into the leg of my pants, seeking out the latex covering beneath. I leap backward, and Ernie shoots me a confused look.

He takes over. "Did it bother you when Rupert left the group?"

"Bother me? No. Was I concerned for him? Of course. We're all free to live our lives however we choose, Mr. Watson, but it saddens me when a dinosaur, so previously entrenched on the road to a meaningful, fulfilling life, strays from the path of truth."

"He seemed happy enough."

"Until he killed himself, you mean?" Point one for Circe.

I step up. "We're interested in your organization. In the next step."

"You wish to join, then? It's not an easy path."

"We understand. But it . . . it *intrigues* us. Though we have some questions."

"Don't we all?" she says. "Please, anything I can do to help is purely my pleasure." Another caress with the tail.

Now a wholly different part of my guise is tightening up, and I have to think about nuns and painful vaccinations and old horses being sent out to pasture in order to relieve the tension. I'm quite glad at this point that I was unable to disrobe earlier; the H-series of buckles wrapped tightly around my groin is keeping me from a world of embarrassment.

"Well, gentlemen," says Circe, "are we going to stand around all night or get to it?"

"Get—get to it?" stammers Ernie. He's flushed, the old dickens! I'm glad to see that it's not just me who's been rising to the occasion.

"You had questions, didn't you?" Circe backs up to a massive beanbag chair on the ground and plops atop it. "I assume some of these questions you have are about your friend."

"And yours, if I'm not mistaken."

She nods and amends her statement. "And mine. Though I must be frank, I did not know your friend very well. We've had a great number of converts in recent years, and though I wish I could get to know them all personally, I am unable to."

"But isn't the goal one of personal communication between dinosaurs?" I say.

"Of unfettered communication, yes. We believe that our costumes—like that guise you're wearing now, manufactured by an impersonal conglomerate somewhere in Japan—"

"Taiwan, actually," I correct. "It's a Nakitara, but from their secondary plant."

"Taiwan, then. These costumes only serve to separate us from ourselves, but perhaps even more importantly, they separate us from our fellow creatures. Did you know that back in the days of our ancestors, we could make positive identification of one another from miles away?"

"I didn't—I mean, I'd *heard,* but it's just an old wives tale, right?"

"Why is it," ponders Circe, "that an old husband is wise, while old wives are full of nonsense? No matter. There are others—old wives, young husbands—who say we were able to communicate with our scents. Not verbally, mind you, but almost in hallucination. In meaning. In spirit." Is she talking directly to me here? Did she feel what I felt back at the party the other night? At the funeral?

"What's the point?" asks Ernie. "We've got phones nowadays."

"And maybe that's a problem, too," says Circe. "We rely on such modern conveniences only because we're following the mammalian construct. We had the ability to create such technology tens of millions of years before the humans climbed down out of the trees, but did we? Certainly not. Because we didn't need to. We had everything we wanted, and none of the problems inherent in this so-called modernized society."

"Sounds romanticized to me," I point out.

"How so?"

"*Everything* was better back in the good old days," I say. "Talk to any geezer, they'll tell ya."

Circe can't help but laugh, a giggle that sends a tingle down to the tip of my tail. "Perhaps you're more advanced than we thought," she says, and leaves it at that.

We chitchat our way through more of the Progressive belief system, most of which revolves around reestablishing closer ties with both the ancestors and their ways, and in doing so, becoming a whole dinosaur. Or something like that; even after a fifteen-minute in-depth discussion on the matter, I'm not quite sure. "Are you saying we're only part dinosaur now?" asks Ernie.

Circe nods. "I'm saying we're but mere fractions of our possible selves."

All of this philosophy has got my head spinning 'round. I stand up from my cushion and stretch my legs. "I must say, it's a fascinating system you've come up with."

"Oh, it's not mine," says Circe. "Any more than the group is mine, or this house is mine. It's all of ours, all of it, but we do owe a lot to our founder."

This must be the one that Jules told us about back at the wax museum—the vacuum-cleaner salesman with the ego complex. "And where is he?" I ask.

"Oh, Raal doesn't come around much anymore," says Circe, and that name strikes a chord with me. Raal. "He's one hundred percent dinosaur natural, and I'm sure you can imagine how difficult it is to maintain such an incredibly high level of Progress living in a mammalian-dominated society."

I assume that "doesn't come around much" is her euphemism for dead, but it's possible that Circe actually believes that instead of moving on to a better place, this Raal simply moved on to a *different* place. "So we can't see him," says Ernie.

"Oh, not until you're further along," is Circe's response. Then she stands up and brushes off the few strands of dust that have clung to her green velvet robe. "I'm afraid the funeral is about to begin. Would you boys like to attend?"

Odds are, there'll be some free grub afterward, so Ernie and I hop after Circe as she makes her way downstairs. Her movement is effortless, graceful, Audrey Hepburn all the way, and I feel like the most awkward of toddlers walking next to her.

As we approach the ballroom, there's a murmur similar to the one from the other night, but this time it's lower, more somber, and behind it is a familiar pop and crackle that I'm currently unable to place. Halfway between a giant bowl of Rice Krispies and the white noise of a radio tuned to a missing station, it almost sounds like . . . like . . .

Fire. Flaming licks of heat steam up from a wide hole carved into the ballroom floor, the air above shimmering in a decadent belly dance of carbon dioxide and ash. The sheer temperature variation pushes me back out of the ballroom for a second, but I steel myself and enter the sweltering area, making myself at home among the horde of other dinos—some in costume, some natural—waiting for the festivities to begin.

I certainly didn't notice anything like this the first time I was inside the ballroom, but as I look closer—shielding my eyes against the glare with the side of my hand—I can see that the floor has been retracted, possibly mechanically, and that the miniature version of Hades ten feet down is filled with what looks a lot like molten lava, if my Discovery Channel memory serves.

"Nice fire pit," Ernie whispers to me.

"Sure is," I reply. "You bring the marshmallows?"

We are shushed by at least five different dinos. Progressives, as a rule, lack the crucial humor gene on their DNA. Then again, if I had to eat raw newts all the time, I'd be pretty miserable, too.

It doesn't take long for the funeral to get started. Circe takes her place atop a slightly raised dais, and begins a long monologue about the deceased, about how she'd found her way in life through Progress, and a bunch of other hoo-ha that has the effect of bringing the crowd to tears.

It is Samuel and another Progressive, a pudgy Triceratops wearing no guise but sporting a pair of Armani spectacles, who wheel out the body of the old Ornithomimus. Yep, she's dead, all right.

"As many of our ancestors met their end in the fires of the Great Showers, so we now admit our sister into the heart of our shared heritage. As the ancestors left this earth, so shall we."

"So shall we," echoes the audience, Ernie and I excepted. No one gave us cue cards.

At this signal, Samuel and the Trike place the deceased atop a long, wooden plank with four wheels and begin to push the improvised gurney toward the open, roaring fire pit. The dead Ornitho's arm drapes over one side, but no one seems to notice, even as her claws scrape along the floor, sending up a terrific screeching noise as the plank draws nearer to its incineration.

"Fire to fire," intones Circe, "ancestor to ancestor."

"Fire to fire," repeats the crowd. "Fire to fire."

With a final shove by the pallbearers, the Ornithomimus and her wooden conveyance slide off the ballroom floor and fall into the pit, wheels clattering for an instant against the marble before the rejuvenated flames tear up into the air, rejoicing at a new source of fuel. The congregants sway back and forth in unison, a massive underwater plant drifting with the current, low gurgles trickling off their throats. And Circe stands above it all, arms held high, tail raised to the ceiling, light from the flames flickering, caressing her body.

I can smell burning flesh. Next to me, a T-Rex is crying and salivating all at the same time. Something has grabbed hold of my stomach lining and is proceeding to twist it into all manner of Boy Scout knots, wringing out my belly like a towel thick with water.

"We oughta get outta here," I gurgle to Ernie.

"You feelin' okay?"

"Let's just—" A burp surfaces, and I'm barely able to suppress the accompanying nausea. "Let's just go." Ernie, God bless him, agrees.

But we're not more than halfway to the door when the crowd parts—aha, an easy exit—and Circe appears, standing in our way. I'd usually be more than happy to see her, but at this point there's not much more I'd like to do than make it to the safety of a restroom or, should it be necessary, a copse of bushes.

"I should have warned you about the smell," she says, instantly diagnosing my problem. "It can be rough the first time out."

And just like that—I don't know if it's the words, the sentiment, or some burst of her own magic scent—my nausea is gone. In fact, I'm starting to feel a little hungry. I'm about to thank Circe for her intervention, but she's already on to the next topic, two small envelopes suddenly appearing in her hands.

"Before you go, I wanted to have a word with you."

"We're in a hurry," explains Ernie.

"One moment, please. We're having a get-together this weekend," she says, "sort of a Progressive convention, and I'd be honored if you two would come as my guests. I'm embarrassed to admit that there's a slight fee involved. . . ."

"That's not a problem," I say immediately. Even if the group isn't in need of money from their recruits, we nevertheless want to fit in with their upper-middle-class member profile. Money should not seem like an issue.

"Excellent," she says. "If you need quick travel arrangements, you'll find some numbers here for a few agents we use over in Santa Monica."

"Travel arrangements?"

"For the flight."

"The flight?"

"To Hawaii," says Circe, and I can feel the cash bottoming out of my pocket already. "You can fly into Maui or Kauai, it doesn't make a difference. The hydrofoil will pick you up and bring you over to our private island in the afternoon, so make sure you book a flight that arrives in the morning."

Ernie's managed to get his invitation open, and he's already gaping, slack-jawed, at the finely printed words on the rice-paper backing. ATTAIN A HIGHER LEVEL OF PROGRESS AT OUR NATURAL-IZATION CONVOCATION, it reads. SPECIAL SPRING PRICE, $4,000, INCLUDES ALL FOOD, DRINK, AND LUXURIOUS ACCOMMODATIONS FOR THE WEEKEND. PREPARE TO PROGRESS!

I take a long swig of self-confidence, follow it down with a jigger of bravado and a dash of foolishness, and wait for the mixture to settle in my belly. "We'll be there."

. . .

"We sure as hell *won't* be there," Ernie is saying as we pull up to the office. "I'm not asking Louise for this kind of cash—"

"Do you wanna find out who killed Rupert?"

"If he *was* killed—and I'm still not so sure of that—then, sure, I wanna find the guy. Or gal."

I let that last bit go. If there's one thing I want to believe, it's that Circe is innocent. I don't know where this impulse comes from—though I must say that the notion is tinted in the same colors as those herb-induced fantasies I've been so prone to lately—but at least 83 percent of my intuition tells me it's true, and majority rules in this brain. "And if you wanna find out who killed Rupert, don't you think his own sister would be willing to shell out a few extra bucks?"

No response from Ernie. I park the car too close to the curb, so I back out and try it again. My contacts are drying out in the arid night air, and I'm forced to blink nonstop like a southern belle trying to land a mate.

"Listen," Ernie says after I've slammed into the curb six or seven times, "I could get the money out of my ex-wife with no problem. I can go upstairs and call Louise and tell her that we've been following up on Rupert's death. And I'll tell you what—for that she'll be pleased. I can tell her that we've begun to view it more as a homicide than a suicide. For that, she'll be intrigued. But if I tell her that we've been associating with the Progressives, if I tell her that we've been socializing with their leader, if I tell her that we want almost ten thousand dollars to give to the very same group that had been draining her coffers for the past two years—for that . . . for that, she'll be nothing more than hurt. And I won't hurt her. Period, paragraph, end of story." Ernie gives me a second to let his little soliloquy sink in.

We climb the stairs in silence, and though I want to bring up the Hawaii trip again, and I think it's not only a good idea but a *necessary* one—we are, after all, investigators, and neither rain nor sleet nor lack of available funds should stop us in our appointed task—I keep quiet out of respect for Ernie's respect for his ex-wife. My reticence won't last long, though—I'm giving it five minutes before I bring the matter up for a second review.

The office door is open.

"You don't think . . ." says Ernie.

"I do."

"Little apefucker . . ."

It's Minsky once again, suit and tie rumpled, wrinkled, all a shambles, and this time he's pacing back and forth rather than sitting nonchalantly on my desk, but the sight of the little guy in our private space is enough to throw me into a frenzy registering 4.3 on the hissy-fit scale.

"How many times do I have to tell you this is illegal?" I bellow, drawing as much out of my natural dino self as possible. I hope to work in a good roar or two. "And how many times do I have to tell you that I don't want to see you again? I haven't had to crack heads in a while now, but you're pushing me, Minsky. . . ."

But he's not even listening to me—if he were, he'd be stumbling backward, away from my advancing claws, rather than coming toward me, his own stubby arms raised beseechingly.

"You gotta get her," he whines, that tinny little voice like a champagne glass shattering across my ears. "The bitch went too far this time."

Ernie's not having any of it. He grabs Minsky by the back of his wig—attached with some incredibly strong epoxy, it seems, because the whine turns to a howl in no time—and proceeds to drag the bite-sized Hadrosaur across the floor.

"Waaaait," he whimpers, "it's all different now! It's all different now!"

Against my better judgment, I place a hand on Ernie's shoulder. He's still got Minsky by the hair, but the mousse the midget put on this morning is slicking up my partner's hand. "What is it now?" I ask. "You know we've put a moratorium on doing any business with you."

Ernie loses the battle with Minsky's hair, and the midget falls to the ground. He lifts himself up, doesn't even brush off, and storms back toward me, shaking his finger up at my incredulous expression. "I want you to find her, and I want you to—to—to do whatever it is you do to those people." His face has flushed the guise skin into a deep crimson, and I won't be surprised if I get a chance to use my CPR training in the next few minutes.

" 'Whatever it is we do'?" echoes Ernie. "I don't think you're asking us what I think you're asking us. . . ."

"Are you telling us to hurt Star?" I ask.

Minsky's sneer of revulsion is genuine. "Do what you have to."

"I think you've got us pegged wrong," I begin, though I'm sufficiently intrigued by the little guy's anger to hear him out. "We don't do that sort of thing. Violence. I mean, sure, if it comes at us first, or if there's a *really* good reason. Or if I'm in a pissy mood. Or if—"

"Just find her. You do *that,* don't you?"

I nod and set a pot of coffee on the burner. "Of course. Then again, it seems we've been hired to find this girl before, but you did a pretty damn good job of finding her yourself."

"Why don'tcha just use your dick?" Ernie jokes. "Made a pretty good divining rod last time."

Ooh, that's got him going good. The pacing starts again, rapid little pitter-patter steps that shoot him in small circles around the office, anxious as a racehorse at the gate. "Last time, last time— last time doesn't matter. Never happened. I was a fool for going back to that—that—"

A string of profanities rarely heard by these delicate ears follows, and Ernie and I check our watches as the tirade carries on well past five minutes. When he's done, Minsky is out of breath, but a little of that rancor has slipped away from the muscles lining his heart and into the open air. He's out of coronary danger at least.

The coffee has begun to percolate into the pot, hissing with every drip. "She's dropped out again, I take it."

"She has," Minsky admits.

"And this time, it's more than just ether."

"How'd you know that?"

Ernie fields this one. "Last time you weren't this upset. I think last time you wanted us to find her so you could pork her again."

I turn to Minsky, fold my arms across my chest. "What'd she take? Money? More drugs?"

Ernie chimes in. "Your basketball net? Shoe lifts? Stepladder?"

A mumble from the midget, a susurrated slur, and for a second I think I hear what he's saying. No, that can't be it. "Come again?" I ask.

"She took my . . ." Minsky pauses, sighs, stares at us with his hands on his squat hips. "You're gonna make me say it again, ain't ya?"

Ernie clears his throat. "It—it sounded like you said she took your . . . your dick."

The protest I expected from the dentist does not emerge. He just stands there, defeated, eyes glancing the short distance down to his feet, cheeks flashing crimson.

"She stole your shlong?" I ask, my normal voice rising up a notch in surprise. "She pinched your penis? Detained your—"

For once in his weaselly little life, Minsky's eyes are filling with true shame. Stumbling toward the door, little legs pushing hard against the worn floorboards, he slams into Ernie's legs, bounces, rebounds, and makes for the hallway in a flailing blur, shouting, "Forget it, you two just forget it—"

But Ernie catches him with an easy left-field snatch and hauls the pipsqueak back into the room. "This ain't the kinda thing you can just forget," he explains. "It ain't every day a client comes in tells us his Johnson got jimmied."

Ern and I run through a few more good euphemisms for the old trouser snake, then make a quick U-turn back to business. "We're talking the human kind, I take it."

"Of course," says Minsky. "It was a Mussolini."

Ernie's low, impressed whistle echoes through the room. "Musta set you back a pretty penny."

"I inherited it," explains our client. "It was my father's, and his father's before him."

Unfortunately, I'm not doing too good of a job following the conversation. My standard-issue human phallus has always served me quite well, and since most of my romantic trysts take place out of guise—with a few notable drunken exceptions—I don't find that I need to employ its services all that often. Somewhere in the back of the rotting file cabinet of my memory there's a manila envelope with the name Mussolini on it, but the secretary is out of the office today, and there's no hope of retrieving it myself. "What's a Mussolini?" I ask, expecting a barrage of incredulous stares.

I get them. "Only the finest handcrafted human phallus in existence," Ernie says, shocked at my naivete.

"A mere seventeen left in the entire world," Minsky says proudly. "Three in America. Benito Mussolini's half-brother, Alfredo, handcrafted them during a four-year period just before the Second World War, and to date there is no finer instrument. It's like a glockenspiel, only longer. Precision ball bearings, clock-work timing, dual-thrust motion sensors. We're not just talking pricks—we're talking phallic perfection."

"They're worth millions," Ernie tells me. "But nobody ever sells."

"They're priceless," Minsky clarifies. "Priceless."

I get it—I think. "And Star . . . she took it?"

"We were sleeping after one of our . . . Anyway, we were sleeping—at least, *I* was sleeping—and when I woke up, she was gone. And my Mussolini was gone. I looked down at my guise, and all I saw was this. . . ." He starts to choke up, tears welling in his squinty eyes. "All I saw was a big gaping *hole* . . . where it used to be."

"You think she plans to hock it?" Ernie asks.

"I think she plans to use it. She loves that thing, can't get enough of it. I tried to take it off once, to have sex with . . . you know, with my real . . . Anyway, she wouldn't go for it. She has to have that Mussolini. And now . . . now she does."

Oh, super—my favorite kind of case: retrieve the golden dildo. When I got into the PI business, I expected to have to pay my dues, to spend a lot of time in cars and crappy apartment buildings, eating take-out food and snapping off cheap photos, but it's very possible that Minsky's case will sink me to a new investigative low.

"And you want us to retrieve it?" I ask.

"You have to. You find her, you grab hold of that no-good, rotten . . ." Once again, Minsky's union-truck-driver alternate personality emerges, and the profanities spring forth from his lips like a filthy, frothing fountain.

By the time he's done ranting, the coffee is ready. I dole out the cups, and we all have a nice sip of java to get our nerves jangling good and hard once again. "Partner, can I see you alone for a second?" I ask.

"Sure, kid," he responds. I've asked him not to call me *kid* in front of clients before, but as it's meant as an endearment I let it go. Undermines my authority a little, but you gotta give up something in the name of bonding.

We step out of the office and into the hallway, making sure to ensconce ourselves in an echo-free area. I've had an idea brewing ever since I put that pot of coffee on the fire, and I think it's just about time to serve it up.

"You think he'll go for it?" Ernie asks once I've laid out the basics for him.

"I think he wants his fake dick back so bad he'd sell his own real one to get to the girl."

"Think it'll come to that?"

"Hope not," I say. "But let's not count it out."

We step back into the office, plastic grins plastered across our faces. "We've got some good news for you," Ernie announces, and the grin that springs to Minsky's face is half joyous, half crazed. "We've got a lead on where she might be, and we think we can find her, not to mention your whang."

"Whatever it costs, do it."

"Cost is an issue, yes. We'll most likely have a good deal of expenses . . . at least ten thousand dollars' worth, maybe more."

"Anything," he says. "Find her, bring her back, throw her to the cops, and get my Mussolini back. That's all I care about."

"It may take a little bit," I point out. "A week or so. Longer, perhaps."

"Didn't you guys hear me?" says Minsky. "Whatever—it—takes. I want you to get her and get her good."

"Are you sure about this?" Ernie asks, completing the triumvirate of double-checks.

"Sure as a pile of shit behind a dead-eyed Diplodod," says Minsky, and though I don't exactly know what this means, I'm pretty darn sure that he's pretty darn sure. And when it comes to the amount of cash we're talking about, that's good enough for me.

The next half-hour is spent getting Minsky to sign documents and budget agreements that pretty much let us spend whatever we need wherever we need to in order to get the job done.

The next two hours after that are spent at my condominium as I rifle through my drawers and closets, trying to pick out and pack the proper clothing for our upcoming adventure. For the first time in some time, I'm actually at a fashion crossroads—I haven't got a clue what to wear.

Aloha, native Hawaiian girls. This is one Velociraptor who is ready to get leid.

First things first, work before play. It's a hell of a way to live, but the taskmaster who resides in my brain doesn't put away the whip until I've got things tied up in a neat little package for him. In the few remaining hours before our flight to Hawaii, the land of sugarcane and coconuts—the most potent of aphrodisiacs for any Diplodocus female, for some reason—there's a stop I need to make closer to home. West Hollywood comes before South Pacific.

Jules has come in useful for favors before, down-and-dirty details that a dino in drag—especially one who works in the reconstruction business—has more access to than a straight bum like myself, and I need to hit her up one more time for a little assistance on the case. But she doesn't pick up the phone, even after I let it ring for nigh on three minutes. Doesn't answer the private line at home, either, which can mean only one thing: Jules is helping out her friends.

The Shangri-La is a small nightclub perched on the west end

of West Hollywood, barely dangling over the line between undifferentiated LA and highly differentiated Beverly Hills. The owner is an Iguanodon named Patrick who, though not gay or a cross-dresser himself, has a sweet spot in his heart for those whose friends and families don't understand or appreciate their lifestyle. Word on the street is that Patrick gives out more in food, drink, and spending money than he takes in. Must be true, because when I arrive out front, a huge spray-painted banner hanging over the club entrance reads: SHANGRI-LA GRAND CLOSING TONIGHT! EVERYONE MUST GO!

But despite the demise of the only dino drag club in greater Los Angeles, the party inside rages as hard as ever. Music blasts from speakers recessed into the walls, green confetti rains from the ceiling in an unending torrential downpour, and a bevy of beautiful dinosaurs of indeterminate gender bop and hop on stage, on the dance floor, at the bars, in the bathrooms. This is truly hedonism at its finest.

"Jules around?" I ask the bartender, a passable Audrey Hepburn I haven't seen around here before.

"Who's asking?" she shouts over the noise, her voice low, gravely, the kind of thing you hear out of construction workers. Needs some practice if she's gonna make it as Holly Golightly.

"Rubio," I tell her. "I'm a friend."

Audrey gives me the once-over, and, after deciding that I must not be that much of a threat, nods her head toward the back door. "You know the knock?"

"My favorite tune," I drawl, but sarcasm is wasted on the gal.

A quick knuckle-rap of the theme from *Yentl*, and soon I'm granted entrance to the smallish dressing room tucked behind the stage. Jules is here, done up nice for the event, a short, black skirt showing off a pair of finely shaped legs I know to be surgically enhanced. In fact, I was there when Jules was shaving off the final layer of epoxy from them a few months ago, but the knowledge only increases my admiration of her talents. The matching halter top hides little of the ample chest attached to her guise, and as she bends over to pick up a dropped bobby pin, I nearly fall into the Grand Canyon of her cleavage. "Gotta hand it to ya," I say as I enter the dressing room, "you're making a lot of real human women look bad."

"I'm not here to boost egos, honey," she replies, consciously replacing her initial smile with a cultivated pout. "I'm here to shine."

After a hug, a peck on the cheek, and a full-body embrace, I am quickly bombarded by a host of others who want a piece of the Rubio action. Jules's friends have always been a hoot, every one a dear, and I've done my share of work for them in various capacities, never charging more than the bottom line, often throwing in a free snoop shoot or two for good measure. I think they get off on the fact that I'm a real PI, Bogie-made-flesh, tail notwithstanding.

"Darling!" cries one such friend, a dead-on double for Judy Garland's raven-haired daughter who, when he's not masquerading as Liza Minnelli up in WeHo, is actually Hector Ramirez, a Coelophysis and toxic-waste shift worker at a chemical plant in Carson. In her best *Cabaret* strut, Liza sidles up to me and throws a sculpted leg around my waist, squeezing tight. "You've come for the action?"

All around me, male dinosaurs are buckling up more than their fair share of dangling appendages (using an improvised P-clamp, for obvious reasons) and shoving themselves into female human costumes, all in the name of fun and a little bit of soul-searching. It weirds out most of the dinos I know, but to me a guise is a guise is a guise.

"I've come for help," I explain. "I need Jules to help me out with a few things on this dog of a case."

"Jules is busy," coos Liza, to which my plastic surgeon friend—pins stuck between her lips, hands fiddling with a piece of loose flesh—nods her head. "Besides, if you want the dirt on a fellow, who better to ask than me?"

"I'm sure you could crack the Pentagon, doll"—they love it

when I talk this way, makes them feel like they're inside the movies they try so hard to emulate—"but I'm gonna need Jules's help on this one."

Jules looks up from her work—trying to stitch up Rita Hayworth's rump, the pinup model's glutes squirming all over the place, refusing to let the master do her job. "Whatever you need, I'll do it," she mumbles, a needle clutched between her thick, red lips. "I've got two mask lifts today and this butt-cheek implant, but as soon as Rita stops fidgeting, I'm here for you."

"The information might be a pain in the ass to get," I warn her.

"Best kind."

"And you might have to cross a few Progressive paths. . . ."

"It's only getting better."

Eventually, Jules finishes up her work and sends the redhead sensation wiggling back out to the dance floor. "Okay," she says, sticking the needles back into an apple-shaped pincushion, "lemme tell you something about your Progressives."

"They're not mine—"

But she's not interested; the gal's already on a roll. "I've got three girls who are all bent out of shape 'cause of those bastards, you know that? Whitney won't go on tonight because she's nursing a black eye, and even though I offered to sew on a new cheekbone, she's too rattled to perform."

"What—what happened?" I ask.

"Progress happened," she drawls. "I was working on some costumes back at the Wax Museum for some of the ladies, and when they left, they headed up Hollywood way. Next thing they knew, they were down some alley, and a herd of blueshirts were on 'em, slamming away, shouting that they were freaks, they were unnatural, they were making it harder on the rest of us . . ."

"I'm—I'm sorry," I stammer, unsure of whether or not to apologize for a group I personally dislike yet in whose company I am about to spend the next three days.

"Forget it. I've got to go stage-manage in five minutes. But for you, I'm around. Any way I can help you bring down these pre-historic pieces of crap?"

I run down the details we've accumulated on the Progressives, omitting the more personal details such as my occasional hallucinations and more than favorable impressions of Circe. Recently I've been trying not to admit them even to myself.

"You think it's smart to go to this thing?" she asks me once I'm all done. "Seems like a hard place to keep your head screwed on straight."

"I'll try," I promise. "But I need some help from you. You know photos, right? You've got scanning equipment and all that?"

"Beyond the beyond, darling."

"Good. I've got photographs—" and here I produce the meager few shots I was able to get a hold of in the past few days: Jay with his waffle-loving dad; Crystal, the gal who met the wrong end of a rifle at the hands of bungling warehouse thieves; a few other Progressive expats who made it to safety before completing the journey to the great beyond. And in every photo, their loyal deprogrammer, those who helped free them from the mental ravages of Progress.

"This one's a nice shot," she murmurs. "Good light work."

"I need you to try and identify everyone in these shots. Get beneath the guise, give me some idea of who's down there."

"Whatcha lookin' for?"

"No idea," I say with all honesty. "I was hoping you'd stumble onto something."

Jules scoops the photos into a bundle, rolls them up tightly, and stuffs them into her blouse, much as she did with the cash Ernie handed her a few weeks ago. I wonder if she's got a safe down there. "I can do some extra snoop work if you want me to," she offers.

"Thanks, Jules, but I can handle that."

"You sure?" she asks me. "I'm itching to get after those sons of bitches, and my friends are always ready and willing to help. Gina's on the force out in Riverdale, you know."

"She's a cop?"

"Shhh, keep it down. They don't take to us all that well, so she keeps it a secret. Twice-decorated lieutenant. I made her a special set of tits with a hollow inside so she could hide her handcuffs. They're fabulous. She could be a real help—"

"Thanks, but—"

"Ain't nobody like a drag queen can move in and out of a place without being noticed."

"Liza's already offered," I explain, "but I'll be okay. See what you can do for me, and I'll call when we get onto the island."

We end with a hug and a promise to each other to be careful. I give her Dan's number at the LAPD in case she should run into trouble, then make my way back through the Shangri-La, snaking through the dwindling crowd. There's dancing and singing and tasting and loving and all sorts of naughtiness going down tonight, but as I'm leaving, it feels more like a wake than a true party. It's all a mask atop the mask—behind the laughter and the smiles is the knowledge that six hours from now, there will be no place left in Southern California for these folks to hang their wigs.

· · ·

Notwithstanding the myriad articles on the subject produced over the years by the world's greatest academics, I can say with all certainty that right here and right now is truly a Velociraptor's natural habitat: lush, leafy trees, temperatures hovering somewhere in the mid-seventies, water lapping at my feet, subservient creatures scurrying around (though never underfoot), enough fresh herbs to last a lifetime. And a blended virgin daiquiri with extra coconut shavings and a massive multicolored parasol of which even Mary Poppins would be envious.

Jurassic, my ass. The Westin Maui Hotel and Suites is where it's at.

We got to Hawaii a day early—my idea—ostensibly in order

to prepare ourselves for what is sure to be a trial by fire, but really just to get out of Los Angeles before Minsky realized we conned him into bankrolling another client's case. Which is not to say that it's entirely impossible that Star Josephson has fled to the enchanted islands; it's just highly unlikely. Better chance finding her in another flophouse in North Hollywood, but you've gotta start an investigation somewhere, and Maui's as good a place as any.

I'm all by my lonesome out here, soaking up the rays, sipping my drink, and clearing my mind of detective effluvia. It tends to build up after a while, junk information clogging my neurons, and I should really hire a housekeeper before it clogs the entryway with a pile of false leads and red herrings. Ernie was sunning himself here on the pool deck for some time, but he recently picked himself up and waddled away, complaining about the heat building up inside his guise. I suggested to him a long time ago to upgrade his old Americraft guise to a newer Japanese model with PoreRight breathable skin, but the old wanker's resistant to change.

The pool is a remarkable feat of engineering achievement, a series of waterfalls and plastic slides interweaving through one another into a giant Gordian knot of liquid entertainment, and I'm sure I'd be more enthused about it if it didn't attract such a young clientele. A mess of bratty little human children scamper by one by one, strobing out the sunlight on their way to the local splash-fest, their screams piercing an otherwise tranquil afternoon. As one toddler stumbles by, my nostrils inform me that he's already made a mess of whatever diaper is beneath that bathing suit; as he jumps headlong into the pool, I resolve to stay dry for the rest of the day, or at least until the chlorine has had a chance to work its delousing magic.

I brought a book, a nice thick tome by some fellow with an unpronounceable middle name and astounding linguistic skills, but I'm barely into the second page when I catch a whiff of pine. Instinctively, I raise my eyes, shielding the glare from the sun with an outstretched hand. Before I know it, that hand is grabbed, pumped, released, and grabbed again. I've got just enough time to sit up before I'm shaken once more.

"Good to meetcha," says one of the silhouetted figures in front of me. "My name's Buzz."

"I'm Vincent," I mumble.

"Wendell," says the other one, his voice eerily similar to the first.

My eyes take their own sweet time in adjusting to the light; when I was a kid, these peepers went from pitch-black to screaming halogen in milliseconds, but with every passing year my aging pupils lose a bit of their edge. Eventually, I'm treated to a view of a tall, lithe fellow with an elongated face and protruding chin in a shrieking Hawaiian print shirt and baggy shorts—

And another tall, lithe fellow with an elongated face and protruding chin in a shrieking Hawaiian print shirt and baggy shorts. With the same hair. And the same eyes. And the same nose. And the same voice.

"We're twins," they sing in unison. The chorus effect is astounding.

"I see that."

"Smelled ya from over there, I did," says Buzz.

" 'Bout the same time *I* smelled ya," Wendell chimes in. "We're like that."

"Aha." Their scent is practically the same as well—a little acetone, some burning sugarcane—and their movements are similarly synchronized. As Buzz pulls up a chaise lounge to my left, Wendell drags one over to my right. They sit, flanking me, big goofy grins etched into those long faces.

It's not odd for dinosaurs to come out in multiple identical births—I knew a set of Triceratops triplets, in fact, who treated me to a triumvirate of titillation at their aunt's beach house in Ventura—but they tend to artificially distinguish their guises from one another once they're past puberty and tired of the myriad tricks that can be played on others when you've got a look-alike sibling. Yet Buzz and Wendell don't seem to have moved past this stage in their relationship. The closer I look, the more I believe that they've never even bothered to order two separate guises; most likely, they use one or the other's ID number and just ask for two of the same costume to be manufactured each time they have to reorder.

"Is this your first time at the hotel?" Buzz asks me, pulling himself closer. "With . . . us? With our kind?"

"Yes," I say, hoping this will end it, "it's my first time." I pointedly lift my book back to eye level and attempt to get in a few sentences; it's pure show in the hopes that they'll get the hint and excuse themselves, but I don't have much faith in its efficacy.

"We've been here three times," Wendell whispers to me, as if such a thing might be taboo. "We love it."

Buzz grins, ear to mawkish ear. "Absolutely love it."

"Three times . . . wow . . ." I'm trying to muster up interest, but it's just not happening. "You don't say."

"You know how we paid for our plane fare?" Wendell asks me, a childish excitement spinning his words into small, individual chuckles of delight.

"Can't say that I do."

"We saved it up," says Buzz.

"In change—"

"—in a jar—"

"—a big snowman jar—"

"—with pennies and dimes—"

"—and quarters and nickels. And three half-dollars that we got from our Uncle Joe."

It's the verbal equivalent of a tennis match trying to listen to these two, my neck twisting back and forth, trying to keep up with the shifting audiological focus. I opt for staring straight ahead and letting my ears do all the work.

"That's a lot of change," I say.

"We've been collecting since last year's trip."

"We always stay here before the journey," says Buzz.

"The journey?"

Wendell shakes his head. "I like to call it an adventure. Buzz says journey, I say adventure. We're different that way."

"Of course you are." I put on my best grin, beam it out to the twins, and start in on reading my book again. But it's a little hard to concentrate with the brothers sitting to either side of me, snickering over some inside joke, mouthing whispered syllables to each other. Tweedle-Dum and Tweedle-Dumber are starting to irk me, but I'm loathe to adopt an overtly hostile demeanor while ensconced in such a sedate environment.

I put the book back down. "And what journey would this be, then?"

The twins shoot each other a short glance, their slightly protruding eyebrow ridges raising in question to one another. "The great journey," says Buzz.

"The mystical adventure," says Wendell.

"The path to enlightenment."

"The way to salvation."

Oh, good. I was worried that I might not make my loony bin ratio today. "You guys here to preach to me?" I ask.

"Preach to you?" cries Buzz, clearly offended. "No! No, no, no . . ."

And then, as if in the same breath as his brother, Wendell scopes the area, sits back in his chaise lounge, and asks me, "Have you found Progress, brother?"

I sigh and toss my book in the pool. Nice vacation while it lasted, but the shop is open again and ready for business.

.   .   .

"They're on the same flight out tomorrow morning," I tell Ernie as we make our way down the hallway of the Westin Maui, nodding to the other tourists as we pass. There's some type of virus going around the islands—forces complete strangers to smile and nod affably at one another, and I'm afraid I've got a bad case of it. I may need to go to New York for the cure. "Talked my ear off for an hour."

"First-timers?"

"Fourth-timers. From what I gathered, they've already spent about sixty grand on these convocations."

"Sixty grand apiece?"

"There is no 'apiece' with these two."

"That's a lotta spare change."

"You don't know the half of it," I say, and leave it at that. "Point is, I think I might have made some inroads with them; once we're on the island, I'd like to try to get to know them better, see if they can give us some of the inside scoop. Maybe they knew Rupert."

"Good thought," says Ernie. We reach the elevator bank and wait for a lift to arrive. Dinner's already started, and I fear we're going to miss out on the good seats. Buffet-style food is of no use to me if I have to walk more than thirty feet to get it. At that point, I expect a waiter to do the messy work.

"Meanwhile," Ernie continues, "while you were sunning it up with the Bobsy Twins, I had myself a chat with the hotel desk clerks. Showed 'em Rupert's picture—"

"And?"

"And I got nothing. But the valet was listening in and caught up to me in the hall afterward. He knew our boy—not well, but he'd carried his bags once or twice—and said that the last time he came, he'd checked in with a lady friend."

That's a new one; as far as we knew, Rupert hadn't been seeing anyone for quite some time. Most of his relationships had been severed once he joined the Progressives, but it's wholly possible that in the intervening years, he'd shacked up with another truth-seeker. Nothing like the warmth of another body to keep the spiritual fires stoked.

"Something to look into," I say, and Ernie agrees. "Any description?"

"Stock. Asian, pretty, leggy."

"Welcome to Hawaii. Scent?"

"No clue," says Ernie. "Valet was a mammal."

We curtail the conversation on the way down, the rest of the elevator cab filled with humans and their own . . . *special* odors.

The doors can't open soon enough, and we pour out into the lobby, only to be shoved back a second later by a mass of redolent bodies. Dinos, all of them, and each one ruder than the last. They push, they shove, they make their way onto the elevator without letting us step off; we squirm and twist as we try to exit to the lobby.

"Big crowd," I mutter as we spawn our way through to the other side.

"Progressives?" suggests Ernie.

"I don't think so," comes a familiar voice from behind us. I turn to find Buzz and Wendell dressed in their finest Hawaiian livery, decked out head to toe in delicately strung flowers. They look like floats in the Rose Bowl Parade, and I suck up a good amount of air to keep myself from laughing. No doubt I will be burping soon, but it's worth it.

I do the introductions all around, and soon Ernie is inviting Buzz and Wendell to eat dinner with us at the hotel-sponsored luau. My initial instinct is to slap him across the back of the head—he doesn't know what it's like to talk with these two—but once again, my partner's got the right idea. If we can get in good with the twins now, it will be that much easier to get to them once we're on the island together.

"There's a convention in town," Buzz says as we head out of the hotel and down to the beach. "Accessories, mostly. Guise manufacturers, the big boys."

Does he mean the major manufacturers or just those who create plus-size guises? My grandmother, Josephine, who suffered from a glandular problem that, as far as I could tell, forced her to eat everything in sight, was a regular patron of the Lane Bronto catalog, and I spent many a night listening to her prattle on about the difficulties of finding appropriately sized guises that also suited her refined tastes.

From a hundred yards away, the smells of the dinner buffet begin to work their way through the Hawaiian air and up into my nostrils, and for a moment, I catch a whiff of something that's distinctly neither food nor drink. It's herb—fresh, sweet herb— and enough of it to flash me back to Circe, to her own intoxicating aroma, to our brief, unreal romps through an impossible jungle. But there's no seductress here, nothing in the way of yielding flesh and soft tail; there's simply pu-pu platters, coconut rum, and all the foliage I can stand.

I think I'll go get drunk now.

.   .   .

They roast pigs underground here. I don't mean in a little as-seen-on-TV rotisserie or wimpy So-Cal backyard fire pit, either— we're talking six feet down, Egyptian-mummy style, wrapped in foil, covered with sand, slowly cooked atop a pile of smoldering coals, and the resultant flavor sets off firecrackers of delight against my taste buds. And somehow, those bursting M-80s are managing to scurry their way off my tongue, up through my sinuses, and into the backs of my eyeballs, setting off a resplendent display of exploding reds and blues before my astonished eyes. Then again, it might just be the banana leaves talking.

"Good luau," I mumble to Ernie. My speech hasn't been affected quite as much by these leaves—the powers of which I never knew I was susceptible to until about twenty minutes ago—as has my vision, which continues to produce stunning hallucinations, mostly of an abstract variety.

"Good luau," Ernie echoes. He's morosely sipping at a fruit drink and pining away, probably for Louise. We're sitting at a small table set up right on the beach, the plastic legs of my chair sinking into the sand, the water lapping up against the shore no more than thirty feet away. Above, a multitude of stars gather themselves into the predictable patterns: Big Dipper and Orion for the human set, Baobob Tree and Luna the Lizard for my own species' zodiac.

Buzz and Wendell are also half in the bag, clucking their tongues like two farmers surveying their property, long rosemary branches dangling out of their mouths. "Whassa matter, Ernie?" asks Buzz.

"Don'tcha want some?" offers Wendell, plucking the spittle-coated weed from his mouth.

But Ernie just pushes it away, shakes his head, and returns to his drink. Slurp, pout, and slurp again.

"You gotta perk up," I find myself telling him. "Find a dame. Have a go at it."

A hard stare from my partner, almost a slow burn, but he can't bring himself to draw it out to any effective length. I grin right on through. "Have another banana leaf, kid," he mutters.

"Seriously," I continue. "How long's it been since you've got some in the sack?"

Now I'm getting the slow burn. And an impressive one, to boot. "In my day, we didn't go around asking each other how we were feeling and how long it'd been since we'd been with a broad—"

"It's a new age, Ern," I tell him. "You don't have to fess up, but you gotta deal with the rest of us."

I try to get Ernie to open up that Pandora's box of a heart of his, but the majority of my attention is suddenly, violently yanked across the back lawn of the hotel, past the volleyball net, the rent-a-snorkel booth, beyond the pool and the waterfall and the swim-up bar, all the way back to the hotel's veranda—

It's a Velociraptor. It's a female. As Ernie would say, it's a broad.

And what a broad. Her tail is long, curvaceous, enchanting, a Nile River of flesh. The snout strong and powerful, teeth flashing out like a row of diamonds. Eyes that glint with emeralds and the hint of more to come, a torso that holds the package together in just the perfect way, at just the perfect height.

She's naked. And she's coming this way.

"Ernie—" I stammer. "Ah—there's—"

"Knock it off, kid."

Making her way through the throng of humans, none of them paying her a lick of attention as her tail whips across their legs, their backs—raising great red welts on their flesh—her sight set on the luau, and, if I'm not mistaken, on our table. Two hundred feet and closing, Captain.

"Guys . . . ah, Ernie . . ."

"Knock it off, kid."

"No—Ernie, listen—"

"Two years, okay?" my partner barks at me. "It's been two years. You happy now?"

Two years? My god—I think I'd explode after two *months* without a little release. But even his admission of sexual dormancy isn't able to break through my shock at watching an unguised Raptor walk smack-dab through the middle of the Westin Maui Friday Night Luau, past the pu-pu platter and on her way. She's taking a long, serpentine path through the array of tables set up here on the beach, but I can tell from the set of flashing green eyes locked on mine that we are, indeed, her final destination. "Not that, Ern. Check it out."

I nod toward the approaching dino—something odd, now—is that a hint of clothing I see? And where did the tail go?—and Ernie takes a glance. "Nice looking, I guess," he says, and goes back to his drink.

By the time she's arrived at our table, the hallucination has dissipated. What was once a stunningly nude Velociraptor female is now nothing more than a fully guised female dino of undetectable lineage. The guise is impressive from a mammalian standpoint—native Hawaiian, mocha skin, thick lips, long limbs, straight black hair down to her petite mid-back—but I'm disappointed that my mind has chosen this moment to wake up on me.

"Mr. Rubio?" she asks, tapping me on the shoulder. It takes

me a moment to wrest control of my body—*hyah, steed, hyah!*—and nod my head in the appropriate gesture.

"There's a phone call for you," she says. "They've been paging you for half an hour."

I blink, hoping to see that nude dino appear before me once again, but the Hawaiian mammal look-alike remains. "On your way back," mumbles Ernie, "grab me another one of these." And he returns to the solitude of his drink.

We walk across the sand, arm in arm, my legs a little wobbly either from the recent surprise or, most likely, the continuing effects of the banana leaves. "You knew who I was."

"Why do you say that?" she asks. Her voice is soft, light, inflected with a slight Hawaiian accent. Perfectly melodic.

"I saw you coming for me back there. Did someone point me out?"

A light blush spreads across the skin. Nice capillary action on that guise. "I smelled you when you registered. I like your scent."

I smile back and say, "I like yours, too." But in all honesty, I'm having a difficult time finding one. The pine is there, certainly, but beyond that I'm a little lost. My olfactory detection skills are always slightly hampered by the usual vices—fenugreek dries my nose up something fierce, clogs my sinuses like I'm drowning—and I assume these banana leaves are having a similar effect.

"I asked the desk clerk for your name," she admits. "I remembered you."

"So when they needed someone to come find me—"

"I volunteered. Yes."

Fair enough. Nothing like a nice little ego boost this late in the evening. I decide to play it out. "Is this what you do? Find guests who've been paged?"

She giggles, shaking her head coyly. "I'm in special sales, but I'm off for the night. This is just a favor to a friend at receiving."

"You like to do favors?"

"Depends on who's asking."

"And what if I asked?"

A hair toss, a light shoulder shrug, nice human moves for a dino. "Then we might need to work out a deal."

We've arrived at the hotel lobby, where I'm directed to a green courtesy phone. "You'll wait for me?" I ask my new Hawaiian friend. "You can teach me to hula."

The phone call is mercifully short. It's from Samuel, and he wants me to know that the hydrofoil will be picking Ernie and me up at the dock at three o'clock the following afternoon.

"Unless you'd prefer to take the ferry," he says. "It's not quite as rough a ride as on the hydrofoil."

"Might be nice," I muse. "Open water, peaceful trip."

"Takes about four hours, leaves from the port of Kauai."

"That's another island," I point out.

"Right."

"And how do we get there?"

"Hydrofoil."

They're not making this easy. "Forget the ferry; we'll go straight from here. Hey—can you give me an idea of what toiletries I should bring? I'd like to leave some stuff here on Maui to lighten the load, but—"

"No toiletries," he says.

"No, no, I'm talking about toothpaste, toothbrush, that sort of thing—"

"Exactly. No toiletries needed."

"Oh." I'm surprised—didn't expect a full-service resort on a tiny private island. "So you'll provide soap and whatnot?"

"Vincent, you're getting back to nature," says Samuel. "Don't concern yourself with such matters. The only things that need to get on that hydrofoil tomorrow afternoon are you and Ernie."

"And our check."

A pause, but certainly not a long one. "Yes. And the check."

When I hang up the phone and stroll back out into the main part of the lobby, I find my Hawaiian girl waiting for me on a plush tapestry-covered papasan chair. She matches the decor perfectly, and I wonder if the hotel ordered her out of some special catalog. I'd like to get myself put on *that* mailing list.

"I don't know your name," I tell her as I approach. "But when I ask a woman out, I always try to do it in a formal style."

"It's Kala," she says coyly.

"Thank you. Would you be so kind as to accompany me for a drink, Kala?"

"You drink?"

"For nourishment only. I do, on the other hand, enjoy a chew. . . ."

She holds aloft a small black clutch purse, bursting with unknown pleasures. "I brought my own," she purrs.

I feel like a teenager again as we huddle in a service nook off the lobby and tuck into the herbal delights Kala produces from her bag. A fair amount of locally grown date leaves—this is what they meant when they called it Maui Wowie—and some other native elements with which I have little prior experience quickly make their way through my digestive tract. There was a short period between the banana leaves and the phone call from Samuel when I had decided to quit the herbs altogether—even on a social level—go cold turkey, but in no time, I'm back off the wagon and rolling around in the mud below.

There's a lot of touching, a little squeezing, a heap of kissing, and a growing desire to rip off my guise right here, right now, and have at it. We're banging noses, bopping heads, uncomfortable enough in our costumes without herb-enraged lust complicating matters even further. My tongue delves into her mouth, seeking and finding the same, now snaking around hers; the caps pop off, allowing us free reign. I can taste the epoxy that holds that damned mask around her lips.

A minute later, laughter sets in. It's always that way—first, the slow, mellow rush of the drug working its way through the system, waving a friendly hello at all the organs as it passes on through; then, with certain herbs, the sexual rise, but by the time it's begun to knock on the brain's front door, the giggling takes over. Speaking is relegated to a second-class activity; what with all the kissing, it's difficult to breathe, much less get a full sentence out, "What—what is—whadda we got here—"

"Sugarcane. Bark."

"Ruff."

This sets off another twenty minutes of laughing and fondling, during which time we're asked by an overly officious member of the hotel staff to take it outside or upstairs. This sobers us up for but a moment.

"Outside?" I ask her.

"Upstairs?"

A little sidelong glance at each other, some unspoken agreement on the delightful future of this delightful evening—and we race through the lobby, hand in hand, barreling through tourists and not giving a good goddamn about it.

We're alone in the elevator, which is fundamentally good and right. Desire leaps up sixteen notches with every floor we pass, and it's amazing that our guises are still on. I hate kissing through this mask, these teeth, but even lust can't get me to violate the daily code of conduct—yet. If this elevator should stall, I'm fully certain that when the mechanic finally opens up the doors, he'll find two overgrown lizards going at it with all the primordial fury they can muster.

But the lift makes it all the way to the top and soon we're stumbling down the hall, our lips locked, mumbled nonsense syllables welling up from our chests, muted groans of craving that don't—and shouldn't—mean anything. My wild, wild hands are roving, trying to dig deep beneath that odd hourglass human guise in search of the true shape beneath, but every time I reach for her buttons or zippers, Kala whispers, "Not yet . . . not yet . . ."

We've reached the hotel room. It better be *yet* already.

As we crash into the room and stumble past an opened suitcase lying on the floor, I trip and go down hard, landing, with exquisite luck, faceup on the bed. Air whooshes out of me for a moment like a balloon with its knot untied, but by the time I've regained my breath I'm already laughing, calling out for Kala, reaching to pull her down with me and continue what is likely to become one of the better evenings in my considerable years of experience. But she's curiously absent from my grasp, and as I sit up, the room not so much spinning as it is line-dancing, I call out, "You still here?"

"In the bathroom," comes the reply, and I sigh and plop back down. Of course—time for the primping and the preening. In that respect, the female of the dino species is no different from that of the humans, except with the dinos there's less makeup and more basic hide care.

"Worked here long?" I call out, knowing that if I don't keep up a steady stream of chatter, I'll pass out good and hard. As if on autopilot, my hands begin unbuttoning my guise, ripping off clamps and girdles, tossing the foul things to the beige carpet below. My natural flesh ripples as it comes in contact with the damp Hawaiian air, and my groin is waiting for similar treatment.

"No," she replies. "You're on vacation?"

"Working vacation," I answer. There's a nice odor invading the room, perhaps some potpourri coming in through the air conditioning, or maybe streaming in from outside. The foliage on these islands is like nothing else we've seen on the mainland, and I've been having a great time sniffing around like a dog looking for the perfect place to poop.

"What do you do?" she asks me.

This always gets 'em. "I'm a private investigator," I say proudly. "I'm working a case for a friend."

"That's interesting."

"It's a job." Part of my humble routine. Works like a charm.

But there's no charm going on in here to match the one this Hawaiian beauty is working on me. There's the unmistakable click of a lightswitch being flicked off—my wooziness intensifying with the sudden lack of light, head sinking into the pillow, arms leaden and motionless—come on, Vincent, this is something you're gonna want to stay up for—and a tail flicks out from the darkness and slowly caresses my chest, the tip working its way down, down, knowing just where to go, just how hard to press, just when to release—waves of desire rising, lifting me off the bed, rising, straining, stretching—my mind fluttering away, letting itself drift, drift, and enjoy . . .

I hope Ernie doesn't wait up.

A hangover, I can deal with. A pasty, numb mouth that tastes like I've eaten stale carpet—fine, no problem. Ringing in the ears, in the head, jaw aching, body trembling at the 3.0 Richter mark—okey-dokey by me. A nauseated feeling deep in the pit of my stomach, a family of hamsters scurrying around in my intestines—not fun, but acceptable.

It's the memory loss I could do without.

"You don't even know if you slept with her?" Ernie is chiding me as we trundle our bags through the marina on the way to the hydrofoil that will take us to the Progressives' island. We're a little late—half an hour by my watch—due to my inability to wake up and meet Ernie by noon, and the frantic pace has got me ready to lose what little lunch I was able to shove down on the way out of the Westin Maui's front door.

A tip: Poi is not appropriate hangover food.

"The act itself? No, no, I don't remember that."

"Nice habit you've got there, kid."

"Don't lecture me, I'll throw up on you. Look, I remember the foreplay. I remember the aftermath . . . sort of. It's that middle part that's a bit hazy."

All of it's a bit hazy, actually—the fondling before, the pillow talk afterward—but it's true that the actual act of sexual congress has completely escaped me for the moment. This has happened before, once or twelve times, mostly after a night of frolic and fun and bingeing. I'm sure there's a repository in some alternate dimension bursting with all of the things I've forgotten over the years, but it's probably filled more with algebra equations than sexual relations.

"What was she?"

"In what sense?"

"In the only sense," Ernie says. "Carno, Raptor, what?"

"I . . . I don't remember."

"Of course. You tell her why we're in Hawaii?"

"I'm sure I didn't."

"You're *sure*?" Ernie checks.

"Sure I'm sure. Sure." Not in the least. I could have given her my name, rank, serial number, and favorite breakfast foods for all I know. The only thing I'm positive about is that Kala was gone this morning when I woke up. Probably for the best. "Hell of a gal," I say. "A real firecracker."

"As far as you remember."

We make it to dock seventeen only thirty-nine minutes after our scheduled departure time, and the other passengers on board are not exceptionally thrilled with us. Buzz and Wendell, who haven't changed their clothes since last night—unless, of course, they brought duplicates of those god-awful outfits—make a show of tapping their feet, checking their watches, but the twins are too grateful for our friendship to work up any real negative emotion.

"We made 'em wait," Buzz informs me as the dockhands gather up the mooring lines and prepare to cast off. "They wanted to go, but we said our friends were coming."

"That's what we said, all right. That's exactly what we said."

And that's how the next two hours go, Buzz and Wendell regaling us with tales of their heroic adventure of keeping the hydrofoil in dock. The telling of the story lasts at least three times as long as the actual event, I am sure, but Ernie and I use the time to shut off our brains and take a gander around us at the other dinos who have decided to live life the Progressive way.

Their human guises show no outward signs of mental instability; the hair is mostly washed, combed, and few of them are babbling incoherently. The smells aboard the hydrofoil, though mixed and braided through one another, are strong and don't have the pungent after-aroma so often associated with clinical wackoness. Once upon a time Ernie and I tailed a cat who was so far gone that his usual cookies-and-cream scent had curdled into a stench strong enough to track from twenty blocks away, unassisted. Good thing he couldn't smell himself, or it would have driven him even farther off the beaten path.

But what in the world—this or the next—could possibly be drawing this seemingly random collection of otherwise healthy dinosaurs into a semimystical, full-bunk organization like the Progressives? Is it the camaraderie? The reverence for past generations? Or is it the idea that they may somehow reconnect with their inner selves, that they can become more dino than human once again?

"I can't wait until we get naked," giggles Buzz.

"Me, too," says Wendell. "That's the best."

Indeed, by the time we reach the island, the others have become restless enough to shed their guises, ripping away at the buttons and zippers in a mad nudist frenzy. As I fumble with my own costume, I realize how out of practice I am, and, by extension, how skilled these Progressives are in the fine art of disrobing. As I struggle with the hidden snaps beneath my human pecs—nicely inflated but not too strapping, despite Jules's insistence on pumping them up with a new polymer she ordered from Korea—a G-2 buckle flies out of the crowd, through the air, and beans me on the noggin. A few seconds later, I duck to avoid a tail strap. They're not particularly careful with their guises, throwing the human skin around like a bunch of old rags. Dino mothers are famous for teaching their children to take care of their costumes—*Do you have any idea how much these cost? Do you know how hard your father works so you can buy new legs every year?*—but these superego lessons didn't seem to take with this bunch.

Ernie and I are more sedate in our divestiture of clothing and costume, but in short order we're standing free and clear alongside the others, ready to disembark and begin our Progressive journey. Some small part of me—a part that shrinks with every passing year Ernie and I work together—is reeling off a grocery list of reasons why we shouldn't be here, why our best course of action would be to turn around, reguise, and have the hydrofoil take us back to Maui and a little more of that fresh banana leaf. Daniel into the lion's den, Abel baiting Cain, stepping on a mad dog's tail. But I know the risks, I know the rewards, and I'm here to do whatever's needed in order to get the job done.

"You ready to crash this party?" I mumble to my partner, already knowing from years of experience what his response will be.

"So long as I don't have to dress up."

"Don't worry," I assure him. "We're going casual."

· · ·

The Hum-Vee ride into the heart of the Progressives' island is uneventful, unless you count the multitude of trees we nearly slam into at speeds approaching NASCAR records. Our convoy of military trucks runs roughshod through the jungle, the wide bodies barely able to negotiate the way. Samuel, unguised and redolent, is at the helm of our six-man open-air assault vehicle, his curved green foot heavy on the accelerator, claws digging into the floorboard. Though I've been around dinos all my life, I've never seen one driving a car in the buff, and I have to force myself to stare at something else; don't want to give the guy the wrong impression.

As we rumble down a barely beaten trail, I notice another path branching off to the left; as we pass, the Progressives don't so much look away as they do expressly *not* look away. It's a weird sign, whatever it is, and I take a gander down there as we shoot by at forty-five miles an hour. The jungle vegetation is thick down that road, I notice, and the path soon disappears into the trees. But something at the end of it catches my eye, my brain, and nags enough to get me to talk to Samuel again. "What's down there?" I ask.

"Nothing. More of the jungle."

"Trees looked sorta . . . odd."

"Trick of the eye," he says, and his silence closes off further conversation.

Soon the Hummer slows, and Samuel reaches over and clicks a small button on what looks like a remote control clipped to the auto's sun visor. Somewhere nearby, a thin creaking sound joins the mix of jungle noises. The bumping slows down as we pass onto a section of well-packed dirt.

"What's that?" I ask.

"What?"

"The creaking."

"Animals."

"Creaking animals?"

"Hawaii is a fascinating land."

After a few more minutes of Mr. Iguanodon's Wild Ride, we pull onto smooth terrain, and the glory—perhaps not the appropriate word—that is the Progressive compound is laid out before us. I don't suppose it would have been fair of me to expect another luxurious Xanadu similar to the complex back in the Hollywood Hills—it's a fair enough chunk of change to buy up an island in the Pacific, so I can't begrudge the Progressives for taking it easy on the accommodations—but bare-bones roughing it has never been my bag. It's hard to make out specifics in the all-but-complete Hawaiian darkness, but as the headlights from the wide-track stream over the camp, I'm a little put off by what masquerades as living conditions around here: simple wooden huts dot an otherwise barren landscape, the occasional weed poking up from beneath a thin layer of brownish crabgrass.

"It's . . . nice," I say as the truck drives into the heart of the camp, kicking up a cloud of dust that stings my eyes and chokes my throat.

"This is a simple life," Samuel responds. "It's closer to the way we were meant to live."

"Ah. Without the huts and the Hummer, you mean."

". . . Yes." I think Samuel is finally learning to dislike me. This would not be atypical.

We hop out of the transport, and Samuel leads Ernie and me to one of the larger huts. The wooden door doesn't so much creak as it complains, and I find myself scanning the walls to check the structural security of this ramshackle domicile. There's a lot of bamboo and dried palm leaves, and though this was more than enough to shelter the castaways of Gilligan's Island, I don't put much stock in its ability to protect us should anything stronger than a light breeze decide to come whistling about.

"Any other accommodations?" I ask.

"How so?"

"Something . . . better?"

Samuel cocks his head. "Like an upgrade package?"

Aha, luxury at last! "Exactly. That's *exactly* what I mean."

"No."

Strewn about the floor of the hut are all manner of branches, leaves, and twigs. "What this for?" I ask, lifting a branch, hefting it to test its weight. "Bringing nature inside for us?"

"That's your bed," explains Samuel, the tone a mite more rational than the words.

I shake my head. "I'm really more of a Posturepedic kinda guy."

"Mattresses and frames are human constructs, made for human bodies," he explains. "You will need to make a nest, much as our ancestors did in the wild."

Now, I am fully aware that the currently popular human theory about our species is that we evolved into birds, that our body types and bone densities are more similar to modern aviators than they are to lizards and the like, but this is pure rubbish. What's more, it isn't even a dinocentric theory. Most of the time, we've got paleontological "plants" doing the dirty work for us, injecting theories here and there, but this whole bird concept is a purely human one, and I can't believe that Samuel would be parroting such nonsense.

"You have two hours," Samuel continues, "and then dinner will be served. Circe has invited the two of you to be her guests at dinner tonight, and then to join her during the Ring."

The Ring? I'd ask Samuel what the heck he's talking about, but Ernie is fixated on the nest situation. "You're joking, right? Tell me there's a cot around that corner."

Samuel shakes his head, a missionary overjoyed to be preaching to the heathens. "We all make our nests every night, and take them apart every day. It is what the ancestors did, and it is part of the natural way."

And, as if on cue, our other hut-mates ooh and aah over this afternoon's chore, eagerly rushing forward, fighting with one another for the best pile of sticks. A pair of Compies rush by, beaks chattering in some language I can't understand; I promise myself that wherever they choose to bed down for the night, I will sleep far, far away.

My nest-building skills are not quite on par with, say, my trumpetplaying skills, which are not quite on par with, say, my juggling or fire-eating. Suffice it to say that once I am done tucking and bending and shoving and mushing, my bed for the evening resembles nothing so much as the chaff left over after a once-mighty redwood has been converted into six hundred reams of InkJet paper. Sticks and branches and bristles and all manner of leafy shards stick out in every possible direction, poking me expertly in all the wrong places.

Ernie's nest is, of course, impeccable, a seamless puff pastry of a bed frame, with perfectly rounded edges, downy-soft leaf interior, and a pillow made out of what looks to be bark shavings held together with twisted vine. If this is all just a giant IQ test thrown at us by the Progressives, I'm sure to end up in the remedial class sometime soon.

"You want help?" he asks.

"Screw off," is my only reply. "I like it this way."

Wendell and Buzz, no surprise, make theirs in identical fashion, forming a series of rounded triangles stacked atop one another until they've got an inverted Aztec pyramid in which to sleep. All the while, as they construct, the twins keep up a furious stream of chatter.

"I love this part," says Wendell.

"The beginning of the journey," says Buzz.

"You do this a lot?" Ernie asks as he puts the finishing touches on his nest, gracing the tips with a little cotton fluff.

"Oh, yes, yes," says Buzz. "We make nests every night, and we've been coming here . . . oh, a long time."

"How long exactly?"

"I don't—I can't remember—"

"Give it an estimate," I suggest. "Give or take."

Buzz and Wendell confer among themselves, whispering back and forth like a Senate witness and his attorney deciding to take the fifth, and eventually come back with, "Five years."

"You've been Progressing for five years?" I say. "Well . . . that *is* a long time. Very impressive." The twins beam with pride, and I'm glad I've got them on the right track.

"It's the only way to live," says Buzz.

"The only way to *be*," says Wendell.

I nod, close my eyes, pretending to soak in this valuable information. Then, as if it's the most natural segue in the world, I say, "Actually, I did know one other fellow who was around the group these last few years—maybe you guys knew him."

"I doubt it," says Ernie, catching on. "These boys can't know everyone."

Buzz jumps up and down, his tail slapping the ground with a meaty thunk. "Oh, but we do! I'm sure we do! What's his name?"

"Rupert," I tell them. "Rupert Simmons."

No reaction. Buzz and Wendell don't even make their usual aside to deliberate on the issue; they simply shrug their shoulders.

"I think he was called Granaagh," says Ernie, and I'm impressed with his excellent dino pronunciation.

Aha! Now there's talking and crying and sobbing and condolences and a hearty dose of caring all around. They knew Rupert, all right, and knew him well.

"Like a brother," sobs Wendell, great streams of salt water running from his eyes. "I loved him like a brother."

Buzz is similarly upset, though he seems unable to match his twin in sheer tear production. "What a good soul. I can never understand why he did what he did."

"Kill himself, you mean?"

"Abandoning Progress," cries Buzz. "He was so close. Seventy-three percent dinosaur natural. He was almost ready for the Ring."

There it is again; that phrase keeps popping up. "The Ring," I say. "This is a prize, of some sort?"

"No, no, it's—it's the ultimate test. The test of Progression."

Mumbo, mumbo, and more jumbo. Don't know why I expected anything different. "This something everyone goes through?"

"Eventually," Buzz tells me. "But it takes a true natural dinosaur to make it through the Ring."

Ernie puts an arm around Wendell, a golf-buddy hug of camaraderie. "You boys pass this test yet?"

Wendell recoils from Ernie—whether it's the arm or the question, I don't know—and shakes his head rapidly, as if he's watching a tennis match between hummingbirds. "Goodness no!" he yelps. "We're hardly ready for that."

"Hardly ready."

"The Ring is only for those who are ready to move on to the next level. We won't be there for some time."

"A long time."

Interesting. It doesn't come as much surprise that Buzz and Wendell, friendly though they are, haven't quite made it up the Progressive ladder. Nice kids. Brains like squirrels. On the other hand, it *does* come as a surprise that Rupert Simmons, after such a short period of time with the group, had. Our estimates had made Rupert a Progressive for three years, max, which meant he moved along quite quickly. "So Rupert—he was high up, huh?"

"He was very advanced," says Buzz. "In fact, he led many of our seminars."

Wendell's eyes go wide, that eerie Progressive look of half excitement/half insanity flaring to life. "Remember the one about the mammals?" he gushes. "It was soooo wonderful!"

Buzz turns to me to explain. "He showed us how the mammals were rightfully under us in the food chain."

"Under *us!*" shouts Wendell.

"And how dinos are technically the dominant species, even though we're a population minority."

I cluck my teeth—hard to do when your chompers are sharp as knives, but I've got it down to a science after years of practicing disapproval—and say, "No love lost for the humans here, I take it."

"Why should we care about them?" asks Buzz. And now that casual, friendly tone is conspicuously absent from his voice. It's all business. "They keep us down. They keep us from realizing our true selves."

"They're hideous," Wendell chimes in. "They must be stopped."

Buzz fixes his twin with a hard stare, and Wendell immediately drops his eyes. "He takes it too far sometimes," says Buzz. "My brother's very excitable."

I'm about to go on, to press Wendell along this path, when a distinctive scent begins to make its way through the cracks in the walls, the ceiling. My head is already beginning to float a foot above my body, my sinuses filling with a potpourri of herbs and spices, stretching through my nostrils, snaking down into my throat, nearly choking off my ability to breathe.

"What is it?" Ernie asks, hands on my shoulders. "You okay, kid?"

"Yeah," I manage to gurgle. "It's—it's—"

"You're turning purple—"

"It's—"

The door swings wide, blowing open on a breeze as if it's made from the flimsiest of woods, and suddenly the scent drops to nothing, undetectable, a figment of my imagination the entire time. Air comes rushing back into my lungs and my heart resumes its normal pattern, albeit with a slightly faster beat, the adrenaline rush courtesy of this magnificent creature standing in the doorway.

"Good evening," whispers Circe, her breath tickling my ears even from ten feet away. "I want to show you two something."

14

t's a barn, and nothing more. I mean, it's fine, as barns go, but when Circe said she wanted to show us something, I was hoping for something a little more on the . . . erotic side. And a barn, certain human fetishes aside, is not a particularly sexual place. Then again, the Progressives have already surprised me; perhaps there's a full-tilt party going down inside that barn. That might explain the otherwise inexplicable human attraction for Amish country.

But for now we're standing outside this tall wooden structure, and I don't quite get it. I express my displeasure, muttering, "It's a little cold out here to be looking at the side of a dumb barn." Despite the warm Hawaiian clime, the nighttime temperature has been dropping steadily since we began the climb up this hill, and the brisk wind up here whips the air into icy little pins that manage to send my hide into miniature convulsions. With the exception of a few mutant species who flourished during the first Ice Age—a rather dismal period, I am led to understand—we dinos were constructed for more temperate climes. Very few of us live north of Buffalo.

"This 'dumb barn,' as you call it, is what enables us to maintain this property," she says, "as well as the other properties we hold around the world. Come, have a look."

We enter through a solid steel security door that opens only after Circe has inserted her finger into a hole that looks suspiciously like the one on the side of the bogus Ancestrograph back on Hollywood Boulevard. I'd try putting my finger inside, just to see if it's got that Frigidaire feel to it, but I've already gotten a glimpse of the security in this place, and I'd like to leave the Hawaiian Islands with all of my digits intact.

"Security measures," explains Circe, and I grin stupidly, as if I understand what the hell she's talking about. It's a *barn,* for chrissakes. Since when are horses a classified secret?

Since they've started decking out their stables in gleaming high-tech lab equipment, I guess. A sea of dinosaurs—all unguised, frenzied, sweaty, and reeking—hover over individual workstations and lab tables, furiously applying their skills to whatever the heck it is that they're doing. The interior walls of this simple farm structure have been plastered with metal plates at least three inches thick, the only available light streaming down from six massive overhead halogen fixtures hanging from the ceiling.

And in the middle of it all stands the end product of all this attention, the raison d'être. It takes a moment for my eyes to adjust to the increased luminescence, but once they do, I am compelled to focus on one of the largest dinosaur skeletons I have ever seen, bar none.

Sure, I've seen complete fossils before, and, sure, the Museum of Natural History in LA has a few real gawkers—but they're much smaller, not as well preserved, and of a dinosaur type far more common than this unique creature. It's eighty feet long if it's an inch, double-decker-bus wide, and tall as a California palm. Down on all fours like an ancient Brontosaur, but with a long, spiked tail that twists its way down and around the large, stumpy legs. A jaw full of sabered teeth rounds out the weapon display, sitting firmly in front of a sloped-back head that leads to a long, thin neck and barrel chest.

Bleached-white bones three feet in diameter have been fastened together with large lumps of alabaster putty, support rods jammed into crucial joints and welded to the base beneath, the entirety of the structure further supported by a series of thin cables wrapped around the uppermost limbs and vertebrae and anchored to the ceiling. It's a gigantic marionette of some long-forgotten ancestor, and though I'm a bit taken aback by its presence, I can't think of a more fitting place for such a monstrosity than in the company of these Progressives.

"What . . . what is it?"

"That's Freeangggh," says Circe, roaring with the best of them, "but mostly, we just call him Frank."

"What the hell are you doing with the old guy?" I ask, then correct myself—"the ancestor?"

"We're making him, that's what. He's not really old, actually. Or really dead."

"Not really dead?" I ask, unsure of the specific mechanisms with which one could be classified as not *really* dead. "Looks like a goner to me."

"And that's the idea. That's the idea precisely. Here, come have a peek."

We follow our host across the barn, taking a serpentine path around and about Progressive dinosaurs crouched over desks, across blueprints. Fifty-gallon vats of a strange white bubbling mixture block our way, and Circe warns us to take care as we step around them.

We arrive at the base of the gargantuan fossil, nothing more than ants invading the dead giant's picnic, and it's only while standing in this Goliath's shadow that I come to a startling realization: even if I were somehow able to transport myself back in time to the Jurassic, I'd be stepped on or eaten in seconds flat. A few sharp claws and a wiseass attitude don't get you very far when you're outweighed by twenty metric tons.

I don't recognize the bone structure, though I imagine that this is more a function of my point of view—looking straight up into the beast's nostrils—than my lack of ancestral fossil knowledge. Nevertheless, I hazard a guess. "Brontosaur? Triassic period?"

"No and no, but a valiant attempt. Don't try again—you'll be wrong."

"How do you know?"

"Because this is neither one of the species of dinosaurs that died out during the Great Showers nor one of those that survived. This is an entirely new species of dinosaur, Vincent, and I'm proud to say he's of my own design."

"Your design?" asks Ernie, stepping forward and into the conversation.

Circe takes a seat near Frank's phalanges, stroking his three-foot-long toes as she speaks. "We'd been hearing some rumblings from the paleontological community for some time about the lack of new finds, complaints about grant money going to waste, so we've been preparing for a baby like Frank here for quite some time. Gave me a little head start on the blueprints. But when it comes to the actual construction, we only work under contract, so it wasn't like we were going to go ahead and start the projects on spec. . . ."

"Wait a second," I say, catching the drift as it wafts by. "I get it—you're fossil-makers. You guys make some of the fake fossils they plant out in the desert."

"Some?" Circe huffs. "We're responsible for eighty-seven percent of the West Coast fossil finds, thank you very much. No one has the quality we do."

Ernie gives the dinosaur's shin a little knock. It echoes right on back. "So Frank—this thing here—is a fake?"

"What new fossils aren't? And for that matter, what old fossils aren't? Do you know how hard it is to get a bone—a real bone—

fossilized? It's not like all the ancestors took off time to go search out a peat bog they could die in. There are very specific conditions under which fossilization can take place, and if we relied solely on natural fossil finds to stock the world's endless hunger for new discoveries, there'd be quite a number of museums out there without their endowments."

"My uncle was a fossil-maker," I say, trying to inject a little spirit of camaraderie.

"Was . . . ?"

"He got bought out," I shrug. "Fossil Time offered him a lump sum. Now he just sits at home and writes angry letters to *Reader's Digest*."

"That's us."

"What is? *Reader's Digest*?"

"Fossil Time."

I shake my head. "We must be talking about something different. This is a joint back in Chicago out near—"

"Near Evanston," Circe finishes. "I know. It's one of our outlets—we don't have many in the Midwest, actually, but it's profitable, so we keep it up. We're also Fossils-R-Us and Bone Dry Diggin' and Good Tyme Mineral Creations and about sixty other companies I can't keep track of. Samuel's in charge of the group's business affairs."

This certainly explains where the Progressives get the cash to front such an expensive operation, but it cuts the legs out from under my idea that young Progressives—like Rupert, Buzz, and Wendell—are pumped solely for their moola. Compared to an outfit like this, a thousand bucks from Daddy's IRA is chump change.

"You do good business?" Ernie asks, his mind clearly on the same path as my own.

But Circe's been to school on the matter. "We do all right," she says, and leaves it to our imaginations to conjure up the millions of dollars that must be flowing into Progressive coffers.

She leads us to a workstation manned by three dinosaurs of different lineage—there's an Ankie, an Allosaur, and a Procompsognathus all working together in harmony. I'm surprised that a Compy has the cranial capacity to carry out such detailed work, but hold any outward signs of my disdain in check. The trio of dinos are hunched over a mica-topped table, fiddling with a long, slender bone about three feet in length and six inches in diameter.

We're introduced—the three Progressives having completely unpronounceable throat-clearing growls as their names once again—and Circe gives us a rundown on the task at hand. "The thing about fossils," she says, "the truly crucial thing about attempting to duplicate the beautiful structures of the ancestors, is age."

"Age? What age? They're new," I say.

"But they don't look it, and they don't test it."

"And I don't get it," says Ernie.

"Artificial aging is where most fossil producers come up short. It's a difficult task, to say the least, but nothing short of perfection makes the grade with us, whereas precision is not as important in the other factors. For example, I could take you back to the firing room, where we cast the molds and pour the liquid dentin, and you could appreciate how we come up with the initial shape of the bones. It's fascinating, believe me, but a slight imperfection here or there won't break six weeks' worth of work. We could sand down, we could build out, or we could leave the mistake as is and let the mammals theorize over its implications for years to come. Remember when that paleontology team from USC found a baby Camptosaur out near Palmdale?"

"Sure," I lie.

"Started out as a Hadro, but one of our mixers threw in too much dentin. We figured, what the heck, the world needed a new species, anyhow."

"It did . . . ?"

"We could also take a tour and go back to the design center," she continues, "a delightful section of the business, and I could show you how we determine the exact length and tendon pairing for each individual piece, how we plan to 'discover' a certain number of pieces first, that sort of thing. Again, while this is an important part of the puzzle, there is room for leeway. A Diplodocus jawbone might be scattered a few extra centimeters away from the rest of the skull, but it's nothing that would set off alarm bells in the average ape.

"But this station right here—and the ten others on the floor—this is where the magic takes place. This is where the slightest miscalculation could bring down the whole house of cards."

Ernie shakes his head, lips pursed. He hates being confused. "Still lost me."

"You've heard of carbon dating, Mr. Watson?"

"Measures the age of an item. So . . . what? You put carbon in these things?"

There's the laugh again, and though it's at my friend's expense, I can't help but feel a warm glow at her every giggle. "No, no," she says. "Carbon dating is actually very limited in scope, and it certainly wouldn't help date an object from the ancestors' time. In fact, when human scientists locate a dino fossil, they're not even able to date the object itself—instead, they rely on the age of the rock surrounding the object. And that's where the fun starts."

"We weren't having fun already?"

"Let me explain: There are two main ways to date any rock stratum. The easiest method is by determining its relative location. The deeper the layer, the older it is. Fortunately for us, paleontologists have come up with quite the intricate dating system—most of it determined long ago by Council planners and carefully spoon-fed to the human scientific community until they took it on and accepted it as their own. And they follow it to a T, so it makes our job that much easier. If we want some scientists to find a Raptor thigh from eighty million years ago, then we just go out to the site, dig to the proper layer—don't even ask what those tools cost us—plant, and bury it back up again. You'd be surprised how no one seems to care, and if any human starts to make a fuss, there's always a dino higher than him on the academic totem pole to kick the little ape off the dig site and send him home to teach Archaeology 101 to a bunch of stoned hockey players."

Circe's getting all worked up now, and I can smell the herbs beginning to flow, ebbing in and out as her mood elevates. Oregano first, like we're passing an Italian joint, but soon the basil and marjoram's kicking in as well. I grab the edge of the table firmly so as to keep my mind—and body—from wandering off to a distant forest.

"Second method is a little harder, and that's what my fine brothers and sisters here are working on. Scientists can take the layer of rock surrounding any given fossil and subject it to a test for radioisotope decay—similar to carbon dating, only on a much grander time scale. At least, that's what we've got them thinking, and that's all the help we need. What we're doing here is impregnating the rock chips surrounding the fossil with a certain amount of radioisotope and a larger amount of the substance it decays into, in order to give the impression that the mineral's been decaying over time—"

"And therefore creating the impression of age," I finish.

"Exactly. The paleontologists dig it up, note the surrounding rock layers, and test the substance. Their computers decide it's gone through twelve point six half-lives—or however long we want the computers to tell them—and they dance around for a while, announce the discovery to the world, and prop the old boy up in a dusty showcase somewhere."

"And who pays you for this?" asks Ernie.

"The museums, mostly. Everyone needs visitors, Mr. Watson. The fine example you saw back there is going to be the newest and hottest thing on the paleontology circuit over the next six months. You just watch."

"Six months?" I ask.

"It takes time, Vincent, it takes time. The fossil structure is completed, but we've still got to disassemble the creature, break off the necessary bone chips, ship the whole mess out to Los

Angeles, prepare the burial, truck it out to Utah, scatter and plant every single piece, wait a few months for the sand to cover up our tracks, and convince some influential foundation to take another crack at the area to see if there's anything they might have missed. Have you ever worked with mammals? It's exhausting."

"What are you calling it?" asks Ernie.

Circe dismisses the question with a wave of her hand. "We try not to prename the fossils here. Oh, we had a division a few years back that would come up with some of the labels—they're the ones that thought of Megalosaur, actually—but it's usually better to let the community pick a name by themselves. Gives them a sense of ownership. I'm sure they'll be extraordinarily creative with this one—Largosaur or Tailosaur or some other brain-dead flight of fancy."

"It's all very impressive," I say, "and it's good to see that everyone's so . . . productive."

"That's a part of the Progressive way," Circe insists. "There are no free rides on the path to a natural lifestyle. We gladly participate in deceiving the humans in this manner so that we are able to be free in our choice of non-costume."

"Everybody works, then?" asks Ernie.

"Everybody."

"Even you? Seems to me you do a lot of philosophizing and not a lot of hands-on labor."

"Even me," Circe laughs. "I run the planting sites in Utah and Nevada, mostly, and the work couldn't get any *more* hands-on. Most of the time, I'm down in the holes, digging away at the dust with my own eight claws."

Great—now Ernie's got her pissed off at us. "He didn't mean—"

"Please, please," says Circe, "there are no wrong questions. Everything is open here."

"Great," I say, getting back to the matter at hand. "What did Rupert do, by the way?"

"Who?"

"Rupert—our deceased friend. The one who's frolicking with the ancestors now . . . ?"

"Of course," says Circe, not a stammer in sight. "Forgive me, please. I'm not accustomed to addressing Progressives by their slave names." There's that term again, and it gives me the willies.

"That's fine. What did Gran—Granna—what did he do?"

"He was a bonewright, I believe. They shape the molds, sand the fossils into the proper shapes before they're sent here for aging."

"I see . . ." I don't—not exactly—but such an admission is unnecessary at this stage.

"Did he have friends?" Ernie asks. "Coworkers?"

"Of course."

"Can we talk with them?"

"To ask them . . . ?"

"Just to talk," says Ernie. "To see if he'd been depressed. It's tough, when a friend goes like that."

Circe takes Ernie's hand—is she blasting him with pheromones now?—and strokes it gently. "I understand," she whispers. "It's very difficult, and I grieve with you." Then, volume back to normal, dropping the hand back to its place: "But I'm afraid I can't interrupt our brethren right now. We've got to come through on Frank here within the week or we'll run past deadline. The Coalition of Natural History Museums will have my hide for sure if we don't fill this contract."

"We understand," I say, nudging Ernie away from the fossil and his next series of questions. I'm all for pushing to get answers, but I don't want to blow it with a premature interrogation.

Circe takes a cursory glance at her watch. "Brothers, I believe it's time for dinner. Shall we?"

Circe takes us by the arm—first me, then Ernie—and with a simple tug easily leads us from the barn. The other Progressives continue their work, though I can feel the combined weight of their stares as we are ushered from the building and back into the night air.

."So . . . do you have any more questions?" she asks, once we've cleared the barn area and are making our way back down toward the compound.

"Just one," I say, remembering the newt and snake snack we were treated to the last time we attended a formal Progressive affair. "Is dinner dead or alive?"

. . .

The evening meal is a casual affair. There are no tuxedos. There are no evening gowns. There are no hors d'oeuvres, ice sculptures, string quartets, wandering waiters with toppling trays, or lectures by pretentious people who are famous mostly for being pretentious in the first place.

There is, however, a lot of raw pork.

"It's not a religious objection," I assure Circe. "I think one of my grandmothers might have been Jewish, and I'm sure I've got some Muslim blood in me, but it's really more of a . . . I mean, it's pork. Rare. Raw. It's a pig."

"It's disgusting," grumbles Ernie. He's ready to fast if need be, and, truth be told, he could do with a few days of food restriction. Seeing him out of his guise for the last twenty-four hours has told me more about my partner's body than I ever wanted to know; the nudist lifestyle does not compliment all somatotypes.

"You are worrying about diseases," begins Circe, who is dressed to the nines—well, to the eights at least. She's the only one in the large dining hall to wear anything other than her natural skin: a small emerald pin, the glimmering jewel cut in a tapered oval—an egg shape—that sticks delicately out of her hide just above her tail. Sex-x-x-y.

A long time ago, a Coelo hooker I was tailing on a case let me in on a little trade secret: the two square inches just above the area where a female dino's tail meets her body is the most erogenous of erogenous zones. Pleasure beyond pleasure can be found in that small patch of hide, and over the years, I've used that knowledge to my great advantage with the ladies. And even as I sit here and calmly talk to Circe, keeping my own erogenous zones safely in check, I find myself hoping that later tonight I might get a chance to try a little cult exploration of a different kind.

"Trichinosis is very rare among our kind, Vincent," Circe continues. "And we've never had an outbreak here on the island. I wouldn't worry about it."

I take another look at the dinner table, at the mostly intact pig lying on its back, sides split open by a sharp claw, the meat and guts spilling out onto a bamboo platter. The other diners at our table—a motley collection made up of Samuel, several unnamed dinos from Circe's cadre, and a few other Progressives whom I don't recognize—don't seem to share my rising gorge; they tear into the thing with their claws and snouts, pecking at it like a pack of vultures on a fresh corpse.

"You're sure?" I ask. "About the trichinosis."

Circe nods, looks me in the eye. I could lose myself in those big green globules, though I'm more worried about losing my lunch. "If you want to journey down the road to Progress, you have to take that first step by yourself."

Trite, no doubt, but it does the job. Circe reaches into the pig—puts her hand right inside the damned thing!—and comes out with an unidentifiable bit of organ meat. Without asking, without warning, she lifts the goo up to my snout and gives me a whiff.

Blood-scent. Strong. A sliver of hunger carving its way up through my stomach. I turn to Circe—to ask her to back off with the meal, to request something different, something cooked, something closer to lunch—but suddenly there's a familiar dagger of herbs heading straight for my nose and all is lost. Cilantro and basil whip themselves into a noose around my brain stem—the scent burst short, instantaneous, there and gone again, but that's all it takes.

The forest. The leaves. The running. The trees. Hunting. The joy of the chase. Finishing it off. The end.

There are pig guts in my mouth. Worse still, I believe there are pig guts in my guts. When I regain my senses in the here and now and manage to open my eyes, I find that I'm bent over the dinner table, my snout buried deep inside the dead hog, tongue grasping, licking up loose bits of flesh. The other dino diners have backed off; they sit back, either impressed or disgusted by my sudden porklust.

Applause, led by Circe. Ernie does not join in. Abashed and, to be honest, quite full, I sit back in my chair, wipe the blood from my lips, and let loose with a long, deep belch. Part of me wants to regurgitate, right here, right now. But there's another part of me, smaller yet somehow more intense, that wants a second helping.

"I'm very proud of you," Circe murmurs to me, and her breath on my ear makes it that much harder to keep my groin in check. The naked form is undesirable for males of any species in certain circumstances; what I wouldn't give right now for a pair of Dockers. "Have some more if you like."

Ernie's on the other ear, whispering his own sweet nothings. "You're making me sick, kid. Pull it back a little."

And whereas I want to follow Circe's advice—to tuck in, to really make an animal of myself, figuratively and otherwise—I know Ernie's right. I'm a professional, and I need to act that way. Undercover only goes so far before you get turned inside out.

"I've had enough for now," I tell Circe. "Quite . . . tasty."

Even if I wanted another bite, I don't think I could get a place at the feast. Now that I've backed off, the others have resumed chomping away, huddled around the platter like a gaggle of bargain-hunters at Filene's sweater table, and soon there's not much more than skin and bones left of the once plump porker.

I do notice that aside from Ernie—who has managed to get someone to rustle up a plate of simple white rice for his more discerning palate—there is one other dino, a Stegosaur with closed eyes and calm demeanor, who isn't partaking of the raw animal flesh. He's not partaking of the conversation, either, and if I didn't notice his chest rising and sinking in a rhythmic pattern I'd guess he wasn't partaking of the available oxygen either. "Who's that?" I ask Circe. "You didn't make *him* eat the pig."

"His name is Thomas," she says, this appellation the closest approximation of the throat-clearing hack that is his "natural" dino name, "and he hasn't eaten since he was chosen. He's preparing himself."

"For . . . ?"

"For the Ring. Tonight is his first."

There it is again—this Ring that keeps coming up in conversation. "You chose him for this thing?"

Circe shakes a finger at me. I stifle an urge to lick it. "*Progress* chose him, Vincent."

And with that, she's standing, rising to her full height. There's no audible signal, nothing that tells the crowd of dinosaurs that it's time to listen up, but as one, they turn in their seats, ligaments and intestines hanging from their snouts, their beaks, between their teeth, hands still full of bloody organ meat, and give their full attention to their beloved leader.

"Today is a blessed day," says Circe, her voice expanding to fill all the available space in the dining hall. This is pure natural amplification, and it beats any sound system I've heard save Mariachi Night last summer at the Hollywood Bowl. *That* was six hours of my life I'd like back, by the way.

"Today is a natural day," the dinos chant back.

"The food of the ancestors is within us."

And, again, the audience takes its turn: "The power of the ancestors is behind us."

Circe's tone drops, and though she's speaking at normal levels now, I'm sure it's still perfectly audible anywhere within the cavernous room. "Welcome to the first night of our glorious convocation," she says. "I'm sure you're all ready for a productive, Progressive day tomorrow, so I won't be long.

"Tonight, one of our fellow soul-searchers will be given the opportunity to attain a new level in his Progress. Tonight, he will know what it is to move beyond mammalian constraints, to understand himself as he was meant to be. Tonight, he will become a natural dinosaur."

Circe walks behind Thomas, and his eyes open for the first time this evening. I can just make out his scent, a leather/lime Jell-O mixture, and it seems to me that it's warbling in and out, somehow vibrating in tandem with Circe's. Impossible.

The Stegosaur stands by Circe's side, his gaze transfixed by hers. "Are you ready to accept the challenge of the ancestors?" she asks. "Are you ready to reclaim your dinosaur heritage?"

"I am ready."

Slowly, calmly, as if this ritual is commonplace, Circe places a hand on the back of the Stegosaur's head and draws him into her body, cradling him with her strong, supple arms. I can see his nose searching out the back of her neck, sucking down that alluring scent, his body filling with the maddening aroma.

Minutes pass, and no one dares to speak. No one dares to breathe.

When it's over, Thomas leans away from Circe, his body automatically righting itself, though that vacant stare in the eyes tells me some part of him is no longer inside this dining hall but running free through the wilds of the Triassic.

"It is time," says Circe. "Let us go to the Ring."

15

Contrary to popular opinion, few, if any, professional wrestlers nowadays are dinosaurs. Sure, there was a time when the leagues were full of Raptors and Rexes wrassling to their fake hearts' content, but in modern times it's mostly been freakishly built humans who have taken up the sport. Still, the occasional dino makes his way into the fabled ring, though it's more common in the Spanish leagues—The Pow-Wow from São Paulo comes to mind, as does a Hadrosaur who goes by the name of Pepito el Carnito—and whereas our Latino brothers don't bother to mask the phoniness with extravagant costumes and pounding entry music, they commonly lavish spectacle on the ring itself. Only in the land of the original corrupt prison guard could they come up with the steel cage death match—along with the razor-wire death cage match, the barbed-wire death cage match, and, my personal favorite, the electrified death cage match—and it's served to gain them quite an audience over the years.

Pepito el Carnito would feel right at home here in Hawaii.

Beneath a makeshift tarpaulin canopy stretching for a hundred yards in every direction, tied taut between the tops of some of the tallest trees I've yet to see on this island, lies a single cylindrical cage that I'd guess measures around fifty feet in diameter. Steel bars six inches thick form the walls and the ceiling of the massive cage, with but a single metallic entry portal granting access on the near side. It's like a giant see-through Campbell's Soup can, and though it wouldn't be too effective at holding soup, if it did, the potatoes would be seaworthy.

Rows and rows of hard metal bleachers surround the Ring, eager Progressives filling each and every seat, the preshow murmur growing with every passing second. A few mill around in back, shuffling their feet in the standing-room section, but they don't seem to mind. The crowd knows what's about to happen— at least they have more of an idea than I do—and I sense an odd mixture of excitement and anxiety in the air. Then again, maybe it's just the aroma from my drink.

Ernie and I are away from the maddening crowd, seated on a long raised dais next to the bleachers, our butts comfortably mushed into thick cushions, our thirst slaked by fruity pineapple and guava slushies, each garnished with a delightfully naughty sprig of fresh mint. This fits my night-out plans to a T. If you're going to a show, you might as well go first-class.

Circe sits between us.

"This is an age-old tradition," she says, taking a sip of her own concoction.

"Like, what?" I ask. "Ten, twenty years?"

Disappointment on her face. "There is tradition beyond Progression, Mr. Rubio. What we codify in ritual now was once nothing more than natural."

I don't understand a lick of what she said, but I nod knowingly, if only so she'll quit it with the condescension. I get enough of that from Ernie.

At precisely the same moment, a contingent of four dinos step out from behind the bleachers and march in lockstep toward the Ring. As they approach the door, one steps forward with a set of keys and ceremoniously unlocks the contraption with a showy flourish.

The crowd is hushed. I stifle a burp. Pig-taste wells up in my throat.

The dinos march back toward the bleachers, disappear for a moment, and then return just as quickly, this time with one more added to their ranks. It's Thomas, the Stegosaur who's about to make his debut, and whatever fate the guy's in for, he certainly seems resigned to it. Odd coming-out party.

"He will be escorted to the gate of the Ring by his chosen compatriots," Circe explains to us, voice a low whisper. "And they are the ones who will give him his final blessings and listen to any words he has to say."

"He chose them?" I ask, pointing to the four dinos who are conferring with Thomas down below.

"If it was up to you," says Circe, "to either choose those who could save your life or have them chosen for you, which option would you prefer?"

I mull it over for a second. "That's a hypothetical question, right?"

Down by the ring, the Stegosaur has said all he needs to say to his cohorts. Turning on his heel, he takes a deep breath, sets his tail high in the air, and walks confidently through the portal and into the Ring itself.

Circe continues to narrate the action for us. "Now that he's inside, his compatriots will lock him in and allow him to prepare himself. Meanwhile, they will return to the holding area to fetch his opponent."

"And that would be . . . ?"

"It is different for everyone. Hush."

Indeed, hushing is what the rest of the crowd seems to be doing. All noises—grunting, talking, or otherwise—have ceased, and an eerie silence reigns under the canopy. I keep expecting to see vendors climbing up and down the bleachers, selling popcorn, pretzels, maybe a raw pig's bladder or two, but all I can make out is snout after snout, tooth after tooth, eye after gleaming eye, all of them rapt on the Stegosaur at center Ring.

As Thomas prepares himself for whatever is to follow, I watch as the four dinos he's chosen as his assistants in this endeavor carefully wheel out another cage, this one much smaller than the Ring itself and covered with a bright red blanket. Suddenly there's a burst of audio emanating from the cage, and its origin is certainly not reptilian. A roar, a scream—this one deeper, angrier, more truly *animal* than anything I've heard come out of a dinosaur since the last time I blew off a date with Brunhilde, a Lufthansa stewardess and T-Rex about twice my size.

It sounds feline.

By the time the cage has been affixed to the Ring's entrance via a series of metal bolts, my guess has been confirmed. With a vicious shriek, the animal inside lashes out a tan-and-yellow paw, ripping aside the red blanket and exposing the ravenous mountain lion within. The hulking creature—broad, rippling shoulders, powerful limbs, teeth beyond teeth beyond teeth— paces back and forth in the cage before wolfing down the blanket in two seconds flat, feathers and all.

It is still very hungry.

"That's the opponent?" Ernie blurts out. "Christ, that's not fair."

"You'd be surprised," Circe says. "Lions can be quite strong."

"I mean it's not fair for the Stego. It's impossible—he'll be killed instantly—"

Circe gives me a look—*He's your friend, isn't he?*—and I try my best to reflect it right back at her, though I suspect it comes across more as gas pain than anything else. "When we reach a certain level of Progress," she informs my partner, "nothing is impossible. Besides, we do take precautions."

"Such as?" I ask.

I will receive no answer. On some unspoken signal, the bars separating the mountain lion's cage from the Ring proper are raised, and the great cat springs out of his confines and onto center stage. It's showtime.

Thomas waits for his opponent, his claws fully extended, but his demeanor calm, composed, as if he's simply waiting for the Number 5 bus to come around the corner. The lion, unsure of what to do with prey that won't run away, paces around the Ring, taking slow, deliberate steps, never taking his eyes off the fresh meat in the center.

Slow, barely perceptible movement from Thomas now, as his back begins to bend, curving ever so slightly, his arms stretching out, reaching for the floor, legs curling inward, bracing. With this new curvature of the spine, the plates lining the Stegosaur's back pop an inch or two farther into the air, and the tail makes its way out from between his legs, straightening into a long, fingerlike appendage, waggling back and forth like a giant spiked metronome.

He's down on all fours, small head parallel to the floor, body low, a sponge for all the surrounding gravity, using his own weight to anchor himself in place. There is nothing familiar about the way in which he's standing now, nothing familiar about the way in which his head cocks back and forth. This is not the same fellow who was meditating during dinner half an hour ago. Thomas is becoming something different, something more animal than the mountain lion. It's almost as if he's becoming something he always should have been.

He's becoming a true Stegosaur.

As if it has noticed the change yet is unaware of what it means, the mountain lion takes a tentative step forward, batting a paw through the air. Kitty wanna play. The lion's claws slide in and out, the beast ready for action. Kitty wanna do damage.

In a sudden blur of action, the lion leaps for the Stego, launching itself up and over the dino, aiming for the back of Thomas's neck. It's blindingly fast, and I've barely got time to register the attack before Thomas's tail swings up and over, the spikes glistening, shining as if already covered in blood, and catches the lion behind the front paw, tumbling the cat upside down in the dust.

A new roar, this one from the Stegosaur, a monstrous screech that would send any nearby Japanese scurrying for their Mothra handbooks. A return bellow from the lion, and the enemies have duly stated their intentions.

"When do you stop this?" I ask Circe, who is wholly rapt by the scene below.

"We don't," she says. "Unless . . ."

I assume there's a signal of some kind, but I don't get a chance to ask what it is. With a new series of yelps, the lion is once again on the attack, leaping atop the Stegosaur, straddling the conical spikes lining his spine, planting its teeth into the tough hide protecting the dinosaur's neck and back.

Not tough enough. Blood bursts out of the Stegosaur's hide, and he rears back in pain, his tail flapping through the air, aiming for the lion, trying to make itself useful. But just as the tail orients itself on the attacker, the lion falls from Thomas's back, leaving an open, unprotected patch of skin as an unfortunate target area, and with a sickening squish the Stegosaur flails himself with his own spikes and cries out in what must be horrendous pain. That's gonna hurt tomorrow morning.

The lion is back to stalking his prey, circling the Stego in an attempt to get back up and cause some more damage. A layer of blood has spread across the floor of the Ring, slicking the surface, making the footing slippery. With a sharp jolt to my eardrums, I realize that the crowd has ceased its silence and now shouts unintelligible phrases of encouragement in any number of human languages, as well as some dino dialect with which I am unfamiliar.

Another blur, another furious attack, and this time the Stegosaur's on his back, fending off a rapid series of bites—snapping jaws tearing at the neck, at the arms, at the soft stomach—as his tail swings powerfully, with control, but to little good effect. The bodies roll around the Ring, slamming into the metal bars, limbs entangled, escape impossible for either one.

What I'm noticing, apart from the blood and the bile and the spectacle, is that Thomas is moving like no creature I have ever seen before. His motions are not those of a rational being, nor quite those of a wild animal, either. There are no parries, no formal lunges, no counterattacks, no sense of a defense of any kind—sort of like watching the Redskins play the Eagles. But there is a method to this instinct, a fight-for-life intelligence, and it's fascinating to watch the process develop, which is distinctly *unlike* watching the Redskins play the Eagles.

Now the crowd noise has grown to a frenzy and I find that I'm standing along with them, pumping my fist into the air, shouting out a string of nonsense syllables, grunting in time with the mob. Ernie's on his feet, too, doing the same thing, similarly caught up in the action; only Circe, still sitting between us, remains stoic, though the intensity of her stare tells me she's more into this scene than the rest of us put together.

The Stegosaur plants his tail on the ground and pushes, flipping himself onto his side, throwing the lion off his stomach and to the floor. But the cat's not down for long—it rears back and launches itself yet again, claws extended on all four limbs, shredding whatever flesh manages to get in their way.

Limbs are intertwined, torsos locked, teeth grinding at hide and skin. If there is a victor when all this is over—something I wouldn't be willing to wager on at this time—he will need extensive recuperation. The Ring has become a slaughterhouse, blood sluicing down backs, fronts, tails, legs, and onto the floor an inch deep. A desperate charge at the Stego's neck is stymied by one of the last layers of protective hide, and the lion backs off for a moment, somehow sure that his next bite will indeed be the final one.

Staring. Pacing. The hunt is the only game in town.

A question of speed, perhaps. The mountain lion is faster. It makes the first leap, preparing to nail down final justice and settle in for a nice Stego snack.

But Thomas is ready for the assault, some instinctual part of the brain working to keep that big body fighting despite the life fluids raining out of it at an amazing rate, and he pitches himself backward at the lion's headlong attack, allowing his back-spikes to cushion the fall. In the same move, his tail flips quickly up between his legs—a puppy waiting to be scratched on his belly. The spikes whistle through the air, screaming toward their target, and I can see it coming a split second before it happens:

The tail-spikes sink into the lion's stomach.

A terrible wail of pain cracks the air, and the feline collapses to the ground, blood pouring from this new, gaping wound. Viscera drag on the floor as the lion's bowels let loose, a steady stream of urine soaking the Ring, and a cry of victory errupts from the crowd.

With a pitiful yelp, the mountain lion slinks to the edge of the Ring, trying to find some method of escape. But the bars are too thick to bend and too close-set to squeeze through, and though the lion bites weakly at his confines—teeth grasping the metal struts, mewling pathetically as he tries to snap through steel—there will be no Great Escape tonight. Perhaps the cat can't see that the ceiling of the Ring, twenty feet above, is caged as well, but he makes a few feckless attempts to leap to safety, each time gaining less and less altitude, like a bouncing rubber ball slowing to a stop.

Pain and terror in the creature's eyes, and, throughout it all, confusion. This isn't the way things were supposed to happen. The prey doesn't fight back. The prey should do what the prey has always done, which is sit back and let itself be eaten. Something has gone terribly, terribly wrong.

Compassion has never been a significant part of the animal kingdom, and it's not coming into play now. Before the lion has a chance to mount even a feeble counterattack, the Stegosaur has blanketed him with a volley of tail-swipes and claw-slashes, and by the time I've blinked twice, the lion's carcass has been ripped into a hundred pieces and scattered across the floor of the Ring. The roar of the crowd is thunderous, and I may need to have my hearing checked when we get back to the mainland.

I have a strong feeling that the Progressives are not endorsed by the ASPCA.

The four dinos who acted as Thomas's confederates return to the cage, unlock the door, and lead the blood-splattered victor out of the Ring. It's an odd sight, as Thomas still walks on all fours, an ancient Stegosaur direct from the pages of an encyclopedia, while those who flank him tread along human-style, upright and stiff-backed.

"You understand something of Progress now," Circe says to me.

"I understand the Ring now," I reply. "Progress . . . I don't know."

Thomas disappears beneath the bleachers and into the jungle, a contingent of dinos trailing after him. The lion's corpse is dragged from the Ring, and the crowd begins to mill around, preparing to leave. "What now?" I ask.

"He'll be cared for by a team of doctors, his wounds healed, his body given time to mend."

"And then?"

A momentary pause from Circe, as if she's deciding whether or not to continue this conversation. Her lips purse. "What happens then is not something that can be explained. It must be experienced. Perhaps someday you, too, will be ready."

I'm not sure why Circe has fallen into Yoda-speak, but I am pretty damn positive I'll never be at a point in my life where I need to fight a starving mountain lion in order to feel good about my lineage.

As a host of workers bearing mops and buckets descend upon the cage—what level of Progress nets you the janitor job, I wonder—Circe rises from the dais and prepares to make her way down to the crowd below. But as she begins her descent, a new voice calls out from within the mob of Progressives.

"I am ready!" comes the cry. "I am ready for the Ring!"

The rest of the crowd hushes as Circe climbs back to her chair and peers down at the lone Velociraptor who has made his way into a clearing below. He's big for his race—I'm about average for a Raptor, and he's got at least four inches and twenty pounds on me—and his claws, zinging in and out of their slots, look especially sharp. Too bad his brain doesn't.

"Progress has chosen me!" he shouts up at Circe. "I must be allowed my chance."

The susurration rippling through the crowd is more of appreciation than disbelief, and the Progressives retake their seats accordingly, preparing for an encore performance. Can it be this easy to call destruction down upon yourself?

Ernie reads my mind. "Can he do that? Just announce he wants in?"

Circe nods. "Progress chooses when Progress chooses."

"But he didn't prepare," I point out. "None of that fasting, the meditation, all of the rituals . . ."

"If he is ready for the Ring, then the Ring is ready for him."

Circe, Samuel, and a few other Progressives gather for an impromptu meeting to work out the logistics for the next part of the evening's symposium. The cleanup crew is ordered to abandon their work, and they gladly desert the Ring, its crimson floor still slick with fluid. The Raptor, who has spent the several minutes since his pronouncement in a state of mild hyperventilation, sits on a bench by himself, eyes closed, hands working over each other. This must be his form of meditation, his method of releasing the dino within. Hope it works.

Circe leaves the dais and approaches the young Raptor. "Choose your confederates," she says, and I can hear her perfectly despite the distance between us. The dino quickly approaches four friends— two Raptors, a Diplodocus, and, goodness gracious, a Compy—and they fall into line behind him.

"This is insane," Ernie says to me. "If Rupert was up for the Ring next, I'm glad he got out when he did. Better to die at home than in this . . . nonsense."

Circe repeats the ceremony from the dining hall, announcing that the Raptor is ready to move on to the next level, asking if he's prepared, going through the whole shpiel verbatim. By the time she's fed him a healthy dose of her scent and sent him on his way, Circe has made her way back up to the box. This time, there is no gleam in her eyes.

A cough from the leader, a barely spoken phrase, and though it's but a whisper, I think I can hear her sighing.

The Raptor approaches the entrance, barely keeping his balance, a muscle tremor shaking his left leg as if it's standing on a localized earthquake. But his eyes are steady, his arms calmly by his side, and despite the anxiety welling up in my own chest, this Raptor looks just about as ready to battle untamed beasts as the Stego before him.

A new cage, different from the mountain lion's. This one's covered in a patchwork blanket of blues and blacks, and the four dinos wheeling it toward the Ring have a difficult time keeping it in place, the cage rocking back and forth on its wheels. Whatever's inside that thing is unhappy with its current state of confinement.

The Ring is closed. Locked up tight. The second bout begins.

Once the door between the cage and the Ring has been raised, it takes less than a second for the bull inside to come charging out, six hundred pounds of angry top sirloin aimed at the Raptor's vital organs. Now, I've seen rodeo before—forced into it, actually, by a Hadrosaur I was dating who had a raw leather fetish—but I've never seen a beast like this one. Five feet at the shoulder, horns filed to a dagger point, and mad as an alcoholic who's been eighty-sixed from the IHOP.

Oh. Oh. That's not good. That's not good at all.

The crowd isn't cheering anymore.

I would like to defend my Velociraptor brother, to say that he put up a valiant fight, that he lashed out in a frenzy at the beast, that the total blood loss was equal, but the simple truth is this: the bull gores him right at the get-go.

Without even giving the dino a moment in which to mount a proper defense, the bull charges the Velociraptor, digs its horns into his fleshy side, lifts him into the air with those bulging neck muscles, and easily tosses the Raptor into a heap on the far side of the Ring as if he's nothing more than a used tissue.

It doesn't get any prettier.

I am torn between fascination and repulsion as the fight continues. Mere seconds have gone by, but it feels like this is the end of a twelve-rounder, and I wonder when someone's going to throw in the blood-red towel. I know the last bout on the undercard ended up as a fight to the death, but if it goes that far this time, I doubt the outcome will be so favorable to my species.

It can't be more than ten seconds after the initial goring, and already it's quite clear that the Raptor won't be rejoining the battle anytime soon. He's nothing more than a paper doll to this bull, and just as I'm about to make my objections known, Circe stands and claps her hands three times in succession. At this cue, as if they had been waiting for this all their lives, the four comrade dinos standing by the Ring reach into a long wooden box attached to the bottom set of bleachers. Each pulls out a rifle.

Ernie stands—so do I—so does everyone else in the joint—as the dinos quickly load, take aim, and fire their guns. I expect a sharp report, a typical rifle boom, but all I hear is a swish and a thwip, and suddenly four darts are sticking out of the bull's hide, no more than a half-inch away from one another. Big target, sure, but these were the kind of shots that would make Robin Hood gasp.

With rapid precision—the kind of skill that can only be gained by practice, practice, and more practice—the dinos reload, reaim, and reshoot, and by now the bull has slowed to a halt, lazily glancing around the Ring for the source of these annoying mosquito bites.

The Raptor in the corner is moving, but not in any coherent, connected manner. His claws paw at the steel bars of the Ring, his tongue waggling lazily out of the side of his mouth. The bull turns back to his toy, preparing perhaps to finish it off, but whatever drug they're using works quickly on the bovine beast, and as it takes another step toward the downed dino, the bull's eyes roll up, up, and away, and he goes down hard.

The bull is carted away. The Raptor is carted away. The Ring is cleaned up, polished, sparkling, as if nothing ever happened.

"He will live," Circe says, answering my unasked question.

"He was hurt pretty bad."

"And I've seen worse."

The crowd below is looking up at us, and for a moment, I get the feeling that they're staring at me, as if I somehow caused this to happen to their friend. I want to protest, to proclaim my innocence, but my paranoid delusion wanes as Circe steps in front of me and addresses her followers.

"Progress is a right we all share, yet it is also a responsibility. It must be gained through effort and through introspection, but it is not something which we can choose as we see fit. Progress chooses us; what we do here simply allows it into our lives. This evening, as you lie in your nests, as you replay this evening's events in your minds and wonder if you will ever be ready for the Ring, ask yourself if you can understand the ancestors. Ask yourself if you are capable of releasing your learned inhibitions. Ask yourself: Am I acting through Progress, or is Progress acting through me?

"Goodnight, brothers and sisters. I will see you tomorrow."

And with that, the group disbands. Circe falls back into her seat and watches the crowd stream out of the amphitheater; Ernie and I do likewise, waiting for the right moment to excuse ourselves and hoof it back to our hut and the oh-so-comfy confines of the nest.

Time passes, and soon there are few of us left in the vicinity of the Ring. Circe continues to stare out into space, not quite catatonic but not quite *here*, either, unresponsive to the few acolytes who approach to bid her good evening. There won't be a reception line tonight, it seems, so Ernie and I take this opportunity to sneak off—

"Wait." It's Circe, and I have no choice but to stop. Ernie's got his hands on my shoulders, holding me tight, but I can't help but turn around. A single tear has wormed its way out of the corner of her eye and leaves a trail of moisture as it slides down one delicately rounded cheek, across her face, and between those two luscious lips.

"Vincent, would you like to join me for a nightcap?"

It's not appropriate. It's not proper. And I'd bet half my take-home pay that behind my back, Ernie is blasting his disapproval toward me with a stare that would make Medusa envious.

"I'd love to," I say, shaking off my partner's hands and trotting over to the fragile cult leader. "Your hut or mine?"

16

id I say hut? The Raptor was mistaken. Whatever funds were
not being spent on the overall adornment of the Progressive
compound were obviously rerouted to the construction and
interior decoration of Circe's pleasure palace here in the
center of the island. The walls sparkle with some unidentifiable
substance that is not quite diamond and not quite pearl, but I
have a feeling that a square foot of it would buy my condo, my
car, and all of the basil I could eat for a decade.

Not that there's a shortage of the evil herb. From the moment
we make our way into the main house via the twelve-foot double
doors, my arm interlocked with Circe's, our mood already jovial
from the refreshing half-mile jaunt up the private walkway, we
are surrounded by sycophants bearing all manner of earthly
delights. Platters piled with parsley, trays towering with thyme—
it's available, it's fresh, and, best of all, it's free.

I am not a mooch, but I play one while undercover.

"Help yourself, Vincent," Circe tells me. She's already

downed a quarter-pound of marjoram, and she's onto the fenu-greek without stopping to take a breath. "The cumin is quite good."

I'd like to have a taste of it all, actually, to romp through this spectacular buffet of mind-benders, but part of my reason for allowing Circe to take me back to her place is to do some serious probing—*questions*, probing *questions*—and I'll need a compara-tively clear head if I'm going to pull it off. Still, a lick or two of cumin can't hurt . . .

And some saffron for good luck.

And some fennel, because I haven't tried it in years.

And a few handfuls of basil to take back to Ernie, because that's the kind of guy I am.

Before I realize it, my bloodstream is full to bursting with sprigs and leaves, and Circe and I are out of the foyer and walk-ing down a long, ornate hallway. Through a far door, I can make out row after row of dry-cleaning racks and a host of drooping human guises hanging to the ground. This must be where my costume is being kept; I hope they've got it smelling piney-fresh.

Soon, before my body has had a chance to dart a memo up to my mind, Circe and I are seated in a large leather loveseat, the high back and wide arms encompassing our bodies, cradling us as one. Circe's long legs dangle over mine, her left underclaw scrap-ing lightly against my knee. We're in a study of some sort, the walls lined with old portraits of austere dinosaurs unfamiliar to me.

"I hope you've been enjoying yourself," she says.

I play it coy. "You've got a nice little island. Nice little group. How long has this Progress thing been around, anyway?"

"Has the time come when we ask each other questions?"

Her initial reluctance to answer my offhand remark reminds me why I'm here in the first place. Yet all of this chitchat, the easy access to herbs, and, yes, the close proximity of a perfect dinosaur specimen of my own race and opposite gender has indeed lulled me into forgetting the task at hand. But now you're back on track, Vincent—full speed ahead and no tugging at the brake.

Grunting with the effort—both physical and mental—I remove Circe's legs from my own, stand, and stroll as steadily as possible across the study. "We can play footsie anytime. I'm here to learn, remember?"

"And so you are. And so you shall."

"You get off talking that way?" I ask her.

"It's better than the other way."

"What's that?"

"Grunting."

Strange lady. Strange place. "You've got a nice island."

She nods, smiling. "Thank you. We try."

"Big. Lots of forest. You only seem to be using a small part of it, though."

"The jungle is beautiful," Circe admits, "though we rarely go in. The other side of the island is . . . different."

I nod, pacing slightly. One step forward, one step back, cha cha cha. "Different how?"

"Changed. Mutated. This island was one of the original sites used for early atomic testing."

Instantly, my skin begins to crawl with a thousand radioactive particles, my entire body sending out a furious, massive itch signal to my frantic brain. Isn't this how Godzilla was born?

But Circe can read me well enough to understand my concern, and she's quickly shaking her head, caressing my arm to assuage my fears. "We're fine over here," she insists. "This side of the island is free of radiation; we have bimonthly Geiger counter sweeps."

"So what's over there?" I ask, ever the curious kitten. "On the other side?"

"I don't know. We've declared it off-limits, for everyone's safety."

We stare at each other. She's lovely.

Time to break the silence, if only to hear myself talk, make sure she hasn't pulled an herb trick and charmed me into a mute. "So, *you* go through a test like that?" I ask. "The Ring?"

"At some point, we all have to 'go through' our little tests. Some are different from others."

I scratch my chin, making a big show of it. This is my attentive look. "So you're saying you've never been in the Ring."

"Very perceptive, Mr. Rubio." I think she may be mocking me, but the herbs have made it difficult for me to distinguish sarcasm from sincerity. "Suffice it to say that the Ring would not be a substantial challenge for me, but if I were to test myself in that arena, I would no longer be fit to lead the group down their path to Progress."

"Would you like to elaborate on that?"

"No."

A polished mahogany desk with brass handles has become my new seat; I place my butt on its surface, the cool wood providing a nice counterpoint to the steamy climate. Haven't these people heard of air conditioning? At least the ancestors were bright enough to manufacture a fan or two, I'd imagine.

"Kind of messy back there, that Raptor getting gored by the bull," I say.

"Sadly, it happens."

"Often?"

"No," she says, "but even once is more than I like to see. Our members are eager to reclaim their true identities, and sometimes their enthusiasm gets in the way of good judgment."

"It was a big bull."

"And he was a strong Raptor. When the combatant is ready, I assure you, there are no unfair battles in the Ring. He'll be taken care of by the doctors, and I doubt he will make such an error again. The next time, he will let Progress take its course." Circe slides over on the chair. "Are you ready to take a seat again? There's room."

I ignore the come-on and stay put. "You have Ring competitions every night?"

"Only when they're called for."

"What if some Diplodod wants to go head-to-head with Simba but you're not in Hawaii?"

"We have other Rings," says Circe, "in other locations."

"Where?"

"Some things are better to find out as time passes. Stay with us and you will know in time."

I jump off the desk and start to wander the room, staring up at the oak-framed oil paintings hung on the maroon walls. All manner of dinosaurs have been captured in delicate portraiture, each one a study in wrinkles and creases and worn hides. These dudes are old.

"The ancestors?" I ask.

"Hardly. That one to your left was a university president back in the late nineteenth century; the Coelo next to him is J. Edgar Hoover. Other than that, I don't know who most of them are, to be honest. This was Raal's study."

"*Was.*"

"Yes, was."

"So he's dead?"

A lick of those lips, focusing on the corner of her mouth. "So they say."

Odd how this little duckling keeps changing her story. Earlier, she was quite adamant that he was alive and kicking, just unavailable for comment. "Did you know him?"

"Yes."

"How long did you know him?"

Circe stands and turns away from me, heading to a wet bar jutting out from the far wall. A steady waterfall streams out from a tap there, and Circe reaches out with that long tongue and laps up some of the elixir. Even from here, I can smell the herb infusion. "I invited you up here for a nightcap—"

"—and I'm staying for the company," I finish. "If you want me to stop with the questions . . ."

"Fifteen years. After that, he was gone."

"And you presume he's dead."

"I presume nothing. Raal was nearly one hundred percent dinosaur natural, and he could accomplish quite a great deal more with one flick of his tail than we could do in a lifetime of struggle."

I suggest, "You were his protégée."

"If you want to call it that. He led me into Progress."

"How?"

Seemingly a simple question, I think, but that one syllable sends Circe back to the waterfall to slurp up another gallon of happy juice. Strangely enough, she's not getting drunk off her beautiful behind; if she is, I am unable to notice the least change in her demeanor. I'd be knocking into walls and excusing myself to doorknobs by this point, but maybe she's worked up a tolerance to the stuff.

"Stay here," she says, and then slinks out a side door, leaving me to my lonesome in this boring study; she could have at least left me alone in a game room. A high-backed leather recliner stands behind the desk, a classic power chair if ever I've seen one, brass buttons dotting the extra-thick cowhide, the leather burnished to a high gloss, the fabric nearly as slippery as Mr. Levitt's slipcover formula back in Thousand Oaks. This thing's a lawsuit waiting to happen—I bet if I sit on it right, I can fall off at just the angle to split my head open and let the punitive judgments come pouring in.

But my greed muscle isn't flexing as strong as my snoop muscle today, and so as soon as I take a seat at what must have been Raal's desk, I can't stop my fingers from grabbing a paper clip out of the desk organizer and bending it into a makeshift lock-pick. This is not a matter of choice; it's a reflex that simply takes over at various times, and there is little I can do to halt the action. There are five drawers in this desk—two to either side, one directly in the middle—and all are practically pleading with me to unlock and uncover their hidden treasures. I'm like Geraldo, only without the TV cameras to provide that extra level of embarrassment.

After a few moments of twisting the small bit of metal in the lock, I realize that the damned thing isn't even closed all the way; whoever used it last was negligent in locking it back up tight, and I'm not one to finish others' work. I open it wide.

Accounting sheets. Red ink, black ink, red ink, black ink, it's a mess of gains and losses, income and expenditures, and I can't figure out a lick of it. The last math class I ever took ended with a protractor stuck halfway up my nose—don't ask, don't ask—and since then I've steered clear of the world of numbers.

But there are certain subheadings under which even I can recognize some massive outflows of cash. Something on the order of six and a half million dollars left the coffers of the Progressives no more than a month ago, and though it doesn't say where this money went, there are very few herb dealers who charge more than a few bucks per kilo of basil.

It's not just good old American sawbucks, either. There's lira and deutschmarks and kroner and a number of other types of currency I don't even recognize. Whatever it is they're buying, they're buying it in more countries than just this one; I only wish I knew what the Progressives were paying so much for. But one thing's for sure—no matter the breed, this puppy is global.

I'm about to look further when I hear familiar footsteps making their approach. I quickly shove the papers back into the desk drawer—crumpling them in the process, I am sure—and toss the paper clip in the direction of a nearby trash bin. It misses. My three-point shot needs a lot of work.

When Circe enters the room, she's holding a thin photo album, the cover blank, the spine unwritten upon. Retaking her place on the loveseat, Circe beckons to me. "I haven't shown this to anyone in years," she says softly, "and if you're going to look at it, you might as well sit by me."

Fair enough. Not that it's such a chore, mind you, but I was hoping to keep this professional.

Ah, who am I kidding? No I wasn't.

The scrapbook opens up with a modest three-bedroom house

somewhere in the suburbs. Lawn jockey, pink flamingo, station wagon in the driveway, the works. On the front porch, man and wife, smiling at the camera, picture of domestic bliss. "This was my house," says Circe. "These were my parents."

I'm surprised, mainly because the broad in the photos is all made up good and proper, like she's going out for dinner and a show. Dinosaurs are usually frustrated enough with the morning routine of buckling in and strapping on that the females rarely have the time or patience to apply an extra layer of face paint to a face that's not even theirs in the first place. In fact, the more granola a female, the more likely she's a lizard in ape's clothing. We go for simplification as often as possible; it's no coincidence, for example, that the bra burning movement was started by a Bronto who had dealt with one strap too many.

"They look nice."

She smiles wistfully. "I'm sure they were. They died when I was one."

"I'm sorry. You were an orphan?"

"Not until then." She turns the page. A baby, pink and gurgling—well, mid-gurgle, anyhow—lying in a bassinet, reaching up for the photographer, chubby little fists stretching to the air.

"You?"

"Before my parents ... went away. The guise was a Blaupunkt—it's the one thing I have from my childhood. At least, it's the one thing I want to keep."

The next series of pictures are not quite so rosy. Rows of girls ranging from toddlers to teens lined up in precise formations, smiling robotically at the camera, shabby uniforms and shiny shoes, eyes dead and defeated.

"St. Helena's Home for Wayward Girls," says Circe. "They didn't like me much," she explains. "I got picked on, but that wasn't the worst of it. An orphanage isn't the best place for a young girl—"

"I know," I interrupt, eager to console. "I saw *Annie*."

Laughter—unexpected, but welcome—as Circe shuts the

book and turns toward me. "*Annie* might be the representation of a human orphanage, Vincent—though I doubt it—but the facilities for dinosaurs were even worse than your theatrical version would have you believe."

"That's not—I didn't mean—"

"The sisters who ran the place had decided that since the world was mostly human anyway, they would teach us to be more mammal than mammals. Horrible creatures, every one of them, shrieking at us every time they smelled an iota of scent coming from our bodies. We were forced to wrap our necks in heavy cloths in order to soak up the pheromones, then spray ourselves with Lysol to cover up the remainder. Hot baths were next, steel wool raked against our hides—anything to get rid of the scent.

"All they wanted to do was drill the dino out of us. They wouldn't be satisfied until we were indistinguishable from the apes. I spent every single morning in that place staring at myself in the mirror, at that hideously pointed snout, those terrible claws, that horrendous tail, hating every last vestige of my reptilian heritage.

"My best friend even went so far as to cut off her tail—went into the machine shop one morning, turned on the buzzsaw, and just sliced it right off—and even though she died, even though her desire to be human was stronger than her desire for life, I remember at the time not horror, not revulsion, but thinking *Janine's so cool, why can't I do that?*"

Can't help but swallow, a big throat-clearing gulp. "Why didn't you?" I ask.

"Raal found me before I worked up the nerve. He came to the home, interviewed a few of the girls, and when he found me, he said he was done. He said he'd been searching for ten years for the one who could lead our people out of bondage. He didn't even wait for the adoption papers to come through—he came for me that night, snuck me out of my room, out of the orphanage, and we took off."

"You believed him, then?"

"Not a bit. But he had food, he had herbs, he had freedom, and for a girl about to hit her teens inside an orphanage, he was Moses and Jesus and Keith Partridge all wrapped up in one."

"And then?"

"And then my training began. Years of patience and understanding, of Raal trying to show me who I was—more importantly, *what* I was. Teaching me to use my natural gifts, and teaching me to love myself again."

I can't help myself; maybe it's the story, the late night, or the last remaining herbs in my system, but this thought jumps out of my lips before I can close the drawbridge—"He taught you the scent trick."

"He taught me the scent trick," she repeats, taking my hand in hers, and a fiery tingle shoots up my arm and straight into my chest. "Which is not so much a trick as it is a natural function, like breathing or walking. It's integral."

"How?"

"The scent allows us access to our true selves. Anything is possible—connection, extension, even hibernation. When you are sure of yourself, it fades into the background, becomes part of your system. It's all natural.

"But each dinosaur is different," she tells me. "We all have many things in common, but we're like humans in the sense that we all have varying degrees of talent."

And as she speaks, I can feel her talent beginning to come on strong. Not a quick jab like the other times she knocked me out, but a slow, steady massage, rolling over me in waves of sugar and spice and everything nice. The room begins to waver, the walls shimmying in and out, waving to me as if to say *Goodnight, Vincent, y'all come back real soon* . . .

But I'm continuing with these questions, damn it, and I use whatever strength I've got left to fight past the smells and form the proper words. "And that's why he picked you," I manage to say. "You had it in spades. . . ."

Circe nods, and from my vantage point, it looks like her

whole body is nodding along. The walls are losing their opacity, becoming more and more transparent. "I left the world," she is saying, "and learned from Raal. He said I had a gift he hadn't seen before. He said that together we would free our species from their shackles. He said that the only path to understanding ourselves was tooiagh greaarlar, and by doing so, laareeeeach orrarelearghhh in the wrolaaergh—"

A babble of nonsense yelps and groans pours from her mouth, mixing some foreign tongue with the only language I know. But she goes right on speaking—growling, grunting—as if it's the plainest English in the world.

As the last remaining walls give way, I reach out and try to grab hold of the loveseat—something to keep me rooted in place. My hands encounter fabric, a good sign, but it's not long before it changes to bark. I look down to find my fingers grasping tight to an ancient tree stump, and by the time I look up again, the study is gone.

I'm in the forest again.

You'd think by now I'd know my way around this darn jungle, but it's got a different feel to it this time. In the previous experiments with Circe and her magical scent, the forest was almost as translucent as reality, a not-quite-here slice of un-life, but this tree trunk is real enough to be scratching my butt something fierce, and should the Pterodactyl hovering above me—a creature that should be long extinct—decide to do its business over my head, you can bet I'm not going to sit tight and hope it's all a mirage.

I stand, and the leaves beneath my feet crinkle against my toes, tickling them, caressing them. Unfamiliar sounds—songs, calls, the joyous shout of all this nature—bounce from tree to tree and back to my ears, delighting me every bit along the way. A thick layer of air blankets everything in sight, and I find myself laboring to breathe, relearning the very act itself. I touch another tree, and it, too, is solid. Right here. Right now.

A caress across my chest, a light finger tracing down, down, the motion coming from behind. Hot breath on my ear. "Do you like it?"

It's Circe. "How—"

"Shh. Do you like it?"

"Yesss," I sigh, hissing the last in a long, sharp exhale. This is not the way my relationships usually start out—I am the seductor, not the seductee—but as long as I'm already standing in a world that can't possibly exist, I might as well let nature take its course, no matter how twisted it may seem.

"Let go," she whispers. "The end of days."

Arms grasping me tighter, encircling my body, and I turn to face my new lover, our tongues already seeking out each other, snaking in and out and around, licking sweat, saliva, scent. My arms, rising of their own accord, holding Circe tighter, lifting her off the ground, fingers clenched around the base of her tail, stroking her back, placing her where she needs to be—where *I* need her to be—

And we're moving now, our feet stationary but the ground beneath rippling by, churning ahead as we begin to make love, rocking back and forth as I plunge myself into her, rolling over in a bed of air, the trees streaming past, leaves whacking past our naked bodies, her legs tight around my body, mouth open, calling out—

Speed rising, growing faster, Circe's claws snapping into place, raking down my back, the pain exhilarating, my snout pulling wide, teeth biting down hard on her shoulder, pelvis thrusting into hers, hard as I've ever been, sweat pouring off our bodies, dripping down our tails, onto the ground below, disappearing in that brown-and-yellow blur, head spinning, sky overhead cartwheeling around and about our bodies—

My own smells rising, mixing with hers, our pheromones making their own sort of love as a howl rises up from my chest, matching Circe's own scream of craving, both of us slamming against each other, no simple sex but a furious animal assault of carnal lust—every tree disappearing now, the world going with it, the leaves, the dirt, the ground, the sky, circling, cycling, nothing holding us up as we tuck into each other, claws imbedded, teeth imbedded, my entire body wrapped up in hers and hers in mine—

Mind shutting down, body left on autopilot, thrusting, feeling—

Never-ending—always like this—

Pain, pleasure, pain—

Then a light, streaming from above—a shriek, not animal, not living—the sky, burning, a hole torn in the clouds—heat, fiery heat as I begin to blast my seed inside her, as I grunt and let loose, a sizzling stream, burning me, needling me—Circe pulling me down, pulling me in, mouth open wide, a low moan of horror and of ecstasy—we are together—we are one—and still from above, louder now, that terrible noise, that ferocious noise, that apocalyptic noise—growing closer, the burning larger, larger, encompassing the sky, everything on the verge of everything else, and—and—

Darkness.

17

My pillow tastes like poi, which tastes like nothing so much as . . . nothing. If I've learned anything in Hawaii, it's that both of them—poi and my pillow—are useless gobs of empty nutrition, neither of which should be in my mouth at any point during the day or night. But as the morning light streams onto my face and I awaken lethargically in my nest, Ernie lightly shaking me—then not-so-lightly shaking me as I tell him where to stuff it—I find my arms clutched tight around a roll of twigs and my snout stuffed with leaves and bark shavings.

"Wake up—we're gonna miss breakfast."

"That'd be a shame," I mumble.

It takes another five minutes of poking and prodding before I'm up and halfway willing to face the world. I should have a hangover, but for some reason I've been spared the anguish, and this seems like a good omen for the day. As I climb out of my nest—perfectly formed, by the way, which means that Ernie must have done me a construction favor sometime last evening—my knees popping, my arms automatically stretching, reaching for the sky, I hear Ernie's low whistle behind me.

"Did a number on yourself last night, eh, kid?"

If I did, I certainly don't recall which number that could be. There was a trip to Circe's castle, dining on some herbs, a little Q&A, a little romance, a little dream, and then . . . nothing. "Whatcha talking about?"

"Your back."

"What about it?"

"You can't feel that?"

Still confused, I try to reach an arm up and over my body, hoping to get a feel of whatever Ernie's talking about. No luck. Lucky for me, though, Ernie's got perfect access. He jabs his finger into my spine, and there's a sharp needle of pain, the kind of sting you get when you jump in the ocean and find out exactly where every single tiny cut on your body happens to be located.

"The hell is it?" I ask.

"A scratch. You got a whole crossroads back there. I got a feeling you weren't exactly interrogating the witness, were you?"

Depends on how you look at it. "Sure, I did," I tell him, and then fill him in on the details of Circe's induction into Progress by the ever-elusive and probably dead Raal.

"And the scratches?" he asks.

There's no need to tell him about the forest and the running and the . . . the . . . that last part, with the light and the fury and the explosion. Eventually, perhaps once I figure it out myself, I'll let him in on whatever induced fantasies I've been privy to, but for right now my hallucinations are a private party, and I'm the only one on the guest list. "No clue." Then, to change the subject, I tell him, "I did find a pretty strange ledger, though. Lots of foreign money jumping around this place. Almost as if they're laundering it."

A rising cackle bursts through the walls of the hut and assaults my ears, almost like a trumpet but two degrees more annoying in tone and timbre. And whoever's playing the damn thing doesn't even have the simple dino decency to play "Summertime" or "Take the A Train." No, this is "Louie, Louie." And it's endless. "The hell is that?" I cry, my jaw shaking, my claws zinging out of their slots of their own accord.

No answer from the others, but suddenly the stampede is on. Arms and tails whap me across the face, torsos slam into mine, as I collapse onto my nest, shattering it back into its component parts, a thousand undifferentiated branches and brambles scattering across the ground.

Ernie stands over me, shaking his head back and forth. "Can't go back to bed yet, kid. Breakfast is served."

It takes a good deal of mental effort to stumble naked out of the hut, fighting the urge to guise myself up all the way. Even if I were to give in to the desire to costume my nude body, though, the decision would be moot; our guises have not been returned to the hut. I can only guess that once they're available, Samuel will hang them on the outside doorknob like a hotel dry-cleaner, but there may indeed be some arcane method of guise retrieval in this place.

"Feels strange, huh?" I ask Ernie as we prepare to step outside.

"Been quite a while," he agrees. "Strange doesn't begin to cover it."

Indeed, this weekend may be the first time since my middle school days—rebellious times, wild times—that I have left the confines of a home without my human skin on, the first time I've stepped onto soil without wrapping myself up in interminable buckles and belts and straps and latex and false goodwill for the rival species. At the very least, I'm sure to get a sunburn in some naughty places.

I may like it. I may not. I can't decide yet.

The clearing looks a little better in the bright morning light—now I can see larger structures situated nearby, a few buildings that look like they're made of something more than Lincoln Logs—but it still ain't Fantasy Island. A steady stream of other dinos make their way toward the low, long redwood dining hut set off to one corner of the encampment, and Ernie and I join the herd.

The trumpeter is still bawling for all he's worth, and on the way inside the hut, I lash out with my tail and flick the Hadrosaur making all those god-awful screeching noises across the snout. For a moment, at least, "Louie, Louie" is silenced.

The pheromones are overpowering in the mess hall, but it's nothing compared to how it smelled during last night's dinner. Morning's always a weak time for pheromone production; our glands don't really get moving until the rest of us does, which makes it hard to track malfeasants anytime before nine A.M. But it's still coming strong, the combined fragrance of a hundred "brothers" and "sisters," and it takes all my effort to keep myself from searching out Circe's scent. Time for that later. Eat first, detect next.

Breakfast is served family-style, and Ernie and I take a seat at a long, wooden bench next to a young, strapping Coelo and a not-so-young, not-so-strapping T-Rex. The poor thing's already-shrunken arms have withered away to flappy little stumps, and I wonder how he's going to reach across the table for his food.

Or why he would want to. In the center of the table are a host of large ceramic bowls, each filled to the brim with our breakfast: eggs. Raw eggs. Raw eggs still in their shells.

I look to Ernie, who looks back to me. We stare at each other in quiet desperation. "Maybe there's an omelet line," I suggest.

By way of answer, the other dinos at our table reach for the bowl, grab an egg in each hand, and toss the little boogers into their mouths, shell and all. A furious crunching fills the air, yolk and shell splattering the table, teeth chomping and throats swallowing, my stomach doing topsy-turvies in anticipation of the salmonella to come.

A glance around the room shows me that Ernie and I aren't the only ones who aren't hip to the raw-egg scene. At least two or three dinos at every table are glancing worriedly around the mess hall, looking for someone else—anyone else—who's maintaining a decent level of sanity and hygiene. My eyes meet up with those of a female Triceratops whose frantic mouthings I can read from across the room: *Do we have to?*

Then again, I did eat some version of raw pork last evening, so I shouldn't have any qualms about ingesting something further back along the developmental time line. What's more, I have to play this out like Olivier doing Hamlet if I want to stay in the Progressives' good graces. Sad to say, I live for my job. Look out, lips—watch out, gums—sorry, ol' stomach, 'cause here it comes.

Gooey. Chewy. The shells scratch my throat.

"I like the big ones, myself." A familiar voice, rising behind me.

"I like the little ones."

"We're different that way."

I turn to find Buzz and Wendell hovering over me once again, watching me chew down the excuse for food that has the audacity to call itself breakfast. They're fully unguised, of course, and the twin Carnotaurs let their tails dangle down to the dirt floor below. I've been trying to keep mine aloft since I woke up—I'm not a stickler for cleanliness, but something about a dirty tail has always unnerved me—yet I doubt that the muscular control will last.

"You boys want my share?" asks Ernie, holding out an egg in each hand.

"We couldn't," say Buzz and Wendell in unison. "We shouldn't." Then, after a perfectly timed pause—technically *just* long enough for Ernie to recant—they reach out and snatch the eggs away, much as I imagine my close ancestral cousins, the Oviraptors, might have done millions of years ago. The twins don't even bother munching; they swallow the eggs whole, like giant caplets of Tylenol, and grin all the way.

"Aren't you having a blast?" says Buzz. It is not a question.

"Thrilled," I respond.

"It's the best," says Wendell.

"The best. Are you ready for the training?" Buzz asks eagerly.

I shake my head. "What training?"

"I love the training," Wendell chimes in. "The training is the best part."

A gong sounds at the front of the breakfast room, and before I can turn around to locate the instrument itself, the rush for the doors is on. Brown clouds of dirt rise in the air, and I'm pushed in every direction, battered about by a score of tails and flailing limbs. It's like midnight at Altamont (the rumor, by the way, that all Hell's Angels are Raptors is rude, scandalous, and not without merit), and within seconds, it's just me, Ernie, and a few more dazed souls staring around, wondering what the hell happened to our peaceful little scene.

Guess it's time for training.

· · ·

"The first thing you need to teach yourselves is how to run," our group leader is saying. She's a beast of a Brontosaurus—firm, stocky legs and a tail with muscular definition rippling the thick hide. With inflections somewhere between a loving mother and a Marine drill sergeant, she's been riding us all morning on the basics of her subject.

For this first part of the morning, we've been split into groups by our Progress level. The eighteen first-timers—"virgins," as they're fond of calling us—have been clumped together and thrown headfirst into the rough waters of dino training. As such, we spend a lot of time looking at one another with mystified glances. This is one of those times.

Fortunately, a hand in the crowd shoots up. "Don't we already know how to run?" asks a fellow Raptor, whose own lower body ripples with power.

The Bronto, whose name is Bleeeach—or Blanche, as she instructed us newbies to call her—gives a shrug of those over-built shoulders. "You think you know how?" she asks.

"I ran track in high school," says the young Raptor. "All-State in the hundred-yard dash."

"Impressive. Which state?"

"Utah."

"A lot of good dinos from Utah." No kidding—Joseph Smith was the first to codify the needs of the dino public, but he bathed his group in a spiritual, rather than physical, light so as to avoid detection. The Mormon flight from New York was not at all religious in nature; rather, it was reptilian. "I imagine you believe you could beat me in a footrace."

The Raptor waves his hand through the air, though not in a dismissive gesture. "You're a Bronto," he points out, his tone respectful, embarrassed to remind her that her race isn't capable of achieving the same frightening ground speed as his.

"And? Aren't we all brothers and sisters?"

"Yes, but . . . I'm a Raptor." No response. He elaborates. "We're just . . . faster."

Within a minute, the implied challenge has been accepted and an impromptu racetrack set up. The contestants—Blanche and the young virgin—take their places, our instructor cool and confident, not even bothering to drop into a three-point stance at the line, while the Raptor has tensed himself up, limbs trembling, ready to jump at the sound of the starting shriek. He's a spring coiled and ready to explode, while our trainer is just a loose rubber band dangling on a hook. It appears that the student will eclipse the teacher on this day.

"Down the road, around the far tree, and back," says the Bronto, marking out a trail a good hundred yards long.

"Is that all?" Now he's cocky.

"Still think you can beat me?" she asks.

No time to answer. The designated shrieker, a female Compy whose tea-rose-and-ocean-spray scent is remarkably pleasant for one of her type, marches forward, counts down, "Three—two—" and then issues forth a piercing yelp to signal the start of the race.

By the time the Raptor is clear of the starting line, Blanche is thirty yards down the field, a murky blur kicking up dust. It's hard to tell, but I think she's down on all fours, her legs cycling so fast I can't be certain.

By the time the Raptor has sped a quarter of the way to the tree, Blanche has already made the turn and is heading back.

By the time the Raptor has collapsed in the dust, tripping over a cavalcade of rocks that have managed to fall precisely in his path, Blanche has crossed the finish line, sat herself down on a nearby tree stump, and crossed her arms to wait for his inevitable, groveling finish.

"Now," she says once we've all gathered around and the young Raptor has sucked up all the available oxygen in the air, "is everyone ready to learn how to run?"

At first, there's nothing different about it. It's your basic jog-of-the-mill running, no record-breaking times in my near future—those Hadrosaurs who win the Boston Marathon every year have nothing to worry about. The legs pump, the feet move, the body comes along for the ride. Maybe the tail gets in the way once in a while, but running is running and it's something we've done since we could stand up and take a look around. Don't see how that's going to get us to achieve the supersonic speeds that Blanche displayed.

"Don't think human," Blanche tells us. "It's so ingrained in us to move like them, to walk like they walk, to run like they run. It's not natural for us to worry about how foolish we look with our tails bouncing up and down, or if we're keeping our butts tucked in tight enough. Let loose. Forget humanity."

Forget humanity. There's a dream.

Nothing still. An hour, two hours, and my muscles are fatiguing, throwing off slow, steady waves of pain, demanding of the other parts of my body that they unionize as soon as possible and insist on regular coffee breaks from management.

I ask to be excused. Permission is denied.

But just as I'm about to give up, once I've informed my legs that their services will no longer be needed today, that they can take off and head out to dinner—following hours spent running under the warm Hawaii sun, my tail no longer held aloft, away from the dirt below, but instead released, allowed to dangle to the ground, to push and to thrust and help out if need be—once I'm at that point of complete, dial-911-and-don't-hang-up exhaustion, some part of my body sends a telegram to my brain to the effect that I may very well be moving faster than before.

Trick of the mind. Can't be.

But there it is, an odd sensation of speed, accompanied by a new muscle memory in my legs. I can't explain it, but I can feel it. A loping move, a lurching leap that is anything but natural in the human-inflected world in which I usually live, but that's what it is. I can't say that the motion is pure dinosaur, and I'm sure as heck not going to say that it means I've Progressed, but for the first time in my life I'm running free, unencumbered by all those straps and buckles, my naked face turned up to the sky, the ground flowing strong beneath me, trees streaming by in a steady brown blur, my legs and arms and tail and whole being churning in some motion that should be impossibly uncomfortable but somehow strikes me as purely and simply . . . natural.

It's time for lunch.

. . .

Which is hen. Not cornish, not roasted, but a game hen of some sort, unplucked, uncooked, and very much un-dead. Inside the mess hall, a wooden stake has been hammered into the ground next to each table, and a flock of these hens tied to each one with a single strand of twine. A frenzied squawking and flapping fill the air—these poor girls can sense that it's all over for their little birdy selves, and I can't blame them for going out with as much noise as they can muster. I can't imagine the proper procedure for lunch, but I have a feeling Martha Stewart would not approve.

As the Progressives enter the mess hall, famished from a hard day swimming with crocodiles or some other inane bloodsport, they coo with delight. Hen Day! What a treat! With careful delib-eration, as if they're deciding on the purchase of a new luxury automobile, each dino chooses his or her bird from the buffet post, snaps the tether with a single claw, lifts the hen to a wide, gaping mouth, and bites the poor flapping thing's head clean off before spitting it into a nearby bucket. Once the body has stopped moving, it's time to feast on the goo inside.

"You gonna try that?" Ernie asks me tentatively.

"You?"

"You seemed to like breakfast," he points out.

I can't deny that. Maybe it wouldn't hurt to give this a try; I am famished, after all, and nourishment is nourishment. I've eaten cornish game hen before; perhaps not so animated, but what's a little sentience when it comes to nutrition? The more I watch the others eating, the more my own hunger grows.

Before I've even spoken to the rest of my body about the matter, my arms act of their own accord, reaching out and snatching a hen from the closest post, snipping the wire tethering the bird to its only form of protection.

Somewhere, far in the background, Ernie is asking me what the hell I think I'm doing.

It's as if I'm outside myself, watching a completely different Velociraptor stretch his jaw wide open, drool slavering from between his teeth, and lift a squawking, flapping game hen up to his mouth.

My lips close around the bird before I let my teeth crunch down, and in that moment, I can feel the hen's beak pecking furiously, frantically at my gums. It wants out, in a big way. But I have no control over my jaws; they begin to make the final movement that will snap the head off this bird and send that beautiful, tasty fluid deep into my mouth, my throat, my belly. I will be sated. . . .

A hand on my shoulder. "Vincent!"

I turn, game hen body poking out of my mouth, the bird having stopped his pecking for a moment, as if to listen in. Ernie's disapproval is palpable; he shakes his head back and forth, slowly, deliberately. "Put down the bird, kid."

That's all it takes. Reason suddenly floods back into the void of my brain, and I realize that if I bite off this hen's head, it will most likely continue with its Woody Woodpecker imitation inside my mouth long after decapitation, which will, in turn, make me nauseous enough to lose not only lunch, but probably this morning's breakfast as well.

I gingerly withdraw the hen from my mouth, apologize to my fine friend, dry off its feathers with a few quick puffs of air, and tie the creature back to its tether. Of course, it's no sooner back at the post, its stay of execution granted, than another dino snatches it by the legs and tosses it down the hatch.

Circe is not around today, so there will be no safe and sound mammalian lunch for us. Then again, if she were here, I wonder what direction my afternoon meal would have taken—would she find me some cooked, non-flapping comestible, or would she somehow have convinced me, through pheromones, hormones, or rational debate, to partake of the live bird? Better not to know, perhaps.

Buzz and Wendell make their way over, plucking feathers from the corners of their mouths, wiping up stray drips of blood with long, waggling tongues. "Great seminar today, don'tcha think?" says Wendell, slapping me across the back. "One more, and then it's free time. Lounge around, practice what we've learned."

"Walk around the facilities, work up an appetite before dinner," adds Buzz. "It's a nice time of day to relax."

Free time sounds like an excellent concept to me; perhaps something productive might come of it. "Think you boys would be interested in giving us a tour of the place?" I ask. "During this free time of ours? There's some areas of the island I'd love to see."

"We'd be delighted!" gurgles Buzz.

"Thrilled!" says Wendell.

"Any place you want to go, we'll take you."

"Anywhere?"

"Anywhere," Buzz confirms.

"The other side of the island?" I try.

Wendell pulls his brother aside and whispers a few choice words into his ear hole. "That's off-limits," says Buzz, coming up from the huddle. "Anywhere other than that."

"Why?" asks Ernie. "What's wrong with that?"

"Radiation," whispers Wendell.

Buzz nods hard enough to snap his neck and joins in. "It was a testing site—"

"A nuclear testing site—"

"And the radiation is dangerous—"

"It could kill you—"

"Before you even know it!"

"That's what they told you?" asks Ernie.

"That's what we know," replies Wendell.

I make a big show of clucking my tongue and widening my eyes, but inside the gears are starting up, working off the accumulated rust. Sure, they tested atomics in the South Pacific, and it's distinctly possible that Bikini Atoll had a few brothers and sisters, but why would the Progressive leadership go to such lengths to scare their members away from this area?

"It's off-limits," Buzz tells us for the second time. "But there are some lovely waterfalls just down the way. You'll love them."

But Ernie and I know where we want to go now, and no arbitrary rules are going to stop us. We're going to get to the other side of the island, horrible radioactive mutation or no horrible radioactive mutation. Personally, I'm hoping for the no-horrible-radioactive-mutation option, but beggars can't be choosers.

First, though, I've got to take a swim.

· · ·

Buzz and Wendell have chosen to join Ernie and me for this post-lunch seminar—a swimming class, we've been told—and I think they're becoming attached to us, which is good, in the sense that they'll be easier to manipulate when it comes time to do so, and bad, in the sense that they have a tendency to get severely on my partner's nerves. But despite last evening's festivities with Circe, we're not here for fun; we're on the job.

A quarter-mile away from camp, our group takes a small footpath leading off into a separate part of the jungle. The trees here are different—mangroves instead of palms, for example—and the ground is becoming softer, mushier beneath my bare feet. Soothing, really.

Swampland. That's what it is—a perfect amalgam of the Florida Everglades, the Louisiana bayou, and every nature special I've managed to catch on the Discovery Channel. It's artificial, without a doubt—I can even make out the concrete sides of the large, forboding swimming hole that spreads out before us—but still impressive in its size and scale.

I take a peek into the murky waters below. The surface of the pond is covered in a light blanket of green algae, and I wouldn't be surprised to find out that this is tonight's dinner. "So . . . what? We jump in?" I stand on the edge of the dirt and prepare to showcase my diving skills.

Wendell's hand shoots out to grab me by the shoulder, locking me firmly in place. "Don't," he says sternly, his face not set into a goofy smile for the first time since we met. "If you splash, they'll think you're food."

"*Who'll* think I'm . . . ?" And then I see it, a pair of eyes emerging from the water, two small golf balls floating on the surface, staring out at the swamp, taking in everything with a fierce intelligence and cunning. Next to those, another pair, and behind that, yet another. All around the swamp, the stillness of the water is broken by eyeball after eyeball after eyeball.

Crocodiles.

In a flash, Ernie's turned on his heels, heading back toward dry land. "Tell teacher I ditched class," he calls back.

I catch my partner, haul him back to the edge of the water. If I'm going in, he's going in. If I'm going to become a part of the

crocodile's food pyramid, he's going to become part of the crocodile's food pyramid.

After a few strict rules from our group leader—no sudden
movements, no taunting the crocs, no putting your head in their
mouths like a circus trainer—advice that I would basically consider simple common sense—common sense, that is, *if* you've
willingly chosen to swim with these snappers—we slowly enter
the swamp, letting the water rise inch by inch over our feet, our
legs, our torsos.

Hide, sliding against mine. Is it Wendell's? Is it a crocodile?
The feel is quite similar, I notice, as is their method of gliding
through the water. The more experienced swimmers among us
dive beneath the surface, taking so much air in their lungs they
don't come up for minutes at a time. I prefer to stay safely near
the shore of the swamp, ducking my head under the water every
so often for a glimpse of our cousins swimming merrily beneath
my feet.

Ernie dog-paddles up beside me, his spastic swimming con-
fusing the surface of the water with miniature tidal waves. "I'm
starting to get the feeling that Progress is regress."

"Not my concern right now," I tell him, my attention on a
nearby set of eyes poking out of the water, eyes that are currently
looking in this direction with a decidedly *hungry* look to them.
"Take your splashing elsewhere, please."

The lesson ends with nary a dino eaten, though one of the
Hadrosaurs does get her bum and tail nipped. To her credit, she
neither screams nor splashes about, which is more than I could
say for myself if some sixteen-foot behemoth decided to engage
in a little taste test on my tuchis.

We slowly make our way out of the water. The Brontosaurs
among us are raving about the experience—big wonder, as their
bloated bodies float better than they walk, which, I'm pretty sure,
is why that blowhard Alexandra hasn't moved her fat ass out of
Loch Ness in thirty years—while the rest of us are grumbling

about the stink of algae now clinging to every crevice in our bodies. That's gonna make for a lovely smell in the mess hall tonight.

But first there's free time, and a little jaunt we need to take. Ernie and I approach Buzz and Wendell—still grinning away, wiping the pond scum from their hides—and ask if they'd like to go on an outing. "You can show us those waterfalls," I suggest. "Wash off some of the algae."

The twins are delighted to get the show on the road, and soon enough we're tromping through the underbrush, shoving aside branches and overgrown palm fronds, tearing them with our claws when the path is too tight. We proceed in silence, climbing over rolling hills, avoiding those plants that look like they might either sting, bite, or cause nasty rashes. "So," I begin, wishing to bring a little light conversation back to the jungle, "bummer of a time in the Ring the other night, huh?"

"It was a shame," says Buzz. "Yanni shouldn't have tried to Progress ahead of schedule."

"A shame."

"Lucky those friends of his were good with the dart guns," Ernie points out. "Pretty good shots."

"Definitely lucky," I say.

As Buzz whips his claws through a dense set of foliage ahead of us, he calls back, "There was no luck to it—that was skill, and nothing less."

"We practice," says Wendell proudly. "I can almost hit the bull's-eye on all five shots."

"You practice what? Shooting?"

"Dart guns, mostly," Buzz explains. "But we hear there's a more advanced class once we Progress a little further. I think around sixty percent dinosaur natural you can opt to take a quick-fire seminar."

Without even looking over at my partner, I can tell that he's incensed beyond incensed. I've had a lifelong dislike and, to some degree, fear of firearms, a bias that's instilled in most dinos from birth. We've got enough natural weapons without having to resort to a hunk of metal and blasting powder, and notwithstanding the Crusades and such, everyone pretty much got along before the mammals decided to mass-produce these things. Then again, Samuel Winchester was a Velociraptor who, I believe, had strayed a little too far from his roots, so I can't blame it all on the humans.

But Ernie . . . for as long as I can remember, despite the infrequent but occasional necessity of firearms as a natural part of a PI's existence, Ernie has had a passionate hatred for guns that rivals his passionate hatred for marzipan—don't ask, don't ask—and that dislike runs deep.

"That's . . . that's disgusting," Ernie spits.

"It—it's only a s-s-seminar," stutters Wendell. He doesn't want to upset his new friend, that's clear, but he's stepped into some pretty hot cooking oil this time.

But Ernie's suddenly laughing, a good old-fashioned chuckle, hands covering his head, shoulders shaking in full-on mirth mode. "This—this is great—" he says. "You—you guys preach natural living, getting back to ourselves, our true side . . . and—and you have *riflery* classes?"

The irony is lost on the twins. "In order for us to understand the enemy," Buzz says soberly, "we must try to think like the enemy."

"Is that what they told you?" I ask. "That you practice shooting in order to understand humans?"

"Yes. You think that's wrong?"

I mull it over. "Not entirely."

We arrive at the waterfall. It's large. It's wet. As Buzz and Wendell promised, there are no crocodiles in it.

"Where to next?" I ask, thoroughly underwhelmed.

Wendell jumps up and down. "Oooh, there's another waterfall just up the way, we could go there. Or there's the one down by the—"

"I'm just about waterfalled out, fellas," Ernie interrupts.

"Maybe there's something more interesting to show us." Without even having to take a glance at his eyes, I know Ernie's ready to move on to the next phase. With every year of partnership that we log, our signals are getting easier and easier for the other to read. In the beginning, I practically needed him to hold up huge cue cards, but now all it takes is a stress on a syllable, a certain nuance in his diction.

"Yeah, let's go farther into the island," I suggest. "Somewhere . . . different."

Buzz and Wendell have no clue what we're talking about. They stare at us blankly, a couple of sheep asked to do trig equations.

"The off-limits area," Ernie says flatly. "That should be interesting."

"But it's off-limits," whines Wendell.

I nod along, pretending to agree. "Thus the name. We wouldn't want to go there, Ern."

"No?"

"Nah. I mean, it might be interesting to go *near* there, to go *up to* that point, but we wouldn't actually want to go in."

"Oh, no, not actually *in*," Ernie repeats.

Now I've got Buzz's attention, too, and I think the little bit of bait I've tossed his way has been snatched up nice and tight. "Well, if we weren't going to actually go *into* the off-limits area . . ."

"Right, right," says Wendell, the excitement crawling back into his voice. "Not into, just near, just near . . ."

Within a few moments, Buzz and Wendell have worked themselves back up to a trailblazing frenzy, and we're off through the jungle again, hacking away at leaves and trees on our way to the next destination.

"Hey," Buzz calls back, "you know who showed me this path?"

"No clue," I say honestly.

"Your friend, the one you call Rupert. About two years ago, after Wendell and I grew to fifty percent natural."

"No kidding," says Ernie. "He knew a lot about the island, then?"

"Of course," Wendell says. "He was a guide. He and Rachel and . . . what was that nice Coelo's name, Buzz?"

"Walter."

"Right, Walter. They were all great."

I trip over a low-lying vine, stumble, catch myself on another low-lying vine, and voila, I'm back to walking again. Greystoke, I am not. "You say they *were* all great?"

"They don't come around anymore."

"Did they all . . . die? Like Rupert?"

Buzz shrugs. "We didn't hear much about them. They were here, and then they weren't. We only heard about Rupert through the grapevine. I think Walter may have passed away, too, but I don't know about the others."

Others, eh? "How many dinos do you know who have disappeared?"

"Since when?"

"Last year or two," I say.

"Six?" says Buzz, unsure of his answer.

"Seven, eight, something like that," says Wendell. They're both completely unconcerned with their own answers and go right on hacking through the jungle.

I'm about to point out to them that they might like to hire some personal protection should they ever decide to leave the group when Buzz stops, eyes roving in his head as if he's looking for an answer and might be able to find it somewhere in his field of vision. "You know, come to think of it, last time we came out here, I was pretty sure Rachel was somewhere out here, too, though everyone had heard that she had met the ancestors. . . ."

"You saw her?"

"I smelled her, right here on the island. Very strong scent of lavender and paint thinner, couldn't mistake it." He turns around and starts hiking again. "It was so strange, but . . . then again, I could be wrong."

As we've been hiking, certain small changes in the surrounding foliage have begun to attract my attention. It's nothing much at first—a misshapen leaf here, a strangely twisted twig there—but as we push farther through the forest, I notice that the trees have begun to thin out, the vegetation becoming more scarce. And those few hardy plants that have cared to keep their roots in the area are all different, as if somewhere down the line a twisted gardener traded in his green thumb for an orange one. Examples:

A palm, the fronds thick and wide, stretching out and providing shade for the root system like any good palm tree will do. Unfortunately, it's only two feet tall.

Hedges ten feet high, brambles with thorns like hypodermic needles, vines sporting flowers that are dead before they even get a chance to bloom, petals rotting inside the buds. A jolly old greenhouse as imagined by Dr. Frankenstein himself.

And it's warmer here, the usually pervasive ocean breeze practically nonexistent, as if the air itself is afraid to make an appearance. The forest animals seem to have all gone on permanent coffee break, and the absence of noise is more unsettling than any jungle cat's scream or coyote's howl. Buzz and Wendell grow more anxious with every step, their voices warbling as they try to call an end to the half-day tour.

"Th—this is good," stammers Buzz. "You've seen it."

"Yeah, you've seen it," Wendell joins in. "Let's go back now."

"What's farther in?" Ernie asks. "I think I see some sort of path."

Buzz is already shaking his head, the trembling matching the rest of his body. "No, no, there's no path."

"No path. Let's go back now, guys, okay?"

But there is—if I squint just right, I can make out a beaten dirt road leading into a clearing, and my legs start a-movin' before the rest of the gang is able to stop me. The misshapen plants, the trees reaching out for me, the sand underfoot that somehow feels more like broken shards of glass than anything else, is all forgotten as I make my way toward that odd little path. There's a building down there, a brick building with . . . I can almost make it out . . . a steel door, I think. Set in the middle of an otherwise deserted clearing, the sand around it black, practically onyx, the very essence of this building is, not unlike the women I generally choose to date, sending out two distinct messages: *Stay far away* and *Vincent, I'm yours.* I heed the latter.

Which is precisely when the world explodes. Accompanied by a throaty roar, a tidal wave of dirt rises out of the earth, a tsunami of branches and brambles and soil, and I fall back to avoid the messy onslaught. Something scrapes against the tip of my tail, a tremendous pressure that sends a shard of anguish tearing up my spine, forcing a yelp out of my snout.

"Electric fence," drawls Ernie. "Nice find, kid."

I don't know where it came from, though I imagine I was so set on conquering the building in the distance that I neglected my short-focus vision; but before I have a chance to exact my revenge on this wire monstrosity, there's another voice booming out of the wilderness, familiar but quite unexpected. "What are you four doing out here?"

We all jump as one—I actually keep it down to a mild hop, thank you—and turn to find Samuel and another Iguanodon climbing down out of a camouflaged Hummer. In the back of the vehicle, a wide tarp covers a pile of some bulky substance; it's difficult to make out the exact cargo.

"Where'd you come from?" asks Ernie.

Extract of displeasure streams out of Samuel in waves; he's the God of Stern Disapproval, and is about to dispense a trademark harsh warning. "The two of you," he says, doing his best to stare down Ernie and me, "shouldn't be worrying about things beyond your Progression level yet. And as for you two"—now focusing his attention on a cowering, shaking Buzz and Wendell—"you should know better. I'm going to have a word with Circe about this. Now get in the car, all of you."

In a cloud of petulance, we climb into the back of the Hum-Vee, a bunch of kids caught in a dumb juvenile prank. I half expect Samuel to call our parents and let them know just what it is we did this night, but I think we might get off with just a warning.

During the wordless ride back to the compound, the tarpcovered pile next to me clanks and clinks with every bump, but I resist the temptation to pull the cloth aside and soak in a good look. I'm in enough lukewarm water as it is, and I don't want to get thrown off the island before I've had another shot at Circe. I'm sorry—at interviewing Circe.

When we arrive back at the camp, Ernie and I are sent to our hut and told to prepare for the evening's banquet; Wendell and Buzz head off with Samuel, presumably to get their spanking.

"I'd hate to get the little pissers in trouble," I tell Ernie. "I mean, they were just doing us a favor."

"They'll be fine," my partner says. "Slap on the wrist and off to eat some raw pork. Wait and see, they'll be bothering us again in no time."

. . .

It is two hours later, and Circe has just announced to the dinner crowd that Buzz and Wendell have been chosen by Progress. In a scant forty-five minutes, they will enter the Ring.

And Ernie and I get to help them.

Whispering: "I thought you said you weren't ready for this."

"We must be. We were chosen, so we must be. Right?"

I'm leading Buzz and Wendell down a long corridor and between the two sets of bleachers, acting as their guide as we walk as slowly as possible toward the Ring. The stands are filled with Progressives, and the view from down here is very different from what it was up on the dais last night. From this vantage point, it seems like every dinosaur up there is looking down on us to mock our passage, as if on some hidden signal, they will all leap down and tear us into a million pieces.

But they're just cheering, cheering on their friends who have so valiantly chosen to attempt Progress together. Little do they know that the twins themselves aren't exactly enamored of the idea.

"Call it off," I urge them. "Stand up and say you recant. Did Circe tell you that you should do this?"

But Buzz shakes his head, and I believe him. Still, something—some*body*—has gotten to him since that Hummer pulled away, and though he's clearly petrified of entering the Ring this evening, he refuses to disavow the decision he and Wendell have made. "Progress has chosen us," he says. "We must go."

"How do you know Progress has chosen you?" I ask, hoping to force some logic into a completely illogical situation. "Did Circe tell you that? Samuel?"

"No." Emphatic, truthful.

"Then who did?"

No answer. We approach the Ring.

It was right after the announcement that Buzz and Wendell would be attempting this night's inanities that we were approached by Samuel, taken away from the main dining hall, and informed that the twins had chosen Ernie and me as two of their confederates for the evening.

"The guys who lead them in?" I asked. "The ones with the cage and the—"

"And the dart guns, yes," said Samuel. "It is a great honor to be chosen."

Ernie shook his head. "We don't know how to shoot," he lies. "We can't—"

"To refuse a request like this is to do your friends the greatest dishonor there is." Once Samuel started talking like Bruce Lee, I couldn't back out. I already felt somewhat responsible for getting the twins in trouble earlier on, and now that they'd gone over the edge of sanity, I couldn't stand back and let them leap alone.

"Your job is simple," Samuel explained. "You will walk them out, you will lock them inside. You'll return for a cage, wheel it out. The other two compatriots your friends have chosen are longtime Progressives; they will know what levers to release."

"That's not the part I'm worried about. The dart guns—"

"Should not be needed." Samuel reached into a duffel bag he had brought along and pulled out one of the rifles we saw last night. "Progress has chosen them for this task, and that means they should emerge victorious. On the off chance that something should go wrong, the operation is very simple." He lifted the rifle to his shoulder, locking the stock against his powerful chest. Meanwhile, I was taking mental shorthand at light speed, trying to get all of this information to take root in my brain as quickly and deeply as possible. "Circe will stand, clap her hands twice, and then, simply, you shoot."

Without even taking aim, Samuel's finger depressed the trigger, a shot zinged out of the barrel, and a few seconds later, a light thud on the ground nearby announced the demise of a small red-red robin who would no longer be bob-bob-bobbin' along.

"Great for you," said Ernie, "but we're not skilled at this."

"And it won't be a bird you'll be aiming at. You've seen Ring opponents; they tend to be a little larger. It works like this: point the barrel at the bad thing and press the trigger. That's all there is to it."

From there on in it was a jumble of confusion, accusation, and apologies, Ernie and I trying to ascertain why on earth Buzz and Wendell would want to do this to themselves when they had explicitly stated to us earlier that they were nowhere near ready for the task.

"Now's the time when we tell you whatever we think is important," gulps Wendell. We're at the entrance to the Ring, and the outdoor amphitheater has taken on a hushed, almost spiritual tone.

"Now's the time when you call a halt to this nonsense," replies Ernie.

But they're beyond that point. "If anything happens, tell my brother I love him," Wendell whispers to me.

A few feet away, I can hear Buzz murmuring in Ernie's ear. "Take care of my brother," he says. "That's all I ever wanted to do."

We lock them inside the Ring.

A hundred different emotions and courses of action flip through my mind as Ernie, the two other confederates—both Carnotaurs—and I make our way back toward the clearing where the second cage will be ready for us to deliver. Do we bolt? Do we refuse to release the animal inside? For the first time in a long time, I find myself mired in a swamp of indecision.

What I will do, it seems, is exactly what others before me have done. The cage is waiting there in the clearing, Samuel standing beside it, checking the security of the brown tarpaulin draped across the top. "Are they ready?"

We nod, and the cage is turned over to our possession. As we wheel it through the jungle, toward the amphitheater, I notice that there are no animal noises emanating from within, and it doesn't shake any more than the bumps and breaks in the path would give it cause to. Could the thing possibly be empty? Could this all be one huge practical joke to play on Ernie and me? It's heavy, no doubt, but the cage *itself* is heavy.

I bet that's it. A joke, nothing more than a high school prank. Buzz and Wendell and the rest of them are just screwing with our minds. It's a fraternity hazing, the last step before official initiation, and I almost got tricked.

Well, if it's a joke they want, they've come to the right place. I can play along with the best of them.

We wheel the cage into the amphitheater and the two Carnotaurs begin to hook it up to the entrance of the Ring. I look up toward the dais, catch Circe's eye, and give her a sly wink. *I know your game,* this wink says. *You almost got me, but I know your game.* Her return gaze is inscrutable, but at least my cards are on the table, and I know that she knows that I know, and that makes me all the more willing to play along.

Inside the Ring, Buzz and Wendell are really laying it on thick, their breathing shallow, their faces flushed. It's a great act, and I have to remember to congratulate them on their skills after we're sucking down some basil and joking about it in a few minutes.

"We're ready," one of the Carnotaurs says to me.

I nod my head like a Roman emperor giving the order to execute. This is my chance to don the thespian mantle; the drama club never wanted me—this'll show 'em. "Raise the gate," I command.

Nothing. No animal roar, no ferocious beast rushing out of the cage to attack the hapless twins. Stillness from the crowd.

Ernie, mouthing to me: *What's going on?*

A joke, I mouth back. *It's all a joke.*

Ernie cocks his head—he doesn't understand. I shuffle closer to him and whisper in his ear, "It's a hazing ritual. They're trying to spook us."

"I don't think so," he replies. "This is a helluva long way to go. . . ."

But there's still no action in the Ring, and the crowd is growing restless. "Here," I say, "I'll prove it to you." I take a few steps closer to the cage, reaching out for the brown tarpaulin covering. "There's no danger to Buzz and Wendell, because there's nothing inside this thing."

Like a magician uncovering his latest and greatest trick, I whip the blanket from the cage and turn to Ernie, showcasing the emptiness inside. "See?" I say. "Nothing."

Nothing plus two grizzly bears, that is.

Furious at my sudden intrusion, the bears leap up from their sleeping positions and launch themselves against the bars of the cage—the crowd roaring as the adrenaline hits—and I'm falling backward, away from the massive paws and heavy claws snaking out from between the bars. Scooting away from the cage on my butt, heart pumping a week's worth of blood in a few seconds—the crowd on its feet now as the bears wisely pass on me and reorient their sights on a more accessible target.

Buzz and Wendell are not prepared for the sudden onslaught. The bears don't even bother dropping onto all fours—they stand straight up for the charge, whipping those long, lethal paws through the air—two seven-foot towers of shaggy brown fur that have just found out it's dino-hunting season, and they've got two more to bag and tag before they reach their limit.

One of the bears squares off against Buzz; the other takes

Wendell. I can do nothing but watch, frozen in place, numbed by my incorrect assumption, my moronic bullheadedness, and, yes, by guilt. I'm sure those bears would have attacked the twins sooner or later, but perhaps they wouldn't have been so pissed off about it if I hadn't interrupted what were probably very nice dreams of picnic baskets and honey pots.

Wendell's fighting mostly with his jaws, trying to sink his teeth into the bear's jugular, but every time he gets to snapping near the creature's neck, the bear takes a swat at the Carnotaur's head, sending Wendell scampering backward with long claw marks gashed across his face. Buzz isn't doing much better, but at least he's keeping his opponent at bay, using his tail to carve out a semicircle of protection.

I don't know if there are any rules of combat in the Ring, but even if there are, the bears don't have much use for them. For just as Buzz has advanced on his adversary, almost driving the bear all the way back into his cage, the other one forgets about Wendell and swoops in from behind, biting down hard on Buzz's neck, the teeth sinking deeply into unprotected flesh, and a geyser of blood sprays up and out, soaking the floor.

With a roar of his own that surpasses anything I've heard from the bears, let alone any special-effects wizard in Hollywood, Wendell charges, jaw spread wide, teeth glistening, ready to swallow his brother's attacker whole, if need be.

But a well-placed swat, this one from the other bear, puts a stop to Wendell's charge, and he, too, sinks to the ground. Both dinos are down for the count and barely putting up a fight.

Circe's hands are still. I await the double clap, staring up at Circe, my arms spread wide—*When? When?*—but she deliberately looks away. Samuel is nowhere to be found.

A piercing scream from within the Ring. I can't look.

"Screw it," I say, and reach for a gun.

Ernie's already way ahead of me. I do just like the guy said—point the barrel at the bad thing in front of me and pull the trigger—

Nothing. No click, no whiff, no zing. The bears continue to maul Buzz and Wendell, the twins' battle cries slowly dying to a whimper.

Frantically, I lift the gun again, sight down the barrel—the bear's back directly in front of me, easy shot, point-blank, eighty-year-old woman with cataracts could make this—and squeeze the trigger with all my might.

Zero.

Unable to work this infernal human contraption, I look over to my partner for help, but Ernie's having just as much trouble as I am. I watch as he takes aim and fires, only to have a staggering amount of nothingness take place.

Now the crowd has begun to scream. It is not, I surmise, in joy.

"It's jammed—" shouts Ernie. "The gun, it's jammed—"

One of the Carnotaur confederates rushes over with his own weapon, raising it expertly to the proper level. He lets a dart fly, and it whizzes across the ring, missing the bear by a good three feet. For a moment I think he's missed on purpose, that he swung the barrel around at the last second, but he stares at the gun in awe, like a tennis player checking his racquet for holes after missing an easy shot, and I know he had that thing aimed perfectly.

Inside the Ring, Buzz and Wendell are dying. They've managed to scoot backward, their bodies pressed up against the bars of the massive cage, the brothers holding on to and cradling each other, their blood truly flowing as one. Our chances left to save them are dwindling, but we've not yet exhausted all options.

"Open the gate," I shout to the one Carnotaur who has yet to lift a claw. "Do it, now!"

My tone is insistent enough to frighten the dinosaur beyond his training or common sense, and he leaps to the Ring entrance, fumbling with the keys. I'm right behind him, still trying to force my gun to fire, a task as futile as trying to buy a decent fast-food fish fillet. There's ammo in there, but it won't load, and I don't know how to force it in. But if I can get inside that Ring, I'll pull a Davy Crockett and shove these darts into those bears' chests with my hands, if need be.

"It's stuck—" cries the Carnotaur, and I shove him out of the way. Ernie rushes to my side and we set to pulling on the bars, the Carnotaurs joining in a moment later.

We strain. We pull. We exert every bit of energy left in bodies that have been malnourished and deprived of sleep for two days, the tumultuous blare of the crowd egging us on, goading us to new feats of strength. The bars will twist. The bars will bend. The bars will snap.

But the combined force of four dinosaurs don't mean a hill of beans to an indifferent mass of steel. The door stays firmly in place, absolutely nothing we can do about it. With a final tug, I lose my grip and fall heavily to the dirt, the wind knocked out of me and not coming back for some time. I can't watch, but I can listen, and there's not much mistaking the gruesome sounds that invade my trembling ears. Within seconds, the bears finish off our friends and, after deciding that the overgrown reptiles are inedible, proceed to cross to the far side of the Ring and drift back to sleep.

The crowd continues in its aimless fury, small skirmishes breaking out below the forest canopy, miniature Ring battles of their very own. High above, up on the dais, I can see Circe, head down, shoulders wracked with sobs. Her skin is dry, pale, dull, but her scent—tinged, somehow, with ragweed and pollen, the stuff of sadness—is stronger than ever, pervading the amphitheater, as if trying to draw me away from the anger of the crowd and into her grief. For a moment, I am lost, captive in her melancholia, and I know deep down that Circe knew nothing of this, that whatever has occurred tonight was either a freak accident or rigged without her knowledge. But that moment of clarity and sorrow soon passes, and the tumultuous frenzy of hundreds of my fellow dinosaurs zaps me back into action.

"Vincent! Vincent!" Ernie's calling to me, pulling me through the crowd, away from the guards, away from the dais, away from the amphitheater and into the darkness, and I follow him with a mindless intensity. There is nothing to say to him. There is nothing to say to anyone. This is the only thing I am thinking, and I am thinking it over and over again:

Buzz and Wendell died in each other's arms, and in that, I hope, the pain of their passing was somewhat diminished. But I swear to Raal, the ancestors, or whoever the hell is listening that when I find the creatures responsible for orchestrating this debacle, they will not be so fortunate.

We have spent six hours lost in this jungle, slamming into tree trunks, tree branches, tripping over stumps, over roots, frightening small woodland creatures, and if it takes another six, I'm more than willing to collect whatever bumps and bruises may occur. The other side of the island and the fence blocking access to that off-limits area is around here somewhere.

We've got to break into that building.

Ernie and I snuck away from the amphitheater with little fanfare. Don't even know if they noticed our exit; they'd have a big enough job calming down hundreds of rioting dinosaurs, and two little infidels cannot have been significant enough to worry themselves over. We don't have maps, but no matter. We don't have a compass—no matter. We don't have the vaguest clue as to where we're going or what we'll find when—if—we get there. No matter.

What we do have is a furious anger, a sense that we've been

played for chumps, and a burning desire to get to the heart of the beast, ferret out the weasel, or weasels, responsible, and exact justice. The only problem is that we're naked, and we're lost.

"You been dropping those pine cones?" Ernie asks me.

"Fat lot of good that'll do. Look for the freaky trees, that's the key."

We proceed deeper into the jungle, the moon and stars completely obscured by the canopy overhead, and by the time I'm starting to believe that we're irretrievably, irrevocably lost, that they'll find our bodies in three thousand years, clean up our skeletons, and place us in museums so that schoolkids can marvel at the advanced stage of lizards back in our time and write misspelled thank-you notes to the curator, Ernie's picked up on a scent.

"What is it?" I ask.

"It's . . . it's me," he says, a little abashed.

Great, he's smelling himself again. I thought we'd gotten that habit taken care of back in '89. "I don't get it."

Ernie's moving quickly now, his legs moving independently of the rest of his body, torso coming along for the ride. "When we were out by the fence with Buzz and Wendell earlier on—when Samuel found us—I took the liberty of relieving myself on a few bushes. I think I've caught the scent."

A deep breath, soaking up the jungle air. I've got urine smells coming in, all right, and when you work in the city—especially if you're running a job in downtown Santa Monica—you can't be squeamish when it comes to matters of the bladder. Still, I'm unable to distinguish Ernie's urine from a raccoon's from a blue jay's—at least, not at this distance. But I'm sure Ernie's been tracking it for miles. Even though humans have a rough time detecting their own body odor—the ones with *bad* body odor have an especially hard time at it, natch—and dinos are unable to smell their own pheromones, we've each got a keen sense of our own waste products. Sure, call it disgusting, but anything that'll get me oriented in this jungle is worthy of some respect.

I follow my partner, who is now working a beeline through the forest, and it's not another ten minutes before the trees begin to take on that Brothers Grimm look. Knotholes elongate, forming great, gaping maws, branches reaching out like arthritic fingers ready to pluck me up and finish me off. Of course, Ernie's walking through it all like it's downtown Brentwood at high noon, but then the old fart never did have much of an imagination.

"There's the bush," says Ernie, pointing to the small urine-soaked hedge. I applaud, he bows, and we stare up at the fence looming before us, thirty feet high, completely unscalable by anyone older than ten.

"Now what?" I sit on a stump, my chin falling into my hands.

"How about getting that gate open?"

I shake my head. "No good. I think it's remote control. Remember when we got picked up in the Hummer that first night? Samuel clicked some box near the dashboard, and I heard creaking—"

At which point my partner opens his hand, green side up, to reveal the most beautiful six-inch box of plastic I've ever seen. The white push button on the side glistens in the moonlight.

"I snatched it from the truck before we got out," says my partner, his grin stretching across those wide-set teeth.

"But you've got no pockets."

"Correct."

"Do I want to know where you hid it?"

"No, you do not."

A click, a whirr, and the gate squeaks open, the hinges bitching about it all the way. "The path works in from here," I tell Ernie. "Should be just along the way."

My partner agrees, and after a few minutes of searching in the darkness, we stumble onto a four-foot-wide area of jungle that looks to have been cleared out a little more than the rest. The mutation is even more evident here, the ground slick beneath our feet, buckling up and out from the monstrous roots beneath its surface. A pair of tire tracks still set in the mud clinches the deal—this is the way in, no doubt, and our pace turns quicker as we slog through the mud, a stroll giving way to a spirited walk giving way to a jog giving way to a run.

We're eating up the land, mud churning beneath our feet, and over the smells of the jungle, our sweat, our excitement, I get a whiff of something else. Something familiar and yet slightly foreign. Can't place it yet, but as I concentrate on the path ahead, I'm collecting samples and letting the forensic scientist in my brain sort through the evidence.

New sounds, too. High-pitched squeaking, a gerbil in distress. Only I don't think gerbils are native to Hawaii. Animal calls, echoing off the trees, howls dying in the stillness of the night. And like the prior absence of sounds, these new noises are not soothing.

"Do you smell . . . others?" I ask Ernie.

"Other what?"

"Other dinosaurs. The pine, the dew . . ."

Mid-run, Ernie takes a deep whiff of the surrounding air, pivoting his head in all directions, nearly whacking into a koa tree on the way. "They may be following us," he says, and as one, we pick up the pace.

Almost before we get a chance to slam on the brakes, Ernie and I burst into a clearing, the moon showing its mocking little face once again, and wind up in front of our very own Holy Grail: the redbrick building. The tire tracks we've been following lead right up to the front door and then stop, and we slow to a quick walk and circle the structure, hoping that an easy way in will materialize if we stare hard enough at it.

No such luck. The only entrance remains a steel door set into the brick wall, and the only lock is an infernal finger-hole next to it, an exact replica of the one Circe used on the fossil-making barn. "Can't hurt to try," I suggest. "No other way in."

"Be my guest."

"Oh. I thought maybe *you'd* want to. . . ."

"Go ahead," insists Ernie.

Good luck, finger. Closing my eyes, I tuck my claw back into its slot—remembering the lesson from Bob, our first Progressive contact back on Hollywood Boulevard—and shove my pointer into the hole, gritting my teeth in expectation of some type of searing pain. If it matters, I prefer amputation to electrocution, but I doubt the door will take requests.

No pain. No miniature guillotine, no shock pads. The door doesn't open, but at least I've still got all eight digits intact. "Your turn," I cheerfully say to Ernie, removing my finger from the hole. But his grubbies don't do the job either, and so we're stuck out here staring at the door, twiddling our claws and scratching ourselves.

The animal calls have intensified. And that smell—pine, perhaps, though not herb-infused. It's not Circe, and even if it were, I wouldn't be worried about getting caught in off-limits territory; they've already killed our friends for a seemingly minor infraction, and I don't doubt but that our next interaction with the Progressives, whatever the situation, will be decidedly violent. But Circe's working on a different plane from the rest of them, and I wonder how well she knows and trusts her right-hand dinos.

Ernie runs his hand across the door, looking for any flaw to exploit. There is none.

"We're stuck."

"Still not natural enough," I sigh.

"Not by ourselves, at least."

"Not by ourselves."

I don't know who thinks of it first, me or Ernie, but soon we're both scrambling for the aperture, trying to shove both our fingers in at once. "Move—move to the left," Ernie complains. "Further. Further."

The fit is tight, but we're eventually able to force both of our fingers into the slot at the same time. There's the familiar cooling sensation as some hidden device sucks the pheromones out of our pores, and a whirr as a different mechanism checks our scent level against whatever percentage "dinosaur natural" it has been designed to grant access to.

I doubt this will work. The contraption has got to be able to discern Ernie's pheromones from mine; it can't be this easy to fool such delicate machinery.

The door swings wide.

After we get our fingers unstuck, we tentatively step inside the building, being careful not to set off any alarms. But it seems that the one steel door is the only barrier to the place, and soon we find ourselves in a small, round antechamber, stone floor and low ceiling, the walls plastered with old, yellowed maps. The entire world is duly represented, with small red and green pins stuck into various islands and peninsulas in nearly every country. Whatever they're tracking, it's done a great job of spreading itself all over the globe.

Ernie calls me to the far side of the room—he's pointing to a large crimson pin smack-dab in the middle of the ocean just off Hawaii, and I pluck it out of the map. Nearly eradicated by the pinhole itself is the outline of a very small, very isolated island.

"*You are here,*" says Ernie. "But I can't figure out the rest of these. The red ones, the green ones . . ."

"Other Progressive camps, maybe?" I take a quick trip around the room, trying to locate a chart with Southern California on it. Sure enough, there's a red pin stuck into Los Angeles, up in the Hollywood Hills specifically, and I'm willing to make a leap of logic and agree that each pin represents a different stronghold for the group.

"You're right about the maps," I say. "Check it out."

No answer from Ernie. I turn, but the room is empty. "Ern?" I call out. "Ern?"

The reply, coming from down a long hallway, is hard to hear: ". . . might want . . . see this . . ."

"What? I can't hear you," I call back.

Ernie's voice is stronger this time, warbling slightly—fear, anger, or just the echo from the chamber walls?—"I said, you might want to see this."

Leaving the map room, I quickly make my way through the cold, tight corridor. Ernie's silhouette is sharp against the glare of a single uncovered hundred-watt bulb dangling from the ceiling, his shadow harsh against the brick walls. His shoulders are shaking, but I don't think he's laughing.

"What'd ya find—" I begin, and the words stop halfway up my throat.

Guns. Boxes of guns. Racks of boxes of guns. Guns in piles, guns on the wall, guns strewn haphazardly about the floor. Rifles, revolvers, semiautomatics, fully automatics, large caliber, small caliber, every make of every ballistic weapon I've ever seen is stuffed to bursting inside this twenty-by-twenty room, a weapons stash that would warm the cockles of Charlton Heston's cold mammalian heart.

"These don't shoot horse tranquilizers, do they?"

Ernie and I make our way into the room, stumbling over steel, picking our way through the morass of firearms. Ernie hasn't said a word since stepping inside—he simply walks in a circle, eyes downcast, some silent fury building up within him with every passing second.

Beneath me is a large cylindrical weapon with a grip like a video-game joystick. I lift the thing to get a better look at it—heavy little bastard—and stare down the barrel.

"Grenade launcher," Ernie says, his voice even, dead of emotion.

Ah. I carefully place it back atop the pile, just in case I hit the wrong button and become the latest Darwin Award recipient. "The hell do they need this for?"

"The hell do they need any of it for?" My partner lashes out at a pile of the firearms, kicking them with a bare foot. "This is the sickest fucking thing I've seen since we got here. All this talk about Progress and nature and understanding our true ancestors, and meanwhile they've got a weapons stock that would make NATO jealous."

I can't argue with the guy; these Progressives clearly have their heads screwed on backward, and I can't imagine what would make them want to amass this much firepower in one location. "We'll get back to LA," I suggest, "call the Council down on their ass. See how they take to a bunch of dinos hogging mammal weapons."

Ernie's hide has flared into a bright green hue along with his anger, the sudden rush of blood drawing out his best skin tone. He should definitely wear more fall colors. I doubt he'd appreciate the fashion advice right now, though, so I leave it alone. "That's right," he growls. "Confiscate the island, that house, throw 'em all in the clink."

Without realizing it, we've backed our way out of the gun room, as if our bodies knew more than our minds and forced us to retreat from such an unnatural location. By the time we're back in the hallway and heading toward the map antechamber— I'd really love to show Ernie those dates above the maps, maybe figure out what the hell they signify—I catch a whiff of the smell again, this time much stronger than before. Definitely pine, definitely swamp gas, and we are definitely not the only dinosaurs in the vicinity.

"Shhh," I tell Ernie, who's clomping his way noisily toward the exit.

"Why?"

"Sniff." Ernie takes a whiff, and instantly silences his movements.

Rustling, outside the building. The trees, shifting in the still air, leaves crackling under someone's feet. Huddling in the doorway, Ernie and I try to get a bead on the new intruder, but it's hard to localize.

"From the left," whispers Ernie. "I think they followed us."

"No," I whisper back. "This is something else."

And then another sound from the right. And another in front

of us. The jungle has come alive, trees rustling in every direction, and the smell has only gotten stronger. It's the scent of a roadkill, of towering ferns, of a newborn baby dino, of steaming swamp pits.

Coming in tandem now—a shake of the trees, a burst of smell—and a new addition to the fun, a distinct howl, an animal call of *This way, boys, I found somethin' to munch on*—and I'm hoping that it's just the Hummer again, I'm hoping that it's Samuel come to lecture us and drive us on out of here—but something in me knows that's not the way it's gonna go down.

"Go," I say, my voice lower than I expected, as if my vocal cords know more than I do about the upcoming events.

"What?"

"Go," I repeat, louder this time, rising on panic. "Go!"

Sprinting from the get-go, we burst out of the building and into the jungle, clambering onto the path and letting loose. It's hard to concentrate on anything other than the road ahead, but I try to keep an ear and a nostril open, just in case.

Now the howls have intensified, deep calls of pain and rage, and it spurs me on to greater speeds. And there's another smell separating itself from the rest of them, riding high on the pine. Leather. New, though a part of me recognizes it. No time to think—time to run. But Ernie's lagging behind, panting hard, and I can't leave my partner in the dust. I fight back against the panic and slow my legs down a notch.

It gives our pursuer all the opportunity he needs. With a sudden piercing screech that nearly bursts my eardrums, a Stegosaur bursts out of the underbrush on all fours and slams into Ernie, a headbutt to the midsection tossing him to the ground. My partner goes down hard—rolling over a foothill of roots and landing against a thick tree trunk—but he's up again in an instant, claws sliding out of his fingers and locking into place.

"Wait a second—" I shout, hoping to stop the Stegosaur with some rational conversation.

But the look in its eye is pure animal; it doesn't even have the common courtesy to try and understand what I'm saying. Lunging forward again, its own claws extended, the Stegosaur stumbles toward Ernie, catching its front foot on an outcropping of rock and going down with a thud.

I take the opportunity to let loose—if we're gonna play this way, let's get it on—and leap feetfirst at the beast, my own sharp underclaw aimed for the throat. But a swinging tail catches me off guard, and it takes a midair pretzel twist to avoid winding up with a back full of spikes. Gotta watch all five limbs when dealing with a creature like this one. Adjusting my position, I slide to the left, narrowly avoiding a one-way trip to eternity.

Ernie's got his jaws set around the Stego's neck, his arms tight around the head, gnawing for all he's worth. I'm jumping around to the other side, sliding onto my back, trying to aim for the beast's soft, unprotected stomach, but it's tough going, as this thing insists on fighting on all fours. The multitude of sparring matches Ernie and I have engaged in, combined with the few real-world skirmishes I've gotten myself into, haven't prepared me a whiff for this kind of down-and-dirty battle.

Coming underneath, I'm just about to make a good stab at the stomach when the scent hits me again, snaking its way out of the back of this creature's neck, down and around its bulging belly, curving up my nose, and slamming directly into the recognition center of my brain: leather and lime Jell-O.

It's Thomas. We're fighting the Progressive who made his bones in the Ring the other night, the one who beat back a mountain lion with nothing other than his claws, his tail, and his wits. I understand the whole post-traumatic stress disorder concept—I ate a Pop-Tart with a cockroach on it once and couldn't look at another breakfast treat for months afterward—but this is beyond modern psychology. What the hell happened to this guy?

But my pause to indulge in conscious thought has given this natural dino a chance to escape my attack, and soon I'm forced to roll to my right as the Stegosaur leaps into the air and comes down hard, attempting to squash me beneath his stubby legs. An unfortunate woodchuck takes my place in rodent heaven. Fair trade.

Tucking into a somersault and popping to my feet at the end—those prepubescent Romanian gymnasts have nothing on a Raptor with his dander up—I spin and prepare to renew my assault on Ernie's attacker. But there's another rustle in the trees behind me, and I turn to investigate the new noise—

Just in time to avoid a claw slashing at my throat. I backpedal, throwing my arms up and out, batting away the matchstick arms reaching for my vital organs. Filling my field of vision now, a gaping jaw, mouth dripping with saliva, two sharpened rows of teeth; Jaws has sprung legs and crawled his way onto land for a jaunt in the jungle.

Close enough. It's a T-Rex—I don't recognize this one on a personal level, but I'm sure he was a busboy or ophthalmologist once upon a more rational time—and, like the Stegosaur, it pays no heed to any of my protestations to cut out the nonsense and start acting like an adult. Fortunately, he's inherited his race's propensity for inefficient forelimbs, so I'm able to keep his claws away from the rest of my body while I defend my snout against those snapping jaws. While guised up as a mammal, of course, this beast would have arm prostheses to help him blend into human society, but unassisted like this, he's at a distinct disadvantage. Then again, he does have quite the set of chompers at his disposal. They crack the air with each vicious bite, and I know from one look in his eyes that wherever the Stegosaur's mind has gone, this T-Rex's brain is riding sidecar on the journey.

Can't even see Ernie—no idea how he's holding up—but the space between my ears is filled with howls and shrieks and wails and bellows, a full cat's-night-out cacophony, and I don't know how much of it is coming from my partner, from the Stegosaur, from the T-Rex, or even from myself.

A tail whips out, tripping me from behind, and I flop to the ground, landing squarely on my back, crushing a pile of twigs and leaves beneath me. For a moment I can't even think about the dinosaur reaching down to finish me off; all I know is that oxygen and I have parted ways, and there's little else that currently matters.

Nearby teeth convince me otherwise. As the T-Rex lowers his head, jaw gaping wide in anticipation of victory, I kick out with my leg—still unable to breathe, mind you, so put *this* on your list of impressive feats—slide my underclaw to its fully extended position, and slam it up and clean through the roof of the Tyrannosaur's mouth.

Now he's flailing backward, a wail of pain curdling the air, flapping his runty arms against my leg, trying to dislodge my claw. I'm going along for the ride; my limb is still stuck inside his mouth, but I don't want to leave it there for long. Soon enough, he's going to get the idea to chomp me off at the knee, and I still have many years of plans left for that appendage. I quickly withdraw the hooked claw back into my body and snatch myself away from the bloody-mouthed dino.

"Little help?" I hear Ernie cry over the din.

"Little busy," I reply, fending off a new, feeble blow from the T-Rex.

He doesn't need my assistance, anyway—Ernie's got this Stego outsmarted and outfought. The larger animal is already beginning to tire, his charging attacks coming slower, coming clumsier. Four large wounds crisscross his back, crimson streaks forming new lines to add to the barely healed scars left there yesterday by the mountain lion.

Working our way into a defensive position, Ernie and I wind up back to back, fending off attacks from either side, keeping ourselves in check and lending a claw when necessary. My T-Rex, though certainly vicious, is on the smallish side, but what he lacks in natural ability he makes up for in pure insanity. Every charge is a kamikaze rush, a lunge for my throat, my belly—there's no defensive strategy in sight.

Which gives me an opportunity to work my own brand of

pugilistic magic. I'm ducking and weaving, bobbing and hopping, Muhammad Rubio with a vengeance, and soon the Tyrannosaur is covered with bloody marks of his own, that *gone to lunch, be back at two* look still in his eyes. Ladies and gentlemen, the undercard looks like it's about to come to a close, Watson and Rubio the victors.

Until there's another rustle in the bushes, to my left. And another to my right. And another directly in front.

Until one dinosaur pops into view. And another to my left. And another to my right. And two more directly in front. Raptors. Brontos. Carnotaurs. Hadrosaurs. Ankies. It's the zodiac of dinos, a pantheon of prehistoric pugnacity, and they've come to teach the interlopers a lesson in manners. Taking a quick glance around, I assess the situation and realize that we're completely, hopelessly surrounded. Within a matter of seconds, Ernie and I have gone from Spanish conquistadores to bow-and-arrow targets at Custer's last stand, and I don't like the odds.

The howls drop to low, panting growls as the pack closes in on us. I can almost hear the digestive juices churning. Even the Stegosaur and the T-Rex I was fighting back off and sink into the relative anonymity of the crowd, content to be a small, yet important, part of our upcoming demise. Step by deliberate step, tails wagging in expectation of a kill, the dinos advance, tugging the noose tighter and tighter around me and my partner.

"Suggestions?" I ask Ernie.

He mulls it over for a very quick second. I can almost feel the saliva dripping on my feet, and I take this time to lament the fact that I have to die in so humid a location. I always figured I'd bite the big one in Los Angeles, where at least there aren't any bugs to feed off your corpse. That is, of course, unless you count the agents.

"Run," says Ernie. And we do.

Using my tail as an extra propellant, I leap over the shortest dino in the bunch—a Compy, whose look of genuine confusion as I soar over his head is so comical I nearly break down laughing upon landing—and begin my sprint into the jungle. I hope to hell I'm going the right way.

Ernie's next to me, kicking up leaves as he throws that husky body of his into Carnotaur overdrive. Behind us, I can hear new cries of frustration, drool being slurped back into waiting mouths, and the combined sounds of half a ton of angry dinosaur crashing through the underbrush. It's the kind of incentive that inspires world-record times, and I'm aiming to bring home the gold.

I don't know if that running class did me any good, but I'm hoping some of the lessons sunk into my subconscious enough to keep me zooming along faster than the others. Forget humanity, forget humanity . . . I feel the panting of my partner, his cardiovascular system pushed way beyond the acceptable limits for one of his age, body type, and previous exercise habits (read: none). "You think"—*pant, pant*—"we're going"—*pant, pant*—"the right way?"

"Better be," I shout back. "I'm not turning around."

And it's a good thing, too, because the pack is right on our heels. Taking a cue from our earlier experience with the crocodiles, I flash back to a nature special I caught a few months back on the boob tube. Some Australian fellow who got his kicks out of wrapping cobras around his head and getting his wife to give enemas to rabid gorillas was adamant about one fact: if you're ever being chased by a crocodile, run in a zigzag pattern. Or maybe it was an alligator. No matter; I figure these Progressives have already flipped back to a distant era when alligators, crocodiles, and dinosaurs were just about equal on the great wall chart of evolution, so I resolve to give this evasive tactic a try.

Grabbing Ernie by the arm, I veer sharply to the left, dragging my partner along with me. For a moment, it seems like the trick may have worked, and I resolve to do a lot more televisionwatching should I make it out of this alive. But then there's a sharp pain shooting down and across my back, a trickle of fluid dripping to my feet, and I realize I've just been sliced by a nearby claw.

Time to run straight again.

The fence looms ahead, and with it, the prospect of having to get to the other side. Ernie's frantically slamming his claw into the remote-control button, but we're so far off the beaten trail that the gate might be miles away. There's no time to sit back and pick out the best tree to scurry up; any stalling will give our assailants the chance they need to tear us into tiny bite-sized pieces, and I refuse to be an appetizer. So even as we continue, full speed, directly toward the fence, I'm letting my eyes scan the trees, in hopes that they'll find a means of egress before it's too late.

"Sausage tree," Ernie calls out.

"What?" Has my partner snapped?

"Sausage tree," he repeats, and points to a spot fifty yards ahead, at one of the most bizarre examples of plant life I've ever come across. A good fifty, sixty feet tall, this sizable tree is draped with hundreds of vines dangling down from its wide branches, but that's not the strange part. At the end of each of these vines, hanging there like an embryo from an umbilical cord, is what looks to be a giant kielbasa. Two, three feet long at least. I blink—still in mid-run—and open my eyes again, and the tree remains. This is not a hallucination. I guess I shouldn't be surprised, radiation or not; evolution, after all, has made some weird, seemingly drug-induced decisions along the way. Who would have guessed, for example, that the apes would learn how to use tools or balance their checkbooks? They still can't program VCRs, but they should get that worked out in another million years or so.

Adjusting course slightly, we head straight for the vines, leading the pack over an unbeaten trail. Speeds not as great now—trees in the way, fallen branches to contend with—and the snarling behind us grows closer. We're Frankenstein's monster, they're the mob, and hope for a happy ending is dwindling fast.

Sausage tree in front of us, the vines hanging just above our heads, and I take the mightiest leap these exhausted legs can manage, grabbing on to one of the weiner-shaped fruits and hauling myself heavenward. Ernie's right next to me on a nearby vine, and we shinny up the tree in tandem. My junior-high gym teacher would be proud.

By the time we're twenty feet into the air, Ernie takes a look down. "Hey," he says, a little awestruck and a lot relieved, "they're not following us."

Indeed, the pack of dinos has remained on the ground, staring up at us with famished eyes and slavering lips. They take turns hopping into the air, trying to claw us on a single jump, but they're a good fifteen feet short of the mark every time.

"Why aren't they climbing?" asks Ernie. "Not that I'm complaining . . ."

"Maybe they can't," I say. "Think about it—climbing is ape behavior; we just learned it as kids."

"And they unlearned it as part of Progress."

So they're down there and we're up here, safe for the moment, but it doesn't help the fact that we still don't have any easy way onto the other side of the fence. The only choice is to exercise some more human traits; it doesn't make me happy, but it keeps me alive.

We swing from vine to vine, carefully grasping each thick strand before gingerly building up momentum to get the next one moving again. Tarzan I am not. But after a few minutes of this, we're over the fence and climbing back down to the ground.

Sunlight is beginning to make its way into the jungle, and in the early morning mist, I can make out the gaggle of shadowy figures behind that fence, defeated and shuffling back into their protected compound. Mumbled growls stream into the air and dissipate, and Ernie and I are back on the path to civilization.

"They weren't . . . thinking," Ernie says as we pick our way out of the jungle.

"Agreed. Whatever they've become, Progress has done it to them. And Rupert . . ."

"We got to him just before he went into the Ring," I say. "And probably just before he became one of the pack."

"And they got to him right afterward."

"Exactly."

"But why?" asks Ernie. "What's the point of all the cover-ups, the secrecy? The guns, that building, those maps—"

I can't help but shrug. "I don't know. I've been trying to figure out the whys and hows of this place since we took on the case. But I think I know a way to find out."

It's time to confront Circe.

20

She's not here. The study, the bedroom, the foyer, all empty, and except for the few guards surrounding the pleasure dome, the whole place seems deserted.

We're sneaking our way through a garden outside Raal's once-upon-a-study, when it hits me. "Wait a minute, Ern—what day is it?"

"Sunday, I think," he says, catching on as soon as it's past his lips. "It took us about six hours to get out of the jungle, a few more sneaking in here. Sunday morning."

"They all left the island. Conference over, everyone scatter."

"Which means that Circe's gone back to Maui," he continues. "And then probably back to LA."

Time to boogie on home. I turn away from the mansion, back toward the camp, eager to make my way to shore—

"Wait," calls Ernie, reaching out to stop me. "Our guises."

Right. The guises. I look down at myself, at the natural hide sitting so easily, so calmly on my bones, feeling the warm

Hawaiian breeze caress my bare skin, my tail flapping open, flapping free, and for a second, I want to say, *Screw it all, screw the guise, screw humanity, I'll go join the others back behind the fence. . . .*

But reason floods past desire a second later, and I stomp past Ernie and back into the mansion, muttering, "I know where they keep 'em. Follow me."

No guards are posted outside the guise-check room I saw earlier, and it's an easy entry. Most of the costumes have been removed from the racks—certain nudist clubs exempted, bare hide is usually frowned upon in the real world, so the Progressives have reconcealed themselves behind buckles and straps for the hydrofoil trip back to the main island.

There are no dry-cleaning tickets corresponding to our costumes like back at the house in the Hollywood Hills, nor is there a fetching Ornithomimus to help us out; we're on our own and pressed for time. The rack of guises spins as I hold down a black button, sluggishly cycling through costume after costume.

My guise pops up a moment later—I recognize the strong jaw, an aluminum-dentin blend—and I think I get a glimpse of Ernie's next to it. Without wasting the time to double-check, I pull down guises number 151 and 152 and Ernie and I help each other to strap on the buckles and the girdles and the clamps and the trusses, moving like undercranked footage of the Keystone Kops.

But by the time we've gotten ourselves wrapped up good and tight—the confines of this costume feeling more restrictive after days of unlimited personal freedom than they ever have in my adult life—it is quite obvious that something is wrong.

"Um, Vincent . . ."

"Wait a sec," I say, trying like the dickens to align my mask with my actual eyelids, compressed jaw, and nostrils. I don't know why it's so difficult to get this thing into place.

"Vincent," my partner insists, "I think you put on the wrong costume."

With a rubbery snap, the mask clips into place, and the room comes into view once again. "What are you talking about?" I ask, turning to the mirror across the way. "We look great."

And there I am, dapper as can be. And next to me—in the flesh, a product not of my dreams, my herb-induced fantasies, or some knock-on-the-noggin concussion—is a beautiful, high-cheekboned, mocha-skinned angel whose features, guise or not, I will never forget.

It's Kala.

I leap to my left, away from my partner—is this one of his jokes, dressing up like an ex-fling?—and land hard across the room, staring at another familiar character: me. And when the Vincent Rubio I'm looking at speaks, it's Ernie talking. "Like I said," sighs Ernie/Vincent, "I think you're wearing designer duds, kid."

"Me?" I cry. "What about you? You're gonna stretch that thing out!"

Ernie's just as dismayed to find himself in my skin as I am to find myself in Kala's, though my predicament worries me on other levels. Can I move in this thing? Can I fight, if need be? Can I run?

Reaching up, his rough fingers pulsating behind my unsullied costume glove, he touches the cheekbones on my new face. Ernie asks, "Isn't this . . . are you . . . the girl, the one you . . ."

"Slept with, yes," I finish, angry with myself, angry with everything that's brought me to this point. "Or didn't sleep with. Kala, from the Westin Maui."

"She was a Progressive?"

"She didn't say so. In fact, she *said* she worked at the hotel, and *said* she'd never been off Maui itself."

"So she lied."

"Seems that way."

"So who is it? Who's the dino that fits in there?"

"Me, for now." For a brief moment, I consider going on a Cinderella hunt, traveling the land with a swatch of human skin draped across my arm, forcing maidens into the costume and finding out who fits and who bursts the guise at the seams, but it's probably a mite impractical, given our time constraints. All

I've got time to do is get out of this costume, find Ernie his own flabby guise, and dress again in record time—

Footsteps, coming down the hallway. Ernie and I glance at each other, his eyes going wide—is that what I look like when I'm nervous?—and we scan the room for an exit. There's only one window, not more than two feet wide, but it might have to do in a pinch.

Forget that—pinch me now, the footsteps are coming closer. And with it, another pair, walking in lockstep. Muted voices, laughter, approaching in tandem, and the only way out of here is through that glass. Ernie crawls out first, wiggling his rear—my rear—as he goes, and I'm taken aback at the sheer expansion forces he's putting my poor costume through; my rump is not usually that big. At least, I don't think it is. I'm next, and though it takes a bit to squeeze my new breasts—a C cup, if I know my human sizes—through the aperture, I do a fine job landing on the other side and hauling my tight little ass across the island.

By the time we make it to the marina, the hydrofoil is long gone; even if it were still around, I doubt it would be safe to take it back to Maui. I might be in a different guise, but I still carry my scent around, and I'm sure by now they're on the lookout for us. Maybe not; perhaps they assume we're dead, lost, or both, and couldn't be happier about the matter. I hope that's the case, as I plan on surprising them with a cameo appearance at some time in the near future, and I always enjoy making a grand entrance.

But a few hundred yards farther down the beach is a dilapidated, deserted marina that we find by following the scent of gasoline and salt water, a surefire trick learned during water-skiing lessons at sleep-away camp. It's a short while before we pick out a rickety boat with accompanying outboard motor.

"Probably here for the benefit of the long-termers," Ernie guesses. "Bring food back and forth for those animals behind the fence."

I don't see the natural dinosaurs as take-out or delivery kinda guys, but there's no reason to argue the point. I hop into the boat, these long, tan legs soaking up the warm Hawaiian rays, and for a split second—less than a split second really, maybe no more than a nanosecond, I swear it—I can understand how Jules could feel . . . comfortable . . . in a woman's guise. But the feeling quickly passes as I force myself to think of football, boxing, and stereo equipment.

The creature who sounds like my partner but looks like me pulls the motor to life, and the air ripples with a loud roar. The boat rocks against the dock, wood scraping wood, and slowly eases out toward open water. Bracing myself against the bow with my new, slimmer, tanner arms, I toss my long, black hair in the breeze and point the way toward Maui.

. . .

It is ten-thirty in the morning, and as soon as we can ditch this boat and get on shore, I need to make a few phone calls in preparation for our trip back to the mainland. Our flight back to Southern California leaves this afternoon, and it should take another five hours after that before we touch down at LAX. That will give my contacts enough time to collect the information I need, so that the second we step off that plane, Ernie and I can hit the ground running. There's enough seemingly unconnected conspiracy data bouncing around in my head to make the Warren Commission Report look like a children's book, but something tells me that the link is nearby and drawing closer. No question about it, I want this case wrapped up by midnight.

Unfortunately, the marina where the hydrofoil docks is packed with tourists fresh off their cruise ships and we're forced to take the boat on a roundabout path in order to avoid a possible run-in with any Progressives. We end up making a detour that puts us a few miles away from the main harbor and pull the boat into a small, isolated inlet protected by a semicircle of large, gray rocks that form a natural breakwater.

A few of the local surfers crest by on small waves as we pilot the boat into the cove, whistling at us as we pass. Ernie and I raise a hand in salutation, but they keep coming back around for more, gawking at us like we're some type of new and intriguing sea creature.

One, a blond raggy type who just stepped out of *Pro Surfing Magazine* glides his board directly alongside our craft, grabs hold of the side of our boat, looks deep into my eyes, and says, "Hey, beautiful, wanna learn how to surf?"

I hope the apefucker drowns.

We abandon the boat in shallow water and tread up the beach, Ernie giggling all the way. "Whatsamatter," he asks, "never been hit on before?"

By the time we get to the airport, our flight is almost ready to board. I leave Ernie at the gate and find a pay phone; my first call is a quick one to Dr. Beauregard. If anyone will be able to help me decipher the mysteries of these Progressives, it will be the expert himself. I may have information for him of which he was previously unaware, and it's distinctly possible that my data will combine with his to give us an overall picture we were unable to see separately.

A ring, two rings, three rings, and an answering machine. No time to beat around the bush—I leave a clean, concise message.

Another calling-card charge, another set of rings, and another answering machine. Jules is neither in the office nor at her home, and it's futile leaving a message for her at this stage of the game. I only hope I can track her down once I set foot back in WeHo territory. In the background, I can hear our flight being announced over the PA—*"Flight number 515 to Los Angeles, boarding all rows at gate 16"*—so I hang up, search the change receptacle for any leftovers, and grab Ernie on the way down to the plane.

On the way through the gate and down to the tarmac—the elevated jetway is broken, they tell us, so we have to take stairs down to the runway and another set up into the plane itself—I fill Ernie in on the fruit of my labors.

"We'll check in with Jules as soon as we return," I'm saying. "And once we get Dr. B. to call us back and confirm my suspicions, we should be able to—"

It's just then that I hear a sharp, pinched bang that comes only with the sharp report of a rifle. Another comes, and another, and I'm ducking, running, evading as best I can. But Ernie's not next to me anymore. Ernie's not next to *anyone* anymore.

Twenty feet away, on his knees, grasping his shoulder with one thick hand, Vincent Rubio—Ernie guised as Vincent Rubio— grimaces in pain, blood oozing out from between his fingers, breath coming short and ragged, and the first thing I think is not *My friend is hurt* or *The Progressives have found us* or *I've gotta do something,* but *So this is what it looks like when I get shot. . . .*

"Ern?" I call out, breaking through the throng of other passengers who have gathered around now that the shots have ceased. I drop to my knees beside him. "Where are you hit?"

Ernie moves his hand, and a new river of blood gushes from the shoulder wound. "Fucking . . . guns . . ." he mutters through clenched teeth.

"Rifle?" I ask him.

"Sniper—up on that roof—" Unable to use his left arm, and clutching his shoulder with the right one, Ernie points with my delicate nose to the top of a nearby terminal. "I saw him—running away—tried to call out to you, but—" A grimace of pain cuts him off, and he slumps farther to the ground.

As I understand it from a lifetime of watching fine American films, this is the point where I cradle him in my arms, he tells me some story about how he always had dreams of relocating to Montana, and he passes calmly into oblivion as I gaze furiously up to the heavens and bellow out his name. But it's not gonna go down like that—Ernie's only got a shoulder wound, and while I'm sure it hurts like hell, it's six degrees from fatal.

"You need a hospital," I say. "Can't go on a plane with blood spurting out; they won't let you sit in the main cabin, and then we'll miss the movie."

But Ernie's shaking his head, just as I knew he would be. "I'll be okay. Get—get back to LA and find her. Stop her, whatever it is she's doing."

"It can wait," I say. "They can—"

"It can't. Whatever—whatever they're doing—you have to stop it—"

I'd argue, of course, if I had more time. Play the good partner, stay by his side, forgo the investigation for the sake of sticking by a friend. But he's right; the plane's about to take off.

I stay by his side until the ambulance and police cars arrive and I can locate one of the dino paramedics on board, inform him of Ernie's special circumstances. At least now I know he'll be safely routed to one of the dino wards of Maui's hospital system, taken care of by the best our species has to offer, his guise expertly mended by seamstresses dressed as nurses and candy stripers.

He's up on a stretcher, the crowd beginning to thin out, the passengers being shuttled back on board, rattled but ready for a nonterroristic flight, and I'm right beside Ernie as he's trundled into the back of an ambulance. "When you find Circe," he says, "give her a good swift kick in the ass for me."

"I'll give her two," I promise.

The paramedics strap his stretcher to the floor of the ambulance and prepare to burn rubber down the runway and to the local hospital. Ernie lifts his head, a modified crunch, and stares me dead in the eye. "Take care, kid—and watch your back. That sniper was too far away to smell me, so he had to go on sight. This bullet was meant for you."

The doors swing closed and the ambulance pulls out, carting away someone who looks very much like Vincent Rubio, Private Investigator.

21

've been shot at before. Never vicariously, mind you, but I have been shot at. So there's nothing new to me in hearing the bang of a gun or feeling a bullet whiz by the ear, barely a millimeter to spare before van Gogh syndrome sets in. Doesn't make it any easier each time it happens, but there's nothing new in the experience itself.

Seeing yourself shot is a different matter entirely—the blood, the wound, the sheer ickiness of it all—and watching Ernie take a bullet that was meant for me has got me unnerved enough to get good and toasted on the flight back to LA. But the stewardesses are out of condiments, and though mustard seeds have in the past sufficed in a pinch, I refuse to suck on one-ounce plastic packets of Gulden's just to get a rush. I'm one of only a few dinos on the plane, too, so such an action would probably net me a lot of discomforting stares.

Then there's the safety factor. I don't know for sure that the shooter was acting alone, and I don't want to do anything to alert any Progressive hit man to my presence inside Kala's costume in case he's also flying the friendly skies this afternoon. Someone in the Progressive organization has decided that my continued existence is no longer required, and it's the direct threat that rankles me more than anything else. If you're going to try to kill me, at least have the balls to do it face-to-face, the old-fashioned way. Then again, I'm the last dino who should talk about having balls right now.

It is with thoughts of Circe, of the Progressives, of the trouble at hand weighing heavily on my mind that I fall into an uneasy slumber. When I wake, the plane is landing in Los Angeles; the pilot announces it's a quarter past eight, and I set my watch accordingly. Westwood is twenty minutes away—*everything* is twenty minutes away if you play it right—but by the time I get my Lincoln out of the U-Park lot, argue with the attendant as to the exact number of days my automobile spent in their substandard facility, and eventually burst through the gate, cracking off a chunk of wooden barrier with my front bumper, it's already nearing nine.

No time to take a quick drive by the office, which is not such a problem since I'm not anxious to meet up with Minsky. It's not that I feel guilty about taking his money and not doing a whiff of work on his missing Mussolini case, but I don't have the time to explain anything to the little tyke just now, let alone why I'm guised up like a geisha. With my luck, he'd kiss first and ask questions later.

Anyway, I'll dissolve into the maddening crowd up in Hollywood, which is just what I need right now. Anonymity with a supermodel figure doesn't come easy in any town, but in LA you've got a fighting chance of being outshone by the next ingenue off the bus.

On the way in, I punch up my voice mail on the car phone and take a listen. Three messages. Number one: Friday, 4:15 P.M. Minsky, calling to check up on our progress a scant half-day after he sent us on the mission to find his floozy, as if he doesn't trust us to get the job done in a timely fashion. The nerve. His high-pitched warble floats through the air—"and when you find her, bring her in to the cops, throw the book at her, but get the Mussolini first, get the Mussolini—" The last thing I need is a Minsky migraine, so I punch number three, erase, and move on with my life.

Number two: Jules, nine o'clock yesterday evening. Worried that I haven't given her a call. I've already taken care of that concern. Skip and erase.

Number three: Dr. Beauregard, today at 10:00 A.M. Aha, now here's a call I've been waiting for. "Vincent, I'm in town helping out another family," he drawls, "a sad case, really, a boy who got himself all mixed up with some humans, believe it or not—and I thought you might be having some more questions for me. I'd be glad to oblige, of course . . ." He goes on in that big, charming, Southern way of his, eventually getting around to giving me the name and number of the hotel he's staying at; it's the Nikko, a Japanese-run establishment just on the other side of Beverly Hills.

A quick return call, and I'm instantly put through to the doctor's room.

No rings, just an answer. "Where were we?"

That doesn't sound like Bo. "I'm sorry," I say hastily. "I must have the wrong room—"

"Vincent?" says Dr. B., and now I can hear the drawl, the syrupy inflections. "Is that you, son?"

"Oh, hey—I didn't—you sounded different—"

"I was talking to my grandkids. We got cut off. Glad y'all are back in town."

It takes five minutes to run through my story, omitting the more graphic details but generally making clear to the doctor that I need some answers, and I need them quickly. "I may need help identifying another deprogrammer, one who may be siphoning information to the Progressives. And there's more. Much more, I think."

"Are you sure?" asks Bo. "That would be highly unethical of any practitioner—"

"We're way beyond ethics, doc. You know a bunch of the others in the field, right, their human guises?"

"Of course, son. If you get me a picture, I'm sure I can identify the man for y'all."

Dr. Beauregard agrees to meet me at a private location, and I suggest a nightclub I know near his hotel. "I need someplace dark," I say. "I think I'm in danger."

"I would not be surprised," says Bo, and this doesn't do anything to assuage my anxiety. "We will be as careful as possible." We set an eleven o'clock meeting time, which gives me an hour or so to get up to Hollywood, squirm out of this costume and into a new one, and soak up whatever information Jules has managed to squeeze out of this town.

"Darling," she cries as I slink my way into the Wax Museum workroom, her eyes roving over my new curves in appreciation and delight, "you've come over to the winning team! I'm so proud of you. . . ."

"Zip it," I tell her, hoping that there's no blush-action veins in Kala's mask. "Last time I came in for work, you made a copy of my guise, right?"

"Down to that cute little navel of yours."

"Could ya get it for me?"

"Why? You look fabulous, darling!"

"Jules—"

"We could use you in the new show. I'm trying to get us booked into Vegas. You could do a hula number. . . ."

Finally, she disappears into a back room and, after a few minutes of rustling around, reemerges with a spare Vincent Rubio draped over her arm.

"How was Hawaii?" she asks as I begin to undress.

"Sticky. And a little bloody, but I don't have time to go into it."

"Where's Ernie?"

"That's the bloody part." I give a quick five-minute rundown of the events, Jules working up a head of steam with every passing detail, and by the time I'm done, she's pacing the workroom, doing

Indy 500 laps around the surgical tables. Meanwhile, I've reguised and chosen a nice slacks outfit from the racks of clothing she's got stashed in one of the many workroom closets.

"I knew something was up with them," Jules is saying, voice rising. "I knew it—"

"No time for an ego check. Tell me what you found."

"What *didn't* I find? I've got newspaper reports, I've got eyewitness accounts, I've got spectroscopic photoanalysis—"

"Let's start there. Can you show me?"

Jules's computer system is state of the art, but for me, it's art of the abstract variety. Folks these days go cruising around the Internet, bouncing from information to information; the closest I've ever come to surfing was that blond-haired dude who tried to pick me up back on the beach.

"Watch this window over here," Jules is saying, her long fingers slapping away at the keyboard like Elton John playing "The Bitch Is Back." When he had that charity auction, by the way, and sold off all of his more lavish costumes, a buddy of mine got a great deal on this Turkish guise that Elton—a Hadrosaur, according to my friend—would use to walk the streets in relative anonymity.

"I scanned in the photos you gave me," Jules is saying, continuing to type as she speaks, "and ran them through a few programs I use to show my clients how the plastic surgery I perform on their guises will meld with the substructure below. You wouldn't believe how many clients I have who simply can't understand that no matter how much liposuction I perform, a Brontosaur is never going to have the same waistline as a Coelo. Work with what you have, I tell them. Everyone can be fabulous."

"Very life affirming," I say. "Back to the computer."

"Okay, so I scanned in the photos, one by one, and checked each for an underlying structure." As she speaks, a series of images—the photos I had given her earlier—pop up on the screen. I pull up a wooden crate stamped NOSES, SWEDISH and take a seat.

Happy families, reunited with their loved ones. Mothers, fathers, siblings, an ex-Progressive grinning out at the camera, and next to him or her, in every picture, an extra reveler, often a deprogrammer, smiling along, arm around his newest success story. Jules has already circled the key element in each photo, and I watch as the computer eliminates all the irrelevant information and hones in on the sweet cream filling.

Photographs whirl around the screen, enlarging and shrinking themselves, superimposing one shot of a deprogrammer atop another. Nothing looks different to me, but Jules is *yes*ing and *aha*-ing under her breath, clearly impressed—either with whatever she's finding or with her own investigative skills. I've been known to high-five myself after a good case, but self-gratification only goes so far.

After a scant few minutes, Jules pushes back from her desk, the chair scooting backward on its casters and clunking into a stack of raw guise flesh behind it. With a flourish, she points to the screen, at the same six pictures that have been up there all along, and declares proudly, "There you go."

Should I be impressed? Should I have any idea what's going on?

Jules notices my confusion and relishes the opportunity to explicate her findings in detail. "Diplodoci, all of 'em. See that slight bulge where the neck joins the back? The indentation at the stomach?" No, but I have a feeling if she takes the time to tell me exactly how she can detect dino lineage beneath the human skin, I'll be late for Armageddon, let alone my eleven o'clock meeting with Bo. "Maybe not the third and the fifth," she continues, " 'cause it's tough to tell with that big costume head—but the rest of these characters are definitely from Diplodod stock."

Does this indicate, perhaps, the presence of a race-based cadre within the Progressives? A group of isolated Diplodoci preying on the others, bending them to their will? Premature assumption, perhaps, but it's what I've got to go on.

"Thanks," I begin—

But Jules won't let me go. "That ain't all, honey. Keep your tush right there, and I'll show you what else I dragged out of the pits."

Jules digs into another nearby box, this one purportedly filled with EYELASHES, KOREAN but actually empty except for a file folder and some stapled pages. "I cross-referenced every Progressive who left the organization and died soon afterward with the amount of time they'd been in the organization. Did the same with those kids who left the Progressives and didn't die. Any guesses as to what I found?"

"Nothing?"

"Everything. Let's look at Rupert for a sec. How long was he in the group?"

I shrug. "Three, four years, they thought. Give or take."

"Fine. Four years, and he's dead. Same with the girl down in Long Beach—she was in for six."

I must be missing the point, because Jules's eyes are twinkling, and I don't think it's due to one of her special New Year's–themed contact lenses. "We knew that already. If you leave the Progressives, you bite it."

"Wrong. I found a lot of kids who left the group and are hunky-dory to this very day. The difference is they got out early."

Jules flips me the papers, and I scan through her information. The trend continues. Four or more years equals death. Two or less equals life. There's not a lot of data for those in the middle, so it's hard to judge exactly where the line between assassination and live-and-let-live actually is, but it's not necessary to confirm my theory: Rupert knew too much.

During his rise up the Progressive ladder, Rupert became privy to more and more information, and by the time we'd cold-cocked him and dragged him back to Westwood, he was too infused with intimate intelligence, too much of a liability to leave dangling out in the real world. You've got two choices when your fine-knit sweater is snagged on a loose bit of wood: you can delicately sew the string back into the weave or cut it off at the base. The Progressives went the easy route.

It must have been the same for the others, which at least means that the cult isn't indiscriminately killing off their errant members; it's just killing off those who can blab about what they're up to—the guns, the brainwashing, the foreign coin jumping from hand to hand.

"This is great," I tell her as I stand, brush a spare nose off my shirt sleeve, and prepare to head back down to mid-city. "Circumstantial, but great. The Council will be interested, I know that much."

But as I head for the door, papers in hand, ready to meet Bo, get his opinion on the situation, and then hightail it to Council headquarters and bring the roof down on the Progressives' miscreant noggins, Jules reaches out an arm to stop me. "One more thing," she says. "And it might not make much of a difference—"

"Everything makes a difference."

"They're not the only ones who went away. The Progressives, I mean." I'm not following her, and she must be able to tell. "I was checking through the papers," she clarifies, "looking at the days around when Rupert and the others died, and for every twenty-something Progressive that bit it, there was another one, someone not in the group, that disappeared that same day, usually nearby."

"Same age?"

"Right around there. Rupert said bye-bye on a Thursday—previous day, some kid named Blish—a T-Rex, only twenty-eight—vanished. Middle of the night. Not that weird by itself, but it happened over and over again. Strange enough for twenty-somethings to be dropping off like that—"

"And stranger still that they're doing it in pairs." Suicide pacts? Assassination clones? Most information focuses investigations; this is only fragmenting it more.

Jules leads me to the door, her hand reassuringly on my back as she gives me a short little hug, pleads with me to be careful, and opens the double deadbolts. "Any idea what all this means?" she asks me. "The photos, the obits, all of it?"

"Got a hunch," I tell her as I check my watch and notice that

I'm running a good fifteen minutes behind schedule, "but there's no time to explain. I'm late for my dinner date." And then, just because I know it will tickle her to the bone, I elaborate: "He's a doctor."

.   .   .

La Brea Avenue, while not mired in gridlock, is still stop-and-go, even at this time of night. It takes a full half-hour to travel three miles, and as I near Wilshire, I can make out the problem: construction. A whole mess of it. And, of course, the city workers, who by all rights should be serving me tea and crumpets as part of their public-servant duties, are instead sitting on their massive mammal behinds, eating doughnuts and sucking down gallons of black coffee. Meanwhile, the rest of us are forced to breathe each others' exhaust due to their inability to get any project done on time and under budget.

The traffic ahead suddenly clears out, and a horn blast from behind spurs my foot toward the gas pedal. I pull away with a lurch, the catcalls and laughter of the construction workers trailing behind. Some part of me is itching for a fight, a full-scale battle to do away with all the human nonsense that gets in the way of our daily lives. *I'll get a freakin' army,* I want to yell out. *I'll go rustle up some of those dinos from the jungle and then we'll see who eats the final doughnut, Mister Homo sapiens, master of the food chain.*

The Tar Pit Club isn't one of your more private locales; it's a rocking joint in the Miracle Mile part of town, just east of Beverly Hills and just west of some areas you don't want to be in too late at night. There's a five-dollar cover charge and a no-drink minimum, so the place is usually packed with dinos and humans of all shapes and sizes flailing away to whatever the music craze of the moment happens to be.

Tonight there's a live ska band jamming out some backbeat rhythms, and the club is filled with Beverly Hills teenagers, desperately hip, whatever the cost. Dancing consists mostly of bouncing up and down, occasionally in couples, but mostly as a group. This isn't how we did it when I was a kid, but I'm sure I looked pretty stupid back then, too.

I told Bo to meet me at a booth in the back-left corner of the club—my usual spot whenever I abandon my solitude for the evening and make the drive out here to mid-city—and sure enough, the doctor is waiting there patiently when I arrive, dressed nattily in a big-shouldered blue suit, the kind plantation owners wore in the wintertime back before the Civil War up and took the market out of cotton. Sliding into the booth, I begin to apologize for my late arrival—

"Y'all aren't that late," he assures me. "I just got here myself. Traffic ain't so bad at eleven at night, but it's still a mite worse than in Nashville."

"Nashville?" I ask. "I thought you said you were from Memphis."

"Memphis is my home now," he explains after a short pause. "Nashville's where I grew up."

"Ah. Got it. You want some basil?" I motion for the waitress, but Bo reaches out and puts my arm down.

"No herbs," he tells me. "I'm driving. Now, let's get down to business—did you bring the photographs?"

I slide the pages across the table into the doctor's eager hands. "I had a spectroscopic analysis done," I say, proud to pronounce the words properly and evincing at least a glancing idea of what they mean, "and I've been told that the dinos beneath those costumes are Diplodoci."

Bo laughs and tosses the pages on the table. "Hell, I coulda told you that, son. You didn't need a fancy analysis."

Sure, tell me *now*. "How can you tell?"

Dr. Beauregard isolates three of the pictures and spreads them out across the desk. Pointing to the deprogrammer in each—one with a mustache, one with a beard, one somewhere in between—he shakes his head and smirks, "I did a fellowship with that one. In these three pictures here, he's wearing his usual guise, just with different accessories. Think he goes clean-shaven normally. . . ."

That's it—Dr. B. has the information I'm looking for. "So you know him."

"I know him well. His name's Carter—Brian Carter, I believe—and the man is a specialist in field paleontology."

"He's a human?" I ask.

"He's a fossil-placer," explains Dr. B.

So that's how he hooked up with Circe—they travel in the same business circles. She must have contacted Carter and convinced him to help out with her plan to keep a tight rein on the Progressive organization.

"Brilliant fellow," Bo muses.

"A brilliant fellow who's also connected to the Progressives," I point out. "Did you tell this Carter fellow anything about your contact with Rupert?"

Bo turns away slightly, avoiding my gaze. "I—I may have mentioned I was coming out to Los Angeles for some fieldwork. . . . May have mentioned Rupert's name, but . . . professional courtesy, a case study, y'all understand—"

I could be harsh on the guy, tell him that his lack of doctor-patient confidentiality may have cost a young T-Rex his life, but there's no point in flogging past indiscretions. If Samuel is at the bottom of Rupert's disappearance, then he'll be the one to pay in the end. "What about these other ones?" I ask, shoving the other photos into his field of view.

"Don't recognize the costumes, but I wouldn't be surprised if it's Carter going with a black-market guise. Boy never had a real fondness for the *rules*."

This Carter, then, is the key to the whole ugly mess. He's the one who's been telling the cult where their lapsed members are located, and he's the one figuring out ways to bump them off in secret. But if I can locate this fellow in human guise and apply the Vincent Rubio interrogation method (read: lots of pain, little mercy), I may very well be able to find out exactly what happened to Rupert and the others, stop whatever insidious plan Circe and her cadre have been cooking up for years now, bring down the Progressive organization, turn them all in to the honchos up at the Southern California Council, and get this case wrapped up by the end of the evening so that I might return home for a solid week of frolicking in the produce section of Ralphs.

"I don't suppose you'd know where to find him?" I ask Bo. He's already been more than helpful in every possible way, but I have a tendency to run favors into the ground. "Carter, I mean."

He's about to shake his head, ready to give me a "no" answer, when I see a little buzzer going off behind those eyes. "Actually," he says, rising higher in the seat, his excitement growing along with mine, "last I heard, he was sponsoring a dig right near here, down in the Tar Pits."

I'm pretty sure he's talking about the Pits themselves, not the nightclub we're presently in, though the sound system would indeed make this a good lecture hall. Ten blocks to the west of us is the George C. Page Museum of Natural Discoveries, a twenty-thousand-square-foot structure dedicated to the La Brea Tar Pits, the large black morass on which it is situated. There isn't a bona-fide dino bone anywhere near the Tar Pit confines, but within this LA landmark, scientists have found a wealth of Ice Age material, everything from saber-toothed tiger bones to woolly mammoths to old, discarded condoms—the nearby park contributes to much of the nonfossil material—and the excavation shelters erected during the halcyon Eisenhower years now serve as stops along many a visitor's tour of the area.

"Can you tell me exactly where he's been leading the digs?" I ask. "Which site?" There are ten or twelve of the shallow basements, and if I can narrow down the information, it will keep me from having to break and enter a dozen times this evening. No chance that Carter is at the park now, but at the very least, I might be able to break into some files or pick up an errant scent.

"I think it's site seven," says Bo. "But I'm not sure. Tell you what: I'm all done up for the night, and this sounds like more fun than watching pay-per-view back at the hotel. I'll come along."

I'm grateful for the company—missing Ernie's presence at my side after only seven hours, like an amputee with nothing but a ghost limb—but I can't put the doctor in what might possibly be harm's way. And even if I find this Carter before the Progressives find me, and even if the only pain incurred is strictly on Carter's side of the equation, Dr. Beauregard doesn't need to know the rumpled details of a PI's life. Better if I run the interrogation solo.

"Thanks, doc," I start out, "but there's . . . there are elements to my job—"

"That ain't a problem—"

"Messy elements," I clarify. "Unsavory elements."

"You think I ain't seen it all?" he interrupts. Leaning forward, pride in his profession, in his status, riding on every word, he confides in me, "I deprogrammed some of the *Manson* kids, son."

. . .

The Tar Pits—a mixture of tar and water, actually—run right next to Wilshire Boulevard along the Miracle Mile, separated from the busy street by only a thin chain-link fence that wouldn't keep out even the laziest vandal. Not that anyone's interested in diving in for a swim, of course, but if they choose to, we'll only know about it in twenty thousand years or so when they dredge up the bodies and prop them up for display.

It's an odd mix of entertainment and education here in the Tar Pits, where on a sunny summer day, the temperature can climb to over a hundred degrees and the resultant Glacier Bay stench can carry for miles. For example, the local curator must have thought the Tar Pits were too bland to attract the proper amount of attention—who wants to look at an oil spill all day?— so in order to spruce the place up, the George C. Page Museum has erected life-sized statues of woolly mammoths and mastodons inside the Pits themselves, depicted in a realistic life-and-death struggle with the imprisoning tar. On a small island of granite poking up from the center of the pit, a concrete baby mastodon watches its mother being sucked under the surface. There's even a hidden sound system bleating out the elephant calls of death and pain; it's a morbid little display, really, but the tourists *ooh* and *aah* at it from a raised viewing station just outside the museum walkway.

Not many tourists here 'round midnight, though. A few of the local homeless, pushing their shopping carts and singing their songs and arguing with the manhole covers, a Russian gentleman who swears that our fortunes can be accurately predicted by his cat, nothing out of the ordinary. Bo and I park in an empty lot and trot across a new stretch of sod; they've just finished a refurbishment of the area, and though it's a lot greener now, there's not much else to show for two years' worth of construction.

"So," Dr. B. asks as we walk, "what else y'all been figuring out on these Progressives?"

"A lot. Nothing. Everything. I've seen more than I'm supposed to, I know that much—dinosaurs running wild, reverted back to some primal version of themselves. A storage hut full of weapons—"

"Guns?" he asks incredulously.

"Rifles, pistols, bazookas, you name it." Okay, technically, I didn't see any bazookas, but it's the kind of minor exaggeration that can make a story more interesting, so I go with it. "They have something planned—something international, I believe."

"I've been studying the Progressives for years," he says, "but I never heard anything like this."

"Believe it, doc. I plan on filing about six hundred motions with every Council I can find once this is all over with. Hell or high water, the Progressives are going down."

No response from Bo; I hope I haven't worried him with my John Wayne side. I can be pretty intimidating sometimes.

We arrive at the excavation site, just a hole in the ground sur-rounded by more wire-link fence; a metal staircase leads down into the viewing area overlooking the pit. It's impossible to tell if the small room is currently occupied—note previous comment on used condoms—but I take the chance of being the *interruptus* in some unlucky couple's *coitus* and descend, Bo right behind me.

A single lightbulb hangs from a wire in the center of this three-walled room, and I flick it on, illuminating the decrepit viewing area with a burst of harsh white light. To my left, right, and behind me are ten-foot-high metal walls, the steel floor beneath littered with soda cans and beer bottles. Strangely, the smells of the tar aren't as strong down here, perhaps because the constant shade keeps the sun from baking the stench into the air.

Where the fourth wall should be, there's nothing but a guard rail and a plaque, and beneath it, the pit itself. EXCAVATION 7, reads the sign. OPENED JULY 12, 1959. Squinting into the dark-ness of the pit down below, I can make out a heap of tar, but nothing in the way of fossils or mummified creatures.

"Pretty boring place for a lecture," I say. "I thought it would be more . . . open."

Bo is beside me, also gazing into the pit; he picks up a pebble and drops it down, watching it thunk onto the surface ten feet below. The pebble does not sink; it simply sits on top of the black goop and waits to be sucked under. Death by delay. It's like waiting in line at the DMV, only it smells better down here.

Dr. Beauregard leans back against the far wall. "These places . . . they're very isolated, aren't they?"

"From what I can tell. Hey, you know if that Carter guy lives in the area?"

I've put him off guard—Bo flusters. "I—I don't know—"

My cell phone is out in a heartbeat—I'm the fastest draw in the west when it comes to mobile communications—and I'm dialing Dan's home number. I'm sick and tired of being routed and rerouted every time I call his LAPD office, so, hopefully, I'll get through this time. "I'm calling Dan—Sergeant Patterson," I tell Dr. B. "You wanna talk to him, say hi?"

"No—no, you feel free . . ."

Two rings, and a real, honest-to-goodness voice—"Yello . . . ?"

"Praise the Lord, he's home," I say into the phone. "You are one hard Bronto to get in touch with."

Instantly contrite, Dan is apologizing all over the place for not speaking with me earlier. "I tried over the weekend," he says, "but you weren't answering, and I didn't want to leave a message—"

"Forget about it," I tell him. "Let you off the hook if you do me a favor."

"Anything."

"I need the address, priors, and whatever you got on some guy named Brian Carter. A doctor, I think."

"Sure, no problem. What's up?"

"Just a little investigation," I say, giving a wink to Bo. He does not wink back. I turn, staring into the tar pits as I speak. "I'm out here with the deprogrammer you turned me on to."

"Huh?"

"Dr. B. Bo. Beaumont Beauregard." How many times does he want me to say the name for him?

"I don't know what the hell you're talking about, Vincent."

I sigh loudly, then carefully explain, worried for my friend's failing memory. "When I called you, back about three weeks ago, I asked you to recommend a cult deprogrammer—"

"And I said I'd get back to you, I know, I know. But that's why I'm apologizing—I kept forgetting to tell you, I don't know anyone who can help."

"What? No, no, I got a call from the doctor, and he said that you—"

"This Dr. Beauregard you're talking about . . ." says Dan, "I have no idea who he is. I've never heard of him in my life—"

It's right about then that the pain begins, a bursting pressure starting in my sinuses, traveling through my nose and up into my head—my entire body suddenly stuffed full to bursting with every imaginable scent: carnivals and Cracker Jacks, carburetors and cola, a cavalcade of smells wracking every muscle, every ligament—

I can barely turn around, vision dimming, the viewing area fading, dissolving away, that prehistoric jungle quickly vibrating into place—Dr. Beauregard, standing in front of me, here but not here, carefully taking the cellular phone out of my hands—Dan's voice, calling in the distance, *"Vincent, can you hear me? Vincent, hello, are you still there?"*—an ancient oak blasting up from the ground, plants popping into existence, mosquitoes the size of eagles materializing, laughing, and flapping away—Dr. Beauregard tossing the phone into the tar pits below—a strange, content smile spreading across his wide, kind face—and I'm wondering if the phone is still on, if Dan is still talking, if my cellular company is going to charge me for the extra minutes—

Another sudden burst of scent, and now I can smell the herbs forcing it along, the basil and cilantro spreading into every pore of my body, my nostrils the gateway to this wonderful, horrible experience—and soon there's nothing else except for me, Dr. Beauregard, a single metal rail, and a prehistoric world alive with a billion natural specimens running wild, running free.

A push on my chest, a trip, a stumble, and I'm over the railing and falling backward, floating on a cloud before I come to a landing in something wet, something sticky. Dr. Beauregard is so far away now, high above me, and he's looking down, waving to me, waving *bye-bye, bye-bye.*

"Goodbye, Mr. Rubio," says the good doctor. "Give my regards to the ancestors."

I will, Bo. I will . . .

There is a strong possibility that I am dead.

. . .

It's not so bad.

. . .

I am myself in here.

. . .

Some time later, whenever that might be—*time* has about as much meaning in this place as *restraint* does in Las Vegas—I find that I am unable to move, unable to breathe, unable to do any of the things one normally associates with living, but somehow I know, instinctively, that I am not dead. This is a new step for me. My last will and testament has been written and rewritten in my head a hundred times since Dr. Beauregard, or whoever he is, bade me farewell, and the really sad part is that there isn't much I have to say. Ernie gets most of my stuff; a nephew of mine in Topeka gets some pocket change and a humidifier for his asthma.

I've also been counting—first up to a hundred, then up to a thousand, then ten thousand, and so on. I lost track a while back, but I think I abandoned the plan somewhere around 16,800 or so. It wasn't even making me sleepy, as I had forgotten to associate sheep with every passing digit.

Tar surrounds me on all sides. At least, that's my current belief. It's distinctly possible that I'm dead and just in denial or reincarnated as a lucky boy's pet rock, but the tar explanation suits me better for the moment.

Fortunately for me, I have remembered the one interesting fact I learned during my first visit to the George C. Page Museum ten years ago: The more you struggle in a tar pit, the faster you will die. Your movements will only help suck you farther beneath the surface, and even if you're able to live without air—a feat I seem somehow to be accomplishing—the lack of food and water will get to you eventually.

Also, fortunately for me, much of the polar ice cap has gone and melted away over the last few millennia, which means I have a distinct advantage over the saber-toothed tigers who found themselves trapped with no means of escape: a high water table. And I'm buoyant, baby.

Allowing myself to sit completely still is a difficult task, especially with an itch on my nose that refuses to go away. But if I reach up to scratch it, I run the risk of aggravating the tar and sinking farther into the pit; better to lie still, deal with the maddening prickling on my proboscis, and let the water help me rise to the surface.

I feel like an errant Monopoly piece when it comes to this dog of a case; every time I start to round Ventnor and Marvin Gardens and prepare to hit the really good part of town, something or someone sends me scurrying back to Baltic Avenue, and I have to start all over again. There's only so much a dino PI can take, and

I'm one and two-ninths of the way past my limit, a mixed fraction for God's sake.

A bright speck of light before me—is this the tunnel that will take me to greet the ancestors? Is my Uncle Ferdy going to leap out of the grave and into the spotlight any second and start up the vaudeville act that used to bring down the house in the twenties? The light does, indeed, grow closer, stronger, more intense, but for the moment, at least, my dead relatives stay put.

Suddenly I can feel the cool night air touching parts of my bare hide, and something in me snaps. It feels like a switch has been thrown, like the fuse box has been fixed, and all of my organs turn on at once. My eyes flick open of their own accord—the bulb in the viewing area burning brightly overhead—and I let out a hacking cough, expelling a thick wad of tar from my esophagus. A deep, gasping breath follows, and my lungs expand with the most tar-and-parasite-infested air I've ever come across. It's the sweetest thing I've tasted.

Everything is revving up once again, coming back to normal. It's as if I was simply sleeping that whole time and needed a few moments in the morning to stretch and work out the kinks. Still, I'm not out of the woods yet. I wait until the water table has pushed me well up over the surface of the tar, being careful not to squirm around any more than necessary. My ideal plan would be to stretch my arm over the surface of the pit, grab on to the side wall, and gradually, carefully, roll myself up and out of the tar. But as I slowly reach for the nearest outcropping, I realize that it's not going to work that way—my arms are far too short to make the trek.

The legs and toes are long enough but don't have the proper dexterity required to do the job. Jaw is too far away from the railing to consider biting my way to safety, and I don't relish having to wait for a flabby tourist with ice cream stains on his Sunset Boulevard T-shirt to fetch me out of this quagmire. The tail will have to do.

The only problem is, it means I have to turn on my side in order to free the dexterous slab of meat from its costumed confines. Rolling to my right like a mother hen carefully sitting on her eggs, I slowly expose my side to the tar, being careful not to stick my arm any farther in than necessary.

With my mammal bum exposed to the open air, I reach back and attempt to unsnap the G-3 series of tail buckles with only one hand. I was especially adept at this in my younger days, only it wasn't my own buckles I was undoing at the time. The task is made more difficult by the layers of clothing and fake skin between my digits and the strap, as well as the omnipresent threat of the thick molasses of death waiting to gobble me up whole.

My tail suddenly springs loose, the open buckle flapping around inside my polysuit. If I get out of this pit, it's going to look like I've got a load in my pants, but no matter; I'd rather be embarrassed than dead any day of the epoch. Now all it takes is a few more snaps at the waist skin, a gentle tug to the hips—

And my tail is free, a small part of me natural and Progressive all over again. Working quickly and assuredly, I elongate my tail as far as it will go and wrap the tip around a chunk of rebar poking out of the Pit wall. Rather than try to force myself up all at once, I use my tail like a fishing rod, reeling it around and around the bar, slowly dragging my body out of the tar and onto dry land.

Wasting no time, I get my tail in on more action, using it as a balance as I leap up and out of the tar pit and into the safety of the viewing area. I reguise myself rapidly, tucking the tail back into its confines and loosely fastening the buckle in place before bounding into the park, a tar baby with vengeance on his mind.

It's all starting to come together now—the murders, the rituals, the doctor who really isn't. I may need some assistance on this one—at the very least, I need someone to bear witness to my knowledge—and since Ernie's still laid up in Hawaii, I need to get to Jules, and I need to get to her fast. But as I lurch into the parking lot, my thighs sticking together—now I know how Oprah feels—there's a curious lack of Lincoln where my Lincoln should be, with nothing but a pool of oil to remember her by.

Okay, *now* it's personal.

With my car stolen, there's no way to get up to Hollywood short of public transportation, and I strongly doubt that our friendly neighborhood bus drivers will let the Swamp Thing come on board, even if he has the required eighty-five cents, which I believe I do not. A taxicab is out of the question as well, if only because they're about as frequent in Los Angeles as trust-fund babies driving Pintos, and if I lift the handset of a public telephone in order to call one, I may become stuck to it for good.

Walking it will be, then, squishing along as fast as my crude-oiled legs will take me. If someone were to come along and scrape my shins, they could power Manhattan for weeks. I stick to alleys and shadows, hoping to avoid contact with any other forms of life. On my way into Hollywood, I pass a mongrel sipping God-knows-what out of an old soup can; the pitiful critter looks up, takes in an eyeful, and promptly scurries away, fearful of losing his Most Decrepit status to a shuffling, panting dino.

But the trip is taking me forever, and this is not my only destination of the night. I've managed to make it up near Beverly Boulevard, surprised to find the streets not quite as desolate as they should be this time of evening. A steady stream of street-walkers prowl the sidewalks, wobbling on three-inch heels, tucking glitter skirts up and in so that the average hemline comes to somewhere just below the neck.

They reek of strong perfume—not the somewhat appealing, somewhat repulsive feminine musk that a lot of human women give off, but a cannonball of potpourri shot directly at the sinuses—and I have to cover up my nose in order to block out the stench.

But it's that smell, the eau de whore, that sets off a series of rapid-fire thoughts in my mind. Soon enough, I've got the semblance of a plan, and my sniffer is released back into the open once more to do its dirty work.

Bringing in the cool night air, I let my schnoz filter through the stronger, bigger bullies of human-made perfumes, searching for the one scent that might be cowering down in the olfactory region as if to blend into the crowd. As I travel up La Brea, I know I should locate it soon enough, if only because this is her usual stomping grounds, and tonight is prime time for eager johns. Unless, of course, she's already retired to the Chateau for the evening. . . .

Every step is another deep breath, another cleansing exhale. Every non-dino smell rejected out of hand, not what I'm looking for tonight. Not what I'm looking for *any* night.

And then, faint but sure, there it is. Pine, autumn air. That's it—that's the basic odor. Quickly then, refining it further, separating the wheat from the chaff, and soon it's a perfect olfactory portrait: bubble gum and sod.

And there she is, strutting her stuff for the clientele who drive by with their windows down and their libidos out, shaking her costumed rump for all to see. Body tightly packed into a red mini-mini, a sleeveless number with a skimpy top and nearly nonexistent bottom. Silver stilettos, makeup caked, fake fingernails as long as her heels and capable of some serious dorsal damage. She's by herself, walking all alone past shadowy side streets and empty storefronts.

I sneak around a back alley and come up right behind this hooker I know so well. "Star," I whisper in her ear, "it's time to pay the piper."

Before she can react, before she gets a chance to alert the other ladies of the evening that anything is amiss, I clap my hand around her mouth and pull her back into the darkness of the alleyway. She tries to bite down on my fingers, but the tar gets stuck in her mouth, and she spends the next two minutes spitting out the foul substance.

"I've been looking for you," I say, keeping my voice low but firm. "You're a hard bird to catch."

"The fuck are you?" she spits.

"My name's Rubio, we met once before. Nice little party at your place."

"Yeah, so, like I said—who the fuck are you?"

"Don't like that answer? Okay, how 'bout this: I'm the guy that's gonna keep you from spending the next year breakin' rocks in the hot sun. Betcha there ain't a lot of johns down at County. A few Janes, I'd imagine . . ." It's this kind of bad-cop, bad-cop confrontation I could really get into; too bad they only come along once a year or so.

"Keep talking," she says, suddenly interested.

"I believe you have my client's penis."

She tries to shake off my grasp—"What? I don't—"

"A very valuable penis, I'm led to understand. A Mussolini."

"You can't prove it—"

"And I don't have to," I tell her. "For that matter, I don't want to. You don't worry about that. All I'm asking of you is a favor. If you do it, I stop looking for you, and I make sure Minsky stops looking for you, too. I know you like that . . . thing, and it's all yours if you do what I ask."

"And you'll protect me from the cops?"

"Just on this," I tell her, making clear my intentions. "Anything else, you're on your own. But maybe I can put a good word in for you down at the station. I know some people."

I give Star a few moments to think it over, but there's no easier decision than this. "Whaddaya want?" she asks, softening up a touch.

She has a pen in her purse, and I grab a pamphlet from the street advertising some new punk band up at one of the Sunset clubs. "Bend over," I say, and Star willingly assumes the position. She begins to lift her dress, allowing me access—

"Keep your goddamn skirt on," I shout, then lower my voice again. Softer: "I'm not interested in—look, I don't want sex, I just want to write a note."

"That's it?" she chirps, and for a split second, I can see the little girl that once held sway over this young mind and body. An innocent relief spreads across her features, softening her eyes, her grin. Then it's all gone, and the streetwalker sneer returns to her ruined face. "So I can keep the dick, right?"

"Right. I write the note, you deliver it, we're even."

A hastily scribbled letter to Jules, detailing all I know and all I think I know and a hasty plan of action for the evening. If I don't come back from this little journey, I want to make sure someone goes to the Council, the cops, to anyone who can bring these bastards down. Folding the letter into fourths, I tuck it deep into Star's purse and make her swear not to peek. I'm guessing that she probably will anyway, but she won't understand half of it. I can only hope that Jules does.

That taken care of, I send Star and her Mussolini on their way and plot a course for my next destination: a certain piece of neo-classical architecture nestled up in the Hollywood Hills. And this time, I hope to be coming back with a few party favors.

.   .   .

It's been hard going, my feet directed, as they are, on the sticky side of the street, but with every passing mile, the tar has worn thinner, the trip grown easier. A digital display outside a bank I passed on the way into the Hills told me it is nearly five o'clock in the morning, which means I must have been lying dormant in the tar pit, not moving, not *breathing,* for just over two hours. Can't think about that now.

On my way through a poorly tended backyard—this must be where the rich white trash of the Hollywood Hills hang out—I snatch a few clothespins off a laundry line and shove them deep down into my tar-filled pockets. There is a serious doubt in my mind as to whether or not they'll ever make it out of these pants again, but if the need arises, I'll pull with all my might. The Hills provide a bit of cover, and I find myself sneaking through more and more backyards in order to remain hidden behind the trees and shrubbery. Along one small stretch of land, it almost feels like I'm back on the Progressives' island, caught in that jungle once again.

Up ahead is the Progressive compound, and inside are the

players in tonight's performance; little do they know I am no longer an understudy. But the curtain's going to fall early unless I can figure out a quick, painless way into the theater. There are sure to be sentinels posted somewhere on the grounds, and I only hope that my current state of camouflage—tar black is in this year—will do the job.

A low brick wall is the only perimeter, but I look before I leap, making sure there isn't a pit of snakes or a rabid guard gorilla on the other side. Nothing would surprise me when it comes to this group.

No snakes, no gorilla, no booby trap of spikes and monsters. Sticking to the trees, I make my way across the acreage, marveling once again at the sheer extent of the land. Fifty, sixty, a hundred acres might be a postage-stamp lot out in Iowa, but in the Hollywood Hills it's practically enough to split off from the union.

In time, the main house comes into view, the blazing white columns and archways beginning to wake up to the first light of dawn, preparing to sparkle and blind the hell out of anyone who has the misfortune to look in their direction, a perfect blend of architecture and protection. The parking lot is filled with cars of every make and model, each space filled and those in between squeezed as tight as they can go, double-parked to the limit. Makes the overfill lot at the Hollywood Bowl look like the Serengeti.

Much like our entrance into the palace back on the island, sneaking into the mansion is a heck of a lot easier than, say, crashing Spago's post-Oscar bash, and results in many fewer bruises—don't ask, don't ask. Soon enough I'm slipping down the main hallway, sticking to the shadows, keeping my eyes and nose open and ready. There's a great tumult emanating from within the main ballroom, and a cacophony of smells intertwined with the noise. But that's not where I'm going. Not yet, anyway.

Footsteps behind me, clomping down the hall, and I fall back into a darkened niche, pressing my body up against the marble walls. Cold. I control the shivering with a good, solid tongue bite, and watch as a couple of dinos in guise—two businessmen, it looks like, three-piece suits and all—stroll purposefully toward the ballroom. As they walk, the two begin to undress, first removing their human clothes, quickly followed by their human skin. A mask is lifted, latex straining against the epoxy, then snapping free, the Hadrosaur beneath flipping his flexible beak into place a moment later. Tails are unfurled, horns released, and soon I'm walking behind two natural dinos, pacing them from thirty feet back.

". . . said they'll be ready in Europe," one is saying. "Same time we are here."

"On his signal, though—"

"—of course, of course, not without his signal."

And they duck into the ballroom—filled to capacity, my nose tells me. Barring the one time I was erroneously placed in the dino immigration ward down in San Diego, I've never been in one location so tightly packed with our species before. There's a dino density of massive proportions in that ballroom—they must be packed in snout-to-tail in there—and I hope the walls are strong enough to prevent a leak.

I come upon that familiar hallway, and at the end of it, Circe's room. *This is my lounge,* Circe told Ernie and me less than one week ago. *I come here before large events, to . . . prepare, if you will.* Well, we've got a large event brewing downstairs, and my guess is it won't be just Circe preparing inside this room. Of course, there's only one way to find out.

Embedded in the wall next to the door is a finger-hole of very familiar proportions, and I know what I have to do. There is no doubt in my mind that these locking systems, the Ancestrograph, and the rest of the mockery of mechanics utilized by this group, are a scientific crock of shit, technically speaking. *Dinosaur natural* is a term created by the few in order to scare the many, but that's as far as it goes. Yet there is also no doubt in my mind that they *do* measure increased pheromone production, a magic trick the higher-echelon Progressives have learned to do on command, without smoke, mirrors, or lovely assistants.

Now it's my turn. David Copperfield, outta my way.

With Ernie out of the picture, I've got to do this thing myself. Squeezing my finger inside the hole, I try to free my mind of mammalian thoughts. Mortgage payments are the first out my mental window, followed quickly by the rampant spread of computer viruses, my dry-cleaning bill, and the Lakers' hopes in the postseason. All I want to think about is running, eating, sleeping, sex. Jumping, hopping, roaring, sex. Fighting, winning, prancing, sex.

I close my eyes and take myself back to that fern jungle, that place where the past surges into the present, where the Jurassic bursts through the walls and makes itself known, where my feet sink into the soft earth and my cry is a death knell for all the lesser creatures. I try not to feel the cold steel around my finger, growing colder with every second, sucking out my juices. I try to keep it warm, moist, a hot summer day seventy million years in the past, every tree and every bush and every leaf a natural part of my body, warming me, keeping me on my toes—open movement, never constricted, never constrained, loose and running free. My eyes opening, taking in the vibrant, natural colors, unblemished by smog and smoke and gas, my ears drooping back, angling upward to hear the calls of the Pterodactyls, my feet curling inward to feel the long, slimy bugs crawling between my toes, thousands of legs working over my bare hide. A herd of Compies—not crude, not crass, but a pack of simple, beautiful creatures—scampering over the lush, verdant landscape.

And I'm on the run, alone and alive, at liberty to move how I want to move, eat how I want to eat, kill how I want to kill, the consummate hunter with a belly full of hunger and the claws to satisfy it—streaming over the open land, head set against the wind, eager like never before to begin the chase, to begin the hunt, to begin—

The hole suddenly spits out my finger like a kid expelling his rutabagas across the kitchen table, and for a moment I'm stuck in both worlds, the prehistoric world and the modern, superimposed on each other, an acetate overlay atop a brilliant Kodachrome print. The hallways are filled with twenty-foot flowers, the door crawling with thirty-pound beetles. A marble Allosaur statue twenty feet away has filled out with flesh and muscles and skin and a roar that echoes out across the hills and down into the basin.

Boom—with a flash, the jungle shatters into a million pieces before my eyes and dissolves into nothingness, and I'm left in front of an open doorway in the heart of a mansion in the Hollywood Hills. For a moment, I almost think I can perceive the remnants of my own scent—if I whiff the air just right, I believe I can get that Cuban stogie coming through. But I know that such a thing's not possible, and it's foolish to even think it at this stage of the game. As it stands, I was able to produce enough pheromones to get the door open on my very first try; it's good to be an overachiever, but let's take this Progress thing one step at a time, Vincent.

As I enter the lounge, I make sure to leave the door open behind me. Those inside are bound to be a mite upset at my presence, and I don't want to foreclose the possibility of a hasty retreat. I've never had a showdown without Ernie by my side.

The 1970s beanbag theme has remained the dominant motif, unfortunately, but a thick mahogany desk and wide-backed leather chair on the far side of the room—the power side of the room, as management consultants would say—belie the design presence of someone other than Circe. A silhouette on the wall doesn't budge an inch as I step into the room, clear my throat, and announce, "I know what you're doing. Ernie knows what you're doing, too, as do a few friends of mine at the LA *Times*." This last part is a bluff, but it's always good to bring up the media at times like these. "I suggest you give it all up now, come with me, and if you help out with the investigation, the Council might be lenient with you."

No answer from the chair, save for a—a giggle? Is that laughter?

"I'm glad you think this is a joking matter," I say, a portion of my confidence draining out through my feet and disappearing into the cracks in the floor. "Because gun smuggling, kidnaping, and murder are all federal offenses, and that's before we bring the Council into it. They'll want to hear about—"

"Who did I murder?" comes a low, even voice, still tinged with a side order of good humor. "Who exactly did I kill?"

"Rupert Simmons for one," I blurt out. "Try that on for starters."

"Did I? Now, that's odd . . ."

And with that, the chair spins around—he must have known I was here, must have been setting up this chair-spin gag for the last ten minutes just to mock me, the crazy son of a bitch—and I'm suddenly face to face with the reason I took on this god-damned case in the first place.

"I'd say I look pretty good for a dead guy," grins Rupert. "Don't you think?"

23

You—you're dead," I stammer.

"Yes, you keep insisting that," drawls Rupert. He stands up from the chair and walks across the room; unguised and standing tall, the young T-Rex is a good five inches taller than I, his body lean and muscular. Meanwhile, I'm sitting here wrapped in my constricting latex, which is, in itself, wrapped in a continually hardening layer of tar. This is not good.

"We—I saw your body," I tell him, still trying to replay the funeral in my mind. Closed casket, if I remember correctly. Okay, maybe I didn't see his body. But his sister was the one who found him, and siblings don't often make that kind of mistake. "Louise, she—she found you—"

"My sister found me in my room," he finishes. "I'm quite aware. But she found me in costume, didn't she?"

I don't know why it hits me now, and at the same time, I don't know why it didn't hit me before. Damn my intuition to show up at the party ten minutes too late. "The T-Rex who went missing near your house that night," I say. "He's the one—they killed him, then dressed him in your guise. You took a total stranger—"

"Not a stranger," Rupert corrects. "A guy I knew from high school, actually. Dan Blish, an asshole football player who liked tying me to the tackling dummys and giving the offensive line a few whacks at the sled. Trust me, he deserved it."

"No one deserves death," I say. "They—you—the Progressives kidnaped and killed this kid so he could take your place at the funeral."

"Wow," says Rupert mockingly, "you're pretty quick on the uptake—when the whole thing's handed to you. Big deal. I knew my sister was a fool for hiring you in the first place."

"Why?" I ask, going against my better judgment and leaning closer to the boy. "Why would you come back to this?"

"Why would I ever want to leave it? All my life, I've been searching for happiness. I was a miserable little kid, a miserable teenager, and a miserable adult, and now that I've found something that makes me content, everyone wants to take me away from it."

"Because it's wrong," I explain patiently.

"How? How is it wrong to want to be what you are? How is it wrong to be able to come out and sing 'I am dino, hear me roar'?"

"It's—it's not that simple—"

"It *is* that simple," Rupert insists. "It's that simple, and it's nearly complete. You and my ex-brother-in-law took me away before I could compete in the Ring, my final challenge before I was to become truly natural, and for that I can never forgive you. But I can forget. Soon, it all comes down to the final battle. Now we'll know for sure who should dominate the earth: the mammals or the reptiles. Would you like to bet on how it will turn out?"

I shake my head. Haven't placed a wager since I lost twenty grand on the last Foreman fight. Some bum told me he was a Raptor, so I laid it down out of respect for the brotherhood and I'm not going to start up again with a bet on the fate of the world.

"I can't let that happen," I say. "I'm sorry, but I'm going to take you back to your sister."

"You are?" he asks, the cheery tone mocking me from all directions at once. Then, dropping to a lower register, taking a step forward and puffing out his chest like a robin searching for a mate, his hard-earned muscles pressing against his hide, claws flashing in and out like the needle on a sewing machine, he asks, "You and who else?"

Good question. Who else?

"Me, for one."

I turn, expecting to find the media, the governor, anyone—but under the circumstances, it's ten times better. With his arm and shoulder wrapped up in a gleaming white cast and his own guise situated comfortably on his body, Ernie is a model of blasé as he enters the room and struts confidently up to his ex-brother-in-law.

"You're a good kid," says my partner, "but you always were a pain in the ass." And with that, he whips that solid cast up and around, cold-cocking Rupert one last time, sending him to the mat for a final ten-count.

The boy goes down hard.

Ernie's all over me before I have a chance to thank him. "You ever heard of the word 'backup'?" he shouts. "Partners don't go in solo, especially not something like this. If Jules hadn't called the office when your note showed up, I'd still be wandering the city looking for you, and you'd be the raw meat at tonight's dinner."

"How the hell did you get here so fast?"

"I flew out on the red-eye."

I shake my head; a loose bit of tar flies out of my hair and lands on Rupert's prone body. "That wouldn't get you here until a few hours from now—that's not possible."

Ernie's good hand reaches up to feel my forehead, as if he's checking my temperature. "You thinkin' straight, kid? I stayed in the hospital for a few hours, got myself released against doctor's orders, and took yesterday's midnight flight back to the mainland. Got in LA around nine A.M. I've been looking for you all day." His eyes scan me up and down, taking in the torn guise and the frazzled hair and, oh yes, the tar, and I can see those Ernie gears engaging and turning, trying to figure out what kind of mess I'd gotten myself into. "Where the hell have you been?" he asks.

If Ernie's telling the truth—and I don't see any reason for him to lie, except for the fact that everyone else seems to have been lying to me for the past few weeks—then I wasn't in the tar pit a mere two hours; I was there for closer to twenty-four. But there is no possible way I could have survived an entombment that long.

Actually, there is one way.

"I was hibernating, Ern." Laughing now, the humor bubbling up from within, the concept so irrational and yet so right that if I don't laugh I'll start screaming instead. "I'm pretty darn sure I was hibernating."

A crash behind us as the door flies inward, slamming into Rupert's leg. Doesn't anybody knock anymore? "That's a Progressive ability, did y'all know that?" says Dr. Beauregard, stepping over the fallen T-Rex's prone body. "Sustained hibernation—animated suspension, basically—is a very primal trait of ours. It might have been that last burst of scent I gave you back in the pits, but I'm pretty sure your body learned that one on its own. I'm proud of you, son."

"And I'm sick of you," I reply. "I'm sick of the whole damn lot of you."

Circe struts in behind Dr. B., tail wagging lasciviously, hands on her hips and a sad, almost disappointed look on that perfectly formed face. She can't meet my eyes, her gaze wandering away every time I try to snag her attention, and her scent is nearly impossible to discern.

Before they can get out another word—or, worse, another smell—I reach into the one pocket that isn't filled with goo and toss Ernie two clothespins. "Snap 'em on," I suggest, whipping off my human mask so that I can affix mine tightly around my natural nostrils. As my snout expands into place, like a sponge growing with water retention, I place a second pin across the first; the double action stings a bit, but it's a small price to pay for protection.

"I don't know what you think you know, Vincent," Circe begins, now shooting small, hit-and-run glances up at me, "but I can assure you, you're making a mistake—"

"Can it, toots," says Ernie, and I think . . . yes, I do believe he's in the zone. "We've heard enough outta you for three natural lifetimes."

"We know quite a lot," I continue, "and none of it's a mistake, not anymore. How you find kids who are scared, who are lonely, and take them in. How you tell them they're a part of a special group, teach them ways to get back to nature."

"And what's wrong with that?" defends Circe. "It's true, it's all true. You've felt it yourself—you can't deny it. Vincent, you're a beautiful, natural Velociraptor, and no social constraints should stand in the way of your natural powers."

Ernie usually takes the closing argument in these cases, but I figure after this ordeal, it's time to make my bones. "May I?" I ask my partner.

"By all means," he says proudly. "Lay it on 'em."

"We knew something was wrong from the moment we saw the second battle in the Ring, the one where the young Raptor lost out to the bull. The dinos he chose as his confederates, by all accounts your average Progressives, were simply too good with a dart gun. Their aim couldn't have been the result of occasional target practice with a tranquilizer rifle—those shots were made with military-style precision, and you only come by that level of skill through a mess of practice. And why should dinosaurs, especially those who are trying to advance beyond human means, be practicing with any firearms whatsoever?"

I walk behind the mahogany desk and take a seat in the chair, facing my audience with a wide grin. I could get used to this. "Now, let's backtrack for a second and look at what happens to those dinosaurs who make it past the challenge of the Ring and join the ranks of mindless carnivores. They're shut up in a paddock, corralled, and drop-shipped live cartons of pigs and live-stock they can tear apart to their heart's content. But why deal with a whole island full of naturalized beasts? Is that truly the goal, to populate a bunch of islands with dinosaurs forced to live off whatever a hydrofoil can ship in on a daily basis?"

Circe tries to cut in. "No, but—"

"Ah, ah—everyone will get their turn. No, of course it's not. And this started to dawn on me from the moment we saw that building in the jungle filled with those maps, those weapons—"

"Weapons?" Circe interrupts, head vibrating in a speedy spasm. "We don't have weapons. Now you're talking crazy, Vincent—"

"Don't play dumb. Of course, I didn't know what to make of it for a while, and the tidal wave of reason didn't crash over me until I got into a confrontation with some construction workers back here in LA."

"Isn't it always that way, though?" says Ern, always at the ready to pop in with a line.

"So here's the big question: What is the goal of any organization that creates two classes out of its citizens, one skilled and the other brutish?"

No response. These folks don't play along with *Jeopardy!* from the comfort of their sleeper sofas, I bet.

"The goal," I tell them, "is simply this: to form an army."

"What?" Circe is not happy, to say the least. Her hands clench into tight balls of fury, and I'm no longer sure that she knows what I'm talking about.

"Sure," I continue, "it's obvious. And not just one little battalion on one little island. We're talking worldwide, large-scale outposts on every island in every country in every continent in the world. Brontosaurs, Raptors, Steogsaurs, T-Rexes. Dinos marching side by side, mowing their way across the globe, exterminating any and every human in their path. Mammals, beware—it's time for the blitzkrieg."

"Tell ya what—why don't you ask Raal about it?"

Slowly, deliberately, I turn toward Dr. Beauregard, making my gaze and my intention quite clear to everyone in the room. My eyebrow raises of its own accord, and I'm pretty sure some drums should be kicking in right about now.

"Oh, quit it," grumbles Dr. Beauregard, whipping off his beard and mustache, dropping the Colonel Sanders routine altogether. The rest of the guise quickly follows, and I'm not surprised in the least to find that beneath that costume is, of course, a Diplodocus. "Everyone knows who I am. Don't start pretending you're Sherlock Holmes on us now."

Ernie raises his hand. "I didn't know. Not for sure, at least."

"Thanks," I say.

"No problem."

But Circe's not interested in joining the banter; her anger is genuine, and she spins on Raal, hide flushed, eyes flashing. "What are they talking about? Do you know what's going on?"

"It's the final culmination to our plans," insists the Diplodod. "The core of the idea, intact and made real."

"That's not what you taught me," insists Circe. "All those years, you taught me that the core is Progression. The core is getting back to a state of nature."

"Yes," Raal agrees. "And after it, conquest."

Ernie gives me a nod, and I'm glad to concede the floor to the honorable Carnotaur from the great state of California. "You see, Circe, Dr. Beauregard—Raal—isn't content with an island or two like you are. He's not content with feeling good about himself or understanding what he is and how he fits into the evolutionary picture. I was worried about you at first—I even warned Vincent to stay away from you. I suspected your motives were . . . shall we say disingenuous?—but you proved me wrong. I believe now that you believe in Progress. Unfortunately, you're not in charge, and the real leader has some other ideas up his triple-fake sleeves. Progress isn't enough for him. It's not fair, he'd say, that the dinosaurs should only get an island to themselves—"

"It's not—" interrupts the cult leader.

"See. And it's not fair, he'd say, that the mammals should have all this land to themselves. It's apartheid, it's oppression, it's deserving of a revolution."

"I like your style," says Raal. "You should come work for the team."

"I don't think so," replies Ernie. "Because while I'm no fan of the human race—believe me, I'd rather eat dinner with a blind mole rat than one of their kind—it doesn't make me want to commit genocide. This is what you meant from the very start, isn't it, Raal? You found Circe because she had the gift, the ability to use her powers and draw others to the cause, but the real goal was to return this world to the way things were before the humans showed up. All this talk about worshiping the ancestors—you don't want to revere them, you want to *be* them."

Raal issues a tight little grin. "And what's wrong with that?"

"What's wrong with that?" I echo. "How about gun smuggling and kidnaping and murder?"

But Raal is guilt-free; it slides off him like grease off Teflon. "Those who died did so for the good of their kind." Circe, on the other hand, has begun to tremble uncontrollably, though whether it is with rage or fear, I can't say.

"Buzz and Wendell?" I say. "They needed to go? You *had* to rig those guns to fail and the cage to lock in place?"

"They had been talking to you, too close to the information. It had to be stopped."

"None of this—" Circe starts. "It wasn't planned."

"Wasn't planned by *you*, perhaps," I reply, "but I'd take a look in your organization and find out who's loyal to your orders and who listens to the big cheese over here."

"And what do you think tonight is for?" Ernie says, keeping his attention focused on Circe. "This little shindig in the ballroom?"

"It's—it's a meeting," stutters Circe, already unsure of the words, the meaning. "To discuss the next conference."

"It's a rally," I say. "It's a pep talk before the onslaught."

Ernie puts an arm around Circe's shoulders, waving his hand

through the air, spelling out a banner headline. "The day when the dinosaurs shall rise again."

"You really should join up," insists Raal, coming closer to me, his snout within snapping distance of mine. "I'd hate to lose a mind like yours in the cleansing."

Ernie steps between us, a ref breaking two boxers from a clench, and clears his throat. "Enough with the spat. We're done here."

"We are, indeed," I say, turning on Circe. "The love affair is over, babe, the heartache just begun. You used me for the last time."

"Used *you*?" she spits back. "You're a phony. You pretended to be someone who you weren't from the start."

"But it's my job, doll. You're two-faced for fun."

Ernie puts a nice end to the conversation. "Vincent, you wanna cuff 'em or should I?" He dangles four solid rings of metal in the air, offering me the chance to captivate Circe for a change.

"I didn't mean—Raal, you said . . ." Circe's voice trails off, eyes searching for some meaning, some explanation from this Diplodocus she'd revered for so long. "Everything you taught me . . . it was a lie. . . ."

"It was the truth," Raal insists. "All of it. And then an even greater truth lays beyond."

Grabbing a handcuff, I break up the little soap opera. "Enough with the fortune-cookie talk, kids. It's time to go get charged."

"You can't arrest us," Circe mumbles.

"No, but we can haul your ass down to the Council. We're not talking jaywalking, here—your group was planning *the extinction of the human race*, sweetheart, and even though you didn't have intimate knowledge of the plan, you were involved enough to be indicted right alongside your precious leader. You think this is slap-on-the-wrist time? I'd say goodbye to Mr. Sun as soon as we step outside, 'cause it's gonna be a while before you get a glimpse of him again."

A sudden burst of discussion, filtering in from down the hallway, a cascade of casual conversation trickling into the room. I look to Ernie—he looks back—and suddenly I can feel the tide turning again, the undertow starting to drag me back out to sea. "You know what that is?" beams Raal, the corners of his mouth curving up into that pear-shaped head of his.

"Vienna Boys' Choir?"

"That's the cadre coming to get us for the rally," he says. "And there's only one way out of this room. When they see us coming out, I promise you they'll attack."

Enough of this game, the bluffs and counterbluffs. Spinning myself in a wide circle, I grab Raal from behind, whipping out my claw and placing it at his throat. "Let's see how quickly they'll attack now."

Circe steps in. "Vincent, don't—"

But Ernie's right behind her, pressed tight to her back—some guys get all the breaks—and soon we've got the two cult leaders handcuffed, strapped, and ready to transport up to the Valley and the local Council representative. Despite every muscle and tendon in me aching to tell Ernie to let Circe go, my quavering sense of duty says otherwise. Circe may not be responsible for any of the more violent aspects of the group, but it would be patently wrong to allow her to escape unpunished.

From the moment we emerge into the hallway—the five Progressives walking toward us have stopped short at the sight of their leaders being led away in chains—insanity takes control.

"Stay back," warns Ernie, pressing the tip of his claw far enough into Circe's neck that it makes a visible indentation. "I've got an itchy finger."

"Do what they say," Raal says calmly. I'm glad he's cooperating.

Unfortunately, the dinos are not. As one, they begin to advance on us, and Ernie and I find ourselves taking instinctive steps backward. Soon we're trotting back the way we came, through the lounge, and out another doorway. This place is a veritable fun house—hallways, mirrors, more hallways—though I'm not actually having much fun.

The dinos follow us as we lead our captives down a winding staircase and into another, smaller hallway, a single door waiting for us at the end of it. "You don't want to go in there," Circe suggests, but Ernie quiets her with a stern glance.

There's no other choice. The dinos behind us are keeping up the pressure, and this door represents our only hope. With luck, we can exit, get into Ernie's car, and get this all finished up within the hour. Success is climbing up the vine, and already I can feel the comfort of my bed, the gentle hum of a ball game on the radio, the warm caresses of some premium parsley running through my veins.

Then it all breaks down faster than a Yugo.

24

As the door swings wide, vertigo slams into my brain without hitting the brakes, my body reeling as the ballroom thirty feet below rocks and rolls like a rowboat caught in a tsunami. The assembled Progressives glance up as one, hundreds of dino snouts and beady eyes focusing on the soap opera thirty feet above them, and I realize that we've just stumbled out of the pan and into the deep fryer.

With a piercing cackle that nearly vibrates my eardrums to kingdom come, Raal lashes out with a tremendous kick to my shins before landing a firm blow to my midsection. My arms go limp and the elusive cult leader dances away, knocking off my clothespins in the process. With incredible athletic prowess, Raal steps out onto the very platform where I first saw Circe and executes a flying leap into the crowd—which parts as he hits the ground—and rolls to a three-point landing. "They're trying to kill us," Raal cries, his voice carrying across the ballroom. "They're here to kill us—and they're here to take us away—"

In the few milliseconds I have to scan the room, I notice that the giant fake fossil they were constructing back in Hawaii has been relocated to the ballroom, and I'm impressed that they were able to reconstitute him in so short a period of time. A thin grid-work of scaffolding surrounds Frank's tenuously coupled bones; still, his recent reconstructive surgery seems to have come off better than half of Hollywood's. Even at the height of this plat-form, I'm only halfway up his long, curving neck, and I marvel once again at the impressive skills of this misguided group.

Behind me, Ernie's maintaining his hold on Circe, but I don't know for how much longer. As the Progressives down in the ball-room go their own ways—those who only showed up for the free food scattering for safety, wanting no part of this melee, others gearing up for what looks to be a cakewalk for their side—the cadre of dinosaurs in the hallway huddle together, and déjà vu returns one more time as I recall the scene back in the jungle. There's a new pack of beasts after us now, and even though these might understand English, it doesn't make them any less deadly.

But here's where things get interesting:

Before I can make a move myself, even before my claws have flashed to their full length, Circe is leaping away from Ernie, the element of surprise clearly to her advantage, a wellspring of unnatural strength throwing my partner up and away by a good three feet. Hands still clasped tightly behind her but no matter, no matter—her entire body is a single speeding bullet streaming onto the platform, out through the ballroom, aimed at the middle of the crowd, legs and sharp underclaws shoved out in front as if she's doing a sit-up while flying through the air. She slams into the pile of dinosaurs with explosive force, and a whole section of Progressives go down in a heap of hide, blood, and saliva. Now *that's* a kind of bowling that might get better Nielsen ratings.

This must be the cue for the rest of the Progressives to start their engines, because soon Ernie and I are engaged in our own skirmishes, ripping off our guises, sliding down curtains like Errol Flynn, beating back paws and jaws and tails from all sides at once. I'm the Raptor version of Chuck Norris, using the tail from an Ornitho in front of me to fend off the chomping attack from a T-Rex to my right. I'm spinning, I'm flailing, and my turn as the last dino action hero is finally upon me.

Statues and busts crash all around the room as we leap atop whatever furnishings might assist us in winning the battle. Marble flies through the air, small bits of bone and rock peppering my hide, but I'm jumping from side to side, lashing out with my tail, with my feet, trying to keep my attackers directly in front of me, preferably out of tooth-and-claw range. It's a defensive battle, a stalling tactic—

"Where the hell are they?" I call out to Ernie, who's busy breaking a bear hold by a Bronto.

"I—don't—know," he yells back, cracking his head against the other dino's with a sickening crunch. The Bronto's grip on my partner slackens and he slumps to the floor like a drunk being tossed at closing time, just as another takes his place.

I don't know where Circe and Raal have gotten to, and I'm not in a position to find out. Soon enough, I'm surrounded by five snarling dinos who could listen to reason if they wanted to but choose to close themselves off from logic and instead take quick, painful swipes at my head and body. I'm lashing out as well, ripping my underclaws into hides, into flesh, protecting myself as much as I possibly can, but there's only so much a Raptor can do when faced with overwhelming odds.

My back impacts hard on a slab of wood, and for a second I think I've been attacked, that my spine must be severed, and I will be forced to live the rest of my life—if I live—in a wheelchair, my tail up in traction, my legs useless for all eternity. But it's just a piece of scaffolding surrounding Frank's rickety forty-foot skeleton, and I use the same tactic I did in the jungle and climb, climb, climb. I may only be a pseudo-simian, but I can ape monkeys with the best of them.

Unfortunately, so can my attackers, who haven't yet unlearned their more helpful human qualities. As I scramble up the elongated bones, kicking out with my legs at snarling faces and snapping jaws, they zip right up behind me, a swarm of dinosaurs crawling like ants over this brand-spanking-new ancient fossil. The entire structure sways and trembles as we zip across its facade, but there's nowhere to go but up.

A Raptor rears up in front of me, lashing out with a slicing sideswipe, but I leap into the air, catching my tail on a scaffolding bar at the last moment, swinging out and around the open space and landing safely on the other side. I resume my climb, shutting out the commotion around me.

And wind up atop Frank's massive skull, the snout itself longer than my entire body. The head of this fossil perches precariously atop the long, shaky neck, and within moments, two Progressives—a Trike and that Raptor who won't give up—pull themselves up and onto the top of Frank's spine, heading straight in my direction.

I look down for an exit—maybe by hanging off of his nose, swinging down and across the teeth—but scratch that plan when I see a new contingent of dinos swiftly scampering up the scaffolding on that side as well. To my left, an Ornitho and a smallish Stegosaur await my arrival; to my right is a T-Rex.

They close.

There is truly nowhere for me to go. Spontaneous hibernation will not be my ticket out this time around. Now that my demise is imminent, I wish I were at least outside, in the fresh air, sucking up the sweet smell of nature, but if heaven is anything like I suspect, there will be a jungle and soft earth and a bed of ferns in which I can lie down at night and look up at the stars.

I hope Ernie gets there, too, but not for a long, long time.

A sudden rattle at the closed ballroom door, and everything slows down for a moment. Another rattle, an earthquake shake—the dinos around me staring about in confusion, momentarily halting their advance, the noise engaging my curiosity as well, raising my hopes—and suddenly there's mass confusion as the barrier bursts inward with a mighty crash and a storm of figures stream inside. The cavalry has arrived.

"Sorry we're late, darling," calls Jules, decked out in her finest ball-gown livery, "but Marilyn had to do her hair."

Miss Monroe issues a girlish giggle and turns coyly to the side. "But it's my best feature," she pouts, lips working overtime.

Jules stands tall in the middle of the barn, flanked on either side by a contingent of the best dinosaur cross-dressers LA has ever seen in one venue. Their hair is perfectly coiffed, nails impeccably filed, clothing flawlessly tailored. It's a cavalcade of stars, each one a perfect to-die-for diva, right down to the skin tone and beauty moles. They're good, and they oughta be—the ladies pay big bucks for those costumes.

With a smile of her own that would make the devil blush, Jules raises a stylish, sculptured arm in the air and announces sweetly, "Get 'em, girls."

Bette Midler launches herself into a pack of Progressives, who are too startled at the attack by a superstar to fight back. She's carefully rolled up the left leg of her guise, so the Divine Miss M has access to a muscular leg and the sharp claws within. A perfectly timed turn-turn-kick-turn lands three of the other dinos in a heap atop one another, and soon she's off and running to the next unfortunate group.

I'm quickly assisted by Jayne Mansfield and Greta Garbo, both of whom are stunning, graceful, and a whirlwind of fighting prowess. Taking the Raptor and the Stego for myself, I land my own blows while watching these two bombshells make short work out of the remaining Progressives on the scaffolding. At one point, Jayne's wig falls off, and she issues a tremendous scream of anger, disemboweling the T-Rex responsible for the injury before reaffixing that shock of long, platinum hair.

I've just leaped back atop Frank's neck, ready to tag-team with Greta on a pair of Diplodoci intent on having us over for dinner, when a rolling roar streams across the floor. Thirty feet down, a blurry wheel of dino flesh flows across the marble, blood flying out at all angles. I can just make out the lines of this furious Diplodod as Raal grabs hold of Frank's ankle and begins to climb. His eyes are locked on mine, and I've got a pretty good idea of his final destination.

No help from the ladies—they're tied up in their own battles, whacking the remaining Progressives into submission. I look around, trying to find a way out, but there's no easy exit. If I leap from here, odds are I'll break something on the way down; perhaps if I'd gone to the jumping seminar back on the island, I'd be okay, but unfortunately I was forced to ditch class that day.

"You can't stop it. . . ." pants Raal as he drags himself onto the platform, a thin stream of blood trickling from his mouth. Every breath sounds a concomitant gurgle, a surefire indication of internal injuries, but it doesn't seem to be sapping his strength. "You can't stop Progress."

"That's what they say," I point out. "They also say you shouldn't shit where you eat, but you seem to have made a career out of it."

The momentary pause of confusion is all I need to get in the first swipe. With my torso leaning back and tail set at the proper angle to spring me, I leap forward, legs first, letting my natural blades do all the work. But Raal's got a few tricks of his own, and though the Diplodocus genes don't equip their possessors with nearly as many deadly weapons as Raptor DNA, his training in the lethal arts is quite evident. With surprising speed, Raal evades my attack, tucks his head back into his body like a frightened turtle, and slams headlong into my side. We go down in a rolling heap, grabbing at Frank's delicate vertebrae to stop our fall.

I manage to scramble back up the fossilized neck, leaping across the skull and out toward the elongated snout once again. There I stand, waiting for the attack, wondering what the hell I'm going to do if he comes at me again. Every breath I take comes with a bee sting to my side, and I think I may have ordered up the Broken Rib Special.

Down on the ballroom floor, dinos are rolling in ten directions at once, the walls caked with all manner of bodily fluids, the priceless art now in definitive possession of a new designation: worthless. And somewhere, somehow, some skirmish winds up with one soldier or another slamming into what happens to be a very dangerous button:

Forty feet down, the fire pit slides open.

"Ernie!" I call. "Barbra, Liza, Jules—anyone?" But they're all too wrapped up in their own battles—and doing quite nicely—to help; even if they were free and clear, it would take them too long to climb up Frank and offer assistance.

Raal advances.

His scent is strong, stronger than Circe's ever was, an entire vat of Aramis as compared to her meager Pine-Sol, and my first thought is *Jump, Vincent, jump, and it can all be over, over so easily.* . . .

I look down, the fire pit below beckoning, its cleansing flames awaiting my arrival.

But I've been through enough crap over the past week to realize that if I'm really talking to myself, I'll probably recognize the sarcasm. Fighting back against Raal's voice, taking a mental firehose to the overpowering scent, I try to stand tall, stand firm, bracing myself for what will probably be the final attack and my final seconds on Earth. But if I'm going down, Progress is going down with me.

Sinking into a crouch, drool dribbling from one side of his chin, Raal prepares to end the charade. There is nothing rational left in that melon-ball brain of his; I can tell that he is no longer in control of his actions, that he has suddenly Progressed into a purely natural state, more Iguanodon than I will ever be Raptor. I am so very, very screwed.

The pressure comes first, a wrecking ball blow right to the midsection, followed quickly by a radiating burst of pain and the inevitable loss of breath. I'm propelled backward at a tremendous speed, flying through the air, no trapeze in sight, Raal's head tucked deep into my abdomen, driving me up, up, and back down, slamming my back onto the protruding ridge of the giant skeleton's first vertebra.

Claws are digging at my hide, my own arms employed full-time as a shield for my soft underbelly, but it's not long before my strength will give, and my guts are strewn on the floor below. Raal is tucked deep into that embryonic position, legs tucked up, in, all four limbs working at once, claws fully extended, wordless growls and grunts lurching out his throat as he bites for my ears, my snout, my eyes.

"Ern—Ernie—" I try to call, but with every successive attack, the cry is cut short. He'll never hear me; I hope he gives me a nice funeral and keeps the paparazzi away.

Strength is draining out of every pore in my body, and though I'm trying to whip my tail around—catch an eye, an ear, any soft spot I can manage to hit—I'm just not connecting. With a hungry growl, Raal steps up the attack, and already I can feel blood seeping out from my stomach; he must have ripped away part of my hide, making for the insides—

When another ferocious roar joins the chorus, harmonizing for but a split second before breaking off into its own riff of anger and betrayal. Raal's body stiffens suddenly, giving me enough time to squirm out from beneath him, nearly clearing myself of his limbs. But a second later, he's on the attack again, rushing forward—

And getting slammed from behind, and then a second tremble wracks his torso a moment later and a new dribble of blood trickles from his mouth. A cough, a sharp breath, a final mortal shudder, and Raal is falling forward, forward, a gaping wound across his back, his frame teetering on the brink, falling over the side and off of the mammoth fossil—

And taking Circe with him.

I'm leaping even before I realize it, my leg outstretched, my claws extended as far as they can go, hoping that my aim is right and that the bones on which I'm jumping can withstand the force. As I land, I grab hold of an eye socket, grasping the ocular cavity with all my might.

My leg is heavier than it should be, about four hundred pounds more so, I should think. Looking down, I find Circe clinging to my outstretched underclaw, her fingers, still coated with Raal's blood, wrapped around its sharp, finely serrated edges, the blades digging into her flesh. And grabbing on to *her* legs is Raal, still very much alive, still very much enraged.

Below their feet, the fire pit roars with delight, eager to be fed. Herbs assault me from all directions now, not a calm, soothing mixture enveloping my body, my senses, but sharp blows to the head, the body, the mind. I'm battered left and right by Circe's scent, and I don't know if it's fear, anticipation, or some combination thereof, but it's knocking me silly. My claw cannot hold on much longer.

Raal begins to climb, grabbing at Circe's body, his claws digging into her flesh, using her beautiful body as nothing more than handholds. He's coming for me, and he doesn't care if he destroys his protégée along the way. A steady slobber of drool and blood drips from his mouth, the fire raging hard below him, shadows dancing across that insane face.

But it's Circe I'm concerned with, Circe who I want to pull to safety, Raal or no Raal. If I save her, I save him, but no matter; I'll deal with it when the time comes.

"Hold on," I grunt. "Just—hold on—"

She's oblivious. "It was right," she says to me, her eyes dancing a two-step in their sockets. "Progress was right."

Straining my leg muscles, trying to bring them to bear, but the extra weight is so hard to handle. I pull on Frank's eye—the head jostling with my effort—and manage to scoot up no more than an inch. Raal is farther up Circe's body now, his torso even with her legs, and he's coming quick.

"Don't worry about that," I tell her, scooting myself back another few inches. "Just hang tight—"

But she's shaking her head, not paying attention to a word I'm saying. "Remember," Circe whispers to me, her softly spoken words easily cutting through the clamor of the fire, the shrieks of battle. "Remember how it *feels*. . . ."

Another hit of herbs, this one a paprika uppercut that slams my head back against my neck, and I'm in for the standing eight-count. Like an alcoholic rescued from his blackout, this little hair o' the pup reaches into the recesses of my memory, grabs hold of a recent evening, and opens it up before the rest of my astonished brain:

I am in the hotel room at the Westin Maui, and Kala is coming into the bedroom. I am tired, so very sleepy, but holding on to consciousness for the promise of great sex. I'm saying something about my job, something about why we're in Hawaii, and by the time Kala is done in the bathroom, I can't decide what's a wall and what's a painting and what's a tree and what's a prehistoric lagoon. And as she emerges from the doorway, steam rising up behind her, I see a familiar Velociraptor coming toward the bed, hushing me with a long, perfect finger, kissing my lips before I have a chance to react in beautiful, beautiful surprise.

"Love me, Vincent," Circe sighs. "Love me tonight."

And back in the Hollywood Hills, Circe, who has known from the very beginning how I was feeling, what I was feeling, why I was feeling it, gives me a nod. What I have seen is true. My little native girl was here with me all along.

"Hold on," I tell her, redoubling my efforts, grinding my teeth with the strain. "Hold on—"

But Raal is coming up, and coming fast, climbing aboard Circe's back, his claws ripping her body into long, bloody strands, ready to leap atop her shoulders and make the final jump back to safety, but for the first time since we met, Circe is in full command of herself and her senses.

This beautiful Raptor shakes her head, looks me in the eyes, in the heart, and says, "It is time for me to meet the ancestors, Vincent. It is time to become natural."

And as Raal prepares to make his final leap, as he steadies himself for the final and fatal attack on yours truly, Circe lets go. Simple as that. The fall is swift, the flames are hot. There is a moment when I think I can smell singed basil, a brief second when I think I hear the cry of a burned songbird, but it's just my imagination, and it is over in a matter of seconds.

Ernie is next to me; I don't know when he got there, but he's gingerly pulling me away from the side of Frank's head, directing my gaze away from the fire pit below. Greta Garbo, a nice baker from Santa Monica who gives me free bear claws whenever I visit, has made it to the top as well, and the two of them begin to help me down. "That's it, darlink," she says to me in that lilting Swedish accent. "It's finished."

Not quite—Garbo suddenly grabs my hand (this is one time when she doesn't want to be alone) and holds on tight as the skeleton begins to collapse. The giant legs go first, buckling from the vibrations, followed quickly by the hips and torso, the attachment pins shaking out, falling to the ground, wires snapping. The three of us leap for the nearest wall, grabbing tight to a piece of loose curtain and riding it down to the ground just as Frank loses all of his structure and collapses into a giant heap of newly minted bones on the floor of the ballroom, his head cracking apart, the jawbone slipping into the still-roaring fire pit.

The other ladies finish up their shows, propelling themselves in the most graceful manner possible while still managing to inflict a frightening amount of damage. Liza Minnelli has a ferocious uppercut, but her mom is head-and-shoulders above her in the knockout department. Judy takes aim at a T-Rex, judges the distance to that cowardly beast, and knocks him clear past Oz with a sharp blow to the head.

Endgame is over in a matter of minutes, Babs doing most of the cleanup on the few remaining stragglers. There's no doubting the woman's pure power of presence as she dances through the room, collecting bodies wherever she goes. Her skill is so great that there's not an ounce of blood shed, yet she fells every enemy within seconds. And to think I mocked her in *The Prince of Tides*.

Epilogue

The last days of December. I hate this time of year. The holidays have come and gone, good cheer flitting in for a moment and then zipping back out the window with a bing and a bang and a boff, which means that the next few days will consist of nothing but driving to malls and taking photographs of husbands hanging out with the mistresses they missed so much during the more family-intensive Christmas celebrations. *Oh what fun it is to ride in a Lincoln with my camera. . . .*

The last eight months have been a constant struggle to forget what happened to me out there in Hawaii, and remember the more interesting, lascivious parts with as much detail as I can muster. Every once in a while I'll catch myself with my eyes closed, trying to imagine Circe, her smell, that jungle, that fantastic prehistoric scene, and every once in a while I'll let myself go. I'll allow myself to feel the breeze and the air and the moisture and the other creatures. Other times, I snap out of it and eat a candy bar.

The highest-ranking Progressives were remanded to the National Council, Ernie and I gave enough sworn depositions to send ten court reporters' children to Ivy League schools up through their Ph.D.'s, and by the time it was all over, no one wanted to tell us the outcome. We wrote letters, petitions, made enough troublesome phone calls to actually have a restraining order slapped down on us by a judge, but still . . . nothing.

I even got so frustrated with the situation that I up and ran for the Southern California Council a few months back, half on a whim, half on a dare, and ended up getting myself elected as the Raptor representative. Lucky me. Now I get to spend the third Tuesday of every month holed up in Harold Johnson's furnished basement, though I use the term "furnished" very loosely. Harold, the Bronto rep, has an old sleeper sofa and love seat down there, but by the time I'm able to make it over to his ranch house in Burbank, Mrs. Nissenberg and that Oberst fellow have usually claimed the comfy spots as their own, so it's the floor or the top of the washer/dryer for me. Of course the one time I sat myself down atop said washer, I had to be driven to the hospital less than an hour later, my tail up in traction for two weeks—don't ask, don't ask—so I usually opt for standing around instead. Oh, it's a blast. The kicker is that even after all of the hoopla and my new and supposedly influential position, I am still unable to squeeze any information out of the National Council reps. Maybe I'll just have to run for higher office and show them a thing or two.

The Progressives are still going strong, I understand, though their weapons have been confiscated, the military plans disman- tled, and the natural dinos brought back to secret hospital loca- tions, where they're having the human drilled back into them. It's okay with me that the group still exists; most of those kids didn't want war in the first place; they were just there to get a better sense of themselves, which is something I can't complain about.

Rupert is all better, but it took six intense months of depro- gramming—with a *real* doctor this time, one we picked out of a phone book—until he was able to accept the fact that he was no longer going to Progress, that his days of free living were over. The Council let him off with a slap on the wrist, two hundred hours of community service working with dinosaurs who have contracted Dressler's syndrome and now think they're actually humans, and he seems to be enjoying the responsibility. He's working with Jules now, actually, helping her out with basic procedures, but it's nice that the little pisser's learning a trade, even if it's one with which Ernie is still a mite uncomfortable. But he's always been a searcher, a seeker, and unsure of his place in the world, and despite the steady employment, I expect to hear about another cult he's joined any day now.

True to my word, I did not turn Star Josephson in to the police, nor did I disappoint Minsky. After doing a little research on the Mussolini and its intricate construction—these are not your average libraries I attended, mind you—I obtained a number of pictures, diagrams, and blueprints of the phony phallus and brought them to the greatest accessories designer I know. Within a week, Jules had a nearly perfect Mussolini replica ready and waiting for me, and it didn't cost me a cent—she was so happy with the result, she's already added the Mussolini to her surgical repertoire. Six hours after the news hit the street, there was a waiting list ten months long for one of her new creations, and now I can barely get through to the gal on the phone.

The day after I got Jules's first Mussolini reproduction, I went to see Minsky at his office, told him that I had indeed found Star in Hawaii, snatched the penis from her pocket, dragged her into an alleyway—it's always best to have a shred of truth in these tales—and then, at that point in the story, my voice trailed off, allowing the midget's mind to go wherever it might take him. Imagination is always better than the real thing. Minsky quickly backed away from the gory details, reattached his Mussolini—no idea it was a fake, though I was sweating it through those first few moments—and thanked me for a job well done. I don't think he'll be coming around much anymore.

Ernie and I have been relatively busy; the word of our investigation into the Progressive affair leaked out, and big stories like that always increase your caseload for a few months afterward. So we've been shuffling in and out and barely seeing each other, almost like a husband and wife in a two-income shift-worker family.

But I'm in the office doing some paperwork on a new case Teitelbaum has thrown at us when Ernie comes marching through the door, high on something. I assume it's life, as he hasn't touched a sprig of herb since we got back from Hawaii. He's been seeing Louise again, but just as friends. She's in love with the new husband, the dolt, and even though Ernie's not crazy about the guy, he tolerates the T-Rex's presence in order to be around his one and only love.

"Got us a case," he says affably.

"Cases we got," I reply. "Workers we don't. Sit down, have a drink, fill out some of this crap." I toss a sheaf of papers onto his desk, and they scatter across the surface.

Ernie shakes his head and heads straight for the closet. "No time, no time." He's not sleeping at the office so much anymore, but he still stores certain items here. I watch as he lugs out a set of soft luggage and a heavy wool jacket.

"You going somewhere?" I ask him. "I've barely seen you in two weeks."

"And you can see me after New Year's. I've got an easy way to make us ten grand, no problem." He proceeds to tell me about the murder of a big-time financier in New York, some guy who got offed a few days ago. "Now the McBride family is offering ten thousand bucks plus expenses—Big Apple, can't miss it—with a bonus if we nab the perp. This is an offer I can't pass up."

"And it can't wait an extra day?"

"Sure it can, but—"

"Look," I tell him, feeling more and more like the unappreciated wife with every passing word, "we haven't had any time to talk, to . . . to hang out. All this work is great, but—"

"But what's the point if it's just work?"

"Exactly," I say. "I'm just looking for a few hours here."

Ernie stops, looks at his suitcase, and pointedly throws it back into the closet, where it lands with a heavy thunk. "What the hell," he says. "A bit of fun can't hurt."

I edge my way out from behind the desk before he can change his mind and grab my coat. Ernie dons his hat, and we take our leave of the office, locking the door with the etched words WATSON AND RUBIO, INVESTIGATIONS behind us.

"Interested in a movie?" asks my partner. "Hear they've got a *Land of the Lost* marathon down at the NuArt."

"Seen 'em all," I say as we hit the stairs. "How about a show at the Shangri-La?"

"Thought they closed it."

"They did. But Jules is doing so well with the Mussolini biz, she's got the money to start it up again. Tonight's the opening, and all the girls are in the show—Barbra, Greta, Jane . . ."

Ernie shakes his head. "I dunno, kid. . . . It's not really my bag."

"You'll have a blast," I promise. "Besides, we can just stay for the first few numbers. And Liz Taylor's got quite the crush on you, I heard."

And believe it or not, my dear old partner is blushing. "Sure, kid," he says, barely suppressing a laugh. "Let's hit the Shangri-La. Then it's a quick bite of dinner, and back to work. That good by you?"

We reach my Lincoln—a new Mark VIII, now that the insurance money for the stolen one came through—and I open his door to let him in. "That's fine by me, Ern. That's fine." He's right—you can't live on work alone, but we shouldn't let this fun and frolic thing get outta hand.

Me and Ernie, we've got a hell of a lot more cases left to solve.

The Historical Bible

THE LIFE AND TEACHINGS
OF JESUS

ACCORDING TO THE EARLIEST RECORDS

THE HISTORICAL BIBLE

By CHARLES FOSTER KENT, Ph.D., Litt.D.

Professor of Biblical Literature in Yale University

ARRANGEMENT OF VOLUMES:

I. **The Heroes and Crises of Early Hebrew History.** From the Creation to the Death of Moses.

II. **The Founders and Rulers of United Israel.** From the Death of Moses to the Division of the Hebrew Kingdom.

III. **The Kings and Prophets of Israel and Judah.** From the Division of the Kingdom to the Babylonian Exile.

IV. **The Makers and Teachers of Judaism.** From the Fall of Jerusalem to the Death of Herod the Great.

V. **The Life and Teachings of Jesus.** According to the Earliest Records.

VI. **The Work and Teachings of the Apostles.** From the Death of Jesus to the End of the First Century.